THE DEVIL AND THE DEEP BLUE SEA

BLACKWOOD SECURITY
BOOK 17

ELISE NOBLE

Published by Undercover Publishing Limited

Copyright © 2024 Elise Noble

v2

ISBN: 978-1-912888-86-3

Edited by Nikki Mentges, NAM Editorial

Cover design by Abigail Sins

www.undercover-publishing.com

www.elise-noble.com

Hell is empty and all the devils are here.

— *WILLIAM SHAKESPEARE*

1

KNOX

"Cheer up, man. We're basically getting a free vacation."

Knox Livingston swallowed the Tylenol, chased it down with coffee, and groaned. He didn't share his friend and housemate's opinion.

"This is *not* a vacation."

"Stay in the Navy, my dad said. You'll see the world, he said. Well, guess who's stuck on an aircraft carrier in the North Atlantic while we head to the Caribbean?"

Ryder's father, Rear Admiral Metcalfe, was the deputy commander of the second fleet, so he wasn't exactly suffering. And an aircraft carrier seemed like a mighty attractive option right now.

"I'd rather scrub the mess deck with a toothbrush than be trapped on a yacht with Luna Maara. She's the human equivalent of artillery shrapnel." Red hot, but not in a good way. "She bitches constantly, treats people like shit, and if you tell her to get down in a hurry, she's gonna stop and take a selfie first."

"If I can survive a week in the jungle with Sky, then I can

handle a spoiled singer. What is she, five feet tall? Ninety pounds? We can just carry her out of danger."

Sky was the boss's protégé, a foul-mouthed eighteen-year-old who would probably have been in a psych ward if she weren't so good at her job. Knox would rather play Russian roulette with her than spend another second in Luna Maara's presence. Four months ago, he'd shared Ryder's optimism when he set off for Antigua. On that trip, Luna Maara hadn't even been the client—he'd been tasked with ensuring the safety of a minor British royal as she relaxed on the beach—but the pint-sized pop princess had still made everyone's life hell.

When the tail end of a hurricane forced the yacht she was residing on with her mother into port, she'd ended up in the same hotel as Lady Petronella Effingham's party, where she'd pissed off every single member of staff and most of the guests too. On day three, Lady P, a woman so particular that she insisted Knox iron the board shorts he wore off duty, had privately referred to Luna as a "barnacle on the backside of humanity" and "the rotten branch of the family tree." On day four, after the brat asked Her Ladyship to move her sun lounger three feet to the right because its shadow was spoiling the view, Lady P told her that "In the land of the witless, you would be queen." The insult hadn't registered for a good twenty seconds, and then Knox had been forced to step in to stop the catfight. Fortunately, Luna was as shallow as a creek in the desert, and she'd gotten distracted by his guns. Not his semi-automatic; his biceps. Lifting weights sometimes paid off in unexpected ways.

"I'll let you do the carrying. I value my nuts too much to interfere with one of her blog posts."

Before Ryder could agree or protest, a voice spoke from behind them. Confident, snarky, British. The boss had arrived, silently as usual.

"Sorry I'm late—I had to see a man about a hostage situation in South Sudan. Danger tourism has a lot to answer for. Anyhow, I take it the two of you are discussing your next assignment?"

"You need someone to go to South Sudan?" Knox asked. "I'll volunteer."

A few weeks in a restless African nation was more appealing than playing bodyguard in the Caribbean. Saint Vincent might have looked like paradise, but with Luna Maara present, it would turn into a slightly more temperate version of hell.

"Nice try, but no bandana. The client asked for you personally."

What the fuck? "She did?"

"Her mother said she wanted—and I quote—the hot guy with the snake tattoo who was following Lady Petronella around."

"Her *mother* said that?"

"Her mother is also her manager, and if you want my opinion, that's where Luna gets her attitude from. Most clients ask about experience and operational capabilities; Luna Maara just wanted photos. And then she rejected everyone with availability from the executive protection team, so Nick asked if we had the capacity to help with an additional body, and Ryder was first runner-up in the beauty parade. Congrats, I guess."

Seriously?

"It's an eel, not a snake. Does that mean I get a pass?"

"Marine life isn't her strong suit, but no. If it's any consolation, Blackwood didn't want to take the job, so we quoted an outrageous fee, and her mom actually agreed to it. Mind you, it was either that or leave her unprotected after her last bodyguard quit on the spot. I'm pretty sure Luna's running out of reputable companies that will work with her."

"Couldn't you have recommended Sentinel?"

"Nuh-uh. I heard she had a falling-out with them last year and terminated the contract."

"Over what?"

When it came to executive protection, Sentinel was Blackwood's biggest competitor, although in general, they tended to be more conservative in their approach. They didn't have an equivalent to Emmy's Special Projects team, for example. But they were professionals, and Knox couldn't imagine one of their bodyguards doing anything inappropriate enough for a client to fire them. Then again, this was Luna Maara. The love child of Barbie and the Terminator who never, ever stopped being a pain in the ass.

"She overheard an off-duty member of her protection detail referring to her as 'Godzilla in a bikini,' which I personally think was unfair to Godzilla because wasn't Godzilla just looking out for her kids?"

"Depends which version of the movie you watch," Ryder—the resident movie buff—said. "The 2014 remake had a different storyline."

Godzilla in a bikini? A mild insult was all it took to get canned from the job? Knox called his friends worse names than that. But Emmy read his thoughts and shook her head.

"Don't get any ideas—I put a hefty termination penalty in the contract, so she'd be an idiot to pull that stunt again. Not that I think she isn't an idiot, but her accountant's going to step in with that amount of money on the line."

"Does she genuinely need security? Or are we just glorified babysitters?"

"A month ago, I'd have gone with the latter, but apparently there have been a few dodgy messages."

"Only a few?"

Knox wouldn't have been surprised if Lady Petronella had sent choice words herself, written in fountain pen on personalised stationery. Her butler would have ironed the envelope and sealed it with a wax stamp. Luna just had that effect on people.

"I mean, she probably gets thousands, but her mom said these ones are different. The contents suggest that someone's been watching her in person. The last one talked about the way she looked in a green-and-white striped bikini, and she only wore that on a hotel beach in Long Bay. No social media pics. The writer said Luna looked as if she was asking for it, and he'd be happy to oblige."

Okay, that bumped the job into a different category. There was a big difference between escorting a celebrity who only hired bodyguards to pad out their entourage and protecting a high-risk client where the threat of kidnap or assassination was very real. The former focused on maintaining a safe distance from fans and paparazzi and blocking the path of anyone who got too enthusiastic, while the latter meant a constant watch for IEDs, guns, and potential abductors. A crackpot lurking in the shadows meant a change in approach. Tiresome as Luna Maara might be, Knox didn't want to see her suffer physical harm.

Especially on his watch.

"Is she aware of the messages?" Ryder asked.

"Not yet. Her team doesn't want her worrying." Emmy rolled her eyes. "Or doing anything dumb like holding a 'spot the stalker' contest on TikTok."

Yeah, Knox could imagine her doing that. She'd incite a frenzy, and her fans would end up targeting innocent fishermen, cab drivers, and café goers all over the Caribbean.

"How are the messages being sent? By email?"

"Through the contact form on her website. Mack's already taken a quick look. The mystery weirdo is using a

VPN, and we're not contracted for investigative services, only protection. The guy calls himself William, but there's no way that's his actual name."

"What do you think? Is he the real deal?"

"Possibly. The messages are sick and specific. Luna's looking for the usual celeb package: keep the great unwashed out of her way, ditto for the paparazzi—unless she's on a quest for column inches, anyway—and make sure you act suitably intimidating. But keep your eyes peeled, okay? And don't mention the threats in front of her. If there's further communication from this guy, her mom will channel it to us here."

"Understood," Knox and Ryder said in unison.

"The logistics team has prepared a file for you to read on the plane. Risk assessment, routes, locations, personnel. The yacht she's staying on belongs to a hedge fund guy named Crawford Balachandran, but his son's commandeered it. Kory Balachandran, also known as DJ Sykik. That's spelled S-Y-K-I-K. I guess all the good names were taken, or maybe he just flunked English? He got booted from college after the third semester, so who knows? Anyhow, he's headed out to the Caribbean to do whatever it is people with no responsibilities and no ambition do all day, and he's invited a bunch of his friends to join him. Luna's going to hang out on the yacht for two weeks before she performs at the Blayz Festival in the Bahamas, and then she's got appearances scheduled in France, Italy, and London. After that, she's flying to LA to spend time in the studio."

"And we're going with her?"

"The contract is for two months, and hopefully by then, her people will have found some other poor schmuck who's willing to join the team permanently. Remember, neither of you is a pool boy, a bartender, a cab driver, a porter, a masseur, or an extra in a TikTok video, all of which are duties I suspect Luna will ask you to perform. Don't. If you get pushback, stand your ground. If she threatens to call the manager, give her my number. I'll gladly tell her to go Facebook herself."

Two months? They wouldn't be back until mid-April. This was the first year Knox had managed to get season tickets for the Capitals, and now he'd miss the end of hockey season. He couldn't help the groan that escaped.

"I know, I know, you'd rather be tiptoeing around a minefield in Angola, but I included hazardous duty pay in the fee. You'll come back with a suntan and enough money to pay for therapy." Emmy patted him on the cheek. "Just avoid jail time, okay?"

She was kidding, but if Knox had realised how prescient her words would turn out to be, he'd have walked to Angola. Fuck the hazardous duty pay.

2

KNOX

Knox stretched out in the airplane seat and closed his eyes, enjoying one last moment of relative peace before they landed in Saint Vincent. "Relative" because the jet engines were still damn loud. He'd been in this position many times before, flying off to far-flung corners of the world—okay, more often on military transport than a private jet—but he'd dreaded few jobs as much as this one. He'd taken the role with Blackwood because Emmy Black had a reputation for getting things done. For making a difference. For challenging her team to do the impossible.

If he'd known that he'd end up kissing celebrity ass, he'd have worked someplace else.

"Gotta take the rough with the smooth," Ryder muttered as he scrolled through the background file. After the briefing from Lita, a logistics manager who worked with the executive protection team, he'd lost some of his initial enthusiasm.

"Yeah, my mom used to say that."

Usually about Knox's father. Despite everything Knox had accomplished on the battlefield, putting that motherfucker in jail was his greatest achievement to date, although if his mom ever found out what Knox had done, it would destroy their fragile relationship.

"Luna's daddy is an English duke. He hooked up with her mom while he was drunk."

"Yeah, I heard."

After Lady P's "rotten branch" comment, Knox had gotten curious and looked it up. Luna Maara had been causing controversy since before she was born. Her mom, a Vegas showgirl, had sold the story of her wild night with the Duke of Southcott when she was eight months pregnant, and the paternity suit had been covered in salacious detail too. Knox had no idea how much contact Luna had with her father's side of the family, but probably not much if Lady P's acerbic remarks were anything to go by. Luna was her fifth cousin once removed, whatever that meant.

"And her mom used to dance half-naked on stage. Gemma Puckett, better known as Amethyst."

Knox had seen her at the hotel in Antigua, a tall, slender woman with bleached blonde hair and talon-like fingernails who must have had work done to look that good at fifty. Emmy was absolutely right about Luna's attitude—she'd inherited her mom's personality along with her looks. Sure, Mom was more subtle with the demands, but she still had the staff dashing around after her.

"Ambition runs in the family."

And Luna's cousin also worked with her. Jubilee was her name.

"Did you get to the part about the agent? He stays in Las Vegas."

"Smart guy. He gets to milk the cash cow from a

distance while we have to get up close and personal. Ever rethink your career?"

Knox had meant it as a joke, but Ryder appeared to give the question serious consideration.

"Sometimes." And then, more quietly, "I nearly ended up selling tractors."

"What the fuck?"

"Shylah's dad owns Birkley Machinery. It's the largest agricultural equipment dealership in Iowa. After I decided to quit the Navy, she figured we'd go back there, and..." He trailed off. "Man, I just couldn't do it."

Ryder didn't talk about his ex-wife much, but Knox got the impression the breakup hadn't exactly been amicable. Because she'd disagreed with his chosen career path? This life wasn't easy on a family, Knox knew that. It took a special kind of woman to wait in the wings while her man put himself in danger, a true unicorn, and he'd never managed to find one.

Not that he'd looked very hard.

With love came loss, and with loss came heartache. Knox never wanted to experience that devastating pain again.

And Ryder was zero for two. There had been another woman once, a long time ago. Neve. He didn't talk about her much, but one dark February evening, soon after they moved into the house in Rybridge, Ryder had started drinking, and he hadn't stopped. In a rare moment of vulnerability, he'd confessed that he was thinking of the woman he'd lost. His high-school sweetheart, the woman he should have married instead of Shylah. The next day, he'd sobered up and never spoken of her again.

"You wouldn't have lasted six months selling farm equipment." Knox looked out the window to the vivid blue sea, to the distinctive black sand beaches and the runway that was fast approaching. "Although if the guy still has openings, I might be interested."

Thanks to Lita, there was a car on standby at the airport in Saint Vincent, and they transferred their luggage for the ten-minute drive to the marina. There, the yacht would be waiting, along with Luna Maara, Kory Balachandran, and a dozen more twenty-somethings with more money than manners.

The driver didn't seem impressed when Knox told him their destination, more relieved.

"You'll be settin' sail tonight, then?"

"No, we're staying here for a few days."

Was that a grimace?

"Maybe you should try visitin' Bequia? It's a beautiful island. Or Puerto Rico? If you're lookin' for nightlife, you won't find it here."

Knox saw the suggestion for what it was—a not-so-subtle hint to leave. Luna and her friends had upset the islanders already? They'd only been there for three days.

"We're just the hired help, buddy."

This time, the driver's glance was more sympathetic. "Then I hope you're gettin' paid well."

Cleopatra, the hundred-and-forty-foot tri-deck yacht Kory's father had named after his fourth wife, gleamed in the sun at the end of the dock, sparkling water lapping at her hull. A deckhand in a white polo shirt and black shorts polished gleaming brass fittings, and two more staff struggled across the passerelle with an oversized cooler. Dance music blasted out across the marina, and a pair of women in bikinis were dancing on the top deck. Was one of them Luna? Knox couldn't tell from a distance.

"Good luck," the driver said as they unloaded their luggage. Packing had taken longer than it usually did because of instructions such as "all clothing will be black or white," and "no synthetic fibres to be worn by staff," and "toiletries must be vegan and cruelty-free." The rider also specified that staff shouldn't have facial hair, but fuck that. They were contractors, not employees. Ryder was rocking a short beard, and Knox's was a little longer. If he'd known he'd be assigned to this job, he'd have gone full Gandalf. As it was, he'd had to tie his hair back in a man-bun to avoid falling foul of the "no hair past the collar" stipulation.

When it came to weapons, they were travelling light. The logistics team had secured permits for one handgun each, and they'd stashed a couple of knives in their luggage. Plus they had the usual zip ties, binoculars, night-vision goggles, first-aid kit, flashlights, and survival gear, as well as diving equipment in case they got any downtime.

Knox waved to the security guard in the marina office as they walked past. "We're here to join the *Cleopatra*'s crew," he called.

The guard waved back. "Better you than me, man."

Great fucking start.

"Did you bring earplugs?" Ryder asked as they lugged the bags along the dock.

"Yeah. You?"

"A half-dozen pairs. We're gonna need them."

They made it onto the *Cleopatra*'s swim platform, complete with guns, before anyone stopped them, and even then it was only a willowy brunette who definitely wouldn't present a challenge to a deranged fan with ill intentions. A crew member? The clipboard in her hand suggested she was staff, but she was wearing a shapeless blue sundress and Converse.

"Can I help?" she asked.

"Knox Livingston and Ryder Metcalfe here for Ms. Maara."

Whose legal name was Luna Maara Puckett, but she seemed to have erased the surname from her identity.

"Are you the bodyguards?"

"That's right."

"Uh, did you get the briefing pack?"

"Rest assured, our dopp kits are entirely vegan."

"But your hair..."

"We're not cutting our hair for a two-month contract."

"Luna won't be happy about that."

"Seems from the briefing notes that Luna isn't happy about a lot of things. We're here to keep her alive, not to participate in a fashion parade."

That earned them an unexpected smile and a giggle that turned into a snort when the brunette tried to swallow it down.

"I can't say you're wrong." She held out a hand. "I'm Jubilee."

So this was Luna's cousin? The background report said she worked on Luna's social media team, so Knox hadn't expected to see her ticking off arrivals at the back of the boat. Jubilee looked as if she'd be more at home behind the camera than in front of it. Her hair was scraped back in a low ponytail, and instead of jewellery, she wore a rubber bracelet with "You've got this" printed on it. Wishful thinking? Her nails were chewed to the quick.

For a moment, Knox felt bad for not visiting the barber.

"Good to meet you."

"Where's the rest of your luggage?" she asked.

"This is all of it."

"Puzzled" seemed to be Jubilee's default operating state. "Only two bags each? Really?"

"Really."

"Well, okay then. You haven't worked with Luna before, have you?"

"Never had that pleasure." Knox's smile felt like more of a grimace. "But our team has carried out background research, so we'll be able to hit the ground running."

"Background research?" Jubilee didn't have much success with smiling either. "Oh dear. Uh, so I'll show you to your cabin, and then you can go meet Luna in the flesh."

Jubilee hadn't been kidding about the "flesh" part. They found Luna on the upper deck in a tiny blue bikini, perched on the edge of a hot tub as a crew member held two portable fans on her and a guy in a pastel-pink polo shirt and loafers took photos.

"Turn the fans on higher. My hair needs to look windswept, like the yacht's moving. Kory, don't get that ugly fishing boat in the shot. Wait. Wait!" She adjusted her bikini top to cover up two small moles that nestled in the cleavage she didn't have. "Okay, now."

The guy in the polo shirt was DJ Sykik? Knox had expected something edgier. His promo pictures showed him standing behind a dimly lit mixing desk with a pair of headphones around his neck, usually with a crowd in the background and a bunch of glow sticks. In reality, he looked as if he'd taken a wrong turn out of the Hamptons.

"Can't Jubilee photoshop the fishing boat out?" he asked.

"Probably."

"Ma'am, the fans are already at their highest speed."

"Then get another one." Luna spoke to the crew member slowly, enunciating each word as if she were dealing with a toddler. "Do I have to think of everything?" She spotted Knox. "Hey, you—take Jubilee's clipboard and fan me."

Good start.

"Can't do that, ma'am."

"Why not? Don't your arms work?" Then she caught sight of Ryder and narrowed her eyes. "Which part of 'no facial hair' do you two not understand?"

Ryder stepped forward. "The part where our next job could be in a country where a beard is necessary to blend in, and shaving it off could compromise our team's safety as well as our own. Ma'am," he added as an afterthought.

"You're the bodyguards?"

"We are."

"Your agency sent photos, and you didn't have a beard then," she said accusingly. "They don't fit my aesthetic."

"Well, before I joined my current team, my boyfriend and I both shaved our beards for a charity fundraiser. That's when the picture was taken."

Knox's lips twitched, and then he felt a rumble of annoyance that he hadn't thought of the idea first. Pretending to be gay? Genius.

Although Luna didn't share that sentiment. "You're gay?"

"Is that a problem?"

Her mouth set in a thin line. "Just fan me."

"Right now, we have a security audit to perform."

"A what?"

"A security audit. We need to evaluate the environment and assess for possible threats."

"But we're on a boat."

"Yacht," Kory muttered.

"We're aware of that, ma'am."

"Nobody's going to harm me on a boat. We're surrounded by water."

"The two of us just walked on board, no questions asked, no ID requested, and we're both armed," Knox told her. "Changes need to be made around here."

Jubilee hung her head, and Knox felt a little guilty for that, but that didn't alter the fact that she'd let them walk right up to Luna. If the threats against their new client were serious, then he and Ryder had to set feelings aside and focus on the goal: securing her safety. A part of him wondered if the security guard in the marina office actually hoped a bad actor would show up. If a willing kook shot out the speakers, at least he'd get some peace.

"Hold on a minute..." Kory started, but Luna held up a hand, stopping him.

"Shush. I'll handle this." She stepped forward on bare feet and snapped her fingers. "Phone." Like magic, a crew member scurried over and placed it in her hand. "I don't know who you think you are, but how dare you interrupt my day and start making demands? Don't you understand your job? You're here to stop fans from bothering me, and apart from that, you keep out of the way." She jabbed at the screen, then put the phone to her ear. "Mom? We need to get new security."

She spoke smugly, clearly used to making demands. Knox couldn't decide whether he felt sorry for her mom or relished the schadenfreude because Amethyst Puckett had probably schooled her daughter to act that way. Either way, he felt no small measure of joy when Luna's smile faded.

"What do you mean, there's no other security available? Fine. *Fine.* Just get rid of them. I'm not putting up with them and their *changes*."

If thunderclouds were sentient, Luna Maara would have been their pin-up girl. Her expression darkened, and she threw the phone into the hot tub.

"Get out of my sight," she snapped. "I don't want to see you or hear you for the rest of this trip. Jubilee, I need a drink."

Knox glanced at Ryder and tried not to smirk. This was going great so far.

3

KNOX

"Just when I think it can't get any worse..." Ryder said as he dropped into the deckchair beside Knox's. They were on the swim platform, both for security purposes and because it was the quietest place on the yacht. Over the past couple of days, they'd tightened up procedures, meaning the guard in the marina office was no longer waving strangers through, and the crew were questioning anyone they didn't recognise rather than leaving it to Jubilee and her clipboard.

"What did Luna do now?" Knox asked.

"Wasn't her. Kory hit on me outside the bathroom."

Knox's bark of laughter made the deckhand cleaning the windows look across in alarm. But fuck, it was funny. Almost as funny as Kory getting relegated to the lower deck because Luna insisted on sleeping in the master stateroom on the main deck.

Knox's fears about getting propositioned by a woman who hated taking "no" for an answer had so far proven unfounded. Most of the time, she just blanked him, although her inappropriate requests included—but weren't limited to—asking him to take off his shirt to "add ambience" to one of her social media posts, demanding he make her a passion fruit martini at one thirty in the morning, and telling him to stay ten paces back because she didn't like his cologne.

He hadn't even been wearing cologne.

On Tuesday evening, she'd whined about camera flashes ruining her dinner with Kory at the Sugar Reef Brasserie, but she'd also ordered Jubilee to make sure the paparazzi knew she was there. On Wednesday morning, she'd climbed on top of an antique cannon at Fort Charlotte even though the guide asked her not to, and then kicked up a fuss when she got asked to leave. Wednesday afternoon, they'd actually taken the yacht out, and she'd spent the afternoon sipping cocktails in the saloon while Kory and a couple more friends zoomed around on jet skis. The excursion ended sooner than Knox had anticipated— jet skis were banned in Saint Vincent and the Grenadines, and the coastguard had escorted them back to the marina after a "don't you know who my father is" argument with Kory. Fuckin' rich kids.

Today? Today, Luna and Jubilee had talked business over breakfast. Social media engagement was trending in the wrong direction, which Jubilee said could be seasonal, but Luna wasn't a girl who liked negativity. She wanted those numbers up again. Right now, she was brainstorming a plan, and Knox just knew he wasn't going to enjoy the result.

"Did you let Kory down gently?" he asked Ryder.

"I reminded him about my 'boyfriend,' and he said that what happens in Saint Vincent stays in Saint Vincent."

"Next time you pretend you're gay, remember to check whether the client's entitled friend is also into cock."

"It was a 'lesser of two evils' situation. Luna's a

succubus. Beautiful on the outside, but exhausting, and she'd sure as hell turn a man's life upside down."

True. Knox leaned back in his chair and stared up at the blue sky. "Could be worse."

"How?"

"Could be raining."

Ryder's turn to laugh. "And at least nobody's shooting at us."

Footsteps sounded on the stairs behind them, soft, but Knox was attuned to every movement. He turned to see Jubilee hesitate and beckoned her forward. She wasn't smiling, but then again, she rarely did look happy. Was that any surprise, given that she worked for Luna?

"Everything okay?"

She shook her head, then checked behind her, furtive. What was the problem?

"There's been another message," she said, her voice a whisper.

"Message?"

"From the guy."

"I didn't realise you were aware of the... communications." How much did Jubilee know?

"I have access to the inbox. Aunt Amethyst said we shouldn't tell Luna because she'll freak out. I mean, some of the stuff the guy says is really nasty."

It was. The background file included copies of the messages, and Knox had read them on the flight over. The writer called her his pretty little whore and described his fantasies in graphic detail. How he wanted to drag her into the shadows, hold his hand over her mouth, and fuck her while people close by remained oblivious. That was what she craved, right? Why else would she lie out in public almost naked? How he wanted her to sing for him, then grip his shaft as he emptied his balls down her throat on a high note. How he wanted to slice off the tiny dresses she wore and plug every hole while she begged him for more. And she *would* beg. She was gagging for it, wasn't she?

"Show me," Knox ordered.

Jubilee handed over an iPad, and he squinted through the glare on the screen.

You looked so pretty yesterday, my little slut. Were you imagining me as you rode that cannon? Did you think of my dick exploding in your tight little pussy? One day, I'm going to show you what a real man can do. One day soon.
    William S

"He's no Shakespeare," Ryder muttered.

No, he wasn't. But he *was* nearby. He'd been at Fort Charlotte on Wednesday. The pictures Luna had posted on social media showed her standing on the cannon, balanced on one leg with her arms extended in some yoga pose. *War versus peace in St Vincent #Namaste.* She'd gotten forty-three thousand likes so far. But before she began posing for the camera, she'd been sitting astride the cannon's barrel, laughing as Jubilee told her to get off.

And Fakespeare had been there, watching.

Fuck.

Knox usually had a good sense for danger—he needed those instincts to stay alive—but he hadn't felt the man's presence. Nobody standing a little too still, no glances lingering a little too long. Just the usual tourists meandering around, admiring the view and taking photos without standing on historic artifacts.

"This arrived yesterday, and you're only telling us now?" Knox's words came out harsher than he intended, and Jubilee flinched.

"I-I don't have time to read all the messages myself. An

assistant in the US usually looks through them first and flags the important ones, but she was off sick until this morning."

"We can't afford any more delays like that, not with Luna's safety at stake."

"I understand. If Sindee gets sick again, I'll make sure I go through the inboxes. You don't think we should tell Luna what's happening?"

"Personally, yes I do, but it's not my decision to make. Ryder and I are just here to throw ourselves in front of the bullets."

It was meant to be a joke, but Jubilee didn't laugh. Her eyes widened.

"You think someone might try to shoot her?"

"Well, those messages don't seem very friendly. What are the chances of getting her to reconsider her trip to Bar None tonight?"

The nightclub would be difficult to secure, and Luna wouldn't want to sit quietly in the VIP area. Luna didn't sit quietly anywhere. The last time she'd visited Bar None, Kory had played an impromptu DJ set, and she'd joined him on stage in an outfit that made an OnlyFans model look modest. The video on her official Instagram profile suggested her antics had been harmless. The photos in the tabloids of a bodyguard rushing her out of the building, beer bottles flying, after the drunken crowd got out of hand, told a different story. But in Luna's eyes, no publicity was bad publicity, and she'd sure gotten column inches out of the drama.

Jubilee perked up and smiled for the first time since she appeared. "The chances are good, actually. The manager at Bar None won't let Kory play another set, so they're planning to go to San Gallicano instead."

Knox took a calming breath. "San Gallicano? As in a whole other country?"

"I mean, it's not far away. Only a couple of hours by boat. And the last time we were there, Luna took an amazing photo with a turtle and got two hundred thousand likes on Insta."

Knox had seen that one. She'd put a pair of Gucci sunglasses on the poor creature and posed next to it with a cocktail. *Tipsy turtle, lol. #JustChillin #EcoWarrior #SanGalli.* The comments had been a toxic mess of *Hey, that's so cute* and *I love you Luna* and *Are you crazy, turtles are endangered* and *You suck, dumb bitch*.

"Don't we need visas?"

"No, there's a waiver program. Last time, we just filled out tourist arrival cards, and the captain got somebody to stamp them."

"We haven't run background for San Gallicano," Ryder pointed out.

Knox knew little about the place, only that it was an archipelago to the west of Saint Vincent. What were the rules on guns there? And how many bars might Luna get into trouble at? Were there cannons? Did San Gallicano have any ancient monuments for her to defile?

"Does that matter?" Jubilee asked. "It's real quiet there."

On any other day, Knox would have argued against the trip, but spending a few days in San Gallicano could be beneficial. Fakespeare was in Saint Vincent, and by the time he caught up with Luna's movements and followed them across the Caribbean Sea, Luna would probably have gotten bored and they'd be on their way back again. Plus Knox and Ryder were former Navy SEALs. They were used to adapting on the fly and making the best of adverse conditions.

"When do we leave?" he asked Jubilee.

Being realistic, if Luna had made up her mind about

something, a complaint from a minion wasn't going to change it.

"As soon as the beauty therapist finishes Luna's nails."

How long would that be? Thirty minutes? An hour? Why did women paint their nails anyway?

"Okay, we'll work with it."

"Is there anything I can do to help?" she asked brightly.

"Can you convince Luna to wear a kaftan?"

"Oh, I don't think she'd like that."

"Then no, there's nothing you can do to help."

Seven weeks to go, and the end of this job couldn't come soon enough.

4

KNOX

"It's just the way I remember." Luna peered through the window at the front of the main cabin, and for once, her smile seemed genuine. Unguarded, not the fake grin she wore most of the time. "All those empty white beaches. There used to be pirates here, did you know that?"

"Like, real pirates?" Kory asked. "Or Jack Sparrow pirates?"

"Real pirates."

"One of the islands used to be a pirate prison," Jubilee said. "Skeleton Cay. It's meant to be haunted."

Luna shuddered. "We're definitely not going to that one. I just want to chill out for a while. Make some new content and relax on the beach."

Two new blondes had arrived yesterday, Lotus and Chanel, and their sole purpose in life seemed to be sucking up to Luna and Kory. Lotus giggled.

"Oh, totally. We could, like, have a bonfire by the water and tell ghost stories."

Luna gave her a scathing look. "We're not twelve."

A look of panic flashed in Lotus's eyes, but she recovered quickly. "Right. You're so right. Let's just make awesome vids."

This was like being back in high school. How did these people make it to adulthood? If you took any of them out of their bubble of privilege, they'd have no idea how to survive in the real world. Luna insisted on her drinks being served at seventy-five degrees and threw a hissy fit if the AC was too cold. Then, thirty minutes later, she'd get pissy because it was too hot.

Blackwood's logistics team was researching the location, and background was trickling in. San Gallicano consisted of one large island—Ilha Grande—surrounded by over a hundred smaller ones. Some weren't much more than rocks in the sea, but a number were inhabited. The area had once been a pirate's paradise, Jubilee was right about that, and smugglers used the islands as a base on their way to South America. The rabbit warren of cays and inlets was a Bond villain's wet dream.

But illicit activities had declined in the past several decades thanks to proactive policing and a tough legal system. Judges faced reelection every six years, and few locals wanted a return to the bad old days. No, the main source of income came from a loosely regulated banking industry supported by agriculture, sustainable fishing, and tourism. A handful of luxury resorts had sprung up on private islands, putting wealthy owners at odds with locals who preferred a traditional way of life. A culture clash. Scuba diving was a popular pastime thanks to the number of shipwrecks in the area, although conservation regulations meant permits were needed for many popular sites, and sheltered coves with clear water meant paddleboarders were a common sight. San Gallicano was one of the Caribbean's hidden gems, according to the nation's official website. A magical hideaway for those who wanted peace and quiet. They'd have to rewrite their marketing blurb once Luna Maara arrived.

Knox thought they'd head straight for the main harbour on Ilha Grande, a crescent lined with restaurants and stores selling trinkets. But Luna decided she wanted to sail around several of the smaller islands and scout for locations from the yacht before they ate dinner.

"Where are the sharks?" Kory asked the first officer. "We should go look for sharks. That would make a great picture."

"I'll try to find out, sir."

"I'm not going near a shark," Luna said. "Are you crazy?"

"You did that thing with the tiger last year."

"That was on stage in Japan. There was a handler, and I still thought it would bite my freaking arm off."

"Why don't you just snorkel with some fish?" Chanel suggested. "Underwater shots would look amazing. And you wrote that song about floating, right?" She began singing. "Floating on love, we resist the earth's pull..."

Luna joined in, and although she acted like Satan's baby sister, she had the voice of an angel. The whole diva act was unnecessary—she really could sing. "A cosmic connection, so beautiful; Our souls entwined, in the heavens we roam; In this boundless love, we've found our home." Then she rolled her eyes, and the spell was broken. "It was about floating on clouds, dummy. Not in the water."

"So no snorkelling?"

"No snorkelling."

A hundred photos of the sunset later, they arrived in Half Moon Harbour, waited while the captain handled the customs and immigration paperwork, and then rode the tender shore for dinner because Luna refused to wait for boats to shuffle around so they could dock. When she managed to get through three courses without causing a scene or pissing anyone off, Knox began to think they might survive this side trip unscathed. But what had both his former commanding officer and Emmy told him time and time again? *Never assume—it makes an ass out of u and me.* If he'd known what was to come, he'd have bundled Luna back onto the yacht and taken off for Saint Vincent, fuck her protests.

But instead, he climbed into the top bunk, mumbled a "goodnight" to Ryder, and got the last decent sleep he'd have in a while.

Saturday morning started bright. Not a cloud on the horizon, not a whiny complaint from Luna or her entourage. Knox took advantage of the peace to indulge in a quick swim across the bay while Ryder stood watch, but before he could towel himself dry, a trio approached the *Cleopatra.* He tensed, then relaxed as he recognised the harbour master. The two men with him looked like police officers. Neither wore a uniform, but Knox had seen a thousand cops and unless they were undercover, they all moved the same way. A slight swagger and a superior expression seemed to come as standard with the badges they wore on their belts.

"Can I help you, gentlemen?" Ryder asked as Knox grabbed a T-shirt.

"We're here to speak with Luna Maara," the taller of the two cops said.

"Under what authority?"

"Under the authority of the Court of San Gallicano. I'm

Detective Fernandez, and this is Officer Roy." Fernandez produced a folded sheet of paper. "We have a warrant for her arrest."

What the fuck? Knox stepped forward as Ryder took the paper and began to read.

"What did she do? We've been here less than twenty-four hours, and she just rode around in the yacht and ate dinner."

"The warrant relates to a matter last year. She's being charged with illegal disturbance of a wild animal."

"A turtle," Officer Roy added. "She dragged it along the beach and poured it a cocktail."

Blackwood ran an excellent training program. Operators on the Special Projects team spent hours in simulated scenarios, kept themselves in peak physical condition, practised hand-to-hand combat, jumped out of airplanes, kept up their dive certifications, and put hundreds of rounds through a variety of weapons. But never, not once, had they covered the steps to take if two cops turned up to arrest a high-profile client for drinking with a turtle.

What the hell should he do? Rouse Luna and tell her to stand still while they cuffed her? Stall for time? Refuse the officers permission to board and flee for Saint Vincent? Fortunately, he didn't have to make that decision because the devil herself appeared.

"What's all this noise? Who are you people? Don't you realise people are trying to eat breakfast in peace?"

"You're Luna Maara?" Detective Fernandez asked, presumably to be certain he had the correct suspect. On this boat, arresting the wrong bikini-clad blonde would be an easy mistake to make.

"Of course I am. What do you want? A picture?"

"Yes, we do want a picture."

"Well, make it quick. My waffles are getting cold."

"Ms. Maara..." Knox started. "I wouldn't—"

"Oh, be quiet."

He did as he was told. The sound of poetic justice turned out to be two quiet *click*s and a lot of screeching.

"What are you doing? Help! I'm being kidnapped!"

"Ma'am, you're under arrest for disturbing a turtle during nesting season. You're not obliged to speak unless you wish to do so, but anything you do say may be put into writing and given in evidence."

"Hey, snake guy! Don't just stand there—do something. They can't do this."

Ryder held up the paperwork. "Actually, they can. This is a signed warrant."

People were taking pictures now, and several passers-by were videoing with camera phones. Why was Luna so upset? Hadn't she been chasing publicity on this trip? Now she had it in spades.

Jubilee ran down the stairs from the main deck and stopped short when she saw her cousin struggling between two police officers.

"What's going on? Why aren't you stopping them?"

Ryder was trying not to smirk. Knox saw the telltale twitch of his lips. "Not our jurisdiction."

"Call Mom," Luna wailed. "Tell her to send a lawyer."

"Uh, okay."

If the client was being held in a police station, did she still need bodyguards on duty? Or should they take the day off? Knox figured he'd better call Emmy. Occasional hiccups on the job weren't unusual, but this one was going to go down in Blackwood history.

"Wait! Wait!" Luna pleaded. "I need to change my outfit."

"We'll provide you with clothes, ma'am."

An orange jumpsuit? This got better and better.

"We'll make some calls," Knox told her. "Just keep your mouth shut and do as the officers ask. Don't make this worse."

"Worse? How could this possibly be worse?"

Knox had a feeling she was about to find out.

5

KNOX

"**M**s. Puckett, I'm going to give you a choice," Judge Morgan said. "Which is more than you gave that turtle."

Knox wasn't sure he liked the sound of that, and from the expression on the lawyer's face, he wasn't too thrilled either.

Just over a week had passed since Luna's arrest, and in that time, Knox had learned plenty about the San Gallician justice system. Foreigners were automatically considered flight risks and denied bail, so Luna had spent nine nights in solitary confinement at the island's jail, without make-up or a phone. Jubilee had posted a statement on social media, and Luna's fans around the world were holding vigils while insulting Judge Morgan and swearing they'd never visit San Gallicano, like, ever. The locals Knox had spoken with seemed pretty happy about that.

While the bail policy was harsh, it was also fair—Luna didn't get special treatment for being rich and famous, probably the first time in her life she'd been held accountable for her actions, and it showed. As did Amethyst

Puckett, three US lawyers, a rep from Luna's record label, and half of the world's media. Judge Morgan banned the press from the courtroom. When a few hapless reporters tried to complain, he threatened to have them arrested for breaching the peace.

For a case like Luna's, Judge Morgan had explained at the arraignment, the process would be swift. There was no doubt she'd treated the turtle inappropriately, or that she'd carried out the act in San Gallicano, seeing as she'd tagged both herself and the location in her Instagram post. The arguments would be over whether she'd caused the creature undue distress. Luna, of course, claimed the turtle was "super chilled" and "looked kinda smiley." She submitted several more pictures, including one of the poor thing wearing an oversized straw sun hat, in an attempt to prove her point. The prosecutor brought in a turtle expert from the Valentine Cay Turtle Sanctuary who explained that identifying stress in chelonians wasn't easy and the most obvious signs came from their behaviour, but the fact that the turtle had defecated on the beach in the final photo of the series suggested discomfort with the situation. Plus he testified that it was nesting season when the incident took place, and the turtle had most likely been crawling up the beach to lay eggs. Luna's thirst for fame had put an already endangered species further at risk.

This morning, a jury had found her guilty of all charges, and now it was time for the sentencing.

"You can either spend thirty days in jail," the judge continued as gasps echoed around the courtroom, "or you can do thirty days of community service here in San Gallicano. For those who might see that as a soft option, understand that I'd rather see Ms. Puckett give something back to this nation rather than using yet more of our resources. What's it to be, Ms. Puckett?"

"Can't I appeal?"

"On what grounds?"

"Uh…"

Her lawyer spoke up. "Can I confer with my client, Your Honour?"

Judge Morgan glanced at the clock on the wall of the courtroom. "You have two minutes."

Furious whispering ensued, presumably the lawyer telling Luna that having forty million social media followers and a dislike of the legal system wasn't sufficient grounds to appeal. Finally, he addressed the judge.

"My client will undertake the thirty days of community service. If we could agree on an appropriate time for that to—"

"Tomorrow."

"Could you expand on that, Your Honour?"

"Ms. Puckett will commence her community service tomorrow." His gaze shifted to Luna. "Treat this as a learning experience."

"Your Honour, my client has commitments. She's scheduled to sing at the Blayz Festival in the Bahamas the day after tomorrow, and—"

"Mr. Thomson, if your client is allowed to choose when she serves her sentence, it's not much of a deterrent, is it? The whole point of a punishment is to be inconvenient."

"This is outrageous!"

The cry came from the public gallery, and Knox didn't have to turn his head to see who was yelling. Only one woman would have the balls, and that woman was Amethyst Puckett. Beside him, Jubilee put her head in her hands.

"Thousands of people are coming to the Bahamas to see my daughter perform, and you want to deprive them over a damn turtle? What kind of banana republic is this?"

"Ms. Puckett *senior*, if you don't stop this outburst

immediately, I'll hold you in contempt. The law in San Gallicano is clear—sea turtles are protected in our waters, and if a visitor flouts the law, they need to understand there will be consequences. That includes your daughter. Do you realise how many tourists have tried to dress marine life in various items of clothing since she posed for that picture?"

The judge had decided to make an example out of her, hadn't he? Her sentence would be talked about as much as the original photo, and he was hoping the publicity would make idiots think twice about messing with endangered species.

"You should learn to show appreciation, mister. Don't you understand how much free publicity she generated for this stupid island?"

"Ms. Puckett! Sometimes, there are more important things in life than money, a lesson you'd do well to learn."

"Well, you'd do well to learn about the celebrity lifestyle. You want my daughter to do community service? In public? She's received death threats, you know. You'd be putting her life in danger."

Luna gasped. "Death threats? What death threats?"

"We didn't want to worry you, sweetie. Why do you think we hired bodyguards?"

"Ohmigosh! Someone's trying to kill me?"

The judge banged his gavel. "Ladies, this is a courtroom, not *Judge Judy*. I'll do the talking."

"You're just jealous of her success," Amethyst snapped. "That women are taking on the patriarchy and—"

"Enough! Bailiff, take the older Ms. Puckett away to cool off. A period of self-reflection would be beneficial—say, thirty days."

Luna watched on in horror as her mom was dragged kicking and screaming from the courtroom. Literally dragged. Literally kicking and screaming. Luna's support network had gone, and she had no one but lawyers to argue for her now. And they weren't going to risk upsetting Judge Morgan either.

"Now, Ms. Puckett *junior*. I'm a big believer in selecting a punishment that fits the crime." The judge turned to the public gallery. "Mr. Baptiste, are you still taking volunteers at the sanctuary?"

The turtle expert nodded. He'd stayed to watch the case, probably out of morbid curiosity. Franklin Baptiste was an older man with weathered bronze skin, one of the world's most prominent authorities on sea turtles. According to his testimony, he'd started out working for his family's fishing business on Ilha Grande, then gained a PhD in marine biology from the University of Miami and assisted with various conservation projects before moving back to San Gallicano twenty-seven years ago and setting up the turtle sanctuary. He'd dedicated his life to preserving the creatures ever since.

"Yes, sir, we still take volunteers," he said. "Just had a group cancel, as a matter of fact."

"Then would you be willing to allow Ms. Puckett to take their place?"

"Never short of paths to sweep or pools to clean out."

"Good. Then it's settled. Ms. Puckett, you'll be held in custody tonight and report for duty at the Valentine Cay Turtle Sanctuary tomorrow. Your sentence will begin first thing on Wednesday morning. In light of the alleged death threats, I'll permit your security team to accompany you. I trust that will be acceptable?"

Luna nodded. What else could she do?

"I'm also banning you from posting on any of your social media accounts for the duration of your time on Valentine Cay. For every picture of you I see—and I *will* be watching—your period of service will be extended by one day. You'll be there to work, not to become a martyr for your cause."

"But...but..."

"I'll also permit your cousin to join the volunteer program, should she so wish. Although she's not on trial, she bears some responsibility as your photographer." He addressed Jubilee. "You might think you're helping, but by enabling Luna to act as she does, you're doing her no favours in the long term." He banged the gavel again. "This case is now over."

Judge Morgan left the courtroom, and the bailiff took Luna away. As Detective Fernandez followed her out, he threw a smug smile in Knox's direction, but there was no need for that. If Knox was honest, he felt that Luna deserved her sentence. The judge had been fair. What she got wasn't so much a punishment as an educational opportunity. A chance to become a better person, although Knox wasn't certain she'd take it.

"Guess we're gonna learn a lot about turtles," Ryder muttered under his breath. "I'll call base, get them to run an assessment on Valentine Cay. Can you deal with Jubilee?"

Knox cut his gaze sideways. Jubilee hadn't moved since Luna left, and he figured she was in shock. People gave her instructions, and she carried them out. She wasn't accustomed to using her own initiative.

"You okay?" he asked.

"What am I meant to do?"

"First, I'd say you need to decide whether you want to spend a month at a turtle sanctuary. If you don't, we'll find a way of getting you home."

"I...I... What do you think I should do?"

"Only you can make that decision." Knox paused. "Why do you work for Luna? You're smart, and you're organised, and you could probably get a job as a PA somewhere else."

What he actually wanted to say was that she seemed to be the one sane person in the asylum. Luna treated her like dirt at times, and he couldn't imagine Amethyst was much easier to deal with.

"I..." She gave a heavy sigh. "It's complicated. I guess... I guess I owe her. When my mom died, Amethyst took me in so I could stay out of the care system, and Luna was a good friend too." Jubilee shrugged. "Bullies saw me as a target, and she was the one who protected me. She wasn't always this way—so demanding, I mean—and she gave me a job with a good salary when I left high school. Do you think it's crazy that I'm still working for her?"

"Loyalty is a good trait to have, but just be careful you don't lose yourself along the way."

"What if she can't cope at the turtle sanctuary? Luna doesn't do well on her own, and she isn't keen on water."

"Isn't keen on water? Then why did she take a vacation on a yacht?"

"Because it makes a great backdrop for her socials. Heck, she's gonna lose her mind if her stats drop."

"So you want to go?"

"I think I should."

The decision wasn't a surprise. Knox suspected that Jubilee didn't do well on her own either. The two cousins had a relationship that both benefited and harmed each of them. In short, the family was a mess, and how could it be anything else with Amethyst Puckett at the helm?

"Then I'll make the transport arrangements. Don't forget to bring bug spray."

Jubilee closed her eyes, appearing to steel herself for what was to come, and at that moment, Knox felt sorry for her. She'd sure lost out in the genetic lottery.

6

CARO

"Tell me you're not serious?"

I dropped the mop into the bucket and perched on the edge of one of the concrete pools we used for rehab. This had to be a bad joke. Luna Maara, pop psycho and turtle hater extraordinaire, couldn't be coming to Valentine Cay. Why on earth would Franklin agree to that kind of nightmare?

"Judge Morgan asked me personally, and we do need the help."

"A woman like Luna isn't going to be any help. She's going to spend all day on her phone, posting stupid videos and trying to make it look as if she isn't a horrible person."

"The judge banned her from social media, and that cousin of hers is coming too. It'll give us two extra pairs of hands."

I pressed my fingers against my eyes as if that might help with the pounding headache that had started with Franklin's call. This...this was like a shoal of tuna inviting a shark to stay for a month and expecting to swim away unscathed at the end of it.

"You know we need help, Caro. We were counting on those folks who dropped out."

True. That was true. They'd seemed so enthusiastic too, but then they'd scored last-minute tickets to the Blayz Festival and decided to spend a month in the Bahamas instead. So now we were stuck with Luna freaking Maara, who treated wild animals as fashion accessories and didn't care two hoots about the critical conservation work we were doing on Valentine Cay.

When I heard she'd been arrested, I'd been beyond thrilled. So often, tourists disturbed the wildlife and got away with it. Late last year, in one of those rare instances where the culprits were caught, a bunch of idiots on an extended bachelor party had pulled a juvenile shark out of the surf and dressed it up in a sombrero. In the trial—also before Judge Morgan—the groom had cited Luna Maara as their inspiration. To hear she'd claimed in court that her actions did no harm was absurd. The shark had lost its life, along with several turtles and a manta ray that had been found around the islands wearing accessories that ranged from a beaded necklace to a pair of board shorts.

Even though everyone knew what Luna had done, Vince Fernandez had told me over drinks one evening that it was unlikely she'd ever face justice. From what he'd heard, she'd spent most of her first visit to San Gallicano complaining about the time the bars closed, about the lack of retail opportunities, about the amount of freaking sand. Nobody thought she'd come back, and no way would the US extradite her over a turtle.

But then she'd shown up, and when Vince had called with the news, I'd celebrated with a pineapple-and-coconut smoothie and two chocolate truffles from the box I kept in the refrigerator for special occasions. Now? Now, I wanted to puke.

"It's going to be a circus. She'll bring every reporter in the Caribbean with her."

"Vince Fernandez says the coastguard will put extra patrols in the area, and if anyone trespasses on the sanctuary's grounds, they'll end up before Judge Morgan. There's nowhere for visitors to stay on Valentine Cay, anyway."

That was true. No hotel, no guesthouse. A wealthy businessman had tried to buy the sanctuary last year and turn it into a luxury resort, but Franklin had refused his money, even though he barely had two cents to rub together. He was rich in spirit, he said. And so was I. Once, I'd been the girl riding around on the expensive yacht and partying into the early hours, but in the end, it hadn't been as hard as I'd feared to give it all up.

"I'll just have to stay out of the way while she's here."

And heavens above, grant me the strength not to throat-punch Luna Maara because I couldn't afford to end up before Judge Morgan myself.

Even while doing community service, Luna Maara managed to bring an entourage. Not only her cousin but two ridiculously hot "bodyguards" who I bet she'd absolutely hired for their looks and not their defence skills. If they had any kind of qualifications, they'd probably gotten them from the internet. Done a Groupon course or something.

Vince accompanied them on the coastguard boat, presumably because he didn't trust her not to flee the country otherwise. Although I'd heard her mom was in jail for yelling at Judge Morgan, which might throw a wrench into the works. Would Luna abandon her own flesh and blood?

Franklin walked down to the dock to speak with Vince while I watched from the safety of the dining room as the group made their way up the beach. Tango sat beside me, her tail still. Usually, it wagged constantly.

"I know, girl. It sucks."

The black lab had shown up soon after I did, and where she came from, nobody knew. Valentine Cay wasn't a big island, so she wasn't local. Vince thought she'd fallen from a passing boat, but nobody ever came looking for her, so maybe she'd been thrown off instead? Whatever, she'd decided she was staying. She'd graduated from begging for the sardines we fed the turtles to eating cans of dog chow Franklin picked up on Ilha Grande, and although she had a bed in the bunkhouse, half the time, she preferred to sleep on the veranda so she could watch the stars.

Tango whined, and I scratched her head in sympathy.

"One month, and it'll all be over."

The bodyguards went up a notch in my estimation when they made Luna carry her own suitcases. Plural. Six of them. How long was she planning to stay? Less than thirty days, if I had anything to do with it. She should be in a jail cell, not wreaking havoc on the life I'd spent the past three years rebuilding. Back and forth, she went in a pair of bejewelled flip-flops. Back and forth. Finally, she had all the cases piled up at the edge of the shingle path that led to the bunkhouses, and she stood there surveying the buildings, hands on her hips and a faint expression of disgust on her pampered visage.

"Where's my room? And I need a glass of water."

No "Hi, I'm Luna" or "Sorry I've turned your lives upside down." Just another demand. Although to be honest, I hadn't expected anything else.

"There are no rooms," I told her. "There are bunkhouses. One for the men and one for the women. I'm Caro, by the way. I'd say it was a pleasure to meet you, but I'd be lying."

"How dare you speak to me that way?"

"Easy—I open my mouth, and the words come out. Look, I don't get paid to be nice to you. In fact, I barely get paid at all, and the last thing I want to do is spend the next month babysitting your spoiled ass. So stop whining, pick up your many, many suitcases, and come choose a bunk bed."

The nearest bodyguard, the one with the eel tattoo curling up his left arm, snorted and tried to turn it into a cough, but not a very convincing one. His eyes twinkled. The man was entirely too handsome for his own good, and that made him dangerous. I'd already fallen for an egotistical Casanova once in my life, and I'd paid the price for my stupidity. Never again.

He held out a hand. "Knox Livingston, and this is Ryder Metcalfe. We're here to provide security for Ms. Maara."

"Caroline Menefee."

That wasn't my real name, but it was the one I'd begun using almost three years ago. Nobody in San Gallicano knew my true identity, and although Franklin was aware I'd had a bad breakup in the past, I'd glossed over the full story of why I'd left Los Angeles.

"It's good to meet you. I'll apologise in advance for our presence."

"Apology accepted."

Grudgingly, although deep down, I understood that none of this was his fault.

Ryder offered a handshake and a smile as well, complete with dimples. He looked to be the more relaxed of the two, boy-next-door cute with dirty-blond hair rather than devastatingly gorgeous, in his late twenties at a guess. Which deity had he offended in order to get this job?

"My arms hurt," Luna announced. "There's no way I can carry these suitcases any farther."

"It's meant to rain tonight," Knox told her. "They'll get wet if you leave them there."

"Why are you so mean?"

"If you want us to be pleasant, that costs extra."

Hmm, perhaps Knox wasn't quite as unlikeable as I'd assumed he would be?

"I hate you. I hate all of you."

"If you want to try firing us again, then go right ahead."

"I would if some psycho wasn't threatening to hurt me. Jerk," she added under her breath.

Luna's cousin seemed to be the nervous type. If she chewed that lip any more, we'd have to take her to the emergency room for stitches. She was also the peacekeeper.

"Why don't we unpack, and maybe we could get breakfast?" The cousin, who'd brought three suitcases of her own, turned to me. "Do you have alkaline water?"

"Do we have *what*?"

"Alkaline water. Luna drinks it with a slice of lemon every morning."

I didn't know what the fuck alkaline water was, but I did know basic chemistry.

"Lemon's acidic. If you add it to an alkaline, you'll neutralise it."

"You don't know anything about nutrition." Luna spoke to me as if I were a small child. "When you drink lemon water, it reacts in your body and turns alkaline."

"I have a degree in biology, and I'm telling you an ad exec made that up."

"The guy who runs the company is a *doctor*."

The cousin raised both hands. "It's been a stressful week, and everyone's tired. Uh, I'm Jubilee."

Luna fixed her cousin-slash-assistant with a glare. "Don't think I've forgiven you for holding back important information. You can't just change the subject and expect me to forget about it."

What hadn't Jubilee told her? I was curious, but it wasn't my place to ask. Plus I didn't want to get pulled into Luna's drama. Having to spend the next month making sure she didn't put lipstick on a turtle or something equally stupid was quite bad enough.

"Do you want a tour of the place, or would you rather find your own way?" I asked.

Ryder sighed and stepped forward. "Luna, if you take two of the suitcases, I'll bring the rest."

Instead of being grateful, she huffed and grabbed the handle of the smallest case. Wow.

I couldn't help myself. "Isn't that worth a thank you?"

"I pay him." But she did turn back and roll her eyes. "Thank you, Ryder," she said, her voice overly saccharine.

What a piece of work.

7

KNOX

Knox checked the signal on his phone. They had service, thank fuck. Valentine Cay, population six hundred and forty-two, was a heart-shaped sandy paradise nestled among half a dozen uninhabited rocks ten miles from Ilha Grande.

Only a handful of significant islands were farther from Ilha Grande—Starlight Reef, famed for its displays of bioluminescence after the sun dropped; Emerald Shores with its lush forests; Dreadhaven, home to a sunken pirate ship that reappeared every so often when a storm shifted the sands; Treasure Atoll, once a picture-postcard paradise but now ruined by amateur sleuths who believed tales of hidden gold; and Skeleton Cay, the deserted prison isle that lay another eighteen miles to the west.

The Valentine Cay Turtle Sanctuary was situated in the dip at the top of the heart, surrounded on both sides by coconut palms and other greenery. In the centre of the dip lay a spacious dining room made from rough-hewn wood with a kitchen and a small office off to the side. The kitchen was partly open-air. The walls didn't go all the way to the roof, presumably to let out the heat and the smell of cooking. In the dining room itself, there were two tables, one with long benches on each side and the other surrounded by mismatched chairs. Beside the dining room, to the east, was Franklin Baptiste's cabin plus the five "pool rooms" where the turtles lived. Well, one of the pool rooms was still under construction, but it would house more turtles eventually. And to the west were two bunkhouses, each with a modest bathroom attached.

Knox had spent yesterday evening poring over background information with Ryder while Jubilee packed the girls' belongings on the yacht. A barrier reef curved around the top of the island, protecting the sun-kissed waters and sheltering the beach while limiting boat access. A RIB would go straight over the top of the coral, but any craft with a draft deeper than a couple of feet would scrape a hole in its hull unless it went through the deeper channel to the east of the sanctuary. Since most of the boats available for hire in San Gallicano were fishing vessels pulling double duty, the paparazzi would find it hard to get close by sea. The team would just have to watch out for telephoto lenses, but Knox had a semi-automatic and plenty of experience with hitting moving targets.

Relax, he was only joking.

Probably.

In satellite photos, the forest around the sanctuary looked wild and dense, but Knox and Ryder would make a better assessment from the ground. They'd brought a dozen wireless motion detectors that they could place around the camp to warn of approaching trouble. Knox would have no problem escorting overzealous reporters off the property—in fact, he was looking forward to it. The *Cleopatra*'s "fully equipped" gym was missing a heavy bag, and it had been a frustrating week.

After Caro had shown them around, he took pity on Ryder and grabbed two of Luna's suitcases. What the hell did she have in there? Fuckin' meteors? Damn things weighed a ton. They dumped the luggage in the girls' bunkhouse, which was a duplicate of the boys' bunkhouse with the exception of a screened-off corner at the rear that seemed to be Caro's space. Bunk beds lined the walls, five up, five down, and there was a table with chairs in the middle. Someone had added homey touches—a bookshelf full of dog-eared paperbacks, paintings of marine life, and a mirror with "Don't Worry, Be Happy" written across the top. Luna was sitting on a bunk at the front, crying, while Jubilee tried to comfort her.

"It'll be okay," she said. "All you need to do is not get arrested again."

"This is so unfair. They tell me that without publicity, talent doesn't matter, so I get publicity, and then they don't like it?"

"I think it was the whole criminal charges thing. I mean, they loved the original turtle post."

"What happened?" Ryder asked.

Jubilee answered because Luna was too busy hiccuping.

"Julius emailed. You know who Julius is?"

"Luna's agent?"

"Right. Anyway, he emailed and said the label was concerned about reputational damage. A bunch of eco-warriors are boycotting her records as well as all the other artists who are signed to Sonic Flare, and sales have declined dramatically. If Luna messes up one more time, they're gonna drop her."

"I don't see how they can do that," Luna said, sniffling. "We have a contract."

"There's a clause about public behaviour. If you bring

the company into disrepute, they can do whatever they want."

"How do we speak with my lawyer? Mom should be dealing with this."

"I already asked the lawyer, and that's what he told me. That if you mess up one more time, they can sever all ties."

Luna flopped backward onto the bed and sighed dramatically. "That freaking turtle ruined my life."

"Do you ever take responsibility for anything?" Caro asked from behind the screen.

"Why can't you even pretend to be supportive? You don't understand what it's like to face losing your whole career and everything you've spent your life working toward."

"Actually, I do. And I didn't sit around complaining the whole time. Are you going to put proper clothes on?"

"These *are* proper clothes. They made me wear a freaking jumpsuit last week, and it was hideous." Hideous, but probably more practical than the high-heeled flip-flops and crocheted dress she'd chosen this morning. "Where can I plug in my hair straightener?"

"For fuck's sake," Knox and Ryder both muttered at the same time as Caro said, "Give me strength."

"Maybe you could try a messy bun today?" Jubilee suggested. "That's hot right now."

Caro headed for the door, wearing shorts and a T-shirt with "Marine Biologists Do It Underwater" printed on the chest.

"Whatever you do, you'll need to do it quickly. There's a briefing in the dining room in five minutes, and then we have to get to work."

49

Franklin Baptiste gave the briefing, leaning on his elbows over a huge table made from scarred wood. Luna—predictably—had complained that the benches didn't have cushions, and Jubilee had found her a sweater to sit on. The black dog that seemed to belong to Caro snored softly in one corner.

"We got four types of turtle in San Gallicano," Baptiste said. "Green turtles, hawksbills, leatherbacks, and loggerheads, but the loggerheads don't nest here, and we don't see them often. They're all endangered, and hawksbills are on the critical list. They got threats coming from every direction—folks eat their eggs and meat, they get caught in fishing gear, and we're ruining their habitats. Turtles travel hundreds of miles to lay their eggs on the beach where they were born. Now when they arrive, too often they find someone's built on the sand or left deckchairs in the way. Then there's plastic in the oceans, climate change, and the turtleshell trade—all threats to their survival."

"Sometimes, I think it would be better if humans went extinct," Caro muttered, then paused to blow on her coffee. "We ruin everything."

It was a thought Knox had shared many, many times. As a SEAL, he'd seen the worst of human nature. Senseless killing, the hunger for control, the inability to coexist peacefully alongside others. No other species fought wars over differences of opinion.

"I'm with you there," he said. "Is there any hope for the turtles?"

Baptiste's fist clenched around the pen he was holding. "As long as there's still hope, I'll fight until my last breath."

"That's quite a commitment."

"Occasionally, a person needs to put aside their ego and do what's right for the planet."

He was looking at Luna as he said it, and she bristled.

"Hey, that's rude."

Caro rolled her eyes. "Accurate, though. What we do here makes a difference."

"*I* make a difference. When I was hired as a spokesmodel for Elemental Gems, I doubled their sales to the under-thirties market. Do you realise how many grooms pick out an emerald or a ruby instead of a diamond because of my social media posts?"

"Why does that matter?"

"It matters to the brides. Firstly, because Elemental sources their gems ethically, and secondly, because they're available in more colours than diamonds. But what would you know? I bet you've never been engaged because what man would put up with you?"

"You know nothing about my life, and at least I don't spend my days cavorting with half-naked men for likes."

Luna stood and leaned across the table, her face going redder by the second. Knox hoped Jubilee might step in since she tried to curb Luna's outbursts on occasion, but she just fidgeted with her rubber bracelet, gaze studiously averted.

"I do not cavort with men! Those are carefully staged photo ops. Do you even have one clue about marketing? Probably not, seeing as I'd never even heard of this place."

Now Caro was on her feet too, and she was a good six inches taller than Luna and probably forty pounds heavier. Not overweight though, not even a little. Just fit from labouring away at the sanctuary day in, day out, plus she had curves under that baggy T-shirt.

"I don't suppose there's much going on in that closed mind of yours at all."

"Ladies..." Ryder warned.

"Shut up!" they both yelled at him.

"My mind is not closed," Luna snapped. "I travel, I meet

people. You live in a hut and your best friends are amphibians."

"Turtles are reptiles, you idiot."

Franklin Baptiste had been chuckling quietly to himself until that point, but when Luna marched around the table, his eyes widened in alarm. Ryder nodded to Knox, and they acted as one.

"Get off me!" Luna shrieked as Ryder picked her up and carried her back to her seat.

As for Caro, she froze the moment Knox's arms wrapped around her, but she quickly recovered to elbow him in the gut. Which didn't have much impact on abs that did two hundred crunches before breakfast every morning, but Knox would probably have a nice bruise.

"What the fuck was that for?" he asked.

"I don't appreciate being manhandled."

Once Luna was back on her ass, Knox released Caro. She might have spoken relatively calmly, but her chest heaved as she sucked in air, and he'd felt her heart hammering against her ribcage. He figured that suggesting she calm down would only add fuel to the fire.

"Just trying to stop a catfight."

"I can take care of myself." She turned and narrowed her eyes, her gaze locked on his from mere inches away. Her voice dropped close to a whisper. "A catfight? I'm not a pussy."

Time stood still as he stared into pissed-off sea-blue eyes with flecks of green around the edges, and that was the moment Knox realised he was in trouble. He was stuck on an island for the next thirty days alongside a pop diva with an attitude, a ball-breaker who made his dick twitch, and a sense of foreboding that left his lizard brain on high alert.

"I'm glad we got that cleared up."

Ryder cleared his throat. "Maybe we could go over the daily routine? What does Luna need to do while she's here?"

Slowly, slowly, Caro turned around and sank onto her seat again, leaving a faint aroma of vanilla hanging in the air. Shampoo? Perfume? Knox caught himself taking a deeper inhale and gave himself a mental kick. *Step back, asshole.* This was work. Caroline Menefee and her intoxicating mix of fire and vulnerability was firmly off limits.

"We have a list of daily tasks," Baptiste said. "The pools get cleaned out each mornin', and the turtles need to be fed. Some are permanent residents, but most are hawksbills that are part of our 'raise and release' program. Each year, we keep a number of the hatchlings here in seawater pools, and then we release them into the wild when they're older."

"It gives them a better chance of survival," Caro said, speaking normally now, although her hands clenched and unclenched on her thighs. She was stressed, and understandably so. Had she felt what Knox did? Or was she just annoyed at the thought of being stuck here with Luna for a month? "As with so many things, it's a trade-off—turtles raised in captivity are less accustomed to life in the sea, and so they have to learn survival skills, but their larger size makes them less vulnerable to predators. We mark the shells and tag them before release, and overall, the program has been shown to benefit the hawksbill population in these waters. Or at least, it did until two years ago."

"What happened two years ago?" Ryder asked.

"Our surveys have been showing a decline in all turtle species. When I moved to San Gallicano, it was rare to make a dive without seeing at least a handful of turtles, but now, we're lucky if we see one. As Franklin said, we mark those we release so we can track them, and they're just disappearing."

"How do you mark them? Couldn't a tag fall off?"

"We use different methods depending on the size. For adults, we attach a pair of flipper tags and inject a PIT tag—a Passive Integrated Transponder—under the skin. Juveniles are too small for flipper tags, so we use PIT tags and also notch the backs of their shells. People often used to see them swimming around and tell us about it. With hatchlings, we've been using VIE, Visible Implant Elastomer. It's a coloured polymer we inject under the skin that fluoresces in UV light." Caro glanced at Baptiste. "This season feels as if it'll be make or break. We built two extra pools over the winter so we can raise more hatchlings."

"What's causing the decline?"

"Mankind."

Caro didn't have a high opinion of her fellow humans, did she?

"Who hurt you?" Luna asked, and was it Knox's imagination, or did Caro flinch?

She recovered quickly and fired back, "Who made you believe you're better than everyone else?"

Before the two women could face off again, Baptiste raised both hands, stopping them.

"We haven't been able to pinpoint a reason for the decline. Could be due to changes in the sea—the temperature, loss of food sources, pollutants. Could be increased activity in the water and on land, so the turtles avoid the area. Could be because people are takin' them, either as bycatch or on purpose. Smuggling still happens."

"So do idiot tourists," Caro added.

Once again, Luna looked as if she'd swallowed a hornet. "Why do you hate me so much?"

"Because you're still breathing."

How the fuck were these women going to share a bunkhouse without killing each other?

"Turtle meat's always been considered a delicacy," Baptiste continued, ignoring the animosity. "And the shells are valuable even though there are regulations in place to prevent them from being sold. The dwindlin' population might be due to a combination of all of those issues, but we need to do more research."

"Who even cares?" Luna asked. "What's the point of turtles anyway?"

Caro's eyes went from calm to stormy in a second. "They're an important part of the ecosystem. Turtles can live for two hundred years, did you know that? If they didn't eat algae off the coral, the coral would die, and we'd have no reefs. They also eat baby jellyfish. Do you want to get stung every time you swim in the sea?"

"I don't swim in the sea."

"She doesn't swim, period," Jubilee muttered.

"Be quiet!"

Luna didn't swim? Because she didn't enjoy it? Or because she couldn't? Knox mentally scrolled through the background file—there were pictures of her posing in hot tubs and relaxing beside pools—but not a single one of her in open water. She didn't know how to swim, he'd put money on it, and now she was living on an island. Well, damn. At least she couldn't make a run for it under cover of darkness.

"We try to do regular surveys," Baptiste said. "Do any of the rest of you folks dive?"

Knox and Ryder both raised their hands.

"But we're here to protect Luna," Ryder told him. "We can't dive together and leave her behind."

"That's a damn shame. I got a problem with my eardrum, so Caro's been on her own for the past month."

The first rule of diving? Never go alone. If something

went wrong underwater, you were reliant on your buddy to help. Plus Knox wouldn't mind seeing Caro in a bathing suit.

"I don't mind diving in my downtime," he offered.

"We'd appreciate that, son. You PADI qualified?"

"I'm Navy SEAL qualified."

Caro's eyebrows arched in surprise, and Knox wasn't sure whether to be pleased or insulted by that.

"And your friend?" Baptiste nodded toward Ryder.

"The same."

"We don't have fancy dive gear here, just the basics."

"We brought our own. Occasionally, a principal likes a little private time, and we get a few hours to play tourist."

Ridley from the EP team had once told Knox about a job he'd worked in the South of France where the client spent most of the contract in her stateroom, entertaining men who weren't her husband. Each evening, she'd kick Ridley off the yacht with orders not to return until she called him. He'd spent more time in the hotel gym than working. But apart from hanging out with Kory, Luna hadn't shown any interest in men. And Kory wasn't much of a friend—as soon as the trial was over, he'd taken off for the Bahamas without a backward glance.

"We schedule surveys depending on the wind," Baptiste said. "Most of our dives are done from the boat"—he tipped his head toward the wooden dock, where an old but well-maintained C-Dory bobbed gently in the breeze—"so entry and exit don't depend on the tide. Not that there's much of a tide here, only a couple of feet between high and low. We can refill your tanks with the compressor out back."

"Air or Nitrox?"

"We only have air."

Caro took a sip of coffee. "Air is enough for what we do.

Plus we're coming up to nesting season, so we won't get much time for surveys. We'll be too busy collecting eggs and reburying them on the beach here."

"Why do you do that?" Knox asked.

"Because it's easier to keep them safe from predators that way, both human and animal. And when they hatch, we can make sure they reach the water."

"Tourists like to see the babies," Baptiste said. "We show people around the sanctuary in return for a donation, plus we visit schools on the other islands to teach the children about conservation. Some of them have never seen a real live turtle before." He shook his head. "Times have changed. When I was their age, I went skin diving on the weekends, and I could name every sea species in San Gallicano by the time I turned ten."

"We won't have any visitors this month." Caro shot a dirty look at Luna. "Everyone who's called in the last two days has been a reporter; I just know it. Oh, sure, they say they're on vacation, but when you ask them if they liked the hanging gardens at Fort Elizabeth—*every* tourist visits Fort Elizabeth—they all say yes, they loved them, even though the hanging gardens are on Malavilla. Rumour says they're offering hundreds of bucks a day to the charter operators on Ilha Grande."

Finally, Jubilee spoke. "Thank you for keeping the reporters away."

"I'm not doing it for you; I'm doing it because Judge Morgan said your cousin isn't allowed any publicity. So now we're short of donations at our busiest time of the year, and all we have is two helpers who have no interest in wildlife, one of whom can't even swim." Luna didn't contest that assertion, which led Knox to believe it was correct. "I hope you're good at cleaning."

Luna looked faintly sick at the prospect. "I don't know anything about cleaning. Why would I? I have people for that."

Caro grinned like a movie villain. "Not here, you don't. And I'm an *excellent* teacher."

8

CARO

"How do you put up with her?" I asked Knox. I might have been a good teacher—I'd taken over training the volunteers last summer so Franklin could focus on the hatchlings—but Luna Maara was the worst student I'd ever encountered. Probably because she didn't want to learn. She'd already broken a nail this morning, and you'd think it was her femur from the way she complained.

"Money," Knox said. "That's how I put up with her. Is there somewhere on this island that sells Tylenol? I only brought one bottle, and I'm gonna need more."

"That bad, huh?"

"That bad."

"The general store near the harbour stocks generic acetaminophen. Franklin drives over there in the truck a couple of times a week if you want anything. Handcuffs, a gag, whatever."

"BDSM isn't my jam, but thanks for the offer."

Shit. That wasn't what I'd meant at all, but I saw how it could be construed that way. I also saw that Knox was dangerous, and not just Navy SEAL dangerous. No, he was heart-stoppingly dangerous.

"You have a dirty mind."

"I tried cleaning up my act once. Worst three days of my life." Knox nodded toward Luna. "And there's someone else who isn't great at cleaning."

An hour ago, I'd shown Luna how to clean the pools where the older turtles lived—each day, we skimmed any faeces and uneaten food out of the water with a net. Once a week, we changed a quarter of the water to prevent ammonia buildup, and once a month, we cleaned the filters, the rocks, and the walls of the tanks. It never ended. Other jobs were dependent on the time of year, with nesting season being the busiest. And this year, it seemed, I'd have a pop star to babysit as well as all the work to do. Luna was still by the first pool, mindlessly sweeping the net back and forth as she stared at the beach.

"Typical rich kid." I called her a kid, even though she was only four years younger than me. Actions were more important than calendars, and she acted like a spoiled brat. "She's never had to lift a finger in her life."

"You spend much time around rich kids?" Knox asked, and dammit, I had to remember how perceptive he was. Those sparkling eyes missed nothing. Telling a vague truth about my past and then changing the subject seemed like the best option.

"I was a scholarship student. If Luna accidentally landed face-first in the pool, would you have to rescue her?"

"Unfortunately." He glanced across at the brat and Jubilee. "Probably shouldn't say that."

"We're all thinking it." A sigh escaped. "I'd better go educate her."

"Good luck."

Luna glanced up as I headed in her direction, her

expression miserable. Good. How did she think the poor turtle had felt when she interrupted its egg-laying to make it an "online sensation"? I sincerely hoped she'd use this month to learn from her mistakes, but I had my doubts she was capable.

"You're just stirring the dirt around," I told her. "The idea is that you remove it from the water."

Gilbert the green turtle watched from the shelter of his favourite rock with bemused curiosity. He was one of our permanent residents. Several years ago, one of his flippers had been amputated after he got tangled in a ghost net, and to add insult to injury, he'd also been hit by a boat. The dent in his shell was obvious when you got close. Now he'd live out his days here, safe in his pool. We tried to make it a home for him by adding rocks and sand, plus Franklin was experimenting with growing seagrass.

"It stinks."

The smell was barely detectable, and it was just saltwater, not shit. "What did you expect? Chanel N°5?"

"This is slavery—you understand that, right?"

I smiled sweetly. "If you'd rather do nothing all day, you're welcome to go to jail instead. I'm sure they'd give you a room of your own, and I hear the stew they serve for dinner is almost edible."

"You're enjoying this, aren't you? You think it's funny."

"Honestly? I knew before you even arrived that you'd be trouble. You're not doing anything constructive, and you're taking up time I don't have. I've had a hundred calls from reporters today already—no exaggeration—who all want to photograph your sorry ass, and folks would rather go destroy the environment at the Blayz Festival than volunteer to help us here. So no, I'm not enjoying this."

Ryder chose that moment to meander in from the beach with a pair of binoculars in his hand. "There are seven boats out there, and I counted eleven photographers on board. They don't look as if they're planning to come past the reef for the moment, but we should be prepared in case they try."

"You mean I should refresh my lipstick?" Luna asked.

"For fuck's sake." Knox rolled his eyes skyward. "He means that we should be prepared to remove them from the property."

"Is that allowed? One of my ex-bodyguards got sued for pushing a reporter."

"In San Gallicano?" I asked.

"No, in Vegas. You know, back in civilisation where forced labour is against the law."

"You're not in Vegas now, Dorothy."

"My name is Luna, you numbskull."

The joke went right over her head, and without thinking, I copied Knox's eye-roll. *What a dumbass.*

"Well, Judge Morgan tends to be a little more pragmatic with his rulings, plus he's not a big fan of journalists. Or Americans." Not after an intrepid travel writer from Florida criticised his son's hotel for being "too rustic." *Two stars, needs a minibar and in-room entertainment.* Jacob Morgan ran an ecolodge, for Pete's sake. Rustic was the whole point. "I'll call Vince and see if there's a patrol boat nearby."

"Vince?" Knox asked.

"Detective Fernandez."

Luna narrowed her eyes. "You're on first-name terms with the jerk who arrested me?"

"It's a small country. I'm on first-name terms with a lot of people."

"You were probably in on his whole conspiracy to humiliate me." She huffed, then glanced across at the sea. "Why don't I just pose for some pictures? Then they might go away."

Knox snorted. "Are you kidding? If you give them what they want, then tomorrow, we'll have thirty boats out there."

"Shoulda brought limpet mines," Ryder muttered.

Jubilee stepped forward and tried a shaky smile. "Luna, the judge said he didn't want to see any pictures of you."

"On *my* socials. These photos wouldn't be on my accounts, would they? They'd be on TMZ, celebgossip.com, PopSugar, the Hollywood Hotlist... Do you realise how much exposure I'm missing out on?"

Boo-freaking-hoo.

"Think of your family too. Cordelia's worried about the impact this will have on your father's reputation. She's emailed me six times already."

"Only six?"

Okay, I'd bite. "Who's Cordelia?"

"Luna's half-sister," Jubilee explained. "She lives in England."

Luna pulled a face that would have lost her a million Instagram followers. "*Lady* Cordelia. She thinks that just because she has a title and lives in a castle, everybody should bow and scrape at her feet."

"It's actually only a stately home," Jubilee put in, then withered when Luna skewered her with a glare. "Sorry."

"Cordelia lives off family money and does literally zero work, but she still thinks she can tell me how to run my life."

"You're also doing zero work," I pointed out.

"Are you kidding? I've released three studio albums and performed on eight continents, plus I post new content every day."

"There are only seven continents." Unless you counted Zealandia, which was controversial and also mostly underwater.

"Whatever. At least I have a career. Are you going to spend the next five decades picking poop out of pools?"

The dig hurt, but I tried not to show it. Truthfully, I had no idea what the next five decades would bring. Once, I'd been more similar to Luna than I cared to admit, but I liked to think I'd become a better person. Did I want to spend the rest of my life at the sanctuary? Honestly, I wasn't sure. Here, I felt safe, or at least as safe as I could feel after Aiden vowed to find me and make me pay for what I'd done. And I'd feel guilty if I left Franklin. He'd given me a place to stay, helped me to find my feet again. I did care about the turtles, and that would never change, but there were times when I wished there was more to my world than a screened-off bunk bed and a succession of visitors who were just passing through on their way to another adventure.

"At least poop doesn't whine constantly." The phone clipped to my belt vibrated, and I cursed under my breath. "If this is another idiot with a press pass looking for an exclusive..." I jabbed at the "answer" button. "Are you a reporter?"

"Uh, yes? My name is—"

"Oh, go take a hike on Skeleton Cay."

"Skeleton Cay? Is that the place where they found the bodies a while back?"

"It's real nice at this time of year."

"But—"

"Look, nobody's going to talk to you. Luna's here to work, not give interviews."

"Who's Luna?"

"Are you serious?"

"Is this the Valentine Cay Turtle Sanctuary? Mr. Baptiste promised to speak with me regarding the decline in turtle populations, but I think I may have the wrong number?"

Aw, shit. Now I felt like the biggest fool on the planet. The biggest bitch too. I did recall Franklin mentioning an email from an investigative reporter asking about our marine life surveys. She'd done some big story on poaching in Africa a few years ago and won a Pulitzer. What was her name? Tracy? Lacey? Kasey?

I blew out a breath. "Sorry, I didn't mean to snap. It's been a difficult day. Your name is…?"

Luna smirked at the apology, and I wished *she'd* landed up on Skeleton Cay. Alone, with no laptop, phone, or internet connection. Ryder glanced down at my hand, and I realised it was balled into a fist. The brat just had that effect on me.

Thankfully, he took pity. "Luna, I don't think anyone cleaned the breakfast dishes yet."

"And you want me to do it?"

"Yeah, I do."

Miraculously, she let him lead her out of the room, and the knot of tension in my belly loosened enough for me to take in air.

"I'm Stacey. Stacey Custer," the reporter said. *Stacey.* Well, I'd been in the ballpark. "And I'm sorry about your day. A friend of mine wrote an article on stress in the modern world, and constant connectivity combined with a lack of time has impacted mental health in a big way over the past several decades. The phone is a necessary evil."

"Sometimes I wish I could just turn it off. I thought being on an island, I'd get some peace, but the signal is surprisingly good here. You're looking for Franklin? He's out right now, but I can take a number and ask him to call you."

"I was hoping to visit the sanctuary. Do you think that would be possible? He offered me a tour and said we could talk over lunch. I'm writing a story on the illegal wildlife trade—that's my passion project—but I also submit articles to travel magazines."

"Gotta pay the bills, huh?"

"Exactly. So I figured I could kill two birds with one stone. Research for my main project, plus background for an article on volunteering overseas."

"Sure, we can help with that. When were you thinking of coming?"

"Tomorrow? Assuming I can get there. I'm on Ilha Grande, and every person with a boat for hire seems to be busy this month."

Three guesses as to why. I glanced out to the bay, where seven boats had turned into eight, and one of them was perilously close to the reef.

"There's a ferry. Two ferries, actually. Go to Half Moon Bay, and there's a stand at the end with a yellow roof. The catamaran will take you to Malavilla, and from there, it's a short hop over to Valentine Cay."

"Weird, a guy in the grocery store near Half Moon Bay told me there were no ferries to Valentine Cay for the rest of the season. Maintenance or something."

"Did you happen to tell him you were a reporter?"

"I might have mentioned a travel article."

"That's why. There are way too many troublesome reporters in town at the moment."

A pause. "Writing about the wildlife trade?"

"No, no, they write for the gossip pages."

"Yikes. Well, better them than me. My ex used to freelance for celebgossip.com and the Hollywood Hotlist—probably still does, but I avoid those sites like the plague, so I don't know for sure. Maybe the fact that he was an asshole makes me kind of biased? Anyhow, I just assume all those guys are the same. More 'invasion of privacy' than journalism."

"Then I guess I'm biased too, because they're definitely assholes."

She laughed. "I'll see you tomorrow. Mid-morning okay?"

"That works." Mid-morning would give me three hours to get some work out of Luna before I needed respite. "If you can't find anyone to drive you from the jetty to the sanctuary, give me a call and one of us will pick you up."

9

RYDER

D amn, she was pretty.
      Pretty self-centred.
      Pretty hot.
Pretty annoying.
Pretty fucking fascinating.

And also pretty safe because she was the principal, and Ryder wouldn't do anything dumb when it came to work. Jeopardising the safety of a client would jeopardise his career, and his career was his life now.

And then there were the memories... He'd wanted to hate Luna Maara, but the more time he spent with her, the more she reminded him of pain from a past he'd tried hard to get over. Neve had been a tiny little handful, unapologetically larger than life but deeply scarred on the inside. For years, Ryder had thought love would be enough, but now he knew the truth. Love didn't conquer all.

And Luna Maara was firmly off limits.

"Why don't these people have a dishwasher?" she asked. "I thought everyone had a dishwasher."

"A quarter of the world doesn't even have access to safe

drinking water. Didn't you sing at a fundraising concert for Water to the World last year?"

"I don't know. Probably? I sing at a lot of concerts when some pig of a judge doesn't mess with my schedule." She turned, and her sundress slipped off one shoulder. "You looked up my performances?"

"The support team did. I just read the report."

Once upon a time, someone had put money into the Valentine Cay Turtle Sanctuary. The buildings were sturdily constructed, and the stainless-steel appliances in the communal kitchen had been built to last. Power came from an array of solar panels and a small wind turbine, with a backup generator in a lean-to attached to Franklin Baptiste's modest home. The C-Dory tied up at the dock didn't come cheap either.

But at some point, the money had run out. The place was clean but tired, with weathered wood in need of a coat of paint and faded cushions on chairs nobody seemed to have time to sit on. Ryder was no expert, but he thought the shingles on the roof would need replacing soon too.

Luna stared at the old porcelain butler sink as if it contained radioactive material rather than dinnerware.

"Let me guess... You've never washed dishes before?"

"This is so unfair. I only had coffee for breakfast."

"The judge wasn't interested in fairness when he sent you here. He said it's meant to be a learning experience."

"Okay, fine. I've learned not to touch turtles. Why can't I go home now?" When she turned the faucet on full, water splashed everywhere, and she leaped back with a shriek. "Yuck!"

"You need to add dish soap."

"This is gross. Who eats curry for breakfast?"

"The good folks of San Gallicano."

Scrambled eggs, curried beans, and flatbread was a

traditional island breakfast. Locals called it *tres bocados*, which translated from Spanish as "three bites," so Ryder figured intrepid explorers had come up with the dish.

"Aren't there any rubber gloves?"

"I doubt it. Those aren't sustainable. And don't leave the faucet turned on—water is a precious resource."

"You're not my boss."

"That's true. But I assume you'll want to take a shower later, and you won't be able to do that if you let all the water run down the sink."

Her mouth set in a hard line, and she didn't say a word, but she did turn off the faucet. Ryder leaned against the counter and watched as she scrubbed the dishes in silence and stacked them in the draining rack to the side. She didn't like being told what to do, but she also wasn't enough of a rebel that she'd refuse to follow orders altogether.

"There, are you happy now?"

She'd done a better job with the dishes than she had with the pool.

"Are *you* happy?"

Luna stared out the window at the tangle of trees beyond. The lack of maintenance extended to the foliage, but Ryder had to view that as a good thing right now because at least the paparazzi couldn't get any good shots. A long moment passed before Luna finally answered.

"How *can* I be happy?"

She couldn't have been expecting an answer because she stomped off to the refrigerator, leaving Ryder to ponder the question for a moment before he followed. Logic said she was talking about the enforced volunteering, but instinct told him that her words had a deeper meaning. Luna Maara had the world at her feet—or so everyone thought—but there was still something missing from her life.

It was a feeling Ryder understood all too well. He'd

made it through SEAL training, spent nine years on the Teams, and then sidestepped into his dream job. That was everything he'd wanted, right? Everything he'd planned with Neve during those late-night heart-to-hearts in Jacksonville. Despite the mansion, the money, and the prestige of being Henry Fontaine's daughter, there'd been a darkness inside her, but she lit up when they were together. They'd made plans. Ryder wanted to see the world, and Neve simply wanted to get the hell away from home. He craved adventure; she needed stability. Marriage and the military would have given them that.

They'd kept their engagement quiet, a secret between the two of them. She wore the ring on a chain around her neck because her father hadn't been a fan of Ryder's. They'd planned to go to the courthouse, just the two of them, and tell him afterward.

But Neve hadn't been able to hold on.

He'd watched them bury her from the slope at the side of the cemetery, rain dripping down his face. His beautiful Neve. Not a day passed when he didn't whisper into the breeze, hoping that wherever she was, she'd hear his words.

She hadn't liked washing dishes either, and when she did, she'd always let the water run because floating bits of food made her gag. She'd been a vivacious pain in the ass, and he'd loved her with his whole heart.

"There's no ice." Luna's complaint broke Ryder out of his thoughts. "And no soda."

"Soda's bad for you."

"Now you sound like my mom."

Ryder peered over her head into the refrigerator. Fuck, she couldn't have been more than five feet one. A tiny porcelain dictator.

"What about OJ?"

"Do you know how many calories fruit juice has?"

"More than water, less than a milkshake? If you put your back into cleaning the pool, you'd burn the calories."

"I hate cleaning."

"Do you hate cleaning? Or do you just hate being told you have to do it?" Ryder opened cupboards, hunting for a glass. "You think it should be someone else's job? You're a perfectionist and you'd rather not do it at all than make an attempt and open yourself up to criticism?" He took two tumblers from a shelf. "All of the above?"

"Are you a psychologist now?"

"Nuh-uh, I'm just an asshole who asks too many questions. But you remind me of a girl I used to know, and she would have balked at cleaning the turtle pools as well."

He poured two glasses of juice and handed one to Luna. She stared at it for a moment but finally took a sip.

"Ugh, there's pulp."

"That's the best part."

"Bits get stuck in my teeth, and then someone takes a photo, and suddenly I'm the girl who doesn't know how to floss."

"Nobody's gonna take a photo of you here."

"Oh, they'll find a way. They always do." For a media darling, she sounded surprisingly resigned. "They never give up."

"Do you want them to take pictures?"

A shrug. "What I want doesn't matter."

"I thought you liked being the centre of attention?"

"It's better to be famous than to be forgotten."

"And it's better to be nice than to be notorious."

"You're really annoying."

"So I've heard." Ryder drained his glass and rinsed it. "What if I told you I could sneak out to one of those boats and remove the drain plug?"

He meant it as a joke, but when he thought about it, was

sinking a boat the worst idea? Luna deserved privacy, and the coastguard had already warned the reporters off once, but as soon as the patrol boat left, the paparazzi reappeared. Perhaps they needed a little help to get the message? If Caro was right about the amount of money the captains were raking in from their "tours," then they'd be able to afford the insurance excess. All San Gallician boats taking paying passengers were required to have comprehensive insurance coverage—there was a notice stating that in the main harbour.

Maybe Ryder would feel a touch of guilt for ruining someone's day, but only a mild twinge. Those assholes didn't give a shit if they ran roughshod over Luna's privacy.

"What's a drain plug?" she asked.

"The thing that keeps the water out."

"They'd get a hundred pictures of you doing it."

Ryder laughed. "My life doesn't go on Instagram. Are you ready to take on the turtles again?"

Luna stood there for the longest time, staring into her glass of juice as if it held the answers to life. Finally, she spoke, her whisper barely audible.

"All of the above."

"Huh?"

"That's why I don't want to clean the turtle pools. All of the above, but mostly the last one. People never stop judging. Caro hates me, and Knox thinks I'm just a dumb, shallow blonde."

"Caro hates that you dressed a turtle in sunglasses. And when you hired Knox, you asked for the hot guy with the snake tattoo."

"Well, I didn't know his name. I only knew that he was fierce when he protected Lady Petronella, and someone told me what company he worked for."

"It's an eel."

"What's an eel?"

"Knox's tattoo. Plus you picked me out of a photo line-up and told me to shave off my beard. You have to understand why we might have preconceptions."

Luna's haughty expression vanished, and for the briefest second, her eyes turned haunted. Ryder had seen that look before, usually before Neve had spilled the details of some other fucked-up thing a family member had done.

"You...you have kind eyes." Luna swallowed hard. "And the beard thing... I had a bad experience, and even though I try to block it out, I still remember the scratch of his beard against my skin." A pause, and her fire returned. "But fine, just label me as unreasonable the way everyone else does."

Fuck.

"I didn't realise."

"Believe it or not, there are parts of my life that I don't share with the public." She finished the juice and put the glass on the counter, then picked it up again and rinsed it.

"What kind of bad experience?"

"None of your business. Just know that finding out you're gay took a weight off my mind."

Double fuck.

Now what? Ryder could hardly confess he was as straight as the trajectory of a 7.62 sniper round. And what harm would it do for her to carry on believing the lie? It wasn't as if he intended to make any inappropriate moves around her. Instead, he took a step back and leaned on the counter.

"Let me tell you a little about my boss. She never mentions her childhood, but I know she wasn't born into money. No trust fund, no silver spoon. She clawed her way up the ladder in a man's world, smashed through the glass ceiling, and managed to marry a billionaire along the way."

"She married a billionaire, but she still has a job?"

"Last week, she climbed onto the roof at the office to remove a dead bird that was interfering with one of the satellite dishes. Sure, she could have called a maintenance team, but she figured it would be quicker to fix the problem herself."

"She climbed onto the roof? Is she crazy?"

"Yeah, she is. And if she was here, she'd tell you that the surest way to fail is to never fucking try."

"When I fail, everybody knows about it."

"Define 'everybody.' There are only six of us here today." A strand of hair hung over Luna's eye, and Ryder's fingers itched to tuck it behind her ear. He stuffed his hands into his pockets. "As long as a mistake isn't fatal, you can use it as a foundation for future success."

"If the bodyguard thing doesn't work out, you could always get a job as a therapist."

"The bodyguard thing will work out just fine. You don't need to worry about that."

"Ryder?"

"Yeah?"

"I don't want those photographers taking pictures of me here."

"Then keep your head down, don't do anything wild, and Knox and I will make sure they stay out of the way."

"Do turtles bite?"

"They can, but Caro said they won't unless they feel threatened. You didn't ask that question before the sunglasses photo?"

"That one seemed real docile, and it was Kory who picked it up."

"The same Kory who hightailed it out of the harbour yesterday? You didn't tell the cops he was a part of Turtlegate."

"I didn't want to get him into trouble" Luna sighed. "He can be annoying sometimes, but he'd never hurt me."

There was a glimpse of the protectiveness Jubilee had spoken about. Luna Maara did have a heart, even if she hid it under a veneer of entitlement and glossy photoshoots. And Ryder had seen hints of her fragility too. She wasn't as strong as she wanted everyone to believe.

This time when he suggested going back to the turtle pools, she walked ahead of him to the door, head held high. Even if Knox and Caro thought she was a lost cause, Ryder had hope that this month would turn Luna into a better person. By avoiding the public gaze, she'd have time to reflect on her past and consider her future, to decide on the type of person she wanted to become. He had a feeling she was a better actress than people gave her credit for, that she'd been hiding her true feelings for far too long.

Later, he'd wish he was wrong.

If he'd realised just how much pain would come spilling out of the cracks, he'd have grabbed a roll of duct tape, sealed up the flaws as best he could, and cleaned the damn turtle pools himself.

10

CARO

"I understand now why you were so upset when I called yesterday." Stacey Custer took a sip of fruit tea and helped herself to a cookie from the box she'd brought. "A deckhand on the ferry filled me in, although I had to google Luna Maara. I'm more of a jazz fan."

"I prefer rock myself."

"Her mom really got jailed for contempt?"

"Thirty days."

And maybe she'd get another thirty days if she kept raising hell. Vince said—when he managed to stop laughing —that she travelled with her own toilet seat, and when she wasn't allowed to use it in her cell, she'd kicked up such a fuss that Judge Morgan had gone to the jail personally to educate her on the error of her ways. I realised now that Luna's attitude problem was hereditary.

Although she'd been surprisingly compliant this morning. Yes, she'd missed several chunks of dirt, and she'd shrieked when Lola the loggerhead swam toward her, but she'd cleaned five pools to an acceptable standard, and when Ryder suggested she might want to make drinks for everyone, she'd actually done it instead of giving him a mouthful of abuse. Jubilee had managed to clean three pools and sweep the floor in the bunkhouse, which meant my headache had dropped from a nine to a four by the time Stacey arrived.

She was younger than I thought she'd be, only a year or two older than me, but her dark red hair and pale skin suggested she spent more time behind a desk than outdoors. She had a habit of click-click-clicking her pen as she spoke, which was getting on my already frazzled nerves, but I didn't want to whine like Luna, so I just gritted my teeth.

"And those boats out there are full of photographers?" she asked.

"That's right. The coastguard cleared them away yesterday, but they keep showing up like bad pennies. We caught half a dozen men trying to sneak in through the trees in the night as well."

When I said "we," I meant Knox and Ryder. They'd set up motion sensors that sounded an alarm every time they were triggered. At three a.m., I'd been woken by the sound of yelling and stumbled outside in time to see Knox marching a reporter away in an armlock. Somehow, a camera lens had gotten broken in the process. The trespasser —a Texan, judging by his accent—had threatened to sue, and I could just imagine Judge Morgan's glee if the case came up on his docket. He was something of a legend in San Gallicano, and he won reelection by a landslide every time.

"People like that give our profession a bad name. I assure you I'm not interested in Luna, only in your knowledge of turtles."

Franklin walked in with Tango at his heels, and Stacey rose to greet him with a handshake. Usually—in the pre-Luna days, at least—journalists dropped by to write travel guides, not because they genuinely cared about conservation. We generally got worse reviews than Jacob Morgan's ecolodge. The last reporter to inquire about turtle smuggling had ghosted us after we refused to go on record, but what did he expect? Smugglers weren't nice people, especially when their livelihoods were threatened, and Franklin feared retaliation. And me? I had even more to lose. If Aiden found me, I'd be in grave danger, so no way was I agreeing to appear on a podcast, in a YouTube video, or as part of any other kind of content. Stacey had already agreed to those terms.

"Then ask your questions," Franklin said. "We'll answer them as best we can."

"Do you mind if I record our discussion? Just to supplement my notes—I promise it won't be replayed for anyone else."

Franklin deferred to me, and I nodded. "As long as our names and the sanctuary aren't mentioned in any article, I don't mind."

"Great, I really appreciate that." Stacey tapped an app and set her phone on the table between us, then opened her laptop and a notepad. "I thought it might be helpful to give a little background on myself first. I mean, I should tell you why I'm interested in wildlife rather than Ms. Maara." She gave a nervous giggle. "When I was in sixth grade, the teacher asked us to make a poster featuring our favourite animal and share it with the class. I actually thought spiders were pretty cool, but Joey Trent had arachnophobia and I had a crush on Joey Trent, so I picked elephants instead. And what I found shocked me. I cried in my presentation when I talked about the ivory trade—which meant I got nicknamed Booboo until I finished high school—and that project inspired me to become an investigative journalist."

"I read your article on elephant poaching."

"Really? I'm hoping to do a follow-up next year. The

anti-poaching unit I followed has expanded their tracking-dog program, and now they train dogs for other units too."

"What made you switch to turtles? They rarely get noticed, I guess because they spend most of their time underwater, so few people see them in the flesh."

"Truthfully, I knew next to nothing about turtles when I started—my knowledge was limited to the Cumberland sliders in the pond I used to walk past on my way to school —but a friend of a friend suggested the story. Her roommate started investigating a couple of years back—he'd always been fascinated by turtles—but then he just...disappeared."

The hairs on the back of my neck prickled. "Disappeared?"

"Yup. One day, he went to work and didn't come home, and the cops never found any trace of him."

"Sometimes people need a fresh start."

Like me, for example. I'd walked out of Aiden's beach house one morning, driven to LAX, and bounced around the world before I ended up in my current home. I'd been on Valentine Cay for nearly three years now. But I didn't have family to search for me, or many friends either. Only Aiden would be looking.

"No, not Beckham. He left his pet turtle behind, and he doted on her. She's only small, a common musk turtle, but he built her a huge home that took up half of the living room."

The prickle turned into a full-on chill.

"Beckham? Beckham Cheng?"

"You know him?"

"Not exactly. A man with that name contacted us last year about an interview, but after we explained we wouldn't go on record, we never heard from him again. I figured he just lost interest."

"Uh, no, I don't think he did. His roommate gave me all his notes and photos, and...well, I couldn't bring the actual shell in case it got confiscated at the airport, but I took a picture."

Stacey tapped a few keys on the laptop and turned it toward us. It took a moment to work out what I was seeing. A close-up of a turtle's shell, marked with three tiny notches. *Our* notches. Franklin had started using that pattern years ago, two nicks close together and one farther away. The notches were permanent and grew with the turtle.

"Look at the next one," Stacey said, jotting notes with her pen.

I swiped, and nearly puked when I saw the image. One of our beautiful hawksbills had been taxidermied into a macabre ornament. A desk lamp with a tasselled shade. An unbearable wave of anger and sadness washed over me, and I blinked back tears.

"Where did he get this?"

"New York. From a market in Chinatown. Is it one of yours?"

Beside me, Franklin looked about as good as I felt. We'd known for a long time that poaching went on, but to see a majestic creature reduced to this...this...abomination...

"Yes, it's one of ours. Did Beckham report this? Hawksbills are an endangered species."

Stacey shook her head. "He wanted to find out who was behind it first. The people in the market, the stores, the restaurants, they're just the little fish. They buy from middlemen, who get the turtles from a supplier. Based on what I've pieced together from his notes, he believes the biggest supplier in the US was sourcing turtles from the Caribbean, in particular from around San Gallicano. A fresh turtle can sell for a hundred and fifty bucks wholesale, but once it's dried and prettied up"—she tapped the picture—"they can fetch ten times that. There's big money in hawksbill products. In Chinese culture, the sea turtle is a symbol of fortune and longevity. Folklore refers to hawksbills as one of the four celestial guardians. Don't you think it's ironic? Their godlike status has driven demand for turtle products, and now they're heading for extinction."

Franklin had told me all about the importance of turtles in China. They were used as talismans to bring luck, and as ingredients in traditional medicine. Turtle meat was eaten widely. A visiting biologist had once told me that he was more likely to find an endangered chelonian species in a wet market in Guangzhou than in the wild. And as income levels rose in China, the trade only grew.

"Don't most of the turtles consumed by the Chinese come from the Coral Triangle? Around the Philippines and Borneo?"

"Yes, and Malaysia, Thailand, and Myanmar. They're mainly smuggled in through Vietnam. But there's a large Chinese population in the United States, and someone else is catering to that market."

Franklin pushed the laptop away. "A handful of poachers have been caught around these parts, but they're small-time guys. Locals out to make a fast buck."

"Who do they sell the turtles to?"

"That's a question I can't answer."

"I spent yesterday at the courthouse researching all the poaching cases from the past five years. Most suspects claimed they'd caught the turtles to eat themselves, and not one of them gave up the name of a trader, even when offered a lesser sentence to do so. They just took the punishment. What does that tell you?"

"Either they really did use the turtles for their own

purposes or..." The implications pieced themselves together in my head. "Or they were protecting somebody."

"And why would they protect somebody?"

"To preserve their meal ticket? So they could work for them in the future? The sentences for poaching are never long enough."

Despite Judge Morgan's best efforts. He'd once confided to Vince that he'd like to throw the book at every poacher, but poachers had families, and those families voted. Plus turtle meat had once been a staple food in San Gallicano, and some folks still followed the old traditions. Three years was the max for taking a turtle or two. It was far easier to make an example out of a fool like Luna Maara. Most of the locals weren't fond of tourists.

"Or because they're more scared of the person they're working for than they are of prison."

Another chilling thought. San Gallicano looked idyllic, but as with many not-quite-paradises, there was a dark underbelly that mostly stayed hidden from view. With the sea's bounty decreasing every year due to overfishing—the industry was meant to be sustainable, but it really wasn't— unemployment grew steadily higher, and more and more residents were either holding their noses and switching to work in tourism or leaving the country altogether. Ray Perrin, who used to help his parents out at the general store, had taken a job on a cargo ship. Donations to the sanctuary were almost non-existent. People toiled for longer hours, so islanders didn't have time to volunteer anymore, although they'd help to watch the beaches during nesting season.

Nesting season... Last year, we'd worked ourselves to exhaustion and still the numbers had been down. Several times, nests had been raided before we got to them because the eggs were a popular snack too. Some folks believed they acted as an aphrodisiac.

"Are you sure it's safe to be investigating this?" I asked.

"I'm careful. At the moment, I just want to find out who might be involved so I can watch from a distance. I have the names of poachers who've been released from prison recently as a starting point, but have you heard any whispers on the grapevine? This seems like a real tight-knit community."

Franklin spoke up. "Folks are close on Valentine Cay, but there are a number of unscrupulous types on the big island. If you want names, start with them."

He twisted in his seat and nodded toward the boats in the bay. They were almost at the reef now, and I was keeping my fingers crossed they'd read the current wrong. There was a nasty spot with underwater rocks not too far from the nearest vessel.

"The photographers?"

"The men who brought them here. They'll do anything to rake in cash. Outside of nesting season, poachers mainly catch turtles out near the smaller islands, and they need boats to get there."

"So poaching is a problem all year round?"

"It's worse in the summer months. Turtles nest from February to July, with a peak around April to May. Then the babies hatch from July to November. It's easier for poachers to collect turtles from the beach, but it's also riskier because the government organises patrols during the busiest times. Locals keep an eye too."

"You collect eggs to hatch here?"

"We do."

"Have you ever had problems with them being stolen?"

"Once, a few years ago. We have a better fence now, and the reef is difficult to navigate at night. Plus I carry a gun, and Judge Morgan is the type of man who would be sympathetic to me using it."

"Destroying the sanctuary would be counterproductive, don't you think?" I asked. "Without us, the turtle population would decline even faster, and the poachers would have fewer of them to catch."

Stacey crinkled her nose. "In my experience, men trying to feed their families don't always think that far ahead."

A fair point, and the fence hadn't kept the damn photographers out, had it? Okay, so maybe having Luna here wasn't such a bad idea after all. Knox and Ryder didn't seem like the type of men who would back down when faced with poachers. For the next month at least, Franklin and I could sleep easy.

"We'll stay vigilant. Did you want to talk about the results of our population surveys? You mentioned that in your email."

"It can be hard to convince people there's a problem without cold, hard data. Having facts and figures to back up my words is important."

Franklin wasn't too good with figures, but in my past existence, numbers had been everything. I'd helped him to prepare a summary of our survey findings to give to anyone who asked, and now he talked Stacey through the harsh reality of being a turtle in a world ruled by humans. Too often, it felt as if we were fighting a losing battle.

Franklin kept speaking, but I suddenly realised Stacey's attention was elsewhere. She was looking over my shoulder, out toward the bay. I turned to follow her gaze.

"Is something wrong?"

"That blue boat looks as if it's in trouble."

I stood to get a better look, and she wasn't kidding. The boat near the reef was low in the water, its stern almost submerged while its bow rose skyward.

"Holy shit, it's sinking."

Franklin jumped up and ran for the door, and I followed

more slowly because, honestly, if they'd hit the reef it was their own dumb fault. As long as they could swim, they'd make it to the shore just fine, or one of their buddies in another boat could pick them up. Fools, all of them. As I ambled along the path that ran parallel to the beach, squinting through the foliage to see if the boat was still afloat, I almost bumped into Ryder as he emerged from the trees. In the blink of an eye, he grabbed my arm to stop me from falling, then shook water from his hair and grinned.

"Productive meeting?" he asked.

"One of the boats is sinking."

"Relax, the passengers are wearing buoyancy aids."

I took in the T-shirt stuck to his chest and his dripping shorts. "Did you try to help them?"

"Nah. Knox is watching Luna, so I went for a swim."

"A swim?"

"Gotta keep my fitness levels up."

"The currents around here can be pretty strong."

"My old commanding officer said I was part marlin. What's for lunch?"

"Did the boat hit the reef?"

"Number-one rule—always check your drainage plug is securely in place before you set sail."

Ryder walked off whistling, and I stared after him. He hadn't...had he? No, any trespassers really didn't stand a chance.

11

LUNA

Two days down, twenty-eight to go...

The silence was unnerving. Apart from the dog snoring in the corner, the only sound in the bunkhouse came from the waves crashing on the shore. And the whole moonlight thing was spooky too. I was from Vegas—wasting electricity was a way of life. Mom couldn't sleep without the TV on, and Jubilee had a weird body clock that meant she got up at five thirty every morning to do yoga.

I'd never been a good sleeper. Well, not since I was sixteen. Some nights, I used to sneak out of whatever hotel I was staying in and walk for hours, because if I wasn't in bed, then *he* couldn't find me. In those days, I'd been able to stroll around unnoticed, but now I couldn't get ten yards away without the whispers starting. *Is that Luna Maara? Wow, she's so tiny. Hey, Luna, can I get a picture?* This was a Good Thing, Mom said. I had the name recognition to do anything I wanted.

As long as what I wanted fit into her Long-Term Plan, obviously.

Through the window, I caught the glimmer of light on the water, sparkling against the night sky. The photographers had gone. Three of them had bugged out when the idiot from celebgossip.com found himself stranded on the reef—he'd nearly drowned trying to save his camera—and the rest had left before dinner. I could go for a walk. Just to the edge of the sand, no farther.

Jubilee slept like the dead, and Caro had to be tired after yelling at the photographer earlier. I knew firsthand how confrontation sapped your energy. Acting nasty left me permanently exhausted, but the alternative—letting people get close to me—was worse. The dog watched from her blanket as I tiptoed to the door, but she didn't move. I wasn't sure whether I liked her or not. I'd never had a pet, and Mom said dogs were dirty, smelly creatures. But Mom talked a lot of trash, so maybe Tango was okay?

I pulled a sweater on over my camisole. The door creaked, but nobody stirred. I brought my notepad with me, and perhaps if the light was bright enough, I could sit for a while? Write a few words? Words I'd never be allowed to sing because they didn't fit my image, but words I needed to write nonetheless.

The beach was bathed in a soft glow, and I picked my way carefully down the rocky steps. Who knew putting sunglasses on a turtle could bring me to such a beautiful place? It hadn't even been my idea, but I was strangely grateful to Kory for suggesting it, and to Jubilee for cropping and filtering and posting it on Insta. She *had* come to help with the punishment, so I couldn't even be a little bit mad at her. I perched on the bottom step and looked out at the sea. That was quite close enough to the water, thank you very much, but the sound of the waves was strangely soothing.

"Hey."

Holy crap! I jumped out of my skin as Ryder jogged silently down the steps and sat beside me. Ryder, but he looked different. Where had his beard gone?

"You jerk! You nearly gave me a heart attack."

"Sorry about that. What happened?"

"What happened to what?"

"Why are you up at three a.m.?"

"Because I couldn't sleep. Why are *you* up at three a.m.?"

"Figured I'd go skinny-dipping."

What? "Are you serious? It's freaking dark. What if there are sharks? What if you drown?"

"No, I'm not serious. You triggered a motion detector when you left the bunkhouse."

Oh.

"Nobody told me there were motion detectors."

"We put them in place to keep you safe. You didn't hear the yelling last night?"

"What yelling?"

"One of the reporters we escorted off the property didn't take too kindly to being told to leave."

"I took a sleeping pill last night."

"You need those? They're not a good idea, little moon."

"Little moon? Are you making fun of my size?"

"No, I..." He shook his head. "Forget it. I don't even know why I said that. But if you're drowsy and there's an emergency, it makes our job harder."

"Then you'll be thrilled to hear I don't have any more. Jubilee forgot to bring them from the yacht."

Last night, I'd taken the emergency pill I kept in my purse. The rest were in a little silver box in my cabin, so Kory had no doubt given them to his friends by now. They'd take any pharmaceutical product that might lead to a good time. He was probably snoozing in the Bahamas, wasted at the Blayz Festival. The organisers had billed it as a hedonistic paradise, and since they'd promised to let me sing rather than lip-sync, I'd been looking forward to going on stage. But now I was here instead. There would be plenty more festivals, and if Mom and Julius had anything to do with it, I'd be expected to perform at all of them.

"You don't sleep well?" Ryder asked.

"Not without the pills. And don't ask if I've tried meditation, herbal tea, warm milk, or yoga. Yes, I have. No, they don't help."

"I was gonna suggest Jack Daniels."

I gave an unladylike snort, then thanked my lucky stars that nobody was filming me. The last time I'd hiccuped, it went viral on TikTok.

"I hate hangovers. Sometimes, going for a walk helps. At least it takes my mind off things."

"What things?"

"You're a bodyguard, not an agony aunt."

Ryder held up both hands. "Didn't mean to overstep."

And now I felt like a shrew. As usual.

"I struggle to sleep in strange beds, okay? I guess... I guess I worry that somebody's going to come into my room."

"Has that ever happened?"

I closed my eyes and drew in a calming breath. Of all the questions to ask, he picked that one? The obvious solution would be to lie. Lie and change the subject. That's what I usually did. But for some reason, I found myself telling the truth, at least partially.

"That's in the past, but it still gives me nightmares." Before I realised what I was doing, I lifted a hand and traced a finger along his jaw. "You shaved off your beard?"

"I didn't want you to be uncomfortable." Damn, his smile was pretty without all that hair in the way. "Nobody's gonna get near you, moon, not with Knox and me here. You can rest easy."

We'd graduated from "little moon" to just "moon"? Weirdly, I found I didn't hate it. My nicknames were usually much less complimentary.

"So I have to go back to bed now?"

"Not if you don't want to."

"If I stay, you'll just sit here with me?"

"That's my job."

Of course. His job.

"Usually, the bodyguard would be hovering over there somewhere." I waved a hand toward the main building perched on its rocky outcrop. "They don't like getting too close."

"Can't take a bullet from fifty yards away."

"You'd take a bullet for me?"

"It's my job."

"That's not an answer."

"Yeah, it is. But I hope it doesn't come to that. Getting shot sucks."

"Have you ever actually been shot?"

"I got winged by an asshole I can't talk about in a country I wasn't supposed to be in." He inched up the bottom of his shorts, and in the wash of light from the full moon, I could make out the puckered skin that scarred his inner thigh. "Damn lucky it wasn't three inches higher."

"Your boyfriend would have been devastated."

"Right. Yeah, he would. So, are you planning to sit out here all night?"

He'd think I was a freak if I said yes. Who did that? Who sat outside all night waiting for their demons to leave? Jubilee claimed she never remembered her dreams, and Caro struck me as the type of woman who'd punch a nightmare in the face if it dared to disturb her.

Damn, paradise had its downsides. In Vegas, I'd head someplace bright and busy because monsters hid from the light, but even if I was allowed to leave the turtle sanctuary, the bars in this part of the world closed at nine p.m. I was stuck here with my thoughts, but at least I wasn't alone.

Ryder wouldn't hurt me.

Not *that* way.

"What choice do I have? I'm not going to lie in the bunkhouse listening to the dog snoring, and there's nothing to do here. No room service, no TV, no bars, no shows, no gym. How do people live like this?"

"Not a fan of solitude, huh?"

"In my experience, it's never been enjoyable." Then curiosity got the better of me. "Do you like being alone?"

"After you've spent most of your twenties living in barracks, tents, or worse, submarines with a bunch of other motherfuckers, you learn to appreciate a little alone time."

When he put it that way...

"What do you do when you're alone?"

"Run, hike, shoot. Take my motorcycle out for a ride. Sit in a park and read a book. What do you do?"

"Order room service and watch a movie."

And write songs. Pour my pain onto paper and wait for the door handle to turn. Even though I'd bought an alarmed doorstop to use in hotel rooms at night, I'd still catch my gaze drifting in that direction, feel my pulse racing at every sound in the hallway.

"Not a fan of the great outdoors?"

"Not a fan of sunburn, bugs, being chased by the paparazzi, getting lost in unfamiliar cities, or being chided by my management for disappearing. Oh, and I don't want to get kidnapped by a psycho stalker either."

Ryder ticked off the points on his fingers. "Moonburn isn't a thing, most of the bugs are asleep right now, the paparazzi's cameras are a hundred feet down, this island's too small to get lost on, and your mom's in jail. Want me to give you some space? I can keep watch from the tree-line, and you'll still be safe enough."

If Ryder had been from the last bodyguard company, I would have said "yes, get the hell away from me." They'd been painfully polite, at least to my face, but somehow managed to look disdainful the whole time. Whenever they followed me around, I could feel them silently judging my lifestyle.

"The 'hundred feet down' part, did you have anything to do with that?"

"I can neither confirm nor deny."

Which had to mean he'd sunk the boat, didn't it?

"Thank you," I said softly. Nobody had ever fought in my corner like that. Oh, sure, Mom pretended to, but over the years, I'd grown to realise that she was only out for herself. But by then, it was too late to escape this life I was stuck in. All I could do was double down and be the person everyone expected me to be.

A self-centred witch.

Most of the time, it felt as if I were wearing somebody else's skin, and that skin was itchy as all get-out. A onesie made from centipedes, and the shoes weren't too comfortable either.

"All part of the service, ma'am."

"Ugh, don't call me ma'am. I'm twenty-six, not fifty."

"Understood."

I studied him. He had to be nearly a foot taller than me, muscly but not all veiny like those assholes who took steroids and lived in the gym, the ones who approached me in clubs expecting me to fall at their feet. No, Ryder was just strong. Strong with the kind of smile dentists charged a fortune for and lines around his eyes that could have come from laughter or too much sun or both. Now that he'd shaved his beard, I saw that he hadn't grown it to hide a weak chin like Julius, so maybe he'd been telling the truth about needing to blend in overseas?

"How old are you?" I asked.

"Didn't you read my résumé?"

"I think we've already established that I only looked at the pictures."

He chuckled. "Twenty-nine. I'll be thirty in May."

Older than me, but not *too* old. If only the circumstances had been different. If Ryder had been straight and if I didn't recoil at a man's touch, then perhaps I'd have asked if he wanted to have dinner with me or see a show or just hang out. But circumstances weren't different, and I was an idiot for even dreaming of a normal life. No man wanted to date me. Not genuinely. They'd use me to show off to their buddies or further their careers, sure, but nobody liked me for...well, me. Kory was the closest thing I had to a friend—at least he wasn't after my money—but even he had an ulterior motive. His dad was a homophobic bigot, and if Crawford Balachandran found out his son was gay, Kory would probably end up having conversion therapy. Rumours of an on-again, off-again relationship suited both of us.

"Twenty-nine? So you're practically ancient, then."

"Almost prehistoric. That's why I'm a good swimmer—it's not been long since my ancestors crawled out of the primordial sea."

"How old were you when you learned to swim?"

"Six months. Mom took me to baby lessons at the pool on base."

"On base?"

"My dad's in the Navy. Did you take swimming lessons?"

I shook my head.

"Can you swim at all?"

Once again, I shook my head. It was a fact I usually kept to myself, but Ryder had signed an NDA, and I found I wanted to tell him the truth.

"But you took a vacation on a yacht?" he asked.

"They're statistically very safe. And if I fell in, you would have saved me, right?"

"Always. Don't you have a pool in your yard, though?"

"More background research?"

"Our team is thorough."

If only mine was. Then maybe I wouldn't have ended up with a pervert like Julius Whitlow as my agent, and I'd be able to kiss a man without cringing.

"I do have a pool, but I've never used it. Jubilee likes to swim."

"You've never wanted to learn?"

"Do you always ask this many questions?"

"Only when I'm interested in the answers."

Why? Why was he interested? He couldn't sell the information to the papers because I'd sue him. If his background research had been as thorough as he claimed, he'd have to know I'd taken my former housekeeper to court —and won—after she told a reporter that I'd been seeing a therapist. News of my impending breakdown had made every gossip site, and the therapist hadn't even helped. No, she'd basically told me I needed to loosen up when it came to sex and then tried to treat me for an eating disorder I didn't even have. Just because I'd puked after a creep of a talk-show host fondled my boobs didn't mean I was bulimic.

So why did Ryder want to know my secrets? Finally, I decided to simply ask him.

"Why?"

"Why am I interested in the answers?"

"Yes."

"Because underneath the sharp tongue and the attitude, I don't think you're the porcupine of a pop princess that you make yourself out to be."

"Did you...did you just call me a porcupine?"

"There are those prickles again."

"You've got some nerve," I muttered, but I was busy processing his words. He saw through the act? But...but nobody ever noticed the real me. Nobody ever cared enough to look.

"Am I wrong?"

Ryder saw me. "Don't you dare tell anyone."

"Your secret's safe with me. So, do you want to learn to swim?"

I shuddered.

"Are you sure? The judge said this month was meant to be a learning experience."

"He said nothing about drowning."

"You think I'd let you drown?"

Probably not, but my mom wasn't meant to let me drown either. And yet she almost had.

I shrugged.

"Luna, what happened to you with water? Did you fall in when you were a kid?"

"How do you know anything happened?"

"Because your hands are shaking."

Damn the stupid moonlight. I glanced down, and Ryder wasn't wrong. There were so many horror stories squashed into my head that sometimes it was hard to keep up.

"I...I didn't fall in. Mom put me in the tub, one of those big ones with the whirlpool jets. And I was playing with the bubbles, and I...I don't know exactly what happened.

Maybe I hit my head? But the next thing I remember is being on the bathroom floor while she gave me CPR." The memories were like blurry photographs—bath, bubbles, being unable to breathe, the terror on Mom's face—but they'd replayed for most of my life. "I was three or four, I think? When I was older, I asked her about it, and she said it never happened, that I have an overactive imagination, but I'm almost certain it did. And that's why I don't like water, okay?"

When Ryder didn't comment, I began to regret sharing something so personal with a virtual stranger. A secret I'd never told anyone but Jubilee. And of course, Jubilee had given Mom the benefit of the doubt.

"Well? Aren't you going to say anything?"

"Just working out what to say, moon. That's fucked up."

"Welcome to my life."

"Have you..." Ryder paused. "Have you talked to anyone about it?"

"Yes, you."

"I meant like a therapist."

"Therapy is overrated."

"You tried it?"

"My therapist told me that if I just put on a few pounds, I'd feel better about life. Like, I'm here because I have intimacy issues, but hey, thanks for telling me that my weight is the problem. We didn't even get as far as the water thing."

"You have intimacy issues?"

Darn it! This was what happened when I got lost in the moment—my big, stupid mouth went rogue.

"That's not what I said at all. You must have misheard."

More silence. Then, "Sure, moon. If that's what you want to go with, I'll play along."

"Don't be so condescending. Just because you're too tough to see a therapist doesn't mean other people don't need help."

"I've talked to a therapist."

"Like, in a bar or something?"

Or on Grindr? It was hard to believe a man as strong as Ryder would seek out a psychiatrist, but again, he surprised me.

"In an office with a couch."

"Really?"

"Saw some real shit in the Navy. Plus Blackwood hired a shrink last year. The folks in charge figured the doc could consult on cases for part of the time and run sessions if anyone wanted to talk."

"And do they talk?"

"Yeah, she's always fully booked. But when it comes to nightmares, I found that what helped the most was making good memories to push out the bad ones."

"There's no hope for me then. For every good memory, I have ninety-nine bad ones."

"Being a world-famous singer isn't all it's cracked up to be?"

"The singing part is okay. It's the other stuff that makes me want to crawl into a hole."

"If you hate it, can't you quit?"

"You try quitting on my mom, tell me how it works out. One time, I refused to go to some stupid awards show, so she sent me to rehab instead."

"The anger management thing?"

Great. He knew about that. The official statement said I was being treated for exhaustion, but somehow, a new story leaked out, probably also from Mom. She told everyone I needed a break, but she was the one who threw a hissy fit if I didn't get a million likes before breakfast.

"See? Literally none of my life is private."

"I'm beginning to understand that. But this month, we're going to keep you out of the public eye, so let's focus on making good memories, okay?"

"Are *you* secretly a therapist?"

"Nah, I'm just an asshole who's good at swimming."

I was beginning to suspect Ryder Metcalfe was so much more than that. More than once, Jubilee had asked, "Why are the good ones always gay?" and I'd shrugged because Kory was a bit of a dick and so were most of his buddies. I hung out with them because firstly, I wouldn't wake up to them climbing on top of me in the middle of the night, and secondly, they weren't as mean and backstabby as the girls I'd tried being friends with in the past. If I had something stuck in my teeth, they told me. They didn't let me do a livestream and then giggle about it afterward.

But now I realised there might be a glimmer of truth in Jubilee's words.

"Sure, I'll look back fondly on weeks spent scooping turtle poop out of a pool."

Poop. I always had to say "poop," never "shit." Mom hated swearing.

"Forget the turtles; I have a better idea."

"Oh, really? Last time someone had a 'better idea,' I ended up puking on a zip line."

When the pulley jammed, I'd gotten stuck over a river in my version of a living hell. A guy had to slide out on a harness to rescue me. At least when Mom threatened to sue the operator, they'd deleted all footage of the incident.

"Take off your flip-flops."

"What? Why?"

"I realise asking you to trust me is presumptuous, but I promise I won't let anything bad happen."

Oh, gross, was he going to give me a foot massage? The

last man to do that—an actor who hid his sleazy side under a squeaky-clean veneer—had quickly worked his way up to my thighs. But Ryder was gay, so what was his angle?

"I don't like people touching my feet. If I want a massage, I'll go to a professional."

He snorted quietly. "I'm not planning to touch your feet, moon. Although the sand will do a better job on your skin than any foot file, so my sister says."

"You have a sister?"

"She's two years younger than me, and she lives in Naples with her husband, their kid, and a dog named Boris."

"Living the dream, huh?"

"People have different dreams. Flip-flops off, moon."

"You want me to...walk on the sand?"

"No, I want you to walk in the water."

"In the water? Are you crazy? There could be sharks."

"If there's a shark in six inches of water, I guarantee it's in more trouble than you are."

"Six inches?"

"Today, we'll stay right at the edge. I won't let you drown, moon. I'm not going to take my eyes off you. But if you can face your fears, little by little, they won't seem so scary anymore."

I didn't want to walk in the water. And I didn't have to. Ryder worked for me—I could just say "no" and go back to bed.

But Ryder didn't have to do this either. He was trying to help me, but why? What was his ulterior motive? The only thing I could think of was that he needed more work and wanted me to extend the contract. Would that be such a bad thing? Usually, I hated bodyguards following me around, but I felt weirdly comfortable with him in my space.

And I *never* felt comfortable around men.

When I told Ryder I'd picked Knox as my bodyguard

because he was fierce, I'd lied. In truth, I'd picked him because he looked at me with such disgust that I knew he'd never hit on me.

But here I was.

On the beach with a man hotter than all of my backup dancers put together.

"Okay, fine. But if I drown, you're fired."

I kicked off my flip-flops and followed Ryder to the water's edge. The sea looked black in the moonlight, and I shuddered involuntarily.

"What about jellyfish? There might be jellyfish."

"Jellyfish season has barely started."

"But it *has* started?"

"I'm going to walk on the other side of you, so if anyone gets stung or eaten, it'll be me."

"Have you ever been stung by a jellyfish?"

"Once or twice."

"Does it hurt?"

"No worse than a wasp sting. One more step, moon."

I'd never been stung by a wasp either, mainly because I didn't go outside much. As soon as I was old enough to walk, Mom had taught me that sunshine meant wrinkles, and having wrinkles was a Very Bad Thing, according to Amethyst Puckett. I'd gotten my first spray tan at the age of four, right before my first beauty pageant. Sometimes, I went out without sunblock as a tiny act of rebellion. Yes, yes, I knew UV protection was good for me, but telling Mom I was wearing factor fifty when I wasn't made me smile inside. If the cost of that was a few wrinkles, so be it.

I dipped a toe into the shimmering water. The sea was colder than I'd expected, or maybe that was just the sense of dread in my belly?

"A jellyfish sting can't be worse than waxing, can it?" I

muttered, mostly to myself because Ryder wouldn't know the answer to that one.

But yet again, he surprised me. "It isn't."

"You wax?"

"I lost a bet once. Back, sack, and crack. I'd rather swim through jellyfish soup than go through that again."

"I don't have a choice."

"There's always a choice. You could go au naturel."

I choked out a laugh. If I showed underarm hair in public, Mom would send me to rehab again. Which was ironic, considering she was the one with the drinking problem.

"That's not an option."

The water was lapping over my ankles now. Every instinct told me to run, but I didn't want to look like a fool in front of Ryder. How could he act so relaxed? He didn't seem to care that he was in harm's way.

"You okay?" he asked softly, and the question threw me. Nobody ever asked how I was, not and really meant it. Nobody ever cared. How was I meant to answer? Should I gloss over things the way I always did in interviews? Or tell the truth? Someone much wiser than me once said that the truth will set you free, but if I told the truth, who would believe me? Who would believe that I'd rather be working in Arby's than entertaining fifty thousand people at concerts?

"Luna?" Ryder stopped walking. "Are you okay?"

"I haven't been okay for a long time," I whispered, my voice barely audible above the gentle waves. The words popped out before I could stop them. Ryder's expression morphed into pity, and I didn't want him to pity me. I didn't want him to see the many, many bad decisions I'd made, decisions that had led me to this time, to this place, to this damn turtle sanctuary. "I'm done here."

Eyes prickling, I ran out of the water and up the beach,

the pebbles at the top of the steps biting the soles of my feet as I hurried along the path. Ryder followed—I could hear his footsteps and the occasional curse—but I didn't stop. Not until I was back inside the bunkhouse and under my blanket. The dog gave me a curious glance, its head lifted an inch, but Jubilee didn't stir and neither did Caro.

This month promised to be difficult, but maybe not in the way I'd expected.

Soul-searching was hard.

But having a person—a man—look into my depths was harder.

12

CARO

"Take it back. Take it all back. We didn't order any of this."

The reporters had tried coming by boat, and they'd tried sneaking in on foot, and when neither of those approaches worked, they figured they'd try the old Trojan Horse trick? Did they think we were dumb? The truck outside the sagging gates of the turtle sanctuary bore the logo of a furniture company from Ilha Grande, and it was stacked high with goods. The pictures on the boxes showed beds, couches, a dining table, and a hammock, but no doubt there was at least one asshole with a camera hiding in there too.

Probably because the photographers couldn't get to the sanctuary by water anymore. When I went to the store yesterday evening, I'd mentioned to Marica Perrin that the spirits were restless, and Marica—along with a large percentage of the indigenous population—took the moods of the spirits very seriously. Between that and the boat currently resting among the corals, rumours of bad juju were spreading like wildfire.

"I can't take it back," the driver of the truck said. "The purchaser paid in advance and insisted on express delivery."

I bet they did.

"Well, call the purchaser and rearrange delivery to somewhere else." Would the reporter have been dumb enough to use his own name? "Who *is* the purchaser?"

He thumbed through the paperwork. "A Ms. J Puckett. There's no number on here."

J Puckett? Jubilee Puckett? I ground my teeth together so hard my jaw hurt, then realised what I was doing and forced myself to stop. It was a bad habit, and I couldn't afford expensive dental work. Not anymore.

"Okay, so I might actually know who that is." And so did the reporters. Had they borrowed her name for an elaborate ploy, or had she genuinely ordered a truck full of stuff? It had to be the former—why would Jubilee need a freaking bed? We already had beds. "Sorry for snapping. It's been a difficult week."

"So where should I put the boxes?"

"Could you just wait here for a moment?"

"I don't got all day, ma'am."

I was already marching back up the driveway, getting more annoyed by the second. For three and a half years, I'd managed to stay out of Aiden's clutches, and now two stupid women were threatening to unravel everything. It wasn't Franklin's fault—I'd never told him the whole story —but that didn't make things any easier. If we hadn't been so short-handed, if we weren't coming into nesting season, I'd have come up with an excuse and hidden on one of the other islands for a month.

Jubilee was in the third of the five pool rooms, helping Franklin to toss pieces of tuna to last year's hatchlings. They'd grown so quickly, and I knew he was worried about the food bills. Costs kept going up. For years, he'd funded the sanctuary himself, and although he hadn't said as much, I'd long suspected that the money was running out. Meanwhile Luna, who had plenty of money, was sitting on her ass watching other people work.

"There's a truck full of furniture at the end of the drive," I announced, and Jubilee's face lit up. "You ordered it?"

"Yes, from a store on Ilha Grande. The guy said it wouldn't be here for another day at least."

"Why?"

"I guess because they have to take two ferries and it's super slow? There's a place on Malavilla, but they didn't have memory foam."

"No, I meant why did you order furniture in the first place? We already have beds."

"Luna isn't sleeping well. She doesn't find sprung mattresses comfortable."

"The rest of us manage just fine. And you're here to work, not kick back on the couch."

"I-I thought it would be a nice surprise for everyone."

"Well, it isn't. We're having security issues here, or did you miss that part? The truck turned up unannounced, no warning whatsoever."

"I didn't think—"

"Exactly. You didn't think, which is how the two of you ended up here in the first place."

"Hey, don't be mean to her!" Luna steamed over, followed by one of her personal pit bulls. Knox. The hot one. Okay, hot*ter* one. He looked at me, looked at her, opened his mouth, and then closed it again.

"I'm not being mean; I'm being truthful. How much money did she waste on stuff nobody needs?"

"Who are you to know what other people need, Miss High-and-Mighty?"

"I know what the turtles need, and in case you haven't noticed, they're the most important thing around here. If the two of you want to do something useful, then you could contribute toward the new pool room."

"In case *you* haven't noticed, we're here under duress. If you want new pools, go ask people who actually care about turtles."

"Oh, sure, because it's that damn easy. We don't all have ten million Instagram followers."

"It's twenty million, actually. Plus twelve million on TikTok and another eight million on BuzzHub."

"And you only got them by acting like a dumbass and cavorting half-naked in public."

Luna launched herself at me, claws out. Jubilee grabbed her arm and began shrieking, and for the second time this week, I found myself trapped in Knox's vise-like grip. Today, I stamped on his instep, and he muttered a string of curses as Ryder ran in and wrestled Luna away. She sounded like a cat in pain when she was angry.

"Enough with the bruises," Knox muttered.

"Then let go of me."

"Can't do that. If you're trying to claw my client's eyes out, then I'm obliged to intervene."

"I didn't do anything."

"You called me a dumbass!" Luna snapped.

"Which was accurate."

Percy the loggerhead swam up to the edge of his pool and stared at her, no doubt perplexed by the noise. The sanctuary was usually such a peaceful place. Franklin kept a wind-up radio tuned to a classical station, although the charge had run out this morning and nobody had bothered to crank the handle again.

"Ladies..." Ryder tried, but Luna didn't let him finish.

"She's no lady. Jubilee buys new furniture, and is she

grateful? No, of course not. She cares more about turtles than she does about people."

True, but they didn't bite as badly as humans did. "Maybe that's because they're better company."

Luna began struggling against Ryder. "You little—"

"Hey, hey, hey. What's with all the fightin'?" Franklin asked from behind me.

"Our two 'guests' have decided to redecorate the place. There's a truck from the furniture store outside the gates."

"That's mighty generous of them."

"They gave no warning whatsoever. The truck just showed up."

"Well, we'd better get to unloadin' then."

Luna folded her arms, and her smug expression made me want to slap her. Honestly, I wasn't a violent person, but something about her rubbed me the wrong way. The sheer sense of entitlement, even when she was meant to be doing community service. Franklin headed to the door with Jubilee trailing behind, and I tried to pry Knox's hands away. He held firm.

"If I let go, are you going to behave?"

"Define 'behave.'"

"Are you going to do bodily harm to Luna?"

"No." I sagged a little in his arms and screwed my eyes shut so I didn't see her triumphant look. "No, I'm not."

I hated new, uptight Caro. She reminded me of old, uptight Caro, and that was a person I wanted to forget. I'd spent the past three years convincing myself to relax. Convincing myself that Aiden wasn't going to crawl out from under his rock and make me pay for what I'd done. Make me pay, the way he'd promised.

Knox's arms loosened, tentatively, as if he wasn't sure I'd manage to control myself. But I could. I had an iron will when I needed it. For almost a year after Aiden first raped me, I'd submitted to him, smiled at his side and carried on going to work, all while plotting my escape. Finally, the time had come. I'd brought both of our worlds crashing down.

And then I'd run.

I headed for the door, for the gates and the truck, blinking back tears as I jogged along the driveway. My emotions ran so close to the surface these days. Where was Caro-the-ice-queen when I needed her?

"You okay?" Knox asked when he caught up with me.

"If you need to ask that, then you're also a dumbass."

"I understand it's not easy having Luna here."

"Do you? Do you really? Do you know what it's like to be happy one minute and have your life turned upside down the next?"

"Yeah, I do."

I stopped mid-stride and whipped around to face him. "Is that so? A pain-in-the-ass singer just walked into your life?"

"More the reverse." Knox gave a heavy sigh, and for a fraction of a second, his tough-guy mask slipped and I saw a flash of pain in those brown eyes of his. At least, I thought I did. I wasn't exactly the greatest judge of character, especially when it came to men. "You need a break. Let's get out of here this afternoon—didn't you say you wanted to go diving?"

"Don't you have to build flat-pack furniture with Princess Primadonna?"

"Ryder can handle her for an afternoon." Knox nudged me with a shoulder. "C'mon—you know you want to. I haven't dived for weeks, and I hear the reefs off Malavilla are the best in the Caribbean."

"Not as good as the barrier reef around Emerald Shores, but they're easier to reach."

"Is that a yes?"

What I actually wanted to do was crawl into my bed, tuck the covers over my head, and stay there until the Puckett girls had gone back to Vegas or hell or wherever it was they came from. But when it came down to a choice between arguing over which screw went where and carrying out a much-needed marine survey, there was only one answer I could give.

"Fine, if we must."

13

KNOX

K nox had never dreamed of becoming a Navy SEAL. When he was four, he wanted to own an ice cream truck. When he was ten, he longed to be a doctor so he could fix his mom. He'd spent his entire childhood wishing she'd leave his dad, hated her sometimes for staying. He realised now that things hadn't been quite so straightforward, but he still wondered how his life would have turned out if that son of a bitch hadn't used his family as a punching bag.

By fourteen, he'd realised that boys like him didn't go to college, and he'd revised his ambitions downward to becoming a rock star. When that fell apart, he'd run away to join the military. He'd quit drinking. Bulked out. Discovered he could be a sneaky motherfucker when the need arose. After tragedy struck for the second time, he'd moved into the private sector and finally found his place in life, but now it looked as if he was going to embark on yet another new role.

As a peacekeeper.

For Pete's sake, couldn't Caro and Luna quit bitching for five damn minutes?

There was something off about Caro Menefee. Yeah, she was hot as the Lut Desert in July, but she wasn't a happy woman.

Her abject dislike of Luna was understandable—firstly, Luna had exploited one of the turtles Caro devoted her life to caring for, and secondly, Luna was a nuisance in general. But the blow-up over the furniture was extreme. Why would someone get so upset over a free couch? Luna and Jubilee weren't going to ship all the shit they'd bought back to the US when they left, and it was good stuff. A pair of velvet couches, one for each bunkhouse, with matching ottomans. Six luxury mattresses. Linen. Cushions. An outdoor dining set with a giant parasol. Vases, a fancy grill, wooden closets. A pair of hammocks. A fucking toilet roll holder. If Knox's worst enemy had offered to furnish his home gratis, he'd have checked the gifts for hidden hazards and then said thanks very much.

But Caro's first instinct had been to complain.

And then there was her general twitchiness. She watched her surroundings constantly, but not in the careful, considered way that Knox and Ryder had been trained to operate. No, she continually turned to check her six, but the manner in which she did it was almost unconscious. An ingrained habit. She clenched her jaw—hard—and then seemed to catch herself and make a conscious effort to relax. Ditto when she chewed the skin around her fingernails. It was looking pretty damn ragged now.

Maybe time away from Luna would help her to relax? And maybe Knox could get some answers about why she was so uptight? The woman lived in paradise, and San Gallicano had that laid-back island vibe, outside of Judge Morgan's courtroom, anyway. Could the arrival of an admittedly irritating singer truly push a woman so close to her snapping point?

"I'm sorry about the furniture," Jubilee said.

"We been needing new mattresses for a while," Baptiste told her as they carried the flat-packed dining table into the clearing by the bunkhouses. "But there's only so much money to go around."

After Knox checked the truck over for unwanted passengers and devices, the driver had pulled it into the parking area outside the bunkhouses. Now they were unloading the contents while Caro got her dive kit ready. Splitting the two women up for a few hours seemed like the best idea. Ryder would keep an eye on Luna while she watched Franklin and Jubilee assemble the furniture—let's face it, she wasn't going to help—and Knox would find out whether Caro acted any calmer away from the sanctuary.

"I've been thinking about that." Jubilee wiped sweat from her brow with a tissue. "The money, I mean. The sanctuary's social media accounts are...not good."

"Like, really bad," Luna added from her perch on the bunkhouse steps. "You haven't posted anything to Insta for six months, your TikTok account is way too serious, and you don't even have a BuzzHub account."

"BuzzHub?"

"It's new."

"We were thinking that we could help to raise the profile of the sanctuary," Jubilee continued. "Turtles are super popular. Luna's turtle post got— Uh, never mind. People love cute animals, and turtles aren't *totally* cute, but with the right lighting..."

They couldn't even last a week without trolling for likes? "Didn't the judge tell the two of you to stay away from social media?"

"Uh, so technically, he said that Luna couldn't post to

her accounts, and she wouldn't be. We'd use the sanctuary's accounts."

Knox saw Ryder roll his eyes in the background, which was usually Luna's thing, so maybe it was contagious? He *had* spent over an hour watching her on the beach last night. Taking one for the team, he said. But before Ryder could make a suitably sarcastic response, Baptiste broke into a grin.

"You'd do that? Caro usually looks after the computer, but she's been too busy these past few months."

Jubilee mirrored his enthusiasm. "We're great at this stuff."

"There'd be no dressing up the turtles, though."

"I swear, there won't be any sunglasses, not even designer ones. We'll just choose the best angles and lighting, boost the colours, and use the right hashtags."

"I don't know what that means."

"It means the posts will attract more views, and then we can ask for donations. Have you considered a sponsorship scheme?"

"We tried speaking with a couple of the hotels, but tourism isn't real big here in San Gallicano."

"I don't mean corporate sponsors, not at first. They always want to know what's in it for them, and right now, you don't have much to offer. No offence. But individual sponsorships could work. Folks pay fifty bucks to receive a certificate and updates on their turtle. Plus you could do higher tiers with better merch. Plush toys, key rings, stickers, that kind of thing. We can draw up a plan."

"I guess it wouldn't hurt to think about that."

Jubilee beamed at him, and Knox had to concede that it wasn't a terrible idea. The girls were undoubtedly pros when it came to social media, and the sanctuary desperately needed additional income if the current state of repair was anything to go by. And it was a clever move on their part—if they were fucking around with photos and hashtags, they wouldn't have to do so much of the grunt work. Jubilee and Luna Puckett might have been obnoxious, but they weren't bad businesswomen.

But somehow, Knox doubted Caro would be quite as enthusiastic as Baptiste about their scheming. Someone would have to break the news to her. And Knox had a nasty feeling it would end up being him.

Damn, that woman was hot.

Moving into the private sector had many perks, and one of those was watching Caro Menefee as she squeezed herself into a shortie wetsuit. Under different circumstances, Knox would have been doing everything in his power to charm her out of that outfit. She wore a plain black one-piece bathing suit, possibly the most boring choice on the planet, but even that didn't detract from her curves. She had an ass to die for. And he might just end up six feet under if she caught him looking at it.

Today, they'd be diving at Coconut Cove on the west side of Malavilla. The beach was quiet, the entry was easy, and according to Caro, the currents rarely got strong there. It was a good spot for them to get to know each other. As dive buddies, obviously, not in any other capacity. And so far, Caro seemed competent. She'd assembled her kit, and on the ferry across to the island, she'd briefed Knox on the marine survey they needed to undertake.

First, they'd draw a map of the area on plastic slates, making note of the type of seabed and any cover present— seagrass, sediment, coral, and the like. Then they'd note down any sea life they saw and class each species as rare, occasional, or common. Turtles would get special attention —they had to be counted and photographed. Knox had his own state-of-the-art underwater camera thanks to Blackwood, and Caro carried an older model she kept cursing at because the clips on the housing were stiff, and she didn't want to break what was left of her nails. When Knox offered to help, she just glared at him.

But finally, they were ready for their buddy check. BCD, weights, releases, air, final visual. They were using recreational equipment, so they'd start with two hundred bar in the tank and a maximum operating depth of 130 feet. Knox's gear was top of the line. Caro's pink fins were held together with cable ties.

"A nice beach like this, I thought it would be busier."

A hundred yards of pristine white sand, and there were only a half-dozen sunbathers plus a guy walking a dog at the far end. The track to the tiny parking lot was rutted, but so were most of the roads on Malavilla. And a few bumps never normally stopped tourists. In Knox's home state, folks would drive for miles to visit the "Intergalactic Spaceport," a dirt strip in the middle of nowhere that the city council had designated as a landing site for visitors from Jupiter. Because if little green men had travelled millions of miles to get to Earth, Wyoming was surely where they'd choose to go.

"There're usually divers around, but there was a shark sighting on Wednesday, and usually when that happens, the dive school goes to the other side of the island for a week or two. I figured it would be nice and quiet."

"A shark sighting? Here? And you're only telling me now?"

"It was a blacktip shark. They hardly ever attack humans."

"Are there any other snippets of information you've been holding back?"

"No, I don't think so."

"How about the reason you kept checking behind us the whole way here?"

Her answer? She walked into the water; fit her mask, fins, and regulator; and submerged. Which told Knox everything he needed to know.

He smiled to himself and followed.

14

KNOX

Knox had seen a hundred turtles over the past four days. He'd learned what they ate, how long they lived, and more than he ever wanted to know about their mating habits. Put a green turtle next to a loggerhead, and he stood a reasonable chance of telling the two species apart. But nothing compared to seeing a hawksbill in the wild for the first time.

Especially when that hawksbill was hanging motionless in the water, a vicious hook piercing its mouth.

Fuck.

The dive had started out well, or at least as well as could be expected when his dive buddy wasn't speaking to him. Caro swam sedately twenty feet ahead. This wasn't exactly a hardship seeing as she looked good from any angle, and despite her refusal to converse on land, she did keep checking on him as any good buddy should. Scowling through her dive mask, eyes narrowed, tendrils of buckeye-brown hair escaping from her ponytail and floating around her face.

She tapped her slate. Right. They were meant to be working.

Knox studied the profile of the bay, where a curve of sand sloped gently to a steep drop-off forty yards from shore. They'd agreed that they wouldn't be venturing any farther—for every thirty-three feet, they'd be under an additional atmosphere of pressure. At a hundred feet down, they'd go through air four times faster than they did on the surface.

Rocks dotted the sandy bottom, each a mini ecosystem with coral and fish clustered around. He tried making a quick sketch. Damn, it looked more like a banana. He'd have failed art classes in high school if the teacher hadn't been twenty-three and up for a quick fuck in the supply closet. Adult Knox wasn't the type of man a woman would take to meet the family, but if a girl had brought teenage Knox home, her daddy would have been waiting on the porch with a shotgun.

He added rocks, and now the sketch looked like a banana with fungus, so he gave up and snapped a few photos instead. If there was a test, he could just attach those to his report. Ditto for the fish. He quit trying to count blue tangs and took a picture of those as well. Still no sign of any turtles, and...fuck, where the hell was Caro? She'd been beside him ten seconds ago, watching a cowfish as it swam slowly around. Knox turned a full circle, watching for a flash of pink, but there was nothing.

Nada.

Which left only one place she could be. He kicked hard for the drop-off, the steep wall where the reef disappeared into the blue, cursing in his head because she should know better than to go below their agreed maximum. When they got back on dry land, he'd curse her out in person and—

That was when he saw it. The thin line, almost invisible

as it disappeared over the edge of the reef wall. A couple of the jagged barbs attached to it still had bait on them, and when Knox swam into the blue, the horror story unfolded beneath him, written in blood. Four turtles were caught on the line, floating lifelessly in the gentle current, their eyes cloudy. Caro was thirty feet farther down, her leg tangled in the line as a fifth turtle hung beneath her.

Knox's pulse ratcheted up a notch as he dove. He and Caro had both spent years of their lives around water, but while he'd been drilled through every hellish scenario imaginable until he basically became amphibious, she hadn't been pushed to extremes. Her panic was all too evident in her jerky movements.

Calm down, babe. I'm coming.

Her timing sucked, but she'd finally broken her habit of watching her back, and as he got close, a flailing arm knocked off his dive mask. Fucking fantastic. His vision blurred, and it took him two attempts to grab the sinking mask, another five seconds to put it back on and purge the water. Caro was still freaking out, and Knox grabbed her wrists, holding her arms still as he fought to gain control of the situation. For once, she didn't try to do him bodily harm.

Their gazes met, her eyes wide and terrified, and she was sucking in lungfuls of air. *Wasting* lungfuls of air. They were a hundred and thirty feet down now, and they'd need every breath to get out of there safely.

Knox released a hand and pointed two fingers at his eyes. *Watch me.* He'd dropped his dive slate, and there was no easy way to communicate. There were no hand signals for this shitshow of a situation. *Trust me*, he tried to tell her. *Trust me, and I'll get us out of here.*

After a long second, she nodded.

Her breathing slowed.

Knox reached for the knife strapped to his leg. The five-inch titanium blade had been a birthday gift from Slater—Knox and Ryder's colleague and housemate—along with a bottle of Jack Daniels and a stripper. At the time, he'd preferred the stripper, but today, he changed his mind on that. The serrated knife edge sliced through the mess of line easily, and the instant Caro was free, she slipped out of Knox's grip and dove after the sinking turtle.

For the love of fuck...

One good kick, and Knox grabbed her inflator hose. He put enough air into her BCD that she began rising to the surface, not so fast it was unsafe, but rapidly enough that she shot daggers from her eyes as she scrambled for the release valve. He slashed a hand through the water. *Cut it out.* Of course, she ignored him, and he had to grab the toggle out of her hand. She shook her head. He spat out his regulator and glared.

"Up!" he mouthed.

She removed her own regulator, and he figured she was going to try arguing, but what she actually did was start choking. Knox put another blast of air into her jacket, and then she was too busy trying to breathe to fight him again.

The turtle was sinking, but as Knox got closer, he saw it was still alive. A fin was moving, and its eyes were clear. One of those eyes focused on him as he grabbed the end of the line, and in that moment, he felt it. A connection. In the SEALs and then with Blackwood, he'd battled his way out of some pretty hairy situations, and at times, he was sure that only the determination flowing through his veins had gotten him home. And that's what he saw in the hawksbill before him. Determination.

The creature was three feet long, wrapped in the thin nylon rope that had led to the deaths of at least four of its kin. He cut away what he could, then wrapped the remains of the line around one hand. He used the other to inflate his BCD, but it wasn't enough. The creature was a deadweight. He checked his air. Fifty bar left—he should be on the beach by now—but he wasn't letting the turtle go. Knox kicked hard, sending silent thanks to Emmy and her insistence that her team spend an obscene amount of time keeping fit.

Slowly, slowly, he inched toward the surface, his dive computer beeping warnings about air consumption and ascent rate and—since it was a Blackwood custom model— probably flashing a message from Emmy telling him to stop acting like a twat.

He should show the message to Caro because as he rose, he glanced up and saw her coming toward him, fast, too fast. For fuck's sake, couldn't she get the message? She'd emptied her BCD to descend, then run out of air, so now she was sinking with eight pounds of lead strapped around her waist. Knox caught her as they drew level and pointed at his spare regulator—every diver carried one in case of emergency.

Maybe it was the fact that he'd brought the injured hawksbill with him, or maybe it was his "fuck with me again, and I'll drown you myself" expression, but the fight went out of her. Caro gripped his arm as he used a lungful of precious air to inflate her BCD manually using the backup tube. Then he checked his dive computer, relieved beyond measure when it said "No stop." They didn't have the air for any more delays. The message scrolling across the screen said "Get out of the water, you fuckwit," and Knox spent the remaining ascent time getting a handle on his temper. Caro hadn't only endangered her own life; she'd risked his too.

"What the fuck?" he asked as soon as they hit the surface.

"I couldn't leave her down there to die alone."

"So you thought you'd go join her in the afterlife?"

"I wasn't trying to die."

Knox supported the turtle so she could take a mouthful of air and then resumed the argument.

"Well, sweetheart, I guess you just have natural talent. What the hell are we meant to do with this turtle?"

"We need to get her onto the beach and untangle her, and depending on how badly she's injured, we might need to take her to the sanctuary. And the dead turtles..." Caro hiccuped a sob, the first time Knox had seen any emotion other than anger or irritation from her. "We have to get them too."

"No, no, no. We're not diving again today. We didn't make a safety stop, and neither of us has time to get treated for decompression sickness. Are you feeling okay? Any dizziness? Nausea?"

He studied her closely. She'd gone pale and her breath came in pants, but she hadn't vomited, so Knox took that as a good sign.

"Why do you even care?" she asked.

"It's my job to care."

That sounded better than telling her he liked her in a weird "I want to fuck your tits because I have masochistic tendencies" sort of way, which would have been totally inappropriate under the circumstances. Under any circumstances, in fact. But it was the truth, or at least, the only truth Knox allowed himself. Deeper feelings were dangerous.

"I thought you were a Navy SEAL? Isn't it your job to shoot people?"

"Common misconception, but being on a SEAL team is about solving problems, not leaving a trail of bodies in your wake. Which brings us back to the turtle. Should we lift her out of the water?"

Caro shook her head. "Not yet. Picking her up by the shell could do more damage. There's a board in the truck—we can lift her on that."

"Stay with the turtle while I get it."

"No, I'll go. I need to call Franklin and tell him what happened." Caro wiped a hand over her eyes. It might only have been seawater on her face, but Knox was ninety percent sure it was tears. "Four turtles, gone. Leaving baited lines is illegal here. What kind of psycho would do that?"

What kind of psycho? Knox had a feeling he didn't want to know the answer to that question.

15

CARO

"It's okay. You'll be okay."

I'd treated the turtle's wounds with Betadine and named her Lucky, because we'd all been lucky today. When hawksbills were sleeping, their metabolism slowed, and they could hold their breath for several hours underwater, plus they did this weird butt-breathing thing where they could absorb oxygen through their cloaca, which sounded like the kind of bullshit a turtle would spout if it played "two truths and a lie," but was actually a thing.

When they were awake, though, they could only go forty-five minutes without breathing, so Lucky had a close call this afternoon. If I'd taken a few extra minutes to squeeze into my wetsuit, she could have died. And if Knox hadn't reacted as quickly and as calmly as he did, then I would have joined her, just the way he said.

And how had I thanked him for saving both of us?

I'd basically accused him of not caring.

Way to go, Caro.

Three hours had passed since we came up from the worst dive of my life, and I was still shaking. I held a hand out in front of me and stared at it. Yup, shaking. I'd seen dead turtles before, but never so many, and never just...just hanging there like that. Franklin had always suspected that bait lines were being set around the islands, but this was the first time we'd been able to prove it.

After I called Franklin, I'd called Vince. Although he was based on Ilha Grande—all the detectives were—he covered Malavilla and Valentine Cay too. The San Gallicano Department of Emergency Services was small, only seven hundred people, and that included all the civilian employees, the fire department, the coastguard, and San Gallicano's paramilitary force. There were only a dozen detectives for the whole nation. That didn't usually matter because serious crimes were rare—other than the drama out at Skeleton Cay two years ago, there hadn't been a murder for three years, and that time, Vince had found the guy's wife still holding the knife. But it did mean nobody had ever gotten a proper handle on the poaching. And maybe they never would? Budget cuts meant the police department was no longer as proactive as it once had been, and there were bigger problems to deal with, drugs and domestic violence being just two of them. Some officers didn't even see the occasional bit of poaching as a problem, despite the government ban. Turtle meat had been eaten for generations, and who were they to tell islanders to change their way of life?

Vince cared, though. He'd shown up with Officer Roy and cordoned off the beach while we waited for Franklin to arrive with the boat. When I described the baited line, both Vince and Franklin thought it was the work of professional poachers and not a hungry local fishing for his supper. There was discussion about leaving the line in place and mounting a surveillance operation to catch the culprits, and Officer Roy was in favour, but Vince pointed out the small crowd that had gathered to watch the drama and said that word of the discovery of the dead turtles would spread like wildfire. If the poachers had local connections, they wouldn't be back. As for Franklin, he said the turtles deserved a dignified burial, that the spirits wouldn't be happy if they were treated as bait. Yes, he believed in the spirits, and I tried to humour him even though I thought the whole thing was a bunch of hokum.

Franklin had taken Lucky, me, and Knox back on the boat while Vince kept watch on the beach and Jason Roy went home to fetch his dive gear. Then Knox had traded places with Ryder, and Ryder went to recover the bodies with Jason while I treated Lucky.

Now? Now Franklin and Ryder were on their way back, and I just felt drained. And sad. And guilty.

My phone pinged with a message.

STACEY

Any idea what happened at Coconut Cove today? I heard it was something about turtles?

I took a couple of deep breaths, trying to keep my emotions under control. Bad enough that Knox had seen my tears earlier without blubbering through the phone at Stacey. I'd managed to hold myself together while my life fell apart the first time, so dealing with it a second time should be easier, right?

She answered on the first ring. "Oh, hey, how are you?"

"Honestly? I'm not good."

"The turtles...?"

"Four of them died. Four hawksbills. We managed to save a fifth, and I nearly ran out of air, and—" So much for not crying. I sniffled and wiped my eyes with the bottom of my T-shirt. "It was h-h-horrible."

"I'm so sorry. Did the shark get them?"

"No, not the shark. This was all the work of humans." I told her about the baited line, how four turtles had been hooked and drowned, how Lucky had gotten tangled and nearly died too. That she was in the tank beside Gilbert, her belly full of sardines, alive and safe. For now. "If only we'd gotten there sooner, we could have saved the others too."

"How long had the line been down there? I thought Coconut Cove was a popular diving spot?"

"A day or two? I don't know. There was still bait on several of the hooks."

"Putting the line there was a big risk for the poachers. They must have known there was a chance a human would spot what they were doing."

"Maybe they just don't care? The turtle population has declined, but there are always sightings at Coconut Cove. That's partly *why* it's a popular diving spot. Or maybe they heard about the shark sighting and figured the cove would be quiet for a day or two?"

"Are there many sharks around here?"

"There never used to be. In the past several years, they've begun coming closer to shore because we're stealing all their food sources through commercial fishing. Locals who rely on tourists for income are worried it'll scare the foreigners away."

Franklin said that in his first twenty years on Valentine Cay, sharks near the beach were almost unheard of. Then occasional sightings were reported, mainly Caribbean reef sharks, blacktip sharks, and the occasional tiger shark. Last year, someone even claimed to have spotted a great white, but they'd probably gotten it confused with a bull shark. The water here was too warm for great whites.

"We destroy their habitat and then complain when they visit ours?" Stacey said.

"Exactly."

"That happened with the elephants too."

"More and more often, I feel ashamed to be a human."

Although there were a few decent ones left. Knox's face popped into my head. Without his quick thinking, Vince would have had a hella busy week ahead. A part of me wondered whether it might have been easier to drown. The San Gallicano PD would take the death of a human far more seriously than the deaths of several turtles, and I was living on borrowed time anyway. If Aiden caught up with me, he'd do a lot worse than leaving me to become fish food.

"I know how you feel," Stacey said. "I still have nightmares about what I saw in Africa."

"Do you think the turtles in Coconut Cove could be connected to your smuggling ring?"

"Honestly, I don't know. Nobody much wants to talk. Some of them blow me off, and others seem…scared. It's strange—in Africa, it was a clear case of good versus evil, rangers versus poachers. But here… It's more like evil versus apathy. You care, and a handful of the cops care, but nobody's really doing much. There's no organised anti-poaching effort other than the occasional beach patrol during nesting season."

"Which gives the poachers more power." A chill ran through me. "Just watch your back, okay?"

"I always do."

The boat came back. I heard the engine and then Franklin's heavy footsteps on the dock. Knox went out to assist, and Luna and Jubilee must have followed him because I heard a scream followed by retching. For once, I couldn't criticise the girls for overreacting because that was pretty much how I felt too.

I should have gone to help, but I couldn't bring myself to look at the dead turtles again. I only had to close my eyes to see them hanging there. Not only was it a reminder of their loss, but of my own mortality as well. When that line caught around my ankle, I'd panicked, and that had only made it tighter. Then I'd tried to cut myself free, but my hands were shaking so much that I'd dropped my knife.

This was never meant to be my life. I'd only taken the minor in biology because I had a crush on one of the teaching assistants, and then he'd broken my heart by getting engaged to a girl who wasn't me. No, finance was my jam. I'd been a good accountant. So good that I'd managed to unravel the fraud at AquaLux Yachts and report it to the IRS as part of my plan to escape Aiden. But then the slippery son of a bitch had wriggled out of the charges, and I'd had no choice but to run permanently.

I'd grown to enjoy working with turtles, and the conservation of an endangered species was vital, but they weren't my first love. More and more often, I missed my fancy coffee and my air-conditioned office. My beautiful shoes and my BMW. I missed sex, but I didn't miss being mind-fucked by Aiden. *Never fall for the pretty ones, ladies.* At best, they were too good to be true. At worst, they were deadly.

"Hey."

Speaking of pretty ones... I turned to find Knox standing in the doorway, dressed in board shorts and a faded T-shirt two sizes too small. Either he'd taken a shower, or he'd been in the sea again because his hair was wet, tied back in a messy bun on top of his head. The man had better hair than I did. When I didn't answer, he came to sit beside me on the edge of Lucky's pool.

"How's she doing?"

"The cut on her flipper is deep, but it should heal in time."

"And how are you doing?"

Don't cry, Caro. "I got scraped by a hook, but I put Betadine on it."

"That wasn't what I meant."

"Oh, really?"

"Don't play dumb, Caro. You're not dumb. You have to know that people are worried about you. Why don't you let them in rather than pushing them away?"

Yes, Knox was too good to be true, and he was definitely dangerous. He saw through me. Saw the vulnerability I tried so hard to hide. Earlier, I'd managed to avoid his question about why I was always checking behind me, but he'd ask it again. He'd ask until I answered. Knox wasn't the type of man to let something drop.

"Are you saying you're worried about me? You've known me for less than a week."

"I wasn't aware there was a set timescale for caring."

I was about to make a snarky retort when I realised I was being horrible to him again. And Knox didn't deserve that. No, he deserved an apology, no matter how hard it was for me to make it.

"I shouldn't..." I paused to breathe. "What I actually meant to say was 'I'm sorry.' I'm sorry I've been such a bitch. It's been a hellish day, but that's no excuse."

"Apology accepted. Do you want to talk? The problem goes deeper than Luna and the dead turtles, doesn't it? You're running from something."

I nodded. There was no point in trying to lie. Knox had already picked up on my fears, and I felt as if I owed him the truth for saving my life.

"What are you running from?" Knox asked. "I know it's

not anything criminal—that would have shown up on the background check."

The...what? "You *background-checked* me?"

"Standard procedure for anyone a principal will be spending time around."

"That's...that's so invasive."

"We only use publicly available information." When I didn't lose my scowl, Knox flashed a grin. "Relax, it was only a basic once-over. Not the comprehensive probe where we turn your colon inside out."

Sheesh, I hoped they didn't find a photo of the real Caroline Menefee. She was six inches shorter and sixty pounds heavier than me. And if Knox had been checking through criminal records, now he thought I'd been busted for smoking pot when I was seventeen. Great.

"I came here after a breakup, okay? My ex was a real jackass."

"You think he might try to find you?"

"He swore he would."

In an email after I left, before I panicked and deleted the whole account.

"And you believed him? Harsh words can be said in the heat of the moment."

"Oh, he had time to think about it." Several days in jail, in fact. "He holds grudges like no other, and he says I ruined his life."

"Didn't like being told it was over, huh?"

"No, he didn't."

Especially when the news was delivered by a criminal investigator. I'd used the time before he got released on bail to pack up my things and disappear. Oh, and get into a fight with his mistress when she showed up unexpectedly. Then I'd flown to England, to Italy, to Mexico, reluctantly returned to the US after six months to get pulled apart on the witness stand, and finally ended up in San Gallicano.

"How long ago did it happen?"

"Nearly three and a half years."

"Maybe he'll have gotten over it?"

"No, he definitely won't." Not when his daddy was still in prison for tax evasion and he'd been forced to sell off most of the family's assets to pay the fines. I'd read about it on the internet. The Malibu mansion, the house in the Hamptons, the Florida beach house, they'd all gone. Most of the yachts too, and the AquaLux brand was a shadow of its former self. I wasn't even sure if Aiden was involved with the company anymore. The new CEO was Carlos Davila, who'd been a mere salesman when I worked there, and it looked as if he was shopping around for outside investment. Unsuccessfully, so far. "Can we please stop talking about this?"

"Sure. So you're just going to stay here at the sanctuary for the rest of your life?"

I shrugged. "Probably. Somebody needs to care for the turtles, and as long as Little Miss Social Media over there"— I jerked my head toward the bunkhouse where I assumed Luna had gone to avoid any actual work—"doesn't blow my cover, I'm safe where I am."

"Safe as long as you don't decide to disregard safety protocols and get tangled in nylon cord again. Don't you carry a dive knife?"

"I dropped it," I admitted. "Thank you for helping me."

"Get a new one. And if you ever pull another stunt like today's, I'll tie you up myself."

"Why? Do you enjoy that kind of thing?"

The words fell out of my mouth before I could bite my tongue. *Think before you speak, Caro.* Hot guys were trouble.

Knox leaned in. Not touching, but closer than was generally polite. "What kind of thing do you mean?" Another inch. "Are we talking bondage? Or merely discipline?"

I swallowed hard. "Can you forget I asked that?"

"Nah, baby. Do you like being spanked?"

"Stop!" I pushed him back, and was it my imagination, or did he flinch when I touched his chest? "Are you hurt?"

"You caught me with your foot earlier. It's nothing."

Nothing? Really? For a man like Knox to wince, it had to be more than that.

"Show me."

He stared at me for a beat, then lifted the hem of his shirt. Damn, the man had abs. A six-pack. No, an eight-pack. I was so busy counting muscles that I almost missed the huge purple bruise on his pec. It was roughly the size and shape of Ilha Grande.

"Shit! I'm so sorry."

"As I said, it's nothing."

"You and me, we have very different ideas of nothing. Do you want ice? Acetaminophen?"

"How about you just don't press on it when you want to avoid answering my questions?"

"How about you stop asking dumb questions?"

Knox smirked. "Don't think I'm gonna do that."

"Why not? Because you have a brain the size of a fairy shrimp?"

Slowly, slowly, he lowered his shirt. "Because I like getting you riled up."

"You're a real asshole, did anyone ever tell you that?"

"And I think you like it too."

"Why the hell would you think that?"

His gaze dropped to my chest, and…oh. Dammit! Why were my nipples hard? Those traitorous tips were pressing against the fabric of my T-shirt as if they were begging Knox Livingston to suck on them. Urgh. I crossed my arms, but that only made him laugh.

"It's not funny."

"Beg to differ, babe."

"I'm not your babe."

"Not yet, but I'm working on it."

"Don't you ever stop?"

"Most women like my stamina."

Was Knox genuinely hitting on me? I wasn't sure whether to be flattered or annoyed or strip off my clothes and drag him behind the storage shed. Certainly the ache between my thighs suggested the third idea was popular. It had been a really, really long dry spell.

"Don't you have a poor, long-suffering girlfriend waiting at home?" He wasn't wearing a ring, so I was going to assume no woman had been fool enough to marry him.

"Outside of work, commitment has never been my thing." He ran a finger down my arm. Just one finger, and heat flooded through my veins. "If you need that itch scratched, you know where to find me."

"What itch? What are you talking about?" More accurately: how did he know?

He took a step back. "And try not to throttle Luna. She's a pain in the rear end, we get that, but there's enough shit going on without having to pull the two of you apart every five minutes."

"I..."

"And if you're trying to keep a low profile, I should probably warn you that Jubilee's offered to take over the sanctuary's Instagram account while they're here, and Baptiste went for the idea. If you see her coming with a camera, duck."

Knox threw me a salute, and then he was gone.

16

CARO

"What am I gonna do, Lucky?"

When I first arrived at the sanctuary, I'd kept a backpack next to my bed filled with the essentials—clothes, money, passport—just in case I needed to run again. Over the past couple of years, I'd grown complacent, become secure in my little bubble, but last night, I'd begun packing a bag again.

I didn't want to leave. Where would I even go? I'd once read a romance novel where the heroine, an accountant, offered her skills to a Mafia don in exchange for his protection, and a part of me thought that seemed like a mighty attractive offer. If I'd known how to actually get in touch with the Mafia, I might have given it a try. But I didn't, and now I was stuck on an island with two annoying women; two hot bodyguards, one of whom might have sort of propositioned me last night, I still wasn't sure; Franklin; and several hundred endangered turtles.

Lucky swam up to me and raised her head out of the water. Curious? Or hungry? Or just taking a breath? I tossed her a sardine, and she ate it.

What was I supposed to do about Knox?

He'd said he wasn't a fan of commitment, and if a handsome SEAL had suggested no-strings sex in my pre-Aiden days, I'd have pushed him onto the nearest horizontal surface and ridden him like a cowgirl. But that was then, and this was now. Mom had told me I needed to settle down, that I couldn't be a party girl all my life, and with Aiden, I'd thought I was doing exactly that. He'd been a successful businessman, well-respected in the community, and everyone said we complemented each other perfectly. In public, he used to joke that I had the brains and he had the charisma. In private, he'd called me a stupid slut. The only saving grace was that Mom had died believing I was happy. I'd just graduated from college, and the world was my oyster. It would have broken her heart if she'd found out what a dark place I ended up in.

Today, I'd decided avoidance was the best policy. Our four guests were working in the fifth pool room, building the extra enclosures we'd need for this hatching season, while I monitored Lucky and fed the other residents. I wasn't sure whether Knox had said anything to Jubilee and Luna, but they were being vaguely civil today. Jubilee had brought me a mug of coffee while I was cleaning the pools this morning, and Luna hadn't been her usual whiny self.

Or maybe Ryder had spoken with her? When I was quietly stuffing clothes into my bag late last night with only the moonlight for company, Luna had left the cabin and headed down to the beach. A minute later, I'd seen Ryder's silhouette pass the window, following in her footsteps. Were they having a secret midnight tryst? Knox was full of inappropriate suggestions, so it stood to reason that his colleague was a horny prick too, and judging by the way Luna cavorted around in the photos on her social media, she'd probably be up for a little action with her bodyguard.

My phone rang, and it was Stacey.

"Hey, how are the turtles? Is the one you rescued yesterday okay?"

"She's doing well. Living up to her name."

"Lucky by name, lucky by nature."

"But I hate to think how many other turtles won't be found in time. Looking for those bait lines is like searching for needles in a whole prairie full of haystacks."

There were fourteen independent dive schools in San Gallicano, plus five hotels that offered scuba as part of their guest activities, and I'd emailed all of them this morning, asking them to keep an eye out for any lines and emphasising the safety aspect. Plus I'd added a message in the San Galli Aqua Group asking scuba enthusiasts, skin divers, paddleboarders, and snorkellers to speak up if they saw anything untoward. And I made sure to post in the right group this time. When I first arrived on Valentine Cay, I'd accidentally joined the San Galli Watersports Club, and when I'd asked if anyone would be interested in buddying up on a casual basis, I'd received a whole bunch of enthusiastic but very strange replies. Vince had set me straight over dinner—in between laughing so hard that beer came out of his nose—and that conversation went down in history as one of the most awkward moments of my life.

"I have a theory about the bait lines," Stacey said. "But I'm not familiar enough with the islands to know whether it holds water."

"What's the theory?"

"You mentioned a shark sighting and how it kept the divers away from the cove?"

"That's right. Blacktip sharks hardly ever attack humans, but I don't suppose any dive school wants to risk getting sued if they're the exception."

"Right, and their insurance might deny a claim if they visited a dive site knowing a shark had been spotted there recently. So, I got to wondering, what if the poachers are more willing to take risks? If they deliberately set their traps in locations with shark sightings, knowing they were less likely to be disturbed?"

"That's...that's..." Horrific. Dirty. Disgustingly elegant in its simplicity. The kind of scheme Aiden would have come up with if he weren't too busy scamming money from the IRS. "That's possible."

"I saw something similar in Africa. There'd be an anonymous report of poachers, and when the rangers went haring out to hunt for them, the real poachers would be acting somewhere else."

I felt sick to my stomach. "Did the rangers catch them?"

"Eventually, but not before more elephants died. These people are sneaky. Real sneaky. I spent the morning going through the posts on the San Galli Aqua Group, and there have been shark sightings every couple of weeks for the past year."

"I know, I'm a member."

"Did you ever check who was reporting the sightings?"

"Uh...not really?"

"Ninety percent of the reports come from accounts with three or fewer previous posts. I did reverse lookups on the pictures—both the profile pics and any photos of the alleged sightings—and they're all freely available on the internet. The blacktip shark from Coconut Cove? It was actually seen in the Philippines two years ago."

"So they're...making up sightings to clear the sea for their bait lines?"

"It's just a theory at the moment."

But a theory that made sense. And there was only one

way to prove or disprove it—we'd have to wait until the next shark sighting and hotfoot it over to the location. Which meant I'd have to buy a new dive knife and ask Knox for help again.

plan while monitoring the San Galli Aqua Group for any shark-related news. Seemed they'd gotten a hit.

"What does it say?" Knox asked, but Ryder was already leaning over Luna's shoulder.

"'Be careful out there, folks—just spotted a bull shark near No Man's Rock. Didn't get a great picture as I was too busy getting the heck out of there, but it looked like a big one!'"

Knox put down the can of sealant he'd been painting on a newly constructed pool and joined them. As long as the girls were safe in the same room, they could all get some work done. The picture was a blur that could have been a bull shark or a torpedo or a smudge on the lens.

"Where's No Man's Rock?"

Jubilee shrugged, and Luna rolled her eyes. "How should I know?"

Caro jogged in. She'd been keeping out of the way since Saturday. Now it was Monday, and Knox wasn't sure whether she was avoiding Luna or him. Or both. Both was also a possibility. Mentioning spanking had been unprofessional, but fuck, that ass was asking for it.

"Stacey just messaged—there's another shark post on Facebook," she announced.

"We're one step ahead of you. Where's No Man's Rock?"

"At the far end of Spice Island."

"Where's Spice Island?"

"Three miles farther east than Malavilla. When the Europeans first arrived, they set up plantations there. A couple of them still exist, but most of the land has been bought up by rich dicks in the finance industry."

The low tax rates and a reasonable degree of secrecy had led to a thriving business district on Ilha Grande. Rumour said that Emmy and Black owned a bank there, but rumour also said that Emmy could control the weather, so Knox took the story with a grain of salt. If Emmy could control the weather, she wouldn't curse so much when Alex made her run in the rain.

"Are we taking the truck or the boat?"

"The boat is probably easier."

"Lead the way."

Caro borrowed Ryder's spare dive knife, and they set off for Spice Island with Baptiste captaining the boat and a faithful promise that she wouldn't do anything reckless this time. If a turtle needed saving, she'd stay back and let Knox do the honours.

The journalist's theory was an interesting one, and Knox couldn't decide whether he wanted Stacey Custer to be wrong or right. If she was wrong, they'd be no closer to finding the person or persons who set the line at Coconut Cove. But if she was right, they had a much bigger problem. A poacher who'd managed to fly under the radar for at least two years. A poacher who thought outside the box and used innovative methods to hide his tracks. A poacher with the network to dispose of a significant number of turtles. This wasn't an old-school islander fishing for his supper.

Jubilee, pleased to have something to do that didn't involve scooping shit out of turtle pools, had combed through as many online San Galli groups as she could find and noted sixty-three shark sightings that didn't seem entirely kosher. Caro had been horrified when she saw the list. Sixty-three bait lines that each caught, say, five turtles, would be 315 dead animals. A lot when they were talking about an endangered species. And it could be twice that—

Knox had counted at least ten hooks on the line they'd stumbled across.

And then Jubilee had found more shark sightings in Saint Vincent and the Grenadines. In Grenada. In Saint Lucia. In Aruba, Bonaire, Anguilla. A fatal shark attack off the coast of Puerto Rico had made everyone nervous. Well, almost everyone. It appeared as if the poachers had tried the same trick in Tobago, but those posts were filled with comments from excited divers heading out to look for the sharks and later comments expressing disappointment that they were nowhere to be found. The Tobago "sightings" had quickly tailed off.

The poaching problem might be much bigger than anyone had previously imagined.

"Try not to kick me today, okay?" Knox said as they suited up on deck.

Normally, he wouldn't bother with a wetsuit when the water was this warm, but they had hooks and potentially turtles to deal with, and turtles had sharp beaks, so he figured a layer of neoprene couldn't hurt. He'd explained the issue to Emmy, and extra equipment was en route from Blackwood's base in the Bahamas, just in case it was needed. Emmy's words of wisdom? *Don't let Luna do anything stupid. She's paying us to protect her, and that includes from herself.*

Knox only hoped that Ryder had gotten the memo too. His brother-in-arms had been a little cagey about his nighttime jaunts with their client. When the motion sensor had pinged again last night, Knox had offered to take a turn at taming the dragon, but Ryder had waved him away. *I'm already out of bed, bro.* He'd already been dressed too. Had he been waiting for Luna to leave?

The idea of following crossed Knox's mind, but that felt

like crossing a line. Ryder was a professional. Knox had to trust that he knew what he was doing.

"It was an accident," Caro said. "I didn't even realise my foot connected."

"Do we need to go through the rest of the list of things you shouldn't do?"

"Again? No, Dad."

Knox swallowed a chuckle. Under different circumstances, Caro was precisely the type of woman he went for. Feisty, brave, opinionated. He liked a challenge. He also liked the satisfaction of seeing them submit to him in bed.

But Caro would probably bite off his balls.

He checked her kit over and waved a hand toward the water. "After you."

Damn, that ass...

The plan today was that they'd search slowly using a grid pattern. If they found a bait line, they'd record the scene and then remove it.

No Man's Rock was a lumpy sandstone formation on the edge of the shore that sank into deep water, barren on the surface but teeming with life below the waterline. A school of butterflyfish milled around, a lionfish hung almost motionless in the water, and a moray eel peered at them from the safety of a crevice. Diving for pleasure was still a novelty for Knox, and although this afternoon's trip wasn't exactly recreational, at least he had a pretty woman by his side instead of a bearded asshole in a rebreather.

Caro turned and pointed, and he tore his gaze away from her assets in time to see a turtle swim past. A green turtle this time, and the first he'd seen in the wild. He followed its trajectory, and...fuck. He banged on his tank with a metal clip, hard enough to spook the creature. It swam off in a hurry, and Caro was about to start bitching, he could tell, when she saw it too. A thin, almost invisible line sloping down into the deep. Somehow, she managed to look both furious and gorgeous at the same time. Without thinking, he reached across to squeeze her hand, and those pretty blue eyes of hers narrowed. But she didn't snatch her hand away. Hmm.

Knox began filming while Caro swam the length of the line. Nothing was caught up today, and the top appeared to be secured to something on the surface. After he'd recorded the scene, he coiled up the thin nylon rope, and damn, those hooks were sharp. Rather than untying the end, he left a yard or so floating in the water. If the cops had any sense, they'd keep watch from the shore and arrest the culprits when they returned to retrieve their catch.

Back on the boat, Caro called Vince right away. Knox watched as she paced the tiny deck with the phone to her ear, water dripping from her hair and running into her cleavage. His cock twitched when she paused facing away from him, one hand on her hip, and if Baptiste hadn't been mere yards away, Knox might have made another highly inappropriate suggestion just to see the fire in Caro's eyes. Between Lady P, Luna's antics, and a trip to Europe to locate a wealthy businessman's missing daughter—a daughter who was happily shacked up with all four members of a death metal band—he hadn't hooked up with a woman in two months. He was gonna get RSI if he didn't get laid soon.

"Yes, at No Man's Rock. We left part of the rope in the water. All you have to do is—" Caro listened for a moment. "I know you're short of manpower, but turtles are dying, Vince." Another pause. "You know what? I'll do it myself."

She hung up and tossed the phone onto one of the padded seats, and it rang a second later. Her face twisted into a frown, then she sighed and answered.

"If you're going to give me another lecture on staff shortages, I don't want to hear it." After a moment, she smiled. "I'm glad about that. Okay, dinner, and you can pick the restaurant. ... This Thursday? Will you book a table?"

A table? She was going out for dinner with the cop? Knox hadn't been a fan of Detective Fernandez when he arrested Luna, and he liked him even less now. Was he dating Caro? Or was it merely a friends-with-benefits arrangement?

"Vince is going to watch the beach himself, and he might co-opt a junior officer if there's one available."

"He's coming right away?"

"Almost. He has to make a few calls first, and then he's coming."

"Did he try to duck out in the beginning?"

"He said he was too busy, but I can be very convincing."

"You bribed him with dinner?"

Caro shrugged. "It's nothing new. We often go out for dinner."

"Right. So you two are a thing?"

It came out harsher than Knox had intended. More asshole-ish, and of course Caro picked up on that. She closed the distance between them, her chest just inches from his. And then she licked her fucking lips.

"What would you say if we were?"

"I'd say..." He swallowed hard and willed his cock not to react. "I'd say I was disappointed."

"Interesting." She smiled and stepped back. "That's...interesting."

Interesting? That was all she had to say? Apparently so, because she turned and walked into the cabin with Baptiste, ending the conversation.

Or so Knox thought.

They were unloading the boat when Knox stepped aside

to let Caro climb onto the dock, but instead of squeezing past him, she stopped.

"Vince is probably more interested in your friend than in me."

"Huh?"

"In Ryder." When Knox didn't reply fast enough, she poked him in the chest. Not on the bruised part, thank fuck. "Do keep up. Ryder's gay? I heard Luna and Jubilee talking this morning."

What the hell? Ryder still hadn't told Luna he was straight? Then what were they doing on the beach all night?

"Vince is...gay?"

"He's just a friend, okay?"

With that, Caro hopped up onto the dock and disappeared.

18

KNOX

"What are you doing with Luna?" Knox asked.

Ryder looked up from his phone. They were lying in the bunkhouse on new mattresses that were a damn sight more comfortable than the old ones.

"Nothing."

"I don't mean right now. I mean in roughly two hours when the motion sensors go off."

"Still nothing."

"So you wouldn't get upset if I went out to check on her instead of you tonight?"

"No, but she would." Ryder dropped his phone onto the bed and sighed. "We talk, that's all. She's lonely."

"Lonely? But she's surrounded by people. She never goes anywhere alone."

"And she doesn't trust any of them."

"Not even Jubilee? I thought the two of them were close."

"When it's crunch time, Jubilee always takes Amethyst's side."

"So it's Amethyst who's the problem?"

"One of them. Probably the main one. Luna doesn't like talking about herself, but she lets pieces of information slip out."

"Doesn't like talking about herself? We discussing the same woman? Luna Maara, with forty million followers who does nothing *but* talk about herself from dawn through to dusk?"

"She's playing a character."

"Well, she's really fucking good at it."

"Yeah, she is, but that isn't the real her. Jubilee writes most of that stuff anyway."

"So who is the real Luna, if she isn't a work-shy whiner?"

Knox intended to provoke a reaction with his words, and he got one. He'd shared a house with Ryder for a year, and if he'd learned one thing, it was that Ryder tended to bottle things up. But he was like soda—shake him, and he'd explode.

"Shut the fuck up. You don't know a damn thing about her."

"I know she still thinks you're gay." When Ryder merely cursed under his breath, Knox continued. "In your deep and meaningful chit-chats, you didn't think to set her straight?"

Ryder let out a long, low groan. "Shit got complicated."

"This whole job got complicated."

Luna's arrest, the court thing, the dead turtles, and now the fact that every time Knox saw Caro, his dick got hard. Not a good look in shorts, which was another reason he'd decided to wear a wetsuit around her.

"Luna isn't a big fan of straight men. She hasn't gone into the details, but I know a stranger got into her hotel room a while back, plus she had a bad experience with a bearded guy."

"That's why you shaved?"

"That's why I shaved."

Right. And now Knox felt like a shit for ignoring Luna's rider. But there was a scar on his chin that he'd rather forget about, and the beard meant he didn't get constant reminders of a past fuck-up.

"Do I need to shave?"

"She already thinks you're an asshole, buddy. Losing the beard now isn't going to change that. And it's probably good for her to learn that not every man with a beard is going to hurt her."

"What, are you her therapist now?"

"No, I..." Ryder slumped back against the pillow—the new memory foam pillow—and sighed. "Fuck, she reminds me so much of Neve."

Oh boy. "As in, your ex-girlfriend Neve?"

"They have the same vulnerabilities. Neve used bitchiness as a defence too. Man, I just want to help her."

"Does Luna need help?"

"Who the hell knows? Neve said she was fine, feeling better, and then she..." Ryder shook his head and took a couple of deep breaths. On the battlefield, he was one of the toughest men Knox had ever served alongside—he'd walk through fire for a teammate—but Knox knew that Ryder had a weekly appointment with Dr. Beaudin whenever they were in Virginia. He had demons. Maybe even more demons than Slater, who should also have been seeing Dr. Beaudin but had so far refused to do so. "Luna and me, we're not fucking around on the beach. I'm teaching her to swim."

This conversation was a ride. "You're...teaching her to swim?"

"That's the plan, anyway. She's scared of water, but last night, she went in up to her knees."

"She's scared of water? But she vacationed on a yacht."

"She figured that if she fell in, one of us would save her."

That sounded more like Luna.

"So, what's the plan? You spend a month hanging out and schooling her in the art of breaststroke, and then you just walk away?"

There was a long pause. "Yeah."

Sure, and the devil would take up downhill skiing.

"What time is your date tonight?"

"It's not a date, and could you do me a favour?"

"As long as it doesn't involve pretending to be your boyfriend. You're hot, baby, but you're not my type."

"Fuck off." Ryder flipped Knox the bird. "Could you ask Caro to go easy on Luna? She's trying."

"Very trying."

Ryder glared at him.

"Why would you think I have any sway over Caro?"

"Because she likes you."

"She doesn't like me. She doesn't like anyone other than Baptiste and the turtles."

Ryder snorted a laugh. "I'm surprised she even likes the turtles. When she studied marine biology in college, she came bottom of the class."

Bottom of the class? That didn't sound like the Caro Knox knew. She'd spent the trip to No Man's Rock telling him about the symbiotic relationship between turtles and remora fish. The remora cleaned all the shit off a turtle's shell, and the turtle gave the remora a free ride.

"How do you know that?" Knox asked.

"It was in part two of the background file. Agatha sent it over this afternoon. Anyhow, Caro was checking out your package when you were setting your dive computer earlier, so there's at least one part of you she doesn't mind."

"She was probably considering the logistics of removing it."

"Nah, she was smiling."

"I refer you to my previous point."

Ryder chuckled and checked his watch. Counting down the minutes until Luna showed up?

"Try telling Caro that the turtle-sunglasses thing wasn't even Luna's idea. It was Kory's, and she covered for him so he wouldn't get into trouble."

"Seriously?"

"I don't think she has many friends."

"The guy's a dick."

"Yeah, I know. And I asked Agatha to take a look at those shark sightings, see if she could find an IP address for whoever posted them."

"Good idea." As if on cue, the motion sensor pinged an alert on Knox's phone. "Speak of the devil," he muttered.

Ryder jumped to his feet. "Don't wait up."

"Wasn't planning on it."

The door closed with a *creak*, and once again, Knox hoped to fuck that Ryder knew what he was doing. He'd passed the C-SORT to become a SEAL, but sometimes, Knox wondered about his friend's ability to hold up in difficult circumstances. Not in a fight—Ryder had no issues there—but in the quiet moments when he had too much time to think.

Knox waited until Ryder's silhouette passed the window, then reached for his tablet. He should have read the email from Agatha earlier, but he'd been too busy diving, and then when Caro and Baptiste went to collect turtle eggs in the evening, he'd taken over Luna duty so Ryder could have a break. Catch up on the sleep he wasn't getting at night. Luna had barely said a word, not that Knox was complaining about that.

Agatha's report expanded on the initial profiles. Franklin Baptiste had once been arrested for protesting about raw sewage being dumped in the ocean, hardly a slight on the man's character. He deserved a medal, not a night in the cells. And there was a brief write-up on Vincent Fernandez—a decent cop, by SGPD standards, at least, and one who'd been on the force since he graduated from the University of San Gallicano a decade ago. But Knox was more interested in Caro. Her only brush with the law had been an arrest for smoking pot. Agatha's summary said that in her class yearbook, she'd been voted life and soul of the party, most likely to die from alcohol poisoning, and best celebrity lookalike. Who did she look like? Knox scrolled to the next page. Rebel Wilson. What the fuck? Caro was more of a Salma Hayek.

He fired off an email to Agatha: *Can you send me a picture of Caroline Menefee?*

Even if she was lying about her identity, she was unlikely to be a danger to Luna. She'd been living at the sanctuary under an assumed name for years, quietly staying out of trouble.

The steps outside creaked, and a moment later, the door opened.

"She kick you to the kerb already?" he asked, assuming it was Ryder.

"What are you talking about?"

Knox glanced up to see Caro in the doorway, and she didn't look particularly happy to be there. Did nobody sleep in this place?

"Everything okay?" he asked.

Instead of answering, she walked farther into the room. She'd unbraided her hair and changed into soft shorts and a strappy little top. No bra. She was either cold or turned on, and seeing as the temperature was still in the seventies, Knox had to assume it was the latter. He felt his cock hardening again and bent a knee so it wouldn't show.

"You seem like the kind of man who'd carry a condom in his wallet."

Was that a criticism or a compliment? "Safety first."

"Good." She took a tentative step forward. "This is just sex, nothing more."

Knox had either misheard or stepped into a parallel universe.

"What did you say?"

"I'm only here because the dog ate my vibrator."

He burst out laughing. "You want me to sub for your battery-operated boyfriend?"

Caro ticked off the points on her fingers. "One, you keep checking out my ass. Two, your wetsuit really doesn't hide as much as you think. Three, you're a commitment-phobe. This would be a mutually beneficial arrangement."

"Like I'm the turtle and you're the remora?"

"I said nothing about sucking. *You're* the remora."

Never before had a woman—let alone one he didn't much like—walked into his bedroom and offered him no-strings sex. Usually, he had to at least take them to dinner first. And this wasn't just any woman; it was Caro. Or was it? Did the whole "lying about her identity" issue affect things? His cock said not. This would be one small step up from a hate fuck, an activity Slater assured him was worth the aggro.

"So you just want to ride my cock and then pretend it never happened?"

"Exactly. Your roommate's having his own weird brand of fun on the beach with Luna, and they're always gone for a couple of hours at least."

She did make a good argument. Caro wasn't a client, and Ryder was watching the principal. Knox beckoned her forward, and she took a hesitant step. Then another. When she was close enough, he sat up and snaked his arms around her thighs, pleased by her sharp intake of breath. Just because this was a transaction didn't mean he wouldn't enjoy himself.

"I can smell your arousal from here, baby."

"Is that a 'yes' to my proposal?"

"Get those fucking clothes off."

19

CARO

My chest heaved as Knox stared at me, and when he licked his lips, I wondered if I'd made a colossal mistake. Bitten off more than I could chew, quite literally. He moved his leg, and holy crap, that bulge in his wetsuit this afternoon hadn't been the whole thing.

"Get. Them. Off," he repeated.

"For the record, I've never done anything like this before."

And I still wasn't certain why I was doing it now, other than the lure of Knox's godlike body and the ache between my legs that wouldn't go away no matter how hard my fingers tried.

Knox dragged his shirt over his head, and I fought to swallow the lump in my throat. He had muscles on muscles, and those beautiful brown eyes darkened and glittered as he raked his gaze over me. The man could snap his fingers and have any woman he wanted, but for one night, he was mine. My fingers tightened on the edge of my camisole, and I pulled it off.

No going back now.

"And the rest," he said.

"You're still wearing shorts."

Knox got to his feet, trailing his fingertips up my back as he rose. The lightest touch, but it left tendrils of heat in its wake. This time, my shiver was for all the right reasons. Wordlessly, he dragged the shorts down over his hips, and his dick sprang free. Yes, the embarrassment had been worth it. The sleepless nights, the hours spent wondering if I dared to be so brazen. That thing was monumental. The Burj Khalifa of appendages. I'd been there once, to the Burj Khalifa, and now the memories came flooding back. Aiden's hand around my throat as we rode up to the Lounge. His whispered warning that I'd better not embarrass him. Him drinking too much and groping my ass as we looked out across Dubai.

"You okay, baby?"

I shook my head to clear my mind. That asshole had no business being in my thoughts.

"I'm fine."

"You shuddered."

"Just awed by the size of your equipment, stud."

Quickly, I shimmied out of my shorts to avoid any questions. I wanted an orgasm, just one fiery, spine-tingling orgasm to erase the ghost of Aiden's dick and send that wiener to roast in hell where it belonged, and Knox Livingston would be the man to give it to me.

He studied me, really studied me, and I tried not to squirm. My gym membership had died along with my relationship, but I was fit from working around the sanctuary all day. I'd taken a shower and shaved everywhere. Maybe I wasn't the pretty little doll Aiden had claimed, but I didn't look terrible. Knox ran the tip of his tongue along my jaw, and then before I could gather my thoughts, he plucked me off my feet and laid me on the bed.

"Wait there."

"Where are you going?" I asked, but he didn't answer. The door opened and closed, and then I heard his footsteps return.

"I put a sock on the doorknob in case Ryder gets any ideas about coming back early. If you want a three-way, I can take it off again."

"Definitely not." I was nervous enough about sleeping with one virtual stranger. But then I got curious. "Have you had a three-way?"

"Do you think I've had a three-way?"

Why did he have to ask me that?

"Probably?"

Knox pulled me forward so my ass was on the edge of the bed, and then he knelt. What was he...?

"Best view in the world," he said, right before he buried his head between my legs and sucked. Hard. I arched off the bed, a scream rising in my throat before I remembered where I was and who was outside and clapped both hands over my mouth.

"You could have...warned me," I gasped.

"You said I was the remora."

He went back for more, circling my clit with a tongue as capable as the rest of him. I buried my fingers in his hair, unsure if I wanted to stop him or urge him on. This was too much. *Way* too much. His beard scratched at my thighs, and damn, that felt good. Raw. Rough. Aiden hated beards. He used to shave twice a day because he didn't want to "look like a Neanderthal."

"I only wanted sex."

"News for you, baby. I don't fuck until a woman's come

at least twice on my tongue. Or maybe my fingers. I prefer to mix things up."

"I can't come more than once a night. Never happens."

"Bullshit."

"It's true."

"Then you've only dated assholes."

Okay, so that was accurate, but he didn't need to put it quite so bluntly.

"And now I've found another one, except we're not dating."

"Thank fuck for that."

"Can't you just stop talking?"

"You're the one who started the conversation."

What was I even doing? Why had I come here? Hormones, that was it. Stupid, dumb hormones and a bad habit of screwing around with the wrong type of men. Knox Livingston most certainly fell into that category.

"This was a mistake. I should—"

"If you don't shut your mouth, I'll stick my cock in it."

I shut my mouth. His gaze locked on mine, and my pussy clenched so hard I almost came on the spot. Which would have been such a waste. I wanted to come riding him like a— No, scratch that. I'd hit my head on the top bunk. Most of the time, I was happy in my little Caribbean sanctuary, but there were moments when I missed the mansion in Malibu.

Knox went to town on me, eating as if he were starving and I was dessert. Then he added a finger, just one, and I was gone. The orgasm crashed over me in a breath-stealing tsunami, drowning out all rational thought. I needed more. I needed more of Knox. His eyes blazed, the heat searing my skin as he crawled up the mattress and settled next to me.

"That's one. Fuck, these tits are spectacular. I've

dreamed about sliding my cock between them and giving you a pearl necklace, but I think I'd have to gag you first."

"It's a 'no' on the gagging. Ditto for the spanking."

"Have you tried it?"

Aiden hadn't been averse to slapping, kicking, and punching when the mood took him, so any hint of violence was a turn-off. And I needed to be able to speak.

"No, but I know I don't want to."

Rather than argue, Knox shrugged a shoulder. "Okay."

Okay? That was it? Aiden would have ignored me and done it anyway. Or convinced me that any reservations were in my head, that every other woman enjoyed that sort of thing and if I didn't, there was something wrong with me.

Knox? He just pushed my legs farther apart, did a magic trick with his tongue, added a couple of fingers into the mix, and made me come again. What the hell? The look of triumph on his face made me want to kiss him. Or slap him. Possibly both.

"I'm not going to say I told—"

"Then don't," I snapped. Holy shit, my legs were trembling, and I was still getting aftershocks. Some enterprising manufacturer needed to replicate his tongue in battery-operated form.

"Ready for number three? Or do you need a break?"

I needed a break. I really needed a break. Time to recover, time to think. I'd imagined Knox would be all about himself. That I'd be nothing more than a warm body, and we'd both selfishly take what we could before I tiptoed back to my bed and we never spoke of this again. But Knox was a giver. Even the arguing was kind of fun.

"Maybe just a few minutes."

He laughed softly and lay beside me, his head propped on one hand and the other draped across my stomach. Now what? Aiden used to roll over and go to sleep as soon as he was done, and I used to either lie there counting my mistakes or sneak off to the bathroom and finish what he started. Ditto for the men who came before him, well, apart from one, a musician who I was quite smitten with until he called me Angie while we were fucking. Knox reminded me a little of him, actually. Cocky, laid-back, hairy.

"Do you play the guitar?" I blurted, and Knox stiffened. All of him, not just his dick. That was plenty stiff enough already.

"Why?"

"Why am I asking?"

"Yes."

Out with the smile, in with the frown. Gone was playful Knox. He'd turned weirdly serious, and I had no idea what had made him that way.

"Uh, I was just curious. I used to date a musician, and he was the only one of my exes who cared whether I came. So I guess I was wondering whether you shared any other traits."

There was the longest pause. He traced the outline of my lips with a finger, but he wasn't looking at me anymore. No, he was staring into the distance, and I had a feeling his mind wasn't in the room at all.

Finally, he answered. "I used to play the guitar."

"But not anymore?"

"Not anymore."

I wanted to ask why. I was *burning* to ask why. But if I did, something told me he'd shut down completely.

"Well, you still remember what to do with your fingers."

The lines in his forehead eased. I didn't quite get a smile, but his lips did twitch.

"My mom bought me a recorder when I was little," I told him. "Big mistake. Huge. I loved playing it, but I definitely wasn't cut out for a musical career. I thought when the upstairs neighbour stomped on the floor, he was joining in with the rhythm, but it turned out he was just mad."

"If you like blowing things, I have a suggestion."

Normal service: resumed.

"Aw, I never suck dick until the second date."

"So you're saying you want a repeat?"

Think before you speak, Caro.

"You think this counts as a date? You're not even wearing pants."

"What if I pour you a glass of wine and tell you that you're pretty?" He wrinkled his nose. "Do we even have wine?"

"Wine is a luxury I can't afford. Ditto for candles, steak, and fancy shoes."

"If I buy you fancy shoes, will you wear them?"

"Where would you buy them? The general store? They only sell flip-flops and knockoff sneakers."

"Leave it with me." Knox rolled a nipple between his fingertips, not hard enough to hurt but with enough pressure to send a current shooting between my thighs. I gasped at the sudden shock, then nearly swallowed my tongue when he swapped his fingers for his teeth. "I could feast on you for hours."

"We don't have hours. I don't trust the whole sock thing. When I was in college, the sock fell off, and I walked in on my roommate... Never mind. I don't want to think about it, but there were two guys, and I never managed to look her in the eye again."

"So you weren't tempted to join in?"

"Ugh. And you didn't answer my question earlier—have you had a three-way?"

"Yeah, but with two girls."

Double ugh. "Why am I not surprised?"

Knox merely grinned, totally unrepentant, and began stroking his manhood. I couldn't tear my eyes away. I'd never seen a man touch himself that way before, not so unashamedly. Aiden had always pretended he didn't jerk off, even though I knew he did. I'd found out one morning when we rode to the office together. His phone accidentally connected to the Bluetooth speaker in his Porsche, and as we rounded a corner half a mile from home, Lusty Linda began moaning at full volume. Aiden ran a stop sign and crashed into a UPS truck, and somehow—I'd never managed to work out how—it was all my fault. He'd been in a vile mood for weeks.

But Knox just pleasured himself in slow, measured strokes, watching me as he did so. Great. Now I'd *never* get this image out of my head.

"I'm still here, you know."

"I know. But you like watching me."

"What makes you think that?" I spluttered, even though it was true.

"Your pupils are dilated and your cheeks are flushed, and even though you might not have noticed it, you licked your lips."

"Dammit," I muttered.

"Loosen up and enjoy yourself."

"I am not...not *tight*."

Before I could blink, his hand was between my legs, a finger sliding into me with practised ease.

"Baby, you are."

Ugh. I thunked my head back on the pillow and groaned. Why did he have to be so annoying? And so...so... good at this? He did some voodoo with his finger, and another orgasm tore through me, turning my insides into a cosmic soup of sensation. My vision darkened at the edges, and all I could see was Knox looking down at me, saying, "I told you so."

Smug bastard.

I closed my eyes, trying to regain a modicum of composure, but he offered no mercy. I heard the rip of foil, and a moment later, his cock nudged at my entrance. The burn as he pushed inside, inch by solid inch, made my eyes water, but at the same time, it felt *good*. Really fucking good.

"You okay?" he asked, leaning in to kiss me softly. Almost tenderly.

"Mentally or physically?"

"I'm going to ruin you for all other men."

I didn't want to confess that he'd already done that. This was a night I'd never forget, and even if I managed to track down a horse-sized dildo on this godforsaken island, it would never measure up.

Sensations overwhelmed me as he filled me over and over, slowly at first. Then something seemed to snap in him and he surrendered the last scrap of control. I wrapped my legs around his waist, giving in, giving him everything, lost in the moment, lost in Knox Livingston. I knew I'd regret it in the morning, but as he carried on whispering filth into my ear and letting his tongue do dirty things to my breasts, I didn't care.

A fourth orgasm was inevitable. I knew that the moment he slid a hand under my ass, raising my hips and leaving me helpless against the onslaught of dick versus G-spot. I forgot to put a hand over my mouth, and I came with a cry that was part ecstasy, part frustration that this asshole could destroy my self-control so thoroughly. Knox followed me over the edge, jerking inside me before kissing me so sweetly I thought another man had taken over his body.

"We can never do this again," I told him.

He just watched me, sweaty hair flopping over his forehead.

"I mean it. This was a one-off."

Why did he have to be so ridiculously handsome? It wasn't fair.

"So I'll see you tomorrow night, then?" he said.

"Get off me."

I wriggled out from underneath him and quickly realised my mistake as I tried to stand. My knees buckled. I staggered a few steps before Knox hooked an arm around my waist and pulled me back onto the bed.

"You realise I'm the type of man to carry *two* condoms in his wallet?"

"You are?"

I was so going to hell, but at least I'd enjoy the journey.

20

RYDER

"Can I help to collect turtle eggs one night?" Luna asked.

They were lying at right angles on a blanket, and she'd taken to using Ryder's abs as a pillow. She turned her head to look at him, and he flicked a lock of her hair out of the way when it tickled his chest.

"Not sure that's a good idea, moon. Someone might see you."

"But it's dark."

And cameras had flashes. "Maybe one day if they take the truck."

"I could ride in the boat."

"The draft is too deep for the boat to get right up to the beach."

"The draft? I thought that was, like, cold air."

"The draft of a boat is how low it sits in the water. Last night, Caro and Knox had to paddle to the shore, and the water was up to their chests."

Luna was going in the water every night now, walking barefoot across the sand and into the sea while Ryder waded beside her, holding out an arm in case she needed to steady herself. Sometimes, she'd go the length of the beach on her own, and other times, she gripped his hand so tightly his knuckles turned white. He was still trying to figure her out. Luna Maara Puckett was a hot mess of emotions wrapped up in a delicate, doll-like package.

At first, he'd worried about breaking her.

But now he understood that she was already broken.

If her mind was in the present, she'd chat about turtles and sunsets and the beach. But all too often, she'd lose her balance on the tightrope and fall into the past or future, and then her frame would tense and her voice would waver if he pushed that avenue of conversation any further. She communicated, though. There was one thing in life that Luna liked, and that was music. When they were lying there on the beach, she'd start singing softly, not her commercial tracks, but songs that came from her heart.

In the shadow of a dream, I'm living day by day
But my heart's grown heavy, and it's hard to find
my way
She said I'd be a star, her vision set in stone
But the path she's chosen, I can't call my own

I wear these chains of duty; they bind me to the
ground
But deep inside, I'm screaming, I need to be
unbound
I long to spread my wings, to chase my own
desires
But every step I take, she douses all my fire

I see her eyes upon me, filled with hopes and
dreams
But they're not mine; it's not as easy as it seems
I wear this mask of smiles, to hide the tears
I cry
A prisoner of her wishes, beneath this
painted sky

Ryder's chest ached as he listened to the words, and he wanted to hug Luna, to tell her that everything would be okay and she'd find a way to be free. That *he'd* find a way to free her.

But he couldn't.

She was the client, and he was the bodyguard. Not her boyfriend, not even her friend. Her bodyguard. Plus she still thought Ryder liked guys, and guilt ate away at him as they lay there under the stars because he was certain that if she knew the truth, she wouldn't be lying there with her head on his stomach. She wouldn't be talking about the night sky while he plotted to murder a man whose identity he didn't yet know.

Yesterday's verses had been the hardest.

In the haze of neon lights, I lost my innocence
Betrayed by trust in you, my fragile confidence
You wore the face of friendship, but darkness
lurked beneath
Now I'm haunted by your touch, a bitter, cruel
deceit

My tears are hidden in the shadows of the night

I wear a mask of strength, but I'm broken deep
inside
In the silent whispers, I hear your haunting voice
A nightmare that replays, I never had a choice

Bound by circumstance
I'm feeling the weight
Caught in these chains
Can't escape
Every time I try
Every tear I cry
I'm bound by circumstance
It's my fate

In this twisted tale, I'm lost and can't escape
Haunted by the memories of that night's cruel
mistake
I'm fighting through the darkness, I long to
get away
But I still have to face you, in the cold light of
the day

I see you in the hallway, your face a wicked grin
A chilling reminder of the darkness that's within
I thought you were my friend, my mentor, my
guide
But now you're just a shadow, a demon I
can't hide

Someone close to Luna had hurt her, hurt her badly, and Ryder knew what that shit could do to a woman's mind. The toll it could take. He was the first person Neve had told about the abuse, would have been the only person if he hadn't convinced her to go to her father. Over a decade later, he still lay awake at night, wondering if he'd done the right thing. Would she still be alive if he'd just offered comfort and shared her pain? If he'd done as she asked and gotten them the hell out of Jacksonville rather than pushing for justice?

The man who raped Neve had been her brother, and the revelations had torn her family apart. She hadn't been able to live with the trauma, not after her father persuaded her against going to the police and her brother showed up for Christmas as if nothing had happened and raped her again.

This time, Ryder would take a different approach.

But tonight, he just smiled and tucked Luna's hair behind her ear.

"Are you ready to go in the water again?"

"You'll come with me?"

"I always come with you, moon."

"I'm going deeper today."

And she'd come prepared. Usually, she snuck out of the bunkhouse in the shorts and camisole she slept in, but tonight, she'd put a bikini on underneath. When she shucked her clothes, Ryder was the one who needed cold water, and quickly. His attraction to Luna was far more than physical, but he was a red-blooded male. His dick still swelled when she stood in front of him with only tiny scraps of turquoise fabric covering her small but perfect breasts.

But she was oblivious, and that was a good thing. He didn't want to throw her off balance by adding feelings into the mix.

As had become their routine, they walked to the sea side

by side. Ryder went into the water first, giving her time to find her feet and catch up. She squirmed and squealed as the waves lapped over her thighs and up to her hips, but she didn't stop.

"I'm going in up to my waist," she decided.

"Do whatever you feel comfortable with."

The instant the water hit her belly button, she turned and ran back to the beach, but she was laughing. Laughing and smiling, and fuck, that was good to see. Beneath the bitchy, defensive exterior, Luna was just a big kid who'd never been allowed a childhood. Her mom had made sure of that. Amethyst Puckett had entered Luna into beauty pageants from the age of four, drilled her through the routines over and over and over until she started winning. Then she'd leveraged Luna's success into a career as a pageant coach. Luna always sang in the talent portion of the contests, and thanks to Amethyst's dedication to exploiting her daughter, she'd become an internet sensation at the age of fourteen. When Luna hit sixteen, Amethyst pushed her into a record deal, rinse and repeat.

"Tomorrow, I'm going in up to my chest. What happens after that? Do I have to get my hair wet?"

"What happens after that is we float."

"Float?"

"Yup. We just float around, looking at the stars."

Neve had named one of those stars. Ryder bought her one of those novelty gift certificates on the last Valentine's Day they spent together, and she'd toyed around with the idea of calling it "Twinkle McTwinkleface," then switched to "Never"—as in Neve-and-Ryder—before ultimately going with "Bring Back Wonder Burger Breakfast Waffles." It was still floating around out there, somewhere near Ursa Major.

"Float?" Luna asked. "Like, on a pool floatie?"

Ryder burst out laughing. "No, just us in the sea."

"I'll sink."

"No, you won't. It's scientifically impossible."

"Science hasn't met me yet. Can't we try floating in a pool? I might have a hope of not dying that way."

"Sure, you can get in with Gilbert the turtle and I'll throw you sardines."

Luna shoved him, then rolled her eyes when he didn't move. "Don't be such a jerk."

"In all seriousness, it's easier to float in the sea than in a regular pool. The salt in the water gives you extra buoyancy. Haven't you heard of the Dead Sea?"

"No, and I definitely don't want to go there. Is it full of skeletons? Poor souls who thought they'd be able to float and couldn't?"

Luna was clever in many ways, but she wasn't book-smart. Officially, she'd been home-schooled, but in reality, Amethyst had only focused on the parts of her daughter's education that could make her money. Singing, dancing, acting, basic math and English. Luna also spoke pidgin Spanish because they'd had a Mexican housekeeper who spent more time with her in those early days than her mother did. Amethyst had been too busy pursuing the almighty dollar to care for the two girls. Luna could reel off perfect answers to a thousand pageant questions, but she couldn't find Spain on a map, and she had little grasp of science. She had an amazing memory, but she'd confessed that she hated reading because she wasn't very good at it.

"It's called the Dead Sea because it's extra salty, and that means plants and animals can't live in it."

"Why not?"

"The extra salt messes with the chemical balance in their cells, which is also why you shouldn't put too much salt on your French fries."

"I don't eat French fries."

"You don't like them?"

"They have too much fat and too many carbs."

"That just means you should eat them in moderation. It doesn't mean you can't have them at all."

Luna bit her lip. The moonlight glinted off her eyes, and they seemed a little watery. Fuck. Ryder knew that look—she was back in the past again.

"What happened, moon?"

She gave a quiet sniffle. "Jubilee went to Arby's on the way home from school one day, and she brought me fries. Curly ones." Luna smiled at the memory, but the smile didn't last long. "They were delicious. Then Mom came in, and she made me put the ones that were left through the garbage disposal one at a time. Each time I mushed a fry, I had to say 'Fries are bad for me.' And then she put what was left of Jubilee's allowance through the garbage disposal too."

It was abuse. Not the kind that left bruises, but Amethyst Puckett had been messing with her daughter's mind for her entire life. Jubilee hadn't escaped unscathed, but Amethyst's focus had been on the kid who brought in the big bucks.

Where on this island could Ryder get French fries? That was a problem for tomorrow. Tonight, he just muttered, "Fuck it," and pulled Luna into a hug. For a second, she resisted, but then she melted against him and that was the best feeling in the world.

"She's not here," he murmured against her hair. "Your mom's not here, and this month, you can eat anything you want."

"But—"

Luna didn't finish the sentence. A cry made them both stiffen, and Ryder tucked her behind him. He hadn't brought his gun to the beach, a decision he was sorely regretting.

"I think it came from near the bunkhouse," she whispered.

She was right.

"Stay quiet, and stay behind me."

"What if—"

"Shhh."

Ryder gripped her hand as they climbed the rocky steps, alert for any movement. The night was still. As he checked his phone, the loudest sound was his heart beating in his ears, but there was no message from Knox. If there was a problem, he'd send an alert via Blackwood's app, unless he was otherwise engaged or incapacitated. Ryder gave Luna's hand a squeeze and set off along the path, watching, listening. A soft *thunk* came from the boys' bunkhouse, and he stilled. Then he saw the fucking sock and blew out a breath.

"What? What is it?"

He pointed at the door handle.

"So? Is that a sock? Why would someone put it there?"

"Little moon..." Ryder cupped her face in his hands. "When a guy brings a girl—or boy—home, he doesn't want his roommate catching an eyeful of his date's naked ass. So he uses the sock as an advisory."

"So the sock means 'naked asses beyond this point'?"

"Exactly."

"Well, whose asses? Knox's, obviously, but who else?"

"The only other people here are Baptiste, Caro, and Jubilee. Knox is straight, so..."

"Jubilee would never." Luna clapped both hands over her mouth. "That's gross."

"They're two consenting adults." Ryder glanced at his watch. "Wonder how long they're gonna take."

If past form was anything to go by, most of the night. Whenever Knox brought a woman home, they were at it for hours and usually loudly. The house in Rybridge had good soundproofing, but Knox had a habit of picking out screamers.

"How long does sex usually take?" Luna asked.

A perfectly innocent question, "innocent" being the operative word. Fuck.

"You don't know?"

Luna realised what she'd said, and her face morphed into a mask of horror.

"I-I-I..." she stammered. "I don't..."

"Moon, it's okay."

"It's not okay. It's never okay."

She backed away, and when Ryder took a step forward, she held up a hand.

"No! Leave me alone."

"Luna..."

"I'm the boss, and I'm telling you to leave me alone."

With that, she turned and bolted, leaving Ryder in the darkness with a pile of confusion and an avalanche of regrets.

21

LUNA

I'm trapped in not-quite paradise, I don't know
what to say
With a hot guy watching over me, in this sandy
golden bay
I came filled with hope, now I'm lost and alone
But I never planned to spill the secrets I've just
shown

Stuck on an island
Feeling like a fool
Ooh, ooh, ooh, what's a girl to do?

Underneath the palm trees and the starry night
so clear
I let my guard down, and I whispered in his ear
"How long does sex take," the truth slipped from
my lips

Now awkwardness surrounds us in this castaway
eclipse

Stuck on an island
Feeling like a fool
Ooh, ooh, ooh, what's a girl to do?

I'm stranded on this island with a guy who's oh-
so fine
But I wish I could rewind and erase that
awkward line
Now the tension's thick as coconut cream; it's so
hard to breathe
Oh, I'm just a fool on an island, and he's the tide
I can't leave

Two days had passed. Two days of awkwardness where I avoided Ryder's gaze and focused on setting up the sponsorship scheme for the turtles. Avoiding Ryder wasn't easy, though. He was always there, watching and waiting. I considered asking Knox to swap with him, but then Knox would want to know why, and what was I meant to tell him? Of course, I could refuse to give an answer—I was known for being difficult, after all— but then Knox would ask Ryder, and my secrets would be revealed.

"That's not Gilbert; that's Penelope," Jubilee said.

Right. A green turtle versus a loggerhead—I knew the difference now. But I just couldn't *think*.

"I'll swap the pictures."

"Are you feeling okay?" she asked.

"Why wouldn't I be?"

"Because earlier in the week, you kept smiling at Ryder, and now we're on day three of you scowling all the time. Did something happen?"

Normally, Jubilee kept her head down and didn't ask questions, but maybe a taste of freedom was making her braver too? I'd never told her that Julius raped me. We were both so young when it happened, and she didn't need that burden. No, I'd only told Mom, and look how that had turned out.

"I'm just sick of being stuck here, that's all."

"Are you sure? When you ducked out of breakfast the moment he showed up, I thought you were avoiding him."

"What? No, that's totally not true." I steeled myself inwardly and smiled. "Ryder, can you help me to make coffee?"

He seemed slightly surprised—and I couldn't blame him for that—but he nodded. "Sure."

Last night on the beach, he'd sat on the steps while I walked in the sea. Only with the water up to my ankles, but at least I'd managed it on my own. On the way back to the bunkhouse, I'd heard giggling from the trees. Knox and Caro. The two of them were hooking up every night now, and although Knox looked rougher around the edges, he was functioning surprisingly well without sleep. Whenever I went without sleep, I got a lecture about eyebags from Mom.

Although she was the one with the eyebags this week. She'd called Jubilee yesterday, begging her to find a new lawyer and get the jail sentence cancelled. The food was slop, apparently, and they never turned the lights off. Secretly, I was hoping she did something really obnoxious and got another thirty days.

Now Ryder followed me out of the pool room to the kitchen, staying a respectful distance behind.

"You okay?"

"Why do people keep asking me that today?"

"Because you look stressed."

"Oh, and why do you think that is?"

"Being a virgin is no big deal, moon. In fact, I was relieved to hear it because some of the things you said before... I thought a man might have... Never mind. There's nothing to be embarrassed about."

"I'm not embarrassed, I..." I didn't know where to start, or if I even should. "Why are you being nice to me?"

"It's my—"

"Don't tell me it's your job. We both know that's not the reason."

In my head, I said "bullshit," but I never swore out loud. Not since I was seven, when I'd told a friend my stupid shoes looked shitty backstage at a pageant, and Mom hauled me into the bathroom and washed my filthy mouth out with soap. Pageant queens didn't use that kind of language, she said.

Ryder stepped closer and kicked the door shut with a heel. Usually, I felt sick being trapped in a room with a man, but I knew he wouldn't hurt me. Not like the others.

"I've had bodyguards before," I said when he didn't speak. "A *lot* of bodyguards. They're mostly civil to my face and rude behind my back. They don't sit on the beach with me and help me to walk in the water."

He gave the heaviest sigh, as if he carried the weight of the world on his shoulders and he couldn't bear the burden anymore.

"You remind me of a woman I once cared for a great deal."

"Cared for? You don't anymore?"

"She passed away when I was a teenager."

Oh.

"I...I'm so sorry."

"She could be bitchy as hell, but she came from a family where showing vulnerability was considered a sign of weakness." Ryder closed his emerald eyes to hide the pain. "Crying was a sin. So she used her temper as a defence mechanism to hide how much she was hurting inside, the same way you do. Get past the prickles, and she was the sweetest girl you'd ever meet. And you're sweet too, moon. Don't think I don't see it."

Today, it was me who hugged him. I clung to Ryder as I tried to fight back tears and failed miserably. He saw me? He saw the real me and not the caricature I'd become?

"I've only had sex once," I whispered into his chest. "It wasn't voluntary."

His arms tightened around me, and we just clung to each other. He was a sponge, soaking up my misery and giving me comfort in return.

"Tell me he went to jail, moon. Tell me he paid for what he did."

"I still have to work with him."

All the curse words that lived in my head spilled from Ryder's lips. "Are you fucking kidding me?"

"He's a big shot in the music industry, and Mom said I shouldn't let one mistake ruin my life."

Ryder went all weird. Like, he was vibrating. I looked up to study his face and froze at his expression. I'd seen anger before, but this was pure, unmitigated fury.

"You told your mom, and she didn't go to the police?"

"Housekeeping already washed the sheets, and she said it would be my word against his. The thought of a trial terrified me. I was only sixteen, Ryder. What choice did I have? But she makes sure I'm never alone in a room with him anymore, and he's banned from coming to my concerts."

"That's fucked up, moon."

"Welcome to my world. So, anyhow, that's why I don't have a boyfriend. We should make the coffee."

"You're not the first person I've known who changes the subject when she wants to avoid difficult discussions."

"I don't know how to talk about this—feelings and stuff. Usually, I just tell people to get lost, and they do."

"What kind of support network do you have?"

"Support network?"

"Friends, family, people you can confide in. Not your mom, clearly. What about your half-sister? Do you get along with her?"

"Cordelia? Ugh. Bringing the family into disrepute, blah, blah, blah." The only time she called me was to complain. "Apart from Jubilee, I don't have anyone, and Jubilee goes along with whatever Mom says."

"If you want to talk, I'll always listen, but you should have somebody else back home."

"What if I hired you as my bodyguard full-time?"

Yes, that was a perfect idea. Ryder would protect me, listen to me, understand me. A strange warmth flooded through my veins. Not happiness, more...relief. But it was short-lived.

"Wouldn't fly with the boss. I'm qualified to be a bodyguard—overqualified—but I'm only working this job because the executive protection team is short-staffed. Too many new contracts, not enough good candidates."

"Then I could hire you privately? I'd double your salary and—"

Ryder was already shaking his head. "I'm offence, not defence. And I'll be straight with you—if a bodyguard has a personal relationship with the principal, even a close friendship, it's hard for them to do the job effectively. I'd be too busy worrying about your emotional well-being when I should be focusing on the physical."

"Then I could hire you as my therapist."

I framed it as a joke, even though I was half-serious.

Ryder chuckled. "I can help you find a good therapist if you want. Plus we have this month, and I'll give you my personal number when the contract finishes. You can call me any time. If I don't answer, I'm probably dodging bullets."

"Don't say that."

"It doesn't happen often. Let's make the coffee, moon, and the next time we hit an awkward point in the conversation, don't run."

"I won't."

"Promise me."

"I promise. Will you teach me to float tonight? Is Knox getting any sleep at all?"

"Yes, and some. The two of them must have passed out in his bed last night because things went quiet, and Caro didn't slope off back to the other bunkhouse until six."

"You sat outside for the entire night waiting for her to leave?"

"No, I fell asleep in the hammock and got bitten to fuck by bugs."

"If it happens again, just come to our bunkhouse. There are spare beds."

"Without wanting to be crude, it's the girls' bunkhouse, and I have a dick."

"Jubilee won't mind. We've shared a hotel suite with Kory before. Someone told the paparazzi, and they wrote a whole bunch of disgusting stuff, but there aren't any staff here to sell out."

"Maybe."

"I still can't believe Knox and Caro are screwing each

other. Okay, so she hasn't tried to strangle me for the past couple of days, but she's still mean."

"Her story isn't mine to tell, but you're not the only woman wearing a mask around here."

What was he saying? Had she been attacked by a man too? Been engineered into a career she hated? Did her mom micro-manage her until she wanted to scream?

"I don't understand."

And how had she ended up working at the turtle sanctuary?

"Caro has demons. Let's leave it at that."

22

KNOX

Was Luna okay?

Her eyes looked red and puffy, but she was smiling and carrying a tray of drinks. Even Jubilee looked confused. Ryder was walking close behind her, and he gave the slightest nod. Was that "yes, she's fine"? Or "yes, I've replaced her with a cyborg and we can just take the batteries out if she gets snippy"? Caro gave Knox a questioning look, and he shrugged.

No clue here, baby.

He was in the fucking dark, and not only about Luna. Caro was a mystery too. The only things Knox knew for certain were one, she could suck a man's brain out through his cock, and two, her name definitely wasn't Caroline Menefee. Agatha had sent the yearbook picture over with a note: *I thought at first it was Rebel Wilson, but the facial recognition program says no.*

So, who was the sexy blonde who climbed into Knox's bed every night? And he said "blonde" because she needed to dye her roots. There was only a hint of new growth, but she definitely wasn't the brunette she pretended to be. He hadn't gotten much further with unravelling her identity since the first time she showed up in the middle of the night.

Agatha had volunteered to dig into Caro's background, and for a moment, Knox had been tempted to take her up on the offer. But did he really want to know the truth? Their relationship was purely physical—okay, *mostly* physical—and it had an expiration date. What good would it do to dig around in her past? Knowing her real name wouldn't change his attraction to her, although if he knew her ex's name, he'd gladly punch the asshole in the face if their paths ever crossed. Caro didn't talk about him much, but she'd mentioned they used to work together, so when they split, she'd had to leave her job too. The gig at the turtle sanctuary had been a fresh start, Caro following her heart rather than her head for once. She wasn't sure she'd stay on Valentine Cay forever, but at the same time, she had no plans to leave.

And whatever was between them was only casual. She'd gone out for dinner with Vince Fernandez last night, and Knox had spent the evening on bodyguard duty.

"I made coffee," Luna announced. "The unicorn mug has the sugar in it."

Caro claimed the glittery unicorn with a muttered "Thanks," and Knox took a chipped mug advertising Havana Hills Cigars. A trio of local volunteers had shown up to help today—friends who came a couple of times a month, Baptiste said—so Luna and Jubilee were staying clear of the pool rooms. This morning, they were putting the finishing touches to the sponsorship scheme. Jubilee had given the sanctuary's website the makeover it desperately needed and set up a page for each of the permanent residents. For thirty bucks a year, folks could sponsor their favourite turtle and receive quarterly updates on how it was doing. The girls had even created templates for the updates, so all Caro and Baptiste needed to do was tweak the write-up and add some current photos.

"Ugh!" Caro spat her coffee back into the mug. "Are you trying to poison me?"

For a moment, Luna looked puzzled, but then her barriers slammed into place. Ryder swore her bitchiness was a defence mechanism, and at first, Knox hadn't believed him because bitchiness was her default operating state. But over the past few days, he'd been watching her to see if Ryder's theory held water, and he'd spotted a few glimmers of humanity, mostly when Ryder was close by.

"Oh, gee, you're welcome. Why are you always so mean?"

After Knox asked Caro to lighten up on Luna, she'd been mostly civil, but now they were back to square one. Knox sighed.

"Because this coffee tastes like it was made with seawater."

"I used the water from the big plastic jug, just the way you do."

"It's true," Ryder said. "I filled the kettle."

Knox took a sip of Caro's coffee, and his tastebuds went into meltdown. Fuck, that was disgusting.

"Where did you get the sugar from?" he asked.

"From the white canister on the shelf."

Caro snorted. "That's the salt. The sugar's in the blue canister."

"Well, how was I supposed to know? There aren't any labels."

Ryder touched her arm. "Let's go make more coffee, moon."

Moon? He'd given her a nickname? Whatever, Ryder's influence had turned her from an unbearable pain in the ass to mostly tolerable. The two of them headed back to the kitchen, and Caro drank half of Knox's coffee, presumably to take away the taste of her own.

"There are still no more shark sightings," Jubilee said. "I've checked every San Gallicano group I can find. I put together a spreadsheet with the past reports, and they average six days apart, but the minimum is three days and the maximum is fourteen. That's assuming that all the sightings are false ones." She shrugged. "There could be some actual sharks around, which is why I'm never going in the water around here."

"Shark attacks are rare," Caro said. "And they mostly happen when people behave like prey, splashing around on the surface. If you see a shark, stay still and hang vertical in the water."

"Stay still? No way. I'm swimming away as fast as I can."

"The shark will always be faster. They don't even like eating humans—most of the time, they'll just take a test bite and you might lose an arm."

Jubilee shuddered. "I'm only swimming in a pool from now on."

"I spent years of my life in the ocean, and—" Knox started, but then his phone rang. He checked the screen. Emmy. "I have to take this."

He stepped outside into the sunshine and immediately missed the cool breeze from the ceiling fan. The air was still today, a wall of heat despite it being so early in the year. The summer would be oppressive.

"Dude, did you seriously requisition condoms from the Nassau office?"

People said that Emmy knew everything, and they were right.

"They're an important part of our field kit. They keep underwater fuses dry, stop sand from getting in gun barrels, we can use them as emergency canteens..."

"You ordered two hundred of them."

"It's cheaper to buy in bulk."

"I see. And the 'Dracul the Destroyer' dragon dildo?"

Fuck. He'd added a note in the comments field that the goods were for a special hush-hush operation. Didn't the purchasing department understand what "confidential" meant?

"It's a joke gift for one of our hosts. Kind of like an April Fool."

"It's March. And what about the stilettos?"

"I'll cover the cost. It's just really hard to get that shit in San Gallicano."

"Tell me you're not sleeping with the principal."

"I'm not sleeping with the principal."

"Tell me you're not neglecting your duties because you're sleeping with someone else."

"Ryder and I have agreed on an appropriate schedule. He said he was happy to work extra shifts."

"Fucking hell. Tell me Ryder isn't sleeping with the principal."

"Nah, she thinks he's gay. He's teaching her to swim instead."

"You're kidding?"

"Nope."

"How can she think Ryder's gay? The guy oozes testosterone and inappropriate suggestions. Not as many as you, granted, but still an above-average amount."

"Because in the beginning when she was being the diva from hell, he told her he had a boyfriend, but then it turns out he's the Luna Whisperer. I guess now he doesn't know how to set her straight."

"So they're just hanging out on the beach and drinking mai tais?"

"They talk." Knox paused for a moment, considering. "Do you know who Neve was?"

"You think I don't background-check my team thoroughly? Honey, I'd know if you had polyps in your colon. Of course I know who Neve was, and I also know about Bitter Edge."

Deep down, Knox had always figured Emmy must have an idea of his past, but she'd never mentioned his old band, not once. Or the accident. His three best buddies, gone in one night.

"Right," he said.

"You're a different man than you were back then."

Knox had been forced to grow up fast. If he'd carried on along his old path, if things had worked out as they were supposed to, he'd probably be the male version of Luna right now. Hounded by the paparazzi, living in a bubble far removed from the real world. Did he wish things were different? He wished Brent, Eric, and Jayden were still alive, but he preferred his current life to the one he could have had. Good friends, anonymity, and enough money that he never worried about the bills. When he was seventeen, his only goal had been to leave Buttfuck, Wyoming, and music was his ticket out of there. After his bandmates died, he'd joined the Navy because he didn't care whether he lived or died, only to discover it was where he was meant to be all along.

"I was an asshole in those days. But Ryder says Luna reminds him of Neve, and I'm not sure he's changed as much as I have."

"He hasn't. Ryder's been on Blackwood's radar for years. Just stay safe and enjoy the sun, and next time you try to purchase sex toys on your expense account, for fuck's sake email me first. I'll approve it directly instead of having the authorisation request bounce around various supervisors before finally landing on Sloane's desk. She nearly choked on her sandwich, by the way."

"Give her my apologies."

"Will do." Knox was about to say goodbye when he hesitated. Emmy was a good boss. Firm but fair, and she had a sixth sense that could be unnerving at times. "Do you know anything about wildlife smuggling?"

"Not a lot. Wildlife can't usually afford Blackwood's services. Why?"

"Because it's possible someone's stealing turtles." Knox summarised the trip so far, starting with Caro's recklessness on their first dive, running through Stacey Custer's investigation, and finishing with the shark theory. "One data point doesn't make a pattern, so we're waiting for another alleged shark sighting, and then we're gonna check for bait lines."

Emmy blew out a long breath. "Bloody hell. Look, turtles are cute, but you're there to protect Luna. She's our client."

"So you're saying we shouldn't get involved? Because Caro isn't gonna drop it, and Luna's stuck here, so whether we like it or not, we're wrapped up in this until we leave."

"I'm saying you need to tread bloody carefully. What you do in your free time is up to you, but criminals can be vicious when their livelihood gets threatened. Protecting Luna is the priority."

"Got it."

"Ask the cyber team to do a bit of background research, see if anything interesting pops up."

"I already submitted a request to see if they could track down the IP address of whoever made the shark posts, but it hasn't been processed yet."

Since this wasn't an official Blackwood operation, Knox

had assigned the task a low priority. Current wait time? Roughly two weeks.

"Get it bumped up the queue, and I'll sign off on it."

"Thanks."

"And don't wait around for some jackass to make up a shark sighting. Take the initiative, create a fake account, and post one yourself. Control the situation. There's a reasonable chance the enemy will take advantage and throw in a bait line. They can do that from the shore, right? If they don't even need to get into the water, what's the risk?"

Why the hell hadn't Knox thought of that? Create an "OMG, I think I saw a shark!" post and wait for the poachers to bite. They could lie in wait for those fuckers to arrive. Well, he could lie in wait. No way was he taking Caro along—if her actions at Coconut Cove were anything to go by, she'd try to make a citizen's arrest and wind up in the hospital.

"We'll do that."

"Keep me updated, okay?"

"I will."

23

KNOX

Thank fuck for bug spray. Jubilee had a hundred fake social media accounts—seriously, she had a spreadsheet full of names and passwords—and over coffee this morning, it had only taken her a moment to mock up a shark sighting at Butterfly Beach, complete with a blurry image that might or might not have been a dorsal fin.

"Why do you have so many accounts?" Caro asked. Luna had made her a fresh mug of coffee, this time without salt, although Knox suspected she might have spit in it.

"Because people hate on Luna all the time," Jubilee said. "We can't reply to nasty comments as ourselves because that only makes them crazier, so I pretend to be someone else and put them in their place."

"Does that work?"

"Sometimes. Other times, they lose their minds completely, but then everyone else can see that they're unhinged."

Jubilee had scheduled the post for late afternoon so

Knox would have enough time to get to Spice Island and hunker down to wait. They'd picked the location because there was only one access track to Butterfly Beach, and it ran past the Castaway Bar. Caro would stay in the truck in the parking lot—she'd *promised* to stay in the truck—and record the vehicles coming and going. If Knox saw anyone tossing a line into the ocean, he'd shortcut back to the bar, and they'd follow the culprit back to their lair.

Right now, he was lying under a bush, watching the end of the track, waiting for the rumble of an engine. So much for fun in the sun.

"Anything?" he asked Caro. She'd borrowed Ryder's comms device, seeing as he was back at the sanctuary on Luna duty.

"Apart from a whole lot of drunk guys in colourful costumes doing the merengue across the parking lot? No."

"It's possible no one saw the report."

"Jubilee posted it in five places. But maybe they only act on their own sightings? Which is dumb because you're more likely to get struck by lightning than attacked by a shark. They're one of the most misunderstood—"

"Wait a second..."

Knox heard an engine, but it wasn't coming from the track. No, this was the quiet *putt-putt-putt* of a small boat approaching from the south. A local fisherman returning late from a day at sea? Or an enterprising poacher out to make a quick buck? He turned on his night vision and hit "record."

The boat drew closer, a small, light-coloured dinghy, white or pale blue at a guess. Two people were on board, one at the tiller and the other on a seat in the bow.

"What's going on? What's—"

"Shhh."

He *really* needed to educate Caro on surveillance etiquette, but all he could do for now was turn down the volume in his earpiece.

The boat had a shallow draft, and it motored right up to the shore. The passenger jumped out, sprightly as a cat. He had a coil of rope in his hand, and Knox smelled the faint aroma of rotting fish.

"Watch out for sharks," the driver called, and then he laughed. His voice was deep, a little hoarse.

"There are no sharks here."

"A tourist saw one. Today's post, that wasn't David."

David. They had one name and also confirmation that their theory was valid.

"If it was a tourist, they probably saw a tuna. Maybe a barracuda."

"You remember that stupid woman who got bitten by the barracuda last year?"

"Yeah, yeah, she just had to take a close-up, right?"

Another snippet of information: the men had been in San Gallicano for at least a year. Neither Jubilee nor Luna had mentioned a barracuda attack, so the information wasn't posted online. It was exactly the kind of story that would have freaked both of them out.

The men were wearing hoodies, so Knox didn't get a look at their faces. The passenger worked quickly, first tying the end of the rope around a rock, then spearing chunks of fish on the hooks and uncoiling the remainder of the line into the sea. But Knox worked fast too. He'd brought a tracker with him, intending to use it as backup on any vehicle that showed up in case they lost sight of it after it left. Tailing a car wasn't easy on an island this size—too many small turnoffs, not enough traffic to hide in. But the tracker was waterproof.

Knox slipped silently into the sea, ducked beneath the surface, and reached the boat in three smooth strokes. When the two shitbags left five minutes later, they had an extra friend riding along. Stupid motherfuckers. He'd almost feel sorry for the pair if Caro got her hands on them.

"What do you mean, there aren't enough officers? Vince, we're practically doing your job for you—the least you could do is help."

They were back in the truck again, parked behind the Spice Strip, the seafront promenade that was home to many of Spice Island's stores and restaurants, everything from bars pumping out techno music to souvenir shops to the spice market the island was famous for. Tourists and locals of all ages flocked there in the evenings, including their quarry. The blue-and-white boat was tied up to the public jetty at the far end of the street, opposite the health clinic and Manny's Pizzeria. There was no sign of the occupants. Half of the male population seemed to favour hoodies, and most of those hoodies were dark colours.

"I mean that we have two members of the Valetian royal family visiting next week to open the new sailing facility, and half of the San Gallicano PD has been pulled off their regular duties for planning and security. And I *am* doing my job," Fernandez said with more patience than Knox would have had. He liked Caro—liked her a lot—but there were times when she gave Luna a run for her money. "I'm still sitting under a tree at No Man's Rock, waiting for someone to show up and look for this bait line."

"Well, they probably won't be back tonight—they went to the Spice Strip."

"How do you know that?"

"Because we put a tracker on their boat."

Fernandez muttered a string of curses that would have made Emmy blush. "You did what?"

"There's a link between all those shark sightings and the baited lines, Vince. The poachers use fake shark reports to keep people out of the water so they can trap turtles undetected."

"How on earth did you come up with that?"

"By thinking outside the box." Caro gave a brief précis of their findings so far. "And when Knox overheard two of them talking at Butterfly Beach, it confirmed our suspicions. There's at least one more person involved. They mentioned the name 'David.'"

"Why didn't you tell me any of this before?"

"I was going to tell you yesterday, but then you moaned about having to sit at No Man's Rock and hung up on me."

Fernandez sighed. "Do you know how many Davids there are in San Gallicano? When I was at school, there were three Davids in my class alone."

"Why are you being so negative?"

"Because I'm tired, Caro. Tired of being overworked and underpaid. Tired of watching for poachers who never appear. I've averaged three hours of sleep per night this week."

"Okay, fine. *I'll* sit here and wait for these assholes."

"No, you won't. Those people are dangerous."

"I'm with a Navy SEAL, Vince. I think he can manage to keep us safe."

More curses. "Let me make some calls."

"Make your calls, but I'm telling you, I'm not giving up. The turtles need an ally to fight for them."

"What is *wrong* with you? Ever since the court case, you've had a firework stuck up your ass."

"I'll give you three guesses."

"Luna Maara will be gone in less than three weeks. Just chill."

"Chill? Are you kidding me? Just find these damn poachers." Caro hung up with a growl of frustration and thunked her head against the seat. "I get that Vince is busy, I do, but this is important. Why does a foreign dignitary have to come and open a sailing club anyway?"

"If it's the princess from Valetia, I believe she won a sailing medal at the Olympics."

Caro fell silent, and Knox studied her. She was still a mystery. He knew her both intimately and not at all. Usually, that didn't bother him, quite the opposite—the type of women he tended to get involved with had a habit of telling him their entire life stories before dessert, and that made his dick deflate—but with Caro, he found himself getting curious. Who had she been before she came to Valentine Cay? Why had she chosen to devote her life to turtles and not some other cause? What were her goals? Her hopes? Her dreams?

She leaned sideways to check the boat again. Knox had picked a parking spot with a view between buildings, and solar-powered streetlights bathed the area in a soft yellow glow.

"This sucks. They're probably in a bar, getting drunk while turtles die."

"No turtles will die. I removed the line."

"But those assholes think they will, and that's almost as bad. I bet the two of them won't go back to the boat until closing time."

Knox had to agree with that assumption. "Then let's get dinner."

"I don't have the budget for dinner here. Working in a turtle sanctuary isn't exactly a great career move. Franklin basically pays me in food, and I earn a few extra bucks through babysitting in the quieter months."

"I'll buy you dinner."

"Oh, great, this is where I get the pity party."

"No, this is where we do things the wrong way around, and I take you on a date after fucking you for the past four nights."

"A date? Which part of 'just sex' didn't you understand?"

"Is it so bad that I want to get to know you?"

Fernandez's "firework up your ass" comment left Knox intrigued. Caro wasn't usually this explosive? And then there was the whole secret-identity thing...

"Yes."

Her bluntness was strangely refreshing, but it wasn't the answer Knox wanted to hear.

"Okay, baby." He opened the truck door. "See you later."

"Wait, where are you going?"

"To get a pizza. Don't worry, I'll bring you a doggy bag."

"You're leaving me here on my own?"

"A man needs to eat."

Knox made it six steps before Caro hopped out of the truck and ran after him.

"This is *not* a date."

"Yeah, baby, it's a date."

He wasn't dumb enough to try taking her hand, though.

Manny turned out to be a real person, a hulking Latino with scarred knuckles and a Cajun accent who showed them to a cosy table for two overlooking the water. There was a rowdy birthday party inside—the cake and balloons were the giveaway—but only one more couple sitting outside.

Teenagers, and judging by the awkward silences, they were on a first date.

"Guess they don't get much trouble here," Knox remarked.

"Manny used to fight MMA in the US before he founded a religion."

"Don't you mean he found religion?"

"Nuh-uh. His church is right over there." Caro jerked a thumb in the direction of the truck. "It's called the Fellowship of the Sacred Path. Every Sunday, he preaches kindness and tolerance and also gets some excellent tax breaks."

"Isn't San Gallicano a low-tax jurisdiction anyway?"

"It is now, but that's a recent thing. Two decades ago, it had the highest tax rate in the Caribbean, and the infrastructure was above average. But emigration was at an all-time high because people could earn more working in the Cayman Islands or the Bahamas, and the government was struggling to support an ageing population. So they lowered taxes. And then the opposition promised to lower them further. So now every time there's an election, taxes get lower, and nothing gets fixed anymore."

"You think they should raise taxes?"

"I think everyone should pay their fair share. People like Manny aren't the problem. The problem is rich folks hiding their assets and outright lying about their earnings."

The venom in her tone suggested she was more familiar with the issue than the average turtle expert. Knox opened his mouth to press her on the subject, then bit his tongue. Why ruin a nice dinner with questions Caro wouldn't answer anyway? Perhaps he *should* ask Agatha to dig into her background... But Emmy would undoubtedly find out, and while she'd been remarkably understanding about the shoes and the poaching research, Knox wasn't sure she'd be quite so happy about him using company resources to run additional background checks on his fuck buddy.

"When is the next election?" he asked.

"The year after next, but I'm not eligible to vote anyway."

Manny returned with a jug of water, a basket of breadsticks, and a couple of menus. Knox turned his menu over and found inspirational quotes and a reminder that Sunday services started at ten o'clock.

"No wine list?"

Caro shook her head. "But Manny will bless the water if you ask him nicely. Shouldn't we be staying sober? How will we chase down the poachers if we've been drinking?"

Knox hadn't planned to drink, but he'd hoped a nice glass of red might loosen Caro's tongue.

"You're not chasing anyone."

"Oh, really? How will you catch both men if they go in different directions?"

"I won't. I'll catch one man and convince him to talk."

"Vince says none of the poachers ever talk."

"Yeah, well, I use a different interview technique."

A pause, and then her eyes widened a fraction. "Wait, you don't mean...? Actually, forget it. I don't want to know."

Manny returned. "Are you folks ready to order?"

They were. Knox chose a pepperoni pizza with extra cheese, and Caro asked for a Hawaiian. And no, it wasn't a joke.

"Pineapple on pizza?" he asked. "Deal-breaker, baby."

"I wasn't aware we had a deal to break."

Technically, they didn't, but the longer Knox spent with her, the more he felt that there was something to their entanglement besides sex. Yeah, his cock stood to attention whenever she came close, but he enjoyed hanging out with her too. No, she didn't make things easy. If she wasn't the most challenging woman he'd ever met, she was certainly in the top ten, and considering Knox was acquainted with Emmy Black, Ana Petrova, Dan di Grassi, and Sofia Darke, Caro had stiff competition. But Knox kind of liked her.

"Then maybe we should make one," he suggested.

"A deal?"

"In six months, if we're both still single, how would you feel about me taking a vacation in San Gallicano?"

"Just to be clear, are we talking about a vacation in my bed?"

"That's right."

Caro chewed slowly on a breadstick, and Knox couldn't face eating at all. His stomach felt weird. Fluttery. Which must have been indigestion because he didn't get nervous around women.

"I don't hate the idea. But why don't you have a girlfriend? With a dick like yours, I would have thought women would be tripping over themselves to get to your bed. Don't Navy SEALs have groupies?"

"Getting girls isn't the problem."

"So there is a problem?"

In the US, one of his unofficial rules was "never date smart girls." And by "smart," he meant the ones perceptive enough to see through his player bullshit to the man beneath. Caro might just do that if he spent enough time with her, but he couldn't walk away.

"Commitment isn't my thing."

"Why not?"

Maybe if he gave her a piece of himself, she'd reciprocate? Show him the real Caro? Because she wasn't as tough as she made out. Last night, he'd spooned her in bed, but she hadn't slept. In the early hours, he'd heard her sniffle, and in the morning, the pillow had been damp with her tears. Knox wanted to know why. He also owed Ryder a fuck ton of beer for giving them space.

"I've been beaten black and blue, run over by a motorbike, and grazed by a bullet, but there's no greater pain than the agony of losing people you care about."

Caro's mask dropped, and her expression morphed into sympathy. "Who was she?"

"Not she, they. My three best friends. They died in the same car wreck. I would have been with them if I hadn't passed out drunk in a bathroom stall."

"I'm so sorry."

"We didn't normally drink that much, but we were celebrating our first record deal." The emotions Knox worked so hard to keep a lid on overflowed, and he looked away. "I never want to feel like that again."

"So you choose not to care?"

"Easier than choosing which flowers to send to the funeral."

Caro rose and walked around the table, then motioned Knox to move his chair back. When he did so, the legs scraping across the wooden deck, she settled onto his lap and wrapped her arms around his neck.

"Don't take this the wrong way, but I'm really freaking glad you weren't in the car that night."

Her words chipped another crack in his wall, and that was the moment Knox knew he was in trouble. He should have pushed her away. He should have made some glib and possibly hurtful comment. But instead, he hugged her tight and buried his head against her shoulder.

Nobody had hugged him after the accident. Not one fucking person. In fact, he couldn't remember the last time anyone had hugged him at all. Leah at work had groped his ass and given him a peck on the cheek at the last Blackwood Christmas party, but that didn't count. He breathed in the vanilla scent of Caro's shampoo and committed the moment to memory. Something to call on in the dark days. Two lost souls offering comfort for a moment before they both moved on.

"Who was he?" Knox whispered.

When Caro stiffened, he feared he'd pushed her too far. *Don't run, baby.*

"I met him when I was twenty-four. He was my boss, of all the fucked-up romance novel clichés, and I fell head over heels. Love overrode common sense. At first, he was the perfect gentleman, but by the end, I was just his toy. He controlled my life. What I wore, where I went, who I saw. He checked my messages and had access to my bank account. Twisted my words. Made me believe everything that went wrong was my fault. Everyone thought I lived this perfect fairy-tale life, but I had nothing."

"That's fucked up, baby."

"I know that now, but I couldn't see it for so long."

"You got away. Be proud of that."

"I had a brief opportunity to escape, and I took it. So, that's me. Now I live in a turtle sanctuary and wear flip-flops instead of Louboutins, and I'm never getting in deep with another man again."

"Thank you for trusting me enough to tell me."

She groaned. "We're both so screwed up."

"Got that right. You've never considered moving back to the US?"

"If Aiden found me, he'd kill me. He's not a man who takes betrayal well."

Aiden. Knox had a name. And maybe someday, if he found out where the man was, he'd pay him a visit. Caro didn't deserve to spend the rest of her life hiding away.

"Guess I'll be coming back to San Gallicano, then."

Caro's arms tightened, and Knox kissed her on the temple.

"Make sure you pick a week when there aren't any other volunteers."

"We'll work out a schedule."

She picked up her glass of water and held it in the air. "Here's to being on-again, off-again fuck buddies."

Knox clinked his own glass against hers. "Just don't mention the word 'relationship.'"

"Absolutely not."

That's what he said, but he wasn't sure he'd be able to go back to his old ways once he got home. Hooking up with another woman would feel...odd. Uncomfortable. Wrong, when Caro was sleeping alone on Valentine Cay. Blackwood was flexible when it came to time off, and he earned good money. Getting back for a weekend each month wouldn't be impossible. How much did houses go for on the island? Only something small, one bedroom and— What the fuck was he thinking? They were both anti-commitment.

Manny brought their pizzas, and Knox reluctantly let Caro go back to her own seat. This evening felt like a turning point, but he wasn't sure what lay around the bend. A fucking roller-coaster, and it wasn't over yet. They still had to watch this damn boat.

"I need to speak with Ryder. Let him know we're not coming back in a hurry."

"Will he mind?"

"No, but we'll need to be on an early ferry to Valentine Cay. If the poachers don't return to the boat tonight and Fernandez doesn't come through, do you reckon your buddy Stacey would cover a surveillance shift?"

"Maybe? I can ask her."

"All she needs to do is take pictures."

"What about tonight? Manny's a lark, and the restaurant closes at ten."

"We'll eat, then you'll find a hotel room and I'll keep watch until morning."

"But—"

"Don't fight me on this, Caro. I'm used to surveillance; you're not."

"But have you ever done a whole night by yourself?"

"Several years ago, I pretended to be a bush for three days."

"How? I mean the logistics..."

"A ghillie suit, liquid nutrition through a straw, and a hole in the ground to piss in. Isn't this a great conversation to be having over dinner?"

"If I can't afford dinner, then I definitely can't afford a hotel room."

"We've already discussed budgetary constraints." Knox slid his credit card across the table. "The PIN is one-nine-nine-three. The next time your mouth is filled with bollocks, they'd better be mine."

Her jaw dropped, but for once, no retort came out of it.

"Wider, baby. My balls are bigger than that."

"You're such a dick."

"We both know there's so much more to me than that. I also have fingers and a tongue." Caro rolled her eyes, but she was laughing, and that was good to see. "Think of me when you touch yourself tonight."

"Are you sure you'll be okay on your own?"

"I'll rest easier knowing you're in a comfortable bed."

"Stop doing that."

"Doing what?"

"Being so sweet. It's awkward."

Awkward because she might catch feelings? Man, Aiden had really done a number on her. Knox would just have to try and slide the sweetness in when she was looking the other way because he definitely wasn't going to treat her like shit. But for now, he picked up his phone and reserved the best hotel room he could find.

"Go wild with the minibar, baby."

Sunlight glimmered over the horizon as Knox crawled out from beneath the upturned dinghy. No way would that boat ever go back in the water. He'd been able to see the stars through the holes in the bottom. The poachers' boat was still bobbing alone in the current. The bars had emptied out, other boats had been collected, but the poachers hadn't come back. Why not? Did they live around here? Had they drunk too much to steer safely home? A little light alcohol poisoning hadn't stopped the other sailors who'd staggered along the jetty at midnight. One man had fallen into the water, and Knox had almost left his hiding place to save him, but he'd managed to crawl onto the beach and collapse onto the sand. A couple of his buddies had carried him off.

CARO

Are you awake? Do you want to trade places?

It was only six thirty. She should still be asleep.

KNOX

I'm good. Bring me a croissant from the breakfast buffet.

Stacey Custer had promised to be on the first ferry from Ilha Grande, and she'd be bringing her camera plus a notebook so she could set up at Manny's and work on her article all morning. Fernandez was hopeful of finding an officer to take the afternoon shift. But Knox had an odd feeling about the boat. Someone should have returned for it last night, and they hadn't. Ditto for the bait line at No Man's Rock. Either the poachers were really fucking disorganised, or they knew they were being watched. Which meant that they were better at surveillance than Knox was, or an informant had tipped them off. How well did Caro know Detective Vince Fernandez?

24

CARO

"Can I come?" Luna asked, and I swallowed a groan.

Knox had asked me to go easy on her, and I'd been trying, but if she came out on the boat with us, there'd be no escape if she got annoying. Unless I tossed her overboard, of course, although that wouldn't go down too well with Ryder. I'd seen the way he looked at Luna. Knox said the two of them were just friends, but if Ryder wasn't gay, I'd have said he was halfway in love with her. Was he definitely gay? Maybe he was bi?

Whatever, he'd been a calming influence. The sponsorship scheme Luna and Jubilee had been working on turned out better than I'd thought it would, plus donations were trickling in through the link on the sanctuary's Instagram account. TikTok was their next task, Jubilee said. I still wouldn't be listening to Luna's music anytime soon, but I didn't want to feed her to the sharks anymore.

Ryder and Luna seemed to come as a pair these days, and the thought of having a Navy SEAL along for the ride when we went to collect turtle eggs was...comforting. Knox was exhausted. He said he wasn't, but I saw the tiredness in his eyes. He needed to sleep this evening.

And I feared someone was watching us.

Nobody had shown up to retrieve the line at No Man's Rock, and the boat was still tied to the jetty outside Manny's. Officer Beattie was hunkered down on the beach, Officer Roy was eating pizza, and Vince was cursing my name. *How well do you know Vince?* Knox had asked, and the question had shaken me. We'd been friends since I arrived on the island, and he volunteered at the turtle sanctuary when he had the time, although that happened less and less often these days. Vince was always busy. But now I wondered whether he'd had an ulterior motive for those visits, whether his interest in our marine surveys was a cover for something more nefarious.

Knox had laid out the facts—Vince was one of only a handful of people who knew about the bait lines we'd found, and also the cop who never managed to catch any poachers, no matter how much I begged him to act. But Vince was also my friend. We ate dinner together once a month or so, and I looked after his dog when he went on vacation. He was one of the few people who knew I had a psychopath lurking in my background, and he looked out for me.

Now I didn't know who to trust.

The alternative was that a stranger was spying on us, hiding in the darkness and watching our every move.

I wasn't sure which idea I hated the most.

"You can come, but you have to do what I say," I told Luna. "No running around and disturbing the turtles, otherwise we end up with false crawls and we have to do this all over again."

"What's a false crawl?"

"It's where the turtles come onto the beach, but they don't lay any eggs."

"Okay, I'll do whatever. I'm just so bored of sitting around here. I mean, you guys don't even have TV. How do you live without Netflix?"

How did someone go through life being that shallow?

"We have books."

"I don't like reading."

"Well, go stare at a wall or something. We're leaving at seven—don't be late."

"I thought it would be more...I don't know...eggy?" Luna said, peering at the turtle egg in the palm of her hand.

"It is eggy. It's literally an egg."

"But it feels like leather."

"Not all eggs have hard shells. The texture of turtle eggs varies depending on how much moisture they absorb from the environment."

"That's weird. Can someone take a picture?"

"You're not allowed to post on social media."

"Who said anything about social media?"

"Have you ever taken a picture and not posted it on social media?"

"Like, a million of them. I only post the best ones."

"Fine, give me the damn camera."

Ryder had carried Luna from the boat on his shoulders until they hit shallow water, and then she'd walked the rest of the way. Jubilee was still freaking out about sharks, so she'd stayed on board with Franklin even though I assured her that she'd be perfectly safe. Perhaps it was because I didn't truly believe my own words? What if there was somebody out there? Ryder had checked the hull of our boat for trackers before we left the sanctuary, but I was still on edge. I hadn't felt this unsettled since I left Aiden.

"Anything?" I whispered.

Ryder shook his head. He'd even brought night-vision goggles. "Nope."

"What if a boat followed us?"

"It would have to be hella far away for us not to notice."

"Hey, there's another one!" Luna whispered. A loud whisper, but at least she hadn't yelled.

A hawksbill crawled out of the water and began her slow journey up the beach. Many turtles came back to the beach they were born on to lay their eggs, although nobody was quite sure how they managed such a clever feat. One theory was that they used the Earth's magnetic field to navigate. Meanwhile, I managed to get lost even with satnav, although that didn't much matter now that I no longer owned a car.

Luna already had a camera out, filming the turtle's progress, and I put a hand on her arm.

"No closer."

"Whatever. Jubilee's gonna set the video to music so you can use it for promos."

"Right."

"You should run ads."

"Ads need money."

"Jubilee says that once you dial them in, they pay for themselves. Hey, is that a different kind of turtle? Holy shamoli, it's huge."

"That's because it's a leatherback."

"I think that maybe I won't go near that one."

"Good idea."

It was almost dawn when we finished reburying the eggs in the hatchery at the sanctuary, and Luna even sort of helped. Well, she didn't hinder, and that was good enough.

"Tired?" Ryder asked.

"Shattered. Only six more months of this left."

I headed for the bunkhouse, but he caught my arm. "Just go to Knox. Everyone knows you want to."

"What about you?"

"I'll take the spare bed next to yours."

"The girls would be okay with that?"

"It was Luna's idea."

Oh.

Knox said she was a different person under the irritating exterior, and it was possible that he was a tiny bit right. Maybe.

At least, that was what I thought at the time.

If I'd known what a storm was coming, I'd have followed the turtles back to the ocean and started swimming.

25

KNOX

"Ah, shit," Knox muttered.

"What? What happened? What time is it?"

Caro had fallen asleep in his arms, the little spoon to his big one. It was the first night they hadn't had sex, and it was...okay. Weird, but strangely comfortable. He was trying not to grow too attached to her, but she didn't make it easy.

"It's nine thirty, and Luna's stalker happened."

"Huh?"

"He sent another message."

Luna's agent's PA, who was holding the fort in Amethyst's absence, had notified Blackwood, and Blackwood had notified Knox and Ryder. Presumably, Ryder was still asleep in the other bunkhouse. Knox didn't think he'd risk sharing a bed with Luna while Jubilee was around, and as far as Knox knew, Ryder hadn't yet fessed up about his sexual preferences anyway.

"What does it say?"

Knox passed over his phone so Caro could read the note.

I missed you, my love. Did you enjoy your trip to the beach last night? It's been too long since I saw you in person, but you look good. Next time, leave the boyfriend behind and I'll show you a good time.
  William S

She went rigid. "He was there last night? At the beach? Watching us?"

"That's the assumption we have to make. There's nothing mentioned about the egg-collecting trip online."

"Luna said Jubilee was going to make a video."

"If she did, it hasn't been posted yet. Caro, I have to ask —was Ryder doing his job last night?" Fuck, it hurt to say the words. Ryder was his brother, not through blood but by something deeper, but Knox wouldn't be doing *his* job if he didn't question what happened. "Was he paying attention to the surroundings or to Luna?"

"To the surroundings," Caro answered without hesitation. "He was using the night-vision goggles and everything. Luna was mostly with me, watching the turtles."

Thank fuck for that. But why hadn't Ryder noticed anyone? Blackwood's night-vision goggles were state of the art, and they also had a thermal mode. He should have spotted anything bigger than a bird. Unless...unless it was high in the air. Could Luna's stalker be using a drone? The more expensive models were equipped with thermal and night vision—what if someone was watching them from a distance? All the motion sensors in the world wouldn't help with that. The trees at the sanctuary would hide most of the daytime activity, but he could have been filming Luna and Ryder as they walked and swam and did whatever else at night. Oh hell.

"I need to wake the others."

They gathered in the dining room. Knox made coffee while everyone else got dressed, and luckily a couple of local volunteers had appeared today because nobody had the energy to clean out turtle pools as well. Knox showed the message to Ryder, and Jubilee must have received it too, because when she scrolled through her emails, she turned deathly white.

"I can't believe this," she muttered.

That made five of them. Ryder kept glancing out the window, checking for drones, and Luna was huddled against him. Until now, they'd studiously avoided physical contact in front of an audience, but things had changed, and she looked terrified.

"Did you see anyone while we were at the beach yesterday?" Ryder asked Jubilee. "Hear anything? Any buzzing sounds?"

"Uh, no? But the boat engine was turned on, and I was mostly sitting in the cabin."

Luna seemed close to tears. "I hate this. I hate it. The one place I was starting to feel safe, and he's ruined it."

She was acting human today. Vulnerable. "I need to ask—have you participated in any outdoor activities that could cause a scandal if pictures appeared?"

"No!"

Ryder was clearly pissed at the question. "Buddy, I told you I've just been teaching her to swim."

"I'm only double-checking."

But Caro had turned as pale as Luna, probably because she and Knox had been having a little alfresco fun. Mostly under the trees, thank fuck, and not in the past few days, but the idea that someone had been watching... Anger bubbled through Knox's veins, but how the hell were they meant to catch this guy? A signal jammer? Their own drone? He needed to speak with Nate. Nate Wood was a part-owner and director of Blackwood, a Navy SEAL turned geek who ran the tech department. His unofficial title was Head of Gadgets.

"This means I can't go outside anymore, doesn't it?" Luna asked.

"For now."

Jubilee tried to cheer her up. "We can work on the socials. I mean, we've barely started on TikTok yet."

Luna nodded, but she still looked miserable. "This sucks."

In that moment, Knox felt sorry for her. She'd become more bearable throughout the past two weeks, and even Caro had stopped complaining about her behaviour. Sitting with Ryder, chewing her lip, she was a far cry from the larger-than-life diva they'd met on Kory Balachandran's yacht.

Which could only be a good thing. If Knox found Aiden and explained—politely, of course—that Caro was off limits, then maybe she'd come to the US someday. Just to visit. And if she stayed with Knox, then Ryder would be there, and Ryder's obsession with Luna didn't look to be letting up anytime soon. It was possible she'd still be on the scene after the contract ended. If the two women could learn to get along, that sure would make life easier.

Ryder glanced at Knox as he tucked an arm around Luna's shoulders, and his expression said, "Dare you to say something." Knox kept his mouth shut.

"We'll fix this, moon."

But things would get worse before they got better.

Much worse.

26

CARO

Three and a half years had passed since I last had this creepy-crawly feeling under my skin. Then, I'd been tiptoeing around Aiden's home in Malibu, waiting for criminal investigators from the IRS to act. It took them months. Months where I feared every day that he'd find out what I'd done and kill me.

When I started dating him, I'd been in a bad place. My mom had just died, and I was trying to deal with the debt collectors who wanted their pound of flesh as well as earn enough money to survive. The job at AquaLux Yachts had been the answer to my prayers, or so I thought. And when Aiden, the handsome, charismatic COO, started paying me attention, bringing little gifts and staying late to talk, I'd been flattered. He'd offered to assist with the legalities, and I'd been so numb at the time, so overwhelmed by grief, that I'd accepted. He gained access to everything. My mind, my body, all those numbers and pieces of paper that make us who we are.

A year passed before my head cleared enough to understand what he'd done, and by then, it was too late. I was trapped. And I also realised there were shortcomings in the company's accounts. Sales being underreported, expenses being over-claimed. Huge "commission payments" being made to people who didn't exist. Incorrect tax deductions. Weird investments in cryptocurrency that made no commercial sense. I was only a management accountant, but controls were lax, and my login details gave me access to areas of the accounting system I shouldn't have been able to see. As home life became unbearable, I spent more time at work, and a bunch of that time was spent copying evidence to a cloud drive so Aiden couldn't delete it. If there was one plus point, it was that he never thought a woman would be smart enough to bring him down.

And he was right. Two senior finance staff took the hardest fall, and his father went to prison as well, but Aiden managed to wriggle out of the charges by blaming others. The FC had gone rogue. The FD should have had better oversight. His father was the one who'd signed the accounts. A chunk of the money had disappeared offshore, and Aiden was left a free man with access to what I estimated was a million or two in embezzled funds.

Which was why *I* could never be free.

I'd gone from being trapped in a luxury mansion to being trapped in a turtle sanctuary. At least the people on Valentine Cay were nicer. Franklin was the closest thing to family that I had now, although Knox... *Knox*. With every day we spent together, I knew it would be harder to say goodbye.

But he'd be out of here as soon as Luna was released. They couldn't stay. Some freak was watching her, and I honestly couldn't blame her for being terrified. I was scared too. Scared of Aiden, scared of the people who kept killing turtles, scared of the ghoul waiting in the darkness.

My phone buzzed.

VINCE

> Nobody came for the boat. We're going to have to leave this now—there isn't the manpower for an extended surveillance operation.

What was I meant to say? He'd been watching for three full days, and if Knox's theory about a leak was correct, the poachers weren't coming back anyway. I didn't want to believe Vince was the culprit, but we couldn't ask him who else he'd told about our theories in case he *was* guilty. There hadn't been any more shark sightings either—Jubilee had been keeping watch.

I looked down at Lucky in her pool and sighed. She deserved to live in peace without being hunted by humans at every opportunity.

"What happened?" Knox asked from behind me.

"How do you know anything happened?"

"I can see your reflection in the water, and you look as if someone killed your kitten."

"Vince is calling off the surveillance."

"We were expecting that."

"I know, but it still feels…"

"Disappointing?"

"And frustrating. We have no more leads, and a man I thought of as a friend might have been lying to me for years."

"Actually, we have one more lead."

"We do?"

Knox held up his phone. "Our cyber team found the IP addresses for several of the shark posts."

"Really?" IP addresses were linked to a physical address, weren't they? "You mean we know where they live?"

"Not exactly. These assholes seem to be fond of drinking —most of the messages were posted from two bars on Ilha

Grande, and a handful were posted from a third bar on Malavilla."

Most of the bars and restaurants in San Gallicano had free Wi-Fi. Some folks didn't have internet access at home, and tourists didn't want to pay expensive data fees, so the establishments with no Wi-Fi were usually emptier. Those were the ones I favoured on the rare occasions I ate out. It wasn't as if I had friends back home to keep in touch with, and the news just depressed me anyway.

"Which bars?"

"Bar Tropicana and Blue Horizon on Ilha Grande, and Shipwrecked on Malavilla. Maybe one of them will have security cameras."

"Shipwrecked is a dive, so there won't be any cameras there. But Bar Tropicana and Blue Horizon are better. Not great, but they don't water down the drinks, and you probably won't get food poisoning if you eat a burger from their menus."

Knox brought my hand to his lips and kissed my knuckles. "I wanted to take you out somewhere fancy for our second date, but would you settle for a vaguely edible burger? I'll hold your hair back if you need to puke afterward."

My hero. I had to laugh, even though I was worried about leaving the island. "Will it be safe?"

"I'll keep you safe, baby, I promise."

"What about Luna? Don't you need to stay here?"

"I'll speak with Ryder. He'll be okay on his own for a few hours, but you're right—we're thin on the ground. I talked with our boss earlier, and she's agreed to send another guy to help as soon as he finishes with his current job. We just need to hold out until then."

"Another bodyguard?"

"Technically, he's more of a sniper, but he has a broad skillset."

"I'm not sure he'll get a permit for a sniper gun. Don't quote me, but I think they're banned here."

"We'll work within the rules." Knox kissed my forehead. He did that often now, almost as if he couldn't help it. "If we take Bar Tropicana, do you think Stacey would go to Blue Horizon?"

"We should go to Blue Horizon, not Stacey. The bartender there is a real creep."

"If he makes any lewd comments, I can't be held responsible for my actions."

"I can look after myself. The last time I went there, he might have accidentally-on-purpose groped my ass, so I might have accidentally-on-purpose slammed a glass down on his fingers."

Vince had been buying the drinks that night, and when the bartender began yelling about assault, Vince had been left in an awkward position. We hadn't been back there since.

"Good work," Knox said.

"Thanks."

Damn, I really, really liked this man. If I'd met him right after I finished college, if he'd been the one to help me in the wake of my mom's death, how different would my life be now? My eyes prickled at the thought of what might have been, but I blinked the tears away.

The past was the past, and all I had left was the future.

"I take you to the best places, baby."

Blue Horizon—which sounded more like a consultancy

firm than a bar—was even worse than I remembered. The clientele was eighty percent men, and I suspected the women perched on tall stools by the bar were hoping to be paid for their services. Ryder hadn't wanted us to come, and we'd nearly stayed at the sanctuary, but after a long discussion with Knox, he'd relented as long as we were back by nine o'clock. There would be no swimming in the sea for Ryder and Luna tonight.

Reggae music pumped out of hidden speakers, there was a stoned guy passed out in a chair in one corner, and judging by the shards of glass on the table next to us, there had been at least one accident this evening. Or maybe a fight. That was also possible.

"I'm a huge fan of sticky floors," I told Knox.

"And I'm a huge fan of security cameras. Guess they have trouble in this place."

"There are cameras?"

I hadn't seen any, but we'd been here for less than a minute, and I'd been too busy wondering how the woman in the red dress could walk in those shoes. I'd break an ankle if I tried, and I was used to wearing heels. Or at least, I had been in my former life. Tonight, I'd put on sneakers, just in case I needed to run, and I was the only woman in the place wearing jeans.

"Three cameras. Above the bar, by the bathrooms, and on a pole to the left of the entrance. Is that the bartender whose fingers you damaged?"

No, thank goodness. "He must be new."

Knox bought us both drinks—non-alcoholic—and ordered the house special, fat burgers with meat of unknown origin served alongside limp salad and greasy fries. He dug in with gusto while I pushed my food around the plate.

"You're actually going to eat that?" I asked.

"Sure. I've eaten a lot worse."

"Oh, really?"

"When the boss sent us on a survival exercise in Belize, I spent a week eating roasted grubs."

"That's gross."

"If you put enough chilli on them, you honestly can't tell." He lifted the bun off the burger and cut through the middle of the patty. "It's cooked all the way through."

"I think I'll stick with the fries."

As we ate, Knox watched the bartender. He seemed to be in charge, and the two waitresses working with him couldn't have been more than eighteen. One of the girls kept getting molested by the customers, and I wanted to help, but when I moved to get up, Knox put a hand on my arm.

"Time and a place, baby."

"But they're acting so sleazy."

"Not our job tonight." He gave a tiny nod toward the bartender. "It's his."

"I doubt he was employed for his sense of civic duty."

"I'm not so sure about that." Knox lowered his voice. "There's something off about him. And by 'off,' I mean he's not your typical bartender. Watch carefully. He's either an ex-cop or ex-forces."

"How do you know that?"

"From the way he moves. Originally, I planned to offer an employee a few bucks to get a look at the camera footage, but I'm not sure that'll fly now."

"Because if he was a cop, we can't risk alerting whoever's leaking from the police department?"

"Exactly. I'll take some pictures, and we'll try to find out who he is."

"How will you take photos without him noticing?"

"Smile for the camera, baby."

27

KNOX

"Stacey has a lead."

Caro walked in from the next pool room with Tango at her heels, and despite the heat, she'd taken inspiration from the poachers and put on a hoodie. Paranoia was setting in. Few people could be trusted. Only Caro and Baptiste, plus they were giving Stacey Custer the benefit of the doubt as well. The police were likely corrupt. A stalker was waiting in the wings. The poachers were still somewhat of an unknown quantity, but undoubtedly dangerous if cornered.

"What kind of lead?"

Even the hood couldn't hide Caro's smile. Damn, she was beautiful. Knox had already asked Samia, who handled scheduling, to block him out for as many long weekends as possible. He'd work Saturdays and Sundays for the rest of the month, no problem, but now that he'd gotten used to having the same woman in his bed for more than two nights in a row, he wasn't ready to give it up. It was so...easy. He knew Caro's body, and she knew his. Those breathy little gasps when he hit the right spot, the way she closed her eyes and tipped her head back when she was about to come... It was still just sex, he told himself, but great sex. Plus he didn't have to think of a hundred ways to let her down gently in the morning. Or scrub his truck clean when a woman scorned wrote "asshole" across the windshield in lipstick.

"Camera footage from Bar Tropicana," Caro said. "Apparently, the bartender hates the boss, and she's on the verge of quitting. For fifty bucks, she showed Stacey through to the back office where the security system was and let her do whatever she wanted. Although 'security system' is a grand term. There was only one camera."

Knox put down the bucket he'd been using to empty water from one of the pools. He'd moved the residents— half a dozen juvenile hawksbills—into a clean pool while he gussied up their home. Fresh water, extra rocks, a bunch of the sea sponges that hawksbills liked to eat. The sponges were grown by an aquaculture company on Spice Island, and they delivered once a week. Knox had grown fond of the turtles as well as Caro in his time at the sanctuary.

Which meant the poachers needed to be stopped.

With Caro's words came hope, and man, did they need some good news.

"She worked out who posted the shark sighting? Do we have a picture of their face?"

"Two men came in together. The camera was near the ceiling, and Stacey said they never pushed their hoods back, not once. But there was only one man using a phone at the time when the shark post was made, and we do have a good picture of his hands. The camera was at the right angle when he went to buy a drink." Caro held up her phone. "Look. Light brown skin and a distinctive tattoo."

Knox studied the still Stacey had pulled from the video footage. Even with the graininess of a cheap camera, the tattoo was recognisable. It looked like rope coiled around the man's left wrist, ending in an anchor on the back of his hand. Did it mean something significant? They already knew he had a link to the sea, but a nautical tattoo suggested the connection ran deep.

"How many tattoo shops are there in San Gallicano?"

"I have no idea, but Stacey said she was going to find out."

"Tell her *we'll* find out. I'll ask someone from Blackwood's research team to look into it."

"How long will that take?"

"A day or two. And when Slater arrives, one of us can go ask about the guy with the tattoo."

"What if they kill more turtles in the meantime?"

"If they've realised we're onto them, and it seems like they have, then they'll probably need time to regroup and come up with a new strategy."

"I hate waiting."

"I know, baby. But we need to do this the right way. Luna has an active threat against her, so she takes priority right now." Plus she was the client. And, it appeared, Ryder's girl. "Our drone will be here tomorrow, and the tech team is sending a jammer too. We'll find this guy, and then we can focus on the poachers."

And when they did find him, Knox hoped he'd be the one to take the motherfucker down. This was personal for Ryder, and he was pissed enough that he'd end up in jail if he did the honours. Good roommates were hard to find.

"What's that thing?"

The man was barely taller than Luna and roughly as old as time. Wiry grey hair hung to his shoulders in a wild

ELISE NOBLE

tangle, a cross between locs and dragged-through-a-hedge-backward, and his leathery skin had lost its battle with the elements long ago. When the motion detectors began pinging, Knox had found him shuffling along the driveway with a blue-and-yellow parrot sitting on his shoulder. The thing squawked and flapped as Knox came near.

"Sir, can I ask who you are?" He kept a safe distance from the bird. There were no weapons in sight, and the visitor didn't look as if he'd be quick on the draw in any case.

"I'm Lyron." The man pointed at the drone in Ryder's hands. "Why are you flying that thing over my property? Are you trying to kill Veronica?"

"Who's Veronica?"

"This is Veronica," he snapped, pointing at the parrot. "She flew off to take her morning exercise and nearly got mown down by that spaceship."

"By the drone?"

Ryder cut in. "The parrot was at least fifty yards away."

"The parrot. The *parrot*. She has a name, you know. She's right here."

"I apologise. *Veronica* was at least fifty yards away."

"You scared her. She flew right back home, and she wouldn't leave her perch for half an hour."

Caro ran up, puffing slightly because she was wearing flip-flops and who the hell could run properly in those things?

"Lyron? Is everything okay?" Caro spoke to him patiently, but there was an edge to her voice. She clearly knew the man, and Knox suspected this wasn't the first time he'd shown up complaining.

"These cretins tried to murder Veronica."

"I'm sure they didn't do anything on purpose. What happened?"

"They flew their UFO right at her. Like an arrow, except with whirling blades."

Caro petted the parrot, and it bobbed its head, no squawking whatsoever. The bird had good taste.

"Lyron, we've had some problems with intruders lately, and the drone is just to check for trespassers. We won't fly over your property again, I promise."

"We weren't flying over his property before," Ryder said. "Apart from a few minutes over the sea, the drone stayed within the sanctuary's perimeter."

"Young man, didn't anyone teach you that it's rude to talk back to your elders?"

Knox glanced to the heavens and took a calming breath. "Sir, nobody's trying to be rude. We're running security checks on private property."

"Where's Franklin? Franklin won't stand for this nonsense."

Again, Caro spoke, still polite, although Knox noticed her hands ball into fists before she caught herself and relaxed.

"Franklin went to pick up turtle eggs on Spice Island. I'll let him know you dropped by, but he's going to say the same as us—this is private land, and we can fly the drone here."

"We'll see about that. The sky is for God's creatures, not that abomination."

Lyron shuffled off, muttering about aliens under his breath, and Caro rolled her eyes.

"Give me strength. You definitely weren't over his property?"

"Is his place the one with the fence made from string and the piles of broken furniture outside?"

She nodded. "Lyron never throws anything away. People give him old chairs and whatever to use as firewood for his stove, but he keeps saying he'll fix everything up someday and hardly burns any of it. Then he undercooks his food and ends up in the hospital, and I end up taking care of Veronica while they pump him full of antibiotics. She whistles all freaking night."

"Is he going to cause problems?"

"He's more bark than bite, and he usually keeps to himself in his cabin. Franklin checks on him a couple of times a week. Can we possibly avoid flying the drone anywhere near him? Ever since his wife died, he's been unnaturally attached to Veronica."

"This is just fucking great," Ryder muttered.

His sarcasm was well-placed. If it weren't for Caro, this trip would be the perfect nightmare. Jubilee had gotten in touch with Luna's lawyer yesterday and asked him to explain the stalker situation to the judge with the hope of commuting her sentence, but it didn't sound hopeful. Judge Morgan said he'd already taken the stalker situation into account, and that was why she'd been allowed to bring security. Unless something changed drastically, Luna was stuck on Valentine Cay. So were Knox and Ryder. Knox at least had Caro to soften the blow, but Ryder had been bitching for twenty-four hours straight.

"We're halfway. Fifteen days, and we can head home. Also fifteen days until Amethyst gets released from jail, so good luck, buddy."

"Luna's dreading it. Her mom fucks with her head."

"Can't she fire her?"

"She should. I haven't broached the subject, but Luna doesn't have much of a support network. Only Jubilee, and Jubilee always caves to Amethyst."

"It's not easy starting over," Caro said softly. "I wouldn't have done it if I'd had any other choice. Honestly, it's taken years for me to pick up the pieces, and now it feels as if it's all falling apart again."

Knox tucked an arm around her waist. "But you and Luna are running from different things. You cut ties completely; she just needs to stand up to her mother. And is your new life better than your old one?"

A long pause. "It is now." Her voice dropped to a whisper. "But I'm still really freaking scared."

Fuck. Caro had changed in the past two weeks. They'd all changed, and Knox hated that he couldn't snap his fingers and fix everything that was wrong in her world. Ryder had two weeks to convince Luna to stand her ground with the army of leeches who wanted to suck her dry, and Knox had two weeks to find out precisely who Aiden was. He intended to make the most of them.

"Maybe you could drop a few hints to Luna?" Ryder suggested. "Help her to understand that change isn't necessarily a bad option. That sometimes doing nothing can be worse."

"Are you serious?"

"She respects you."

"She does?"

"Yeah, but you also make her nervous."

Caro sighed, but Knox was learning to read her better. When she didn't roll her eyes, he took it as a good sign.

"Okay, fine. I'll try."

28

CARO

"You found him? The tattoo guy?"

I glanced behind me—the habit of a lifetime —but this time, I was checking for Knox. He'd been snoring softly when I left him in bed, but he was also a really light sleeper, and I didn't want him to overhear this conversation and get upset with me.

Knox isn't Aiden.

I'd reminded myself of that a thousand times, but that was also how often I'd been on the receiving end of a man's anger, and the inbuilt sense of self-preservation I'd honed over the past three and a half years wouldn't let me take the risk. Knox had said I should get Stacey to back off while Blackwood did their research, and I'd relayed the message, but I also hadn't argued too hard when she said she wasn't going to. Blackwood's priority was Luna. Stacey genuinely cared about wildlife.

"Not quite," she said, "but I'm closer to finding him than I was before. I never realised how many tattoo places there would be, but the fifth one I visited, the assistant working at the counter recognised the anchor. She's ninety percent sure that her friend dated the guy a few months ago, but she only met him once in a bar, and she can't remember his name. She's gonna call her friend and see if she'll speak with me."

My phone pinged, which meant the sanctuary had another Instagram follower. I could admit—grudgingly—that Luna and Jubilee had done a good job with the social media. I hated that stuff. Posting snippets of my life to be judged by others, and usually found wanting if the number of likes I didn't get was any indication. But the girls knew what to write to get people to engage and, more importantly, to donate. Over fifty people had signed up to sponsor turtles so far. Corky was the most popular, an eighteen-year-old hawksbill with a buoyancy disorder. We had to glue little weights to his shell so he could submerge, and on the rare occasions they fell off, he popped right back up again. Like a cork, hence his name. Anyhow, Corky had twenty-three sponsors, and Franklin said this was the first month in years that the sanctuary wouldn't operate at a loss.

Another ping. *Ping, ping, ping.*

They'd probably posted about baby turtles again. Those did numbers, especially on TikTok.

"Did you get a description of the guy? I mean his face?"

"Kind of. She said he was definitely local, and she remembered him being hot in a dangerous way. Good arms —that's why she remembers the tattoo. The rope design wraps around all the way up to his shoulder."

Ping ping ping ping ping.

"Do you think the girl will call you?"

"Who knows? But at least we can be certain the guy's around, and I have a better description of the tattoo. He can't hide forever."

Ping ping ping ping ping ping ping.

"Just be careful, okay?"

"I always am."

The moment I hung up, I checked the sanctuary's Instagram account, but there was nothing new posted today. Huh. Then why were so many people suddenly showing up in support? Something to do with the mysterious algorithm whose altar Jubilee seemed to worship at? I checked on the turtles in the pool rooms, then headed to the kitchen to make coffee. The one downside of spending nights with Knox was never getting enough sleep, which made caffeine a necessity.

Ping ping ping ping ping ping ping ping ping ping.

Dammit, I needed to work out how to turn the notifications off. At first, it had been cute knowing the sanctuary was gaining recognition, but now it was just annoying.

Tango followed me outside, tail wagging, so I headed to the kitchen, poured a cup of kibble into her bowl, and set it on the floor.

"Good girl. You're such a good girl."

Mistaking my vibrator for a chew toy was the best thing she'd ever done.

We were almost out of coffee, so I added a note to the grocery list on the refrigerator while I waited for the old-fashioned cast-iron kettle to start whistling. Outside, a light wind blew puffy whitecaps across the sea, and I spotted a small boat on the horizon. I watched it for a while, that little knot of tension in my gut tightening, but the craft didn't get any closer. Probably a fisherman. There were usually schools of snapper out there.

Knox was awake when I got back to the bunkhouse, one of his arms flung out to the side. If he was going to come back to visit, maybe I could rearrange the furniture? Switch out two of the single beds for a double? Franklin would be okay with that. He'd apologised a million times for not having better accommodation, but money was tight. His own home was just one room with a tiny bathroom attached.

"Morning." Knox's voice was always hoarse so early in the day.

"I made coffee. At some point, we need to do a grocery run, but it can wait until tomorrow."

He beckoned me closer. "Put the coffee down and come here."

"When you say 'come here'...?"

His smile turned filthy, and he pointed at the tent in the sheet caused by his impressive cock. "I mean *come here*."

Several days ago, a giant box of condoms had suddenly appeared, two hundred of them in every colour, flavour, and texture imaginable, and we'd made a respectable dent in them already. Knox could be an animal in bed, or he could be sweet. Which version of him would I get this morning?

"If you want me to sit on it, you'll have to saw off the top bunk."

His expression suggested he was seriously considering it, but finally, he shook his head. "Take too long."

Ping ping ping ping ping ping ping ping.

I groaned. "Make it stop."

"Why is it pinging?"

"We keep getting more followers on Instagram. Which is a good thing, as long as it happens quietly."

"Give me the phone."

He tapped the screen a few times, then put the phone in the nightstand drawer. "Fixed it."

"What did you do?"

"Deleted Instagram."

My eyes rolled of their own accord. "You're such an idiot."

"Get used to it."

Knox was big all over, six feet tall and built like a tank, but he could move surprisingly quickly. In the blink of an eye, I found myself pressed against the wall with my shorts around my ankles and his head between my legs, and this time, my groan was pure pleasure. My knees threatened to buckle as he sucked hard.

"I can't..." I gasped, but he didn't ease up. No, he added a finger into the mix, then another, and when the orgasm tore through me, he caught me before I hit the floor. Next time, I needed to hold out for longer than a minute. This was embarrassing.

"Why do you have to be so good at this?"

"Is that a complaint?"

"More of an observation."

"Good. Get on your knees, baby. Actually..." He grabbed a blanket from one of the spare beds and tossed it onto the floor. "Use that. I don't want you getting bruises."

Seemed I was getting sweet and animalistic today.

And bruises.

Blanket or no blanket, my knees couldn't survive his efforts unscathed, but sweet Knox made another appearance as he lifted me gently onto the bed afterward.

"The coffee should be cool enough to drink now," he said, passing me my mug before he picked up his phone. This was our morning ritual now. He fucked me into a state of bliss, then checked in with the office. There was an app on his phone with status updates. Usually we chatted, and sometimes he mentioned his colleagues.

But this morning, Knox took a sip of coffee, and then his face morphed into confusion.

Then horror.

"What the fuck...?"

"What? What happened?"

He didn't answer, just pulled on a pair of shorts, still cursing.

"Knox, tell me."

"Luna happened. She couldn't fucking help herself, could she?"

"What are you talking about?"

He passed me the phone, and Instagram was open. Not the sanctuary's page, but Luna's personal account, the one with millions of followers. The first post was a video, and I checked the date. She'd posted it an hour ago.

"I thought she wasn't meant to be using this account?"

"She isn't." He blew out a breath. "For fuck's sake. If I get her to take it down fast, hopefully Judge Morgan won't see it."

"He's an early riser."

Knox muttered another curse under his breath and hurried out the door. I still had his phone in my hand. Luna was frozen on the screen with a baby turtle in her hands, so I pressed "play." How bad would this be?

"Hey, gorgeous people. I just wanted to give you an update, and I'm having a great time here on Valentine Cay learning about turtles. I realise now that I was wrong to dress a hawksbill in sunglasses, even if they were Gucci, because animals aren't toys. They're living creatures with feelings, and turtles are an important part of the ecosystem. Let's introduce you to some of the sanctuary's residents..." She showed her viewers Lucky, and Gilbert, and Corky, and she did all that in a bikini. No wonder the video had over thirty thousand likes already. "All of these turtles are part of the sanctuary's sponsorship scheme, and you can find details by following this link." A QR code flashed up. "But I'm only a visitor here—the real heroes are Franklin and Caro, who work here all year round." My stomach lurched. Oh no. No, she couldn't have... She had. There was a freaking picture of me, standing by Lucky's pool with a basket of sardines in my hand. My whole face was visible. "Their Insta page needs a little extra TLC, so if it gets two million more likes before I leave San Galli, I'll walk down the Strip in a bikini." She blew the audience a kiss. "Love you guys."

I. Was. Going. To. Kill. Her.

29

"Take it down."

"Are you crazy? It's gone viral."

"Thirty-five thousand likes," Jubilee added.

Knox took a calming breath. *Don't kill the client.* "If you remove it right away, there's a chance Judge Morgan might not see it."

"Chill out, okay? I kind of like it here, so I figured I wouldn't mind doing an extra day of work if the judge makes me."

"That's not the problem. The problem is you have a stalker, and we don't want to be here a day longer than we need to be."

"But that's why you guys are here, right? To keep me safe."

For fuck's sake.

"I get that you want to promote the sanctuary, and that's commendable, but this isn't the way to do it."

"Really? What do you know about social media?"

"Nothing, but I know a hell of a lot about predators.

There's no way you're walking down the fuckin' Strip in a bikini. You'll get eaten alive."

Knox had found the girls in the dining room, drinking coffee and eating pineapple slices while they giggled and checked their phones. How long had they spent planning this shit?

"Fine, then I'll hire extra security, but you can't tell me what to do."

Ryder tried to make her see sense. "Moon, this isn't a good—"

But his words were cut off by Caro's shriek from the doorway. Ah, fuck.

"What on earth do you think you're doing?"

Luna dismissed her freakout with a wave of the hand. Red rag to a damn bull. "Getting more likes for the sanctuary, duh."

"You put a picture of me in that stupid video."

"Yes, well, I was trying to be a nice person and not take all the credit."

"No, you were acting selfish and doing whatever you wanted, the same way you always do."

"How was I acting selfish? I picked a good picture. Jubilee even made your teeth whiter and fixed your hair."

"My ex is a freaking psycho, and if he finds out where I am, he's going to kill me. How many people have seen that video?"

Luna opened her mouth, then thought the better of trying to justify her actions and closed it again.

"Uh, four hundred thousand people on Insta and another quarter million on TikTok."

They'd put the damn clip on TikTok as well? Hell.

Ryder put a hand on Luna's arm. "Moon, get rid of the videos."

"But—"

"Do it right now."

"I was only trying to help," she whispered.

"I get that, but you're putting Caro's safety in jeopardy. Jubilee, can you delete those videos?"

Jubilee nodded, and a moment later, she confirmed they were gone, but rather than saying thank you or strangling Luna, Caro ran from the room.

"Baby, wait," Knox called.

"I have to get out of here."

Now the damage control started.

Knox found Caro back in the bunkhouse, stuffing clothing, toiletries, and everything else she owned into a backpack. When she said she needed to get out of there, Knox had assumed she meant the dining room, but it seemed she'd been referring to the whole sanctuary.

"Where are you going?"

"Who the hell knows? Anywhere that isn't here."

"Don't you think you're overreacting a bit?"

"No! You don't know Aiden the way I do."

"The video was up for less than an hour, and nobody was watching it to see the staff at a turtle sanctuary. They all wanted to perv over Luna Maara in a bikini."

Walking down the Strip? What the hell was she thinking? Ryder said she wasn't the fame-hungry brat everyone thought she was, but he'd sure been wrong on that one.

"That might have been their intention, but I was still on there, Knox. What if someone saved a copy?"

"You look different now. You used to have blonde hair, right?"

She huffed out an angry sigh. "I need to fix my roots again."

"I'll speak with the cyber team, see if they can work their takedown magic. They might be able to stop the video from spreading any farther than it already has."

"A viral Luna Maara video? That's like trying to fix a burst artery with a Band-Aid."

"Aiden's not going to get here in a day, so let's make a plan. There's no point in bolting with no money, no backup, and no place to go. Does he have any connections to San Gallicano?"

"I'm not sure. We took a trip here once, but we took trips to a whole bunch of places. He likes to travel."

"Tell me more about him. What's his full name? Where does he live?"

"Oh, please. You want me to tell you my secrets so Ryder can spill them to his girlfriend? If he's gay, then I'm the Queen of Spain, but you don't hear me gossiping about other people's personal business."

"Let me speak with my boss, see if Slater can take over my role with Luna rather than providing additional manpower. Then I could get you settled someplace safe instead of you starting over alone." Caro's well-being took precedence over turtle poaching. Knox grasped both of her hands in his, relieved beyond measure when she didn't pull away. "If you let Aiden maintain this hold on you, he wins all over again."

"You'd really help me?"

Knox had come to terms with flying to the Caribbean to fuck her, convinced himself that one weekend a month wasn't a relationship and he wouldn't let himself get too close. But now they were talking about real commitment.

Going from dipping a toe in the water to jumping in feet first.

He saw the pulse fluttering against Caro's throat and realised his own heart was beating just as fast. No, he wasn't ready for this, he knew he wasn't ready, but the alternative was losing her.

He wasn't prepared for that either.

And what was the SEALs' motto? *The only easy day was yesterday.*

"I hear Canada's nice this time of year."

"My budget won't run to Canada. I don't even own a coat."

"Don't worry about the money. Let me look after you."

His words had the opposite effect to the one Knox intended. Caro tugged her hands free and took three rapid steps back. She'd have taken more if the wall hadn't gotten in the way.

Fuck.

"Baby, what's wrong? What did I say?"

"You said exactly what *he* used to say. I met him after my mom died, and he was all, 'Caro, don't worry about that. Caro, leave everything to me.' And then he took over my entire life and left me with nothing."

Two weeks. Two weeks since Knox, Ryder, Luna, and Jubilee had arrived at the sanctuary, and that was all the time it had taken to break Caro completely. Guilt was a heavy burden to bear, and Knox would carry it forever if she had to start again from scratch.

"Tell me what you want. Tell me what I can do to help."

"I-I don't know." A tear rolled down her cheek. "What do I want? I used to dream of the whole fairy tale—Prince Charming, a castle, a world of pretty things. But then I realised that Prince Charming was actually the Big Bad Wolf and all the trinkets in the world couldn't make me happy. So now I just want to feel safe." She sucked in a ragged breath. "What about the turtles? And Franklin? He's been so good to me, and if I leave..."

A few tears became a torrent, and Knox gathered her into his arms. He hadn't been looking for commitment, but he'd fucking found it.

30

CARO

"There's good news, and there's bad news," Knox said.

I'd spent most of the day cleaning out the turtle pools alone. Luna tried to speak to me at one point, I think to apologise, but given that her apology started with "Why didn't you tell me that your ex was crazy?" I couldn't find it in myself to be polite. When I snapped back that my personal life was none of her business, she'd hotfooted it out the door.

I did speak with Franklin, though. After all he'd done for me, I owed him an explanation for my impending departure. He made me tea in his little cabin, and we reminisced about the turtles we'd rescued together over the years. I'd miss seeing this season's eggs hatch, seeing last year's hatchlings find their flippers in the big wide world. Franklin wasn't feeling so great today, and I worried about adding to his stress, but he said he understood, that he'd been both surprised and happy that I'd stayed so long. Maybe someday I'd come back to visit? Aiden was three years older than me, and he drank more alcohol than was healthy. I'd be cheering on heart disease and cirrhosis from the sidelines.

I steeled myself. "Give me the bad news."

"The bad news is that Slater's been delayed in Africa. I can't go into the details, but let's just say that the target they went to pick up wasn't where she was supposed to be."

"When is he coming?"

"The revised mission is planned for Monday. He should be here next Wednesday."

Almost a week. Could I wait that long?

"You said there was good news?"

He smiled. "There is. The first piece of good news is that the sanctuary only got eleven thousand new likes this morning. So either not that many people watched the video to the end, or they don't want to see Luna walk down the Strip in a bikini." Ryder fell into the latter camp, I suspected. He'd been stomping around with a face like thunder all day. "The videos have popped up in a couple more places, but an intern on Blackwood's cyber team is sending takedown notices whenever he finds one."

I pictured a teenager sitting in an office, drinking coffee and trawling the internet for Luna Maara videos. Poor kid.

"I should send him a thank-you note."

"His name is Lamar. I can give you his contact details. But that's not all—I spoke with a colleague who has connections to a charitable foundation. You'd need to fill in an application form and provide a strategic plan, but there's funding available for building renovations here at the sanctuary plus two full-time members of staff. They'll cover the salaries for five years with the potential to extend later on."

Knox's words took a moment to sink in. Funding? I'd applied for thirty-seven grants during my time at the sanctuary—I knew this because I'd kept a spreadsheet—and spent hours writing plans and justification documents, rejigging the wording for each foundation because they all had different requirements. Of those thirty-seven grants, I'd landed four of them, a grand total of forty-eight hundred dollars combined. Knox had made a phone call to a friend and secured enough money to staff the sanctuary for five years?

"Is this a joke?"

"Baby, do I sound as if I'm joking?"

"I just... Nobody gives that kind of funding."

"They do if you ask the right people. Can you write a strategic plan? I'm no good at that stuff."

"I can absolutely write a strategic plan. I'm a pro at writing strategic plans. What should I tell Franklin? *Should* I tell Franklin? What if the application gets rejected?"

"It still needs to be approved by the trustees, but it'll go through. I already spoke with two of them, and they're on board."

"I think I love you. In a purely non-committal way, of course."

Knox kissed me on the forehead. He said he wasn't interested in a relationship, but when the chips were down, he stepped up. I was beginning to think I loved him a little more than I let on, and the thought scared me almost as much as Aiden did. How could my feelings be this strong for a man I barely knew? I'd avoided asking personal questions in case he reciprocated, sticking to safe topics instead. Turtles, scuba diving, the beautiful nation of San Gallicano. If it weren't for the poaching, I could have passed for a tour guide.

"Mercy said she'd email over the paperwork. That gives you less than a week to write a plan, find two new members of staff, decide where you want to live, and pack your stuff. Can you do that?"

A minute ago, the six days until Slater's arrival had stretched out in front of me like an eternity, but now that didn't seem like much time at all.

"Will Ryder be able to keep Luna in line for the next week?"

"He made her delete her social media apps, Jubilee too."

"I bet Luna's thrilled about that."

"She keeps forgetting and trying to look at her phone. Safe to say the love affair is on the rocks."

For the first time all day, I began to have hope. Hope that I'd be able to live in safety, hope that I'd have a future with Knox Livingston in it.

"When you mentioned Canada earlier, were you serious?"

"Not entirely, but if Canada is where you want to go, then I can work with it. Just make sure your new place is near an airport."

I'd camp in a tent on the freaking runway if it meant I'd get to spend more time with this man.

"Oh, I just love the sound of planes taking off in the morning. Are we really doing this?"

Knox took a deep breath and nodded. "We're really doing it, Caro." But then he rubbed a hand over his face. "Caro... Is that even your name? I know your surname isn't Menefee."

My spine went rigid. How could he know that? The identity was a good one. Had he found a photo? I never had to worry about running into the real Caroline in the marine biology world because as soon as she graduated, she'd gone back to partying. She'd only attended college in the first place because it was one of the conditions she had to fulfil in order to receive her trust fund. If I recalled correctly, she'd get the keys to the kingdom on her thirtieth birthday, and I gave her five years after that to blow the lot. Caroline had no idea how to manage money and no concept of moderation. She wasn't a horrible person—I actually quite liked her—but she'd never had to take responsibility for anything in her life. In many ways, she reminded me of Luna.

But I wasn't about to tell Knox those details. His digging around in my past felt underhanded.

"What makes you think that?"

"I already told you we ran a background check."

"Well, it's still creepy."

"It wasn't personal. Just part of the job."

"That doesn't make it any more acceptable."

"We can't change the way we do things. Last year, a colleague was providing services to a family, and we ran the usual checks. A member of the household staff had a past conviction he hadn't disclosed. Child abuse. There was a four-year-old kid, and the guy had been touching her."

"That's sick."

I mean, Aiden was a monster and even he hadn't stooped that low, at least not that I was aware of.

"Right. So our team shakes the tree, and sometimes valuable information falls out."

I didn't want my tree shaken. If Aiden didn't already know where I was, then someone poking around in my past could tip him off. I knew that in time, if Knox and I continued with our not-quite-relationship, I'd have to trust him with my secrets, but I didn't feel ready to do that yet. Not until I was far away from Valentine Cay. If Aiden came here with revenge on his mind, I feared he'd take his anger out on Franklin if he couldn't make me suffer, and the prospect of that made me feel sick. I couldn't change the mistakes of the past, but I hoped that time and distance might make a difference. Which meant that until I had a proper plan, the fewer people who could let my true identity slip, the better.

"My name really is Caro," I said softly. "I only borrowed the surname."

"What about the rest of your history? If Aiden's a problem, we can help with that."

Exactly what I'd suspected he'd say.

"Trusting people doesn't come easily to me. I'll tell you everything, but I need time, Knox."

"Time for me to prove I'm not the asshole he is?"

Knox understood. He understood, and he wasn't angry.

"Something like that."

He cupped my face in his hands and gave me the tenderest kiss.

"Then I guess I'd better get started."

31

KNOX

"You need to keep your girlfriend on a shorter leash, buddy."

Mid-morning, and Knox and Ryder had just changed the batteries on the motion sensors. Now they were slotting the spent batteries into the chargers they'd set up in the small office off the dining room. One of the sensors had malfunctioned during the night, and it looked as if some kind of animal had mistaken it for a snack. But apart from that, all was quiet. Ryder had taken the drone up at first light, careful to avoid Lyron and his junkyard, but there was no sign of any unwelcome visitors.

For once, Ryder didn't argue with the "girlfriend" tag.

"Fuck, man, I'm sorry. I had no idea what the two of them were cooking up. How's Caro doing?"

"Yesterday, she was ready to cut and run, but she's calmer now."

"Did you speak with Emmy?"

"She's on board with the Slater plan."

The best thing about working for Blackwood was having a boss who was actually human, despite rumours to the contrary. Emmy was wealthy, but morals were more important to her than money, even if those morals were decidedly grey. She expected her team to go the extra mile when the need arose, but she also understood that they weren't robots. Work patterns were flexible. She inspired loyalty, and that loyalty went in both directions.

When Knox had given her a rundown of the Caro situation, it was Emmy who'd suggested funding the sanctuary through the Blackwood Foundation, and she'd spoken with Cora and Mercy to speed up the process. Slater would finish out the contract with Luna while Knox took two weeks of personal leave to get Caro settled in a new place. Canada, South America, Europe, wherever she wanted to go, visa permitting. As for the poaching, that was a more difficult problem to solve—Blackwood had no authority in San Gallicano, and they didn't even have an office there. The best they could realistically offer was research capacity for Stacey Custer's independent investigation, plus a few hours of Slater's time when he arrived. Black, Emmy's husband, would also have words in the right ears in the hope of applying some political pressure.

"When is Slater getting here?" Ryder asked.

"Next Wednesday, assuming the team finds Emily Shadrach on Monday."

Nineteen-year-old Emily Shadrach, daughter of Bernard Shadrach, the mattress king of Oklahoma, had gone backpacking around Africa in her gap year, where she'd had the misfortune to hook up with a so-called wellness guru. Her family couldn't get in touch with her, and videos posted to the guru's social media showed her spaced out, barely able to speak. High on more than love and light. The guru was scheduled to "spread the sacred truth" at a lifestyle summit in Morocco on Monday, and the team was planning to extract her from there, assuming he showed up. He'd cancelled a previous appearance due to an unspecified illness. Two members of the Special Projects team had been following him around the continent for the past three weeks, but he never stayed in one place for long.

"For what it's worth, Luna's sorry for making that post. She tried to apologise to Caro, but she said Caro wouldn't listen."

"Because she tried to make out it was Caro's fault for not sharing private details of her past relationship."

Ryder pinched the bridge of his nose and blew out a long breath. "She's not great at this."

"At what? Saying she's sorry? Treating people considerately? Interacting with regular humans?"

"All of the above. I'm not going to make excuses for her—"

"Yeah, you are."

"Luna's parents fucked her over. Her dad barely speaks to her, and her mom treats her as a cash machine. She doesn't have friends. She never went to school. She's basically isolated, and the only way she can protect herself from the predators who want a piece of her is to push everyone away. She's a bad judge of character because she has no frame of reference for good."

Caro hadn't had a great life either, but she didn't go out of her way to ruin other people's.

"So Luna figures that if her life sucks, she'll drag everyone else down to her level?"

"She thought she was helping."

"By offering to walk down the Strip in a bikini? That's whacked."

"Her whole existence is transactional. To Luna, that's normal."

Why did Ryder keep defending her? Luna had flipped

Caro's life on its head and left her in a position where she felt she had no choice but to start over. A half-assed apology wasn't going to cut it.

"More excuses."

"The genie's out of the bottle now; we can't put it back in. And Jubilee pulled that post down fast—the chances of Caro's ex seeing it were minuscule. Does he even use social media?"

"I don't know."

"Then why don't you try asking your girlfriend? Can't she tell you?"

"Because she's so stressed that she has no idea how to trust anymore. Unfortunately, I'm still working for Luna, remember?"

"Luna's stressed too. She got arrested and taken to court, her mom's in jail—"

"Boo-fucking-hoo. She's a—" Knox caught himself just in time, before he said something unforgivable. Ryder was the closest thing he had to a brother. They shouldn't let women come between them. Bros before hoes, although if he called Luna a ho, Ryder would probably break his jaw, and he'd deserve that. "We shouldn't be fighting. We should be working together to fix this."

Ryder closed his eyes and sighed. "What do you want me to do?"

"An apology from Luna would help. A genuine one, no caveats this time."

"I'll see what I can do." Ryder slumped into Baptiste's desk chair. The fabric seat was fifty percent duct tape now—like the rest of the sanctuary, it had seen better days. Hopefully, the grant money from the Blackwood Foundation could go someway toward restoring things. "Man, this is a mess."

"Women. Can't live with them, can't—"

"Is this a bad time?" Caro asked from the doorway. Fuck.

"What's up?"

"I've been trying to call Stacey Custer for the past hour, but she isn't answering her phone."

"Maybe she's just busy?"

"Maybe." But Caro didn't sound convinced.

"Why would you think otherwise?"

A long pause. "Do you promise you won't be mad?"

He glanced at Ryder, who gave the faintest smirk. *Okay, buddy, you're not the only one with a challenging woman.*

"I promise. What happened?"

"You remember how you said we should wait for your company to research the tattoo shops?"

"Let me guess: she didn't?"

"She got a lead on the guy with the anchor on his hand. Not from whoever did the tattoo, but from someone who worked in one of the shops and thought her friend used to date him. The girl was going to speak with her friend, and Stacey said she'd update me, but she hasn't, and now she's not picking up."

"When did you last speak to her?"

"Yesterday morning. Before the video."

"So over twenty-four hours ago?"

"Yes."

"There's a chance she could just be sleeping, especially if she was up late doing things she shouldn't have been doing."

"I know."

"But you're still worried?"

"Maybe I'm overreacting? The video left me on edge, I understand that, and we're not close friends, but Stacey promised to call with updates."

"Did she mention which hotel she's staying at?"

"Vista Suites in Blue Beach."

"Try calling them—see if a member of staff can check her room. What's her number?"

Caro picked up a pad and pen from the desk. "I'll write it down. The first time I called, the phone rang and rang, but now it's going straight to voicemail. That's not good, is it?"

"We don't know for sure. The battery could have died, or maybe she's in a meeting."

"She might have lost the phone," Ryder added. "Or somebody stole it."

Or she'd asked questions about the wrong people and found herself in a situation that Knox didn't want to voice in front of Caro.

"Let's try the obvious answers first."

Caro clung to Knox's arm and kept her head bowed as they walked through the lobby of Vista Suites. Nobody challenged them. Time and time again, Knox had found that if you looked as though you knew where you were going in a low- to mid-price hotel, the staff didn't ask questions.

When Caro had spoken with the receptionist earlier, the woman sent a colleague to knock on Stacey's door, but there was no answer. She'd also let slip that Stacey was staying in suite nineteen. The suites themselves were small bungalows surrounding a central courtyard with a swimming area in the middle. Like the sanctuary, the place had seen better days. Cracked slabs and faded lounge chairs surrounded the small pool, the cabanas were perilously close to collapse, and the grass was worn through to dirt in many spots.

A maid pushed a cart on the far side of the courtyard,

and two kids squealed as they played tag among overgrown bushes. Knox was pleased to note that the doors still required old-fashioned keys rather than electronic cards.

They approached suite nineteen, and Caro knocked softly. No answer.

"Should we ask the manager if they can open the door?" she asked.

Knox shook his head. "No."

The room had two windows, but the drapes were closed, the air silent. No soft glow of a light, no flickering from the TV. Stacey was asleep, or dead, or she wasn't there. There was a fast way to rule out the first two of those possibilities. Knox pulled on a pair of thin leather gloves and took a set of lock picks out of his wallet.

"What are you doing?" Caro demanded in a harsh whisper. She was nervous as hell, but when Knox had suggested he come alone, she'd been adamant that wasn't going to happen. He'd only agreed to her joining him because a couple raised fewer suspicions than a man on his own.

"Taking a look. Don't touch anything."

"You can't just break in. What if someone sees us? What if—"

The door swung open.

"Shhh," Knox said, and sniffed the air. When it smelled of synthetic florals with no hint of decomposition, he motioned Caro inside. "After you."

Stacey's clothes still hung in the closet, a suitcase stowed neatly beneath them. Her toiletries were on a shelf in the bathroom, and there was half a pizza in the refrigerator. A spy novel sat on the nightstand, a bookmark a third of the way through, next to a blank notepad and a pen. The phone charger was plugged into a socket beside the desk. Either she had a spare, or she hadn't intended to be away for long.

"She's not here," Caro murmured.

And neither was her laptop bag or her purse. She'd brought both with her when she visited the sanctuary.

"Try sending her an email," Knox suggested.

"Is there any point? She didn't reply to a text."

"She has her laptop with her but not her phone charger. It's worth a try."

"What if she doesn't respond?"

Knox took one last look around the room. "Then we'll have to report her as missing."

32

CARO

"Vince, do you have a minute?"

This was the second time I'd tried calling him, but last night, I'd gotten his voicemail. I sensed a theme this week. Knox squeezed my hand across the dining table, and I tried to smile but didn't do a great job of it.

Along with Ryder, we'd had a long discussion about who to call. The two men were convinced there was a dirty cop somewhere in the San Gallicano PD, and that the cop was involved in the turtle investigation. But I still had a hard time believing Vince was a traitor. I'd known him for nearly three years, from the day we met in a bar on Ilha Grande, me terrified of where life would take me, him moping over a beer because he'd just split from his long-term boyfriend. He'd drunk a lot in those days, but now he'd gotten over the breakup and we mostly met for lunch or sometimes dinner with fruit juice. Vince was the one who'd introduced me to Franklin.

But with Stacey's safety at risk and my judgment admittedly poor, we couldn't afford to get this wrong. So before I called Vince, we'd reported her disappearance to the missing persons bureau on Ilha Grande. A bored-sounding guy had asked a few perfunctory questions and assured me someone would look into the matter. I wasn't convinced that they would.

Vince, on the other hand, was dedicated to his job, albeit hampered by a lack of time. He'd once told me that he'd never wanted to be anything but a cop. If he wasn't in league with the very people who could have harmed Stacey, he'd make an effort to find her. And why would he help the smugglers? Money? He lived in a one-bedroom apartment and rode a scooter. If he'd sold out, wouldn't he at least buy the Ducati he'd always dreamed of owning?

"I'll have to call you back later."

"This is important."

"A paddleboarder just found a body on Cinnamon Beach, so I'm afraid that takes precedence right now."

Ice filled my veins. "A...a body?"

"You didn't hear it from me. The doc's on his way."

"What kind of body?"

"A human one, or they wouldn't have called me."

"I mean is it male or female?"

"Caro, I can't talk about this. It's an active investigation."

"Please, Vince. I'm not gonna blab, and my friend is missing. That's why I'm calling you."

"What friend?"

"Her name is Stacey. She's a journalist investigating wildlife smuggling. We just got off the phone with the missing persons bureau, and they said they'd look into her disappearance, but the guy didn't exactly fill me with confidence, so I thought I'd call you, and... Is the body male or female?"

Vince cursed under his breath, and I knew it was bad news because he rarely said more than "heck."

"It's a woman. Youngish, the doctor says."

"What colour hair does she have?"

"Looks brownish red, but it's wet."

A sob burst out of me. I couldn't help it because I knew, I just *knew,* that Vince was looking at Stacey. My worst fears had been realised, and she'd never drop by for fruit tea and cookies again. She'd never finish her article. She'd never win another Pulitzer. Silently, Knox came to crouch beside me and wrapped me up in his arms.

"Her name is Stacey Custer." I paused to wipe away my tears, and Tango licked my knee. "*Was* Stacey Custer. I last spoke with her the day before yesterday, and she was going to follow up a lead on the person who posted one of those shark sightings."

"How did she find out who made the post?" Vince asked. "I took a look myself, and those accounts looked fake to me."

Rats. We hadn't considered this part.

"Uh, she didn't go into the details, but she knew one of them had a tattoo, so she was asking around in tattoo shops."

"And she found the artist?"

"No, but she ran into a woman who thought she recognised the design. Not through her work, but because a friend used to date the guy."

"Hold on a second." Vince spoke to somebody else, something about cordons and evidence and crowds. "Caro, what was the guy's name?"

"Stacey didn't say."

"The woman's name?"

"I don't know that either. We only spoke for a few minutes, and I told her..." I paused to compose myself. "I told her to be careful. Hell, I should have stopped her. I should have—"

"We don't know for sure that it's her, not yet."

"Oh, please. How many missing redheads are there in San Gallicano? And how many were investigating people who think nothing of taking a life?"

"There's a difference between a human and a turtle, Caro."

"Tell that to Stacey."

Before I could think properly, I hung up and slapped my phone down on the table. The stupid screen cracked, and wasn't that a metaphor for my life these days?

"Are you—" Knox started.

"Don't!"

"Don't what?"

"Don't you dare ask if I'm okay. Of course I'm not freaking okay. Stacey's dead, and she was following up on a lead we gave her. If we hadn't told her about Bar Tropicana, if...if..."

If only I'd listened to Knox and talked Stacey out of going it alone. Why hadn't I? I knew firsthand how dangerous men could be. One night almost five years ago, Aiden had come within seconds of choking me. I'd passed out, had to wear a scarf for weeks to cover the bruises, and all because he thought I'd been flirting with another man. I hadn't—we'd met at a party and I'd been polite, maybe laughed at a joke he told—but Aiden saw red, and I paid the price. That was the night I'd vowed to leave, but it had taken me eleven more months to escape. I'd hoped for freedom, but in reality, I'd just traded one prison for another.

"If it is Stacey, and she was murdered, there's nobody to blame but the person who killed her."

"You didn't ask her to come to San Gallicano," Ryder

added. "She'd already started her investigation before you met."

My phone rang, and it was Vince, but I couldn't pick it up. I just wanted to curl into a ball and rock.

"Want me to get it?" Knox asked, and I shrugged.

He took that to mean "yes."

"Knox Livingston speaking." A pause. "Yeah, she's a little upset. Didn't you go to sensitivity training? ... Let me check." He turned to me. "Are you up to doing an interview?"

"I don't have any choice, do I?"

"There's always a choice."

"I'll speak with him."

Knox relayed the message to Vince. "She'll speak with you, but here's a tip—don't act like a cop. That's not what she needs today." Another pause, and then he asked me, "Does Stacey have family? A husband? A partner?"

"I...I don't know. She never mentioned anyone. But I think she grew up in Tennessee, or maybe Kentucky or the southwestern corner of Virginia. She said there was a pond full of Cumberland sliders near her home when she was a kid, and they have a very small range, especially compared to other turtles." I remembered what else she'd said in that initial meeting. "Stacey was the second person to investigate this story. The first guy disappeared, but in the US, I think, not here. His name was Beckham, Beckham Cheng. Stacey's friend was his roommate—actually, no, I think the roommate was a friend of her friend—and if you can find her, she'll be able to tell you much more about Stacey than I could."

Knox passed on the information, and Vince must have asked where Stacey was staying because then Knox said, "Yeah, Vista Suites."

Ryder handed me a tissue, and I realised I'd begun

crying again. When Knox and I had gone to the hotel yesterday, I'd been worried, but I hadn't truly believed that Stacey was dead. Now she was gone, and it was partly my fault. If only I'd thought things through, considered the consequences—

"Stop," Knox ordered.

"Stop what?"

"Blaming yourself. What's happened has happened, and we have to move forward, not backward. Vince is coming over. You need to tell him everything you know."

"I really don't know that much."

"Right now, you know more than anyone else on this island. And at some point, he's going to want a signed statement, which gives us a problem because you're using a borrowed name."

Just when I thought things couldn't get any worse...

"What should I do?" I whispered.

"You have two choices: come clean, or don't sign anything. I'll speak with a lawyer and see where you stand."

I began pacing, desperate to use up my nervous energy. Dead. Stacey was dead. How? Hell, I hoped it had been quick. That was my worst fear with Aiden, that if he got ahold of me, he'd draw things out. Make me suffer. He was exactly the type of man to do that. Mental torture was his thing.

"Stacey was the second person to disappear in this case?" Ryder asked. "Neither of you worried about what happened to Beckham Cheng?"

"She just said he'd disappeared, that was all."

Yes, he'd left his pet turtle behind, but he hadn't abandoned her. He'd left her with his roommate. If I left Valentine Cay, I'd have to leave Tango behind, because what sort of life would she have if I needed to keep running? Better for her to stay with Franklin, who loved her too, than to risk landing in Aiden's clutches. He'd hurt Tango to hurt me.

"But nobody ever saw him again?"

"So? People have their own reasons for walking away, and they aren't always nefarious. I should freaking know."

Franklin appeared in the doorway in his dressing gown. He'd been sick for a couple of days, and he looked terrible, but of course he wouldn't go to a doctor. No, he was drinking some weird herbal concoction Lyron had brought over, right after he came back to complain about the drone again. Not only did the herbs stink, but they didn't seem to be helping either.

"Do you want coffee?" I asked. "Tea? Something to eat?"

"Just tea."

"I'll make it. You need to go back to bed."

"There's too much to do."

"And we'll do it." I forced a smile. "Everything's under control."

Luna and Jubilee were cleaning the pool rooms and feeding turtles. Possibly out of guilt but more likely because Ryder had told them to stay the hell away from me. We weren't collecting enough turtle eggs, but I couldn't stake out beaches as well as writing the business plan, which was more important when it came to securing the sanctuary's long-term future. Local volunteers—a husband and wife—were bringing eggs from Spice Island, so at least Franklin would have some hatchlings to raise this year.

Five days until I was due to leave Valentine Cay, and my world was collapsing around my ears. I couldn't sleep, I couldn't stay awake, and I didn't know up from down. All I could do was make Franklin's tea and hope for a miracle.

33

KNOX

"How's New York?" Knox asked Hallie.

Sunday morning, and he'd rolled out of bed early to feed the turtles and the dog while Caro slept. Ryder, Luna, and Jubilee were finishing off in the pool rooms, making sure the bare minimum got done to keep the turtles alive and healthy and the sanctuary ticking over. Luna had been keeping her head down since the fight with Caro. With the animal care in hand, Knox had commandeered the office to video call Hallie without waking his girl.

"Great! I spend my days eating pizza and my evenings at the cabaret."

"You're on vacation this week? I thought you were working." Knox had asked Hallie to take a look through the background information Agatha was digging up. Hallie was young and new to Blackwood, but she had a good eye for detail. "Is Ford with you?"

"I *am* working. Ford's still in Virginia, but I shipped him some cookies. They have the best cookies in Little Italy.

But enough about me—spill the details of your trip. Emmy said you found a girlfriend?"

"'Girlfriend' is a bit of an exaggeration."

"So you're not moving in with her? I thought you needed time off to find a new place? You're a dark horse, Knox. Nobody saw this coming at all. I mean, Luther doesn't even have a pool running."

"Stop listening to Chinese whispers, sweetheart. Caro is... I don't know what she is, exactly. A long-term hookup? Anyhow, she has a problematic ex, and she relocated to San Gallicano to get away from him. Then our pain-in-the-ass client outed her location on social media, so now Caro has to find somewhere else to live because she doesn't feel safe here anymore."

"How does the murder fit in?"

"Separate issue." Knox summarised the mess so far—the poaching, Stacey's investigation, the body at Cinnamon Beach. "The cops still haven't made a positive ID. The lead detective wants Caro to go to the morgue, but we'd rather avoid that if possible."

Not only would seeing her dead friend be traumatic, but Caro also wanted to avoid putting her name on any official paperwork. Knox wasn't going to push her into revealing her identity. She was already close to her breaking point, and yesterday evening, Vince had questioned her until she couldn't take any more. The preliminary finding was that Stacey had been dumped sometime during the night, presumably in the hours of darkness, when, coincidentally, Fernandez hadn't been answering his phone. Where had he been late on Friday evening? As Stacey was being strangled and left for the fishes?

They knew she'd been strangled not thanks to Vince, but because the guy who delivered the sea sponges for the turtles to eat was friendly with the paddleboarder who'd found the body. When Caro was out of earshot, Knox had asked him what else he'd heard. Stacey's eyes had been missing, but the rest of her face was in reasonable shape, which fit with the ME's estimate that she'd been dumped recently. Apparently, she'd had dark bruises around her neck, which suggested strangulation as the cause of death.

Knox had kept the details from Caro. Last night, she'd stayed up for hours, filling in the Blackwood Foundation's grant application and putting together the sanctuary's five-year plan. Twice, Knox had heard her sobbing softly to herself, but when he got up to comfort her, she waved him away and told him to get some sleep. As if that was going to happen. At four a.m., she'd drunk two glasses of the wine he'd bought and finally closed her eyes.

"There are roughly nine thousand people named Stacey-with-an-e in Tennessee, North Carolina, and Georgia combined. Eleven percent of those are male, so we can eliminate them right away. Only six of the remaining women have the surname Custer, and three of them are over fifty. Another is six years old. That leaves two possibles, one in Wilmington and the other near Winston-Salem. There are far more Cumberland sliders near Winston-Salem."

"Did you—"

"Search for relatives? Yes, I did. Check your email—her parents still live in the same house she grew up in."

"I could kiss you right now."

"Please don't—Ford wouldn't be happy. Is the lead detective the one with the drinking problem?"

"What are you talking about?"

"Vincent Fernandez? The detective you asked Agatha to look at? He attends an Alcoholics Anonymous meeting every Friday."

"How the hell do you know that?"

"Uh... So it looks as if Agatha found his personnel file.

He got a warning for showing up drunk to work, but that was two and a half years ago, and there's been no trouble since."

Knox digested that piece of information. If it was true, then the good news was that Vince Fernandez hadn't spent Friday evening disposing of Stacey Custer's body. The bad news? He'd let drinking interfere with his work, so how conscientious was he?

"Does it say how many murder cases Vince Fernandez has worked?"

"Give me a moment... I need to ask Providence." On screen, Hallie bit her lip and leaned forward an inch. Providence was Blackwood's proprietary investigation software. It saved valuable man-hours by analysing endless swaths of data, summarising its findings, and connecting dots. "Okay, so the average homicide rate per year in San Gallicano is eleven. Vince Fernandez has been a detective for four years, and he's led a total of seven homicide investigations. Of those...all were committed by family members. Six convictions, one acquittal, but the acquittal was for a woman who stabbed her husband in a rage after he refused to help around the house. I guess there must have been a bunch of female jurors? Anyhow, in the past five years, only two murders in San Gallicano have been committed by non-family members. The last serial killer they had was in the 1980s, and he ate three of his victims, which is gross, but on balance, it sounds pretty nice there."

"Nice, apart from the woman lying in the morgue."

"Sorry."

"Based on what you've read, do you think Vince Fernandez is up to the job?"

"It's hard to say. I—" A door slammed in the background. "Oh, Dan's just come back. Are those donuts?"

Dan's face squashed into the frame along with her cleavage. "Hey, sexy. I hear you stumbled into an episode of *Death in Paradise*?"

"Something like that."

"His not-girlfriend's friend washed up on the beach, and we're trying to work out whether the lead detective is competent," Hallie explained.

"Why wouldn't he be?"

"Lack of experience and past performance issues."

"Add in possible police corruption and a Valetian royal visit on the main island," Knox told them. "When Fernandez was interviewing Caro last night, I got the impression they're hoping to keep Stacey's death quiet until Princess Gabrielle and her sister leave on Tuesday."

The detective had told Caro to keep a low profile and avoid antagonising anybody. The words of a caring friend who knew Caro all too well? Or a veiled threat?

Dan bit off a chunk of donut. "Let's take this back to basics. Means, motive, and opportunity. Motive?"

"She was a journalist writing a story about turtle smuggling. Last we heard, she was going to meet a source on Thursday."

"So, the easy assumption is that she pissed off a bunch of bad guys and they wanted to keep her quiet. But the body wasn't found until yesterday, so she could have gone on a date that went wrong or attracted the attention of a maniac. I hear Luna has a stalker in the area?"

"Yeah, she does, because this job doesn't have enough complications."

"But let's use Occam's razor and consider the smuggling angle first. The vic was a journalist? Where are her notes?"

"Caro and I took a look around her hotel room before we reported her missing, and her laptop and phone were gone. No sign of a notepad either—apart from the blank one the hotel supplied next to the phone—so we have to assume she had everything with her. Which would make sense if she was meeting a source. When she came to speak with Caro, she brought all that stuff."

"What about her backup?"

"I didn't see any backup device, but we didn't do a thorough search. Maybe she used the cloud?"

"She probably did that as well, but in my experience, journalists like to have a backup with them, especially when they're working in places where the internet connection could be unreliable. A flash drive or a memory card. Even a portable hard drive if they take a lot of photos. Fifty bucks says it's in her hotel room if the cops don't have it already."

Knox was almost certain they didn't. Vince had said that the crime scene technician—singular—had checked Stacey's room and they were satisfied that it wasn't a murder scene, but her belongings had been taken into evidence. Footage from the security camera in the lobby showed her leaving the hotel at 11:53 on Thursday morning, returning at 15:17 with a pizza box, and leaving again at 18:32. Just in case Vince decided to fast-forward, Knox had been upfront about the fact that he and Caro had visited Vista Suites to look for Stacey, although he hadn't mentioned any breaking and entering.

"I don't think they have it."

"Then I guess you have a fun trip in store this evening."

"Guess I do."

"I can't see anything here." Knox closed the desk drawer— quietly—with gloved hands and poked among the leaves on the fake potted plant sitting on the shelf above it. Rifling through a dead woman's personal space felt wrong. Sacrilegious. As if he risked disturbing her soul, which was absurd because even if Stacey Custer were watching from the afterlife, she'd want someone to get to the bottom of her death. To finish what she started. "But those modern drives are tiny."

"You need to think like a woman."

Dan spoke in his ear, through a mouthful of pizza or cookie or whatever she was eating at ten thirty in the evening. Without Caro along for the ride this time, Knox had bypassed the lobby and hopped over the back wall of the Vista Suites, picked the lock in under a minute, ducked under the single X of crime scene tape covering the doorway, and closed the drapes before he turned on the light. He was wearing a camera so Dan could join the search.

"You mean I should put on lipstick and fancy pumps?"

"No, that's *dressing* like a woman. *Think* like a woman. We're crafty. Check all the pockets in Stacey's clothes. The hems too, and her shoes. Shake the bottles in the bathroom and check for any hidden compartments. If there's a box of tampons, that's always a good hiding place—men have a weird aversion to sanitary products."

"Why is it weird?"

"Let's not have this conversation, sweetie. The toilet tank isn't a great place for hiding electronics, and under the mattress is too obvious. Ditto for the back of the desk drawers. Hey, is that a notepad by the phone?"

"There's nothing written on it."

"Check every page, then tear off the top sheet and bring it with you. Do those drapes have hems?"

"Yes."

"Can you recall what model of laptop she owned? Did it have a card reader? It would help if we had a better idea of what we're looking for."

"No, I don't remember, and Caro wasn't sure either. Do you know if Agatha got anywhere with trying to track Stacey's cell phone?"

"No luck yet. We have back doors into the major carriers in the US and a bunch of other global players, but not SG Telecom. The team is working on it, though. Lift that plant."

"I already checked there," Knox said, but he lifted the pot anyway.

"Not the pot, the plant."

"What do you—" He pulled on the leaves, and the whole plant popped free, revealing a hollow compartment in the pot. *Well, I'll be damned.* "Yeah, you're right. Women *are* crafty. How did you know?"

"Everything else in the room is tired. The flowers look almost new, which is a weird priority when the faucet is leaking and the pillowcase has a hole in it. Go on, what's in there?"

"Cash, two flash drives, a bank card, a driver's licence, and Stacey's passport."

"Bingo. Take the flash drives and the cash."

"Shouldn't I leave the cash?"

"If the cops in San Gallicano are as corrupt as you think they are, it'll never find its way to the evidence locker. We can send it to her family anonymously. Now get out of there before some overly conscientious employee decides to check on the crime scene."

Dan didn't have to tell him twice.

"Did you find any clues?" Caro asked.

She was sitting on the bunkhouse steps when Knox

arrived back at the sanctuary, her arms wrapped around her knees and an oversized cardigan draped over her shoulders. There was a chill in the air tonight, caused by an unusually stiff onshore wind.

"Possibly. Did you manage to avoid pulling out Luna's hair while I was gone?"

"Ugh. She's just been sitting on her bed, scribbling in that little notepad she carries around. Probably writing spells or something. What did you find?"

Knox beckoned Caro into the other bunkhouse and pulled the treasures out of his backpack. The flash drives, the cash, and the sheet from the hotel notepad.

"Don't get too excited—a security-conscious journalist will have used a password. I'll check, but it's likely I'll have to send these drives to our cyber team in the morning."

"How long will that take?"

"A day to get there, and then it's anyone's guess. If the drive is set to lock a user out after a number of incorrect guesses, they'll have to tread with care. If not, and they can use a brute force approach, we're talking anything from a second if she used a short numeric password to a trillion years if she got creative."

Caro groaned. "Stacey always came across as careful. When she typed her password into her laptop, it was, like, ten characters long."

Knox would let Agatha know that. A target to aim for. Meanwhile, Caro was thumbing through the cash, counting it. Knox already knew the total—nine hundred and twenty San Gallican pounds, or roughly four hundred dollars.

"I need a small box or a padded envelope to package these drives in. Do you have something suitable?"

"A cereal box? Plus we have scissors and tape."

"Do you have a pencil?"

"Isn't it safer to write the address in ink? Pencil might rub off?"

"The pencil is for something else."

"Uh, I don't have one, but Luna does."

Turned out Luna had a whole selection of pencils in a pink tin, and an equally impressive array of erasers. She stuffed the notepad she'd been writing in into one of her suitcases and slid the tin across the rickety table in the middle of the girls' bunkhouse—someone had wedged a folded piece of paper under one of the legs so it wasn't as wobbly as it once had been—and asked the inevitable question.

"Why do you need a pencil?"

Carefully, Knox laid the sheet of paper from Stacey's room on the table. Dan had explained the best way to do this on the trip back. Don't use too much pressure, she'd said, and he intended to follow her advice.

"Because sometimes when people make notes, they press hard enough to indent the sheet of paper below," he told Luna. "If we shade lightly with a pencil, it might bring up a hidden message."

She held out a pencil covered in tiny bumblebees. Gold lettering said to "Bee-lieve in yourself." Knox thought she had enough self-confidence for ten people, even if Ryder claimed it was all an act, but that didn't matter right now. What mattered was ensuring she survived the next eleven days at the turtle sanctuary, and thank fuck Judge Morgan hadn't seen Luna's video and made it twelve.

Knox shaded the paper lightly, and words began to appear in looping handwriting. *Havana. Boat. 9 p.m.* What did that mean?

"Was there a boat leaving for Cuba?" he mused out loud. "Turtles being smuggled out of the country?"

Caro shrugged. "Stacey said the stolen turtles were

ending up in the US. Restaurants and markets in New York."

"Then it wouldn't make sense to transport goods via Cuba. Too many sanctions, too much scrutiny."

"How about Little Havana?" Jubilee suggested. "Luna made an appearance there last year, and a boat could easily dock in Miami. Maybe Stacey heard there was cargo leaving and went to check it out."

That was a possibility. "And then got caught."

Ryder tipped back in his seat. "Playing devil's advocate, we don't know when Stacey wrote that, or even *if* she wrote that."

"The writing looks like hers," Caro said. "She was making notes when she interviewed me, and I remember those big old-fashioned loops. And she didn't mention Havana when we spoke, so she probably learned about that afterward."

"Hey, you guys?" Luna had picked up the pencil and begun shading again. "There's something else here."

Annoyance flared that she'd decided to take the evidence without asking, but Knox bit back his irritation because she was right. Everyone crowded in to look. The words at the bottom of the page were fainter, as if they'd been written on an earlier sheet, but several were still readable. *Tattoo. Black Pearl.* The letters *M-O-N*.

"She wrote about Havana after the tattoo thing," Caro said. "That was a recent note. What's Black Pearl?"

Ryder snapped his fingers. "The ship in Pirates of the Caribbean."

"Nice try, but that's fictional. Do they grow pearls in San Gallicano?"

Caro shook her head. "Not that I've ever heard."

"Natural black pearls only come from Tahiti," Luna put in. "I did promo work for a jewellery company, and I had to say that on the video. The rest are all dyed. You think there could be a link to the movie? One of the backup dancers on my last tour had a cousin who worked as a stunt double for Johnny Depp."

"I don't know, but I do know that we need sleep. The research team can work on this overnight, and we'll regroup in the morning."

34

CARO

"The Black Pearl is a tattoo shop in Raystown," Knox's colleague said on screen. She was a small, elfin woman who wore her blonde hair in pigtails and favoured the natural look. "I mean, it's also a pirate ship, but I don't think that's what we're dealing with in this instance."

"Anything on M-O-N? Is that part of the address?" he asked.

"Nuh-uh. It's on Chapel Boulevard. Emailing the details now."

"How about Havana? The boat? Nine p.m.?"

"We're trying to get ahold of the shipping records, focusing on any vessel travelling to either Havana, Cuba, or Little Havana, Florida."

"How long would it take for a boat to get there?"

"The distance between San Gallicano and the Port of Miami is just over eighteen hundred nautical miles, to Puerto de La Habana is a little less. We don't know what type of vessel we're dealing with yet, but if we assume it's travelling at somewhere between ten and twenty knots, the journey would take between four and eight days, and it could have docked as soon as yesterday. Reuben from the Miami office is heading over to the port now. Cuba isn't quite so straightforward, but Nate has contacts there. Are you going to try the tattoo shop?"

"I'll head over there this morning."

Excuse me. "*We'll* head over there."

"Baby, it's safer for you to stay here."

"Stacey was my friend." We hadn't known each other for long, but I'd liked her. She'd been the kind of woman I'd have enjoyed spending time with.

"I understand, but there's no point in making yourself a target any more than you already are."

"If I'm a target, then the safest place for me is right behind you."

Knox's colleague snorted. "She isn't wrong."

Okay, yes, I liked her too.

He blew out a breath. "Agatha, we're supposed to be on the same team here."

"We are. If I was in San Gallicano, I'd want to be standing behind you as well."

"Fine. I can't argue with both of you."

Wow. A man who knew how to give in semi-gracefully. "If I come, I can help—Stacey said she spoke to a woman, and I might be able to build a rapport with her."

Agatha giggled. "Knox can be quite the charmer when he puts his mind to it."

And now I had to give in gracefully too. "Yes, he can."

"Sloane told me she'd found a courier to bring the drives to us in Virginia?"

Knox nodded. "That's right—the courier will be our first stop when we get to Ilha Grande, and you'll have the package this afternoon."

On the rare occasions that I needed to send something

to the US—there were a couple of volunteers I kept in touch with, and we mailed each other birthday cards—I used the economy service at the general store, where the item got loaded onto a boat and arrived several weeks later. Not Blackwood Security. When the package was important enough, they hired a person to walk the item onto a plane and hand-deliver it to their offices. No delays other than a flight change at Miami International. The environmentalist in me was screaming, but I held my tongue—finding Stacey's killer was more important than everything else right now. I'd plant a tree when this was over.

Look on the bright side, Caro. At least they're not using a private jet.

The Black Pearl was more than a tattoo shop. Through a colourful beaded curtain, I saw a single empty chair, but the front of the establishment seemed to house a jewellery store-slash-art gallery. Chunky crystal necklaces fought for space among framed drawings of winged beasts and delicate angels. The artist could have used the girl behind the counter as a muse. She wore a filmy kaftan over tiny shorts and a tank top, and in the light streaming through the window behind her, she looked almost ethereal.

"May I help you?" she asked. "We have a pair of topaz earrings that would match your eyes perfectly."

"We were actually hoping for some information. A few days ago, a friend of mine came here asking about a particular tattoo. She was trying to find its owner."

"A friend?"

"Her name is Stacey." *Was* Stacey. I still struggled to believe she'd gone. Logically, I understood, but I still kept half expecting her to call again, asking for more facts and figures on the turtles. "Do you remember her?"

"Uh, not really? I mean, she was here, but we didn't speak much."

Knox squeezed my hand, and I wasn't sure whether that meant "You're doing good, keep going" or "Thank goodness we're in the right place." But a wave of relief washed over me because I had his support.

"She said you had a friend who dated the guy?"

"Well, I thought so, maybe, but I was probably wrong. We have some lovely necklaces, if you'd like to take a look?" She slid a tray out from beneath the glass counter. "This pink agate would definitely suit you."

"Did you speak with your friend?"

"Uh, I... I shouldn't get involved."

"We need to get in touch with her. Stacey disappeared the day after she came here, and your friend might be the last person who spoke with her."

The girl had been pale to start with, but as soon as I mentioned the word "disappeared," she turned the colour of sun-bleached bone.

"D-d-disappeared?"

"We're not sure whether the two things are connected, but if your friend didn't call her, it would help if we could rule that out."

"Sh-sh-shouldn't the police be looking into this?"

"We filed a report, but the guy on the missing persons desk basically said that they were all busy with the royal visit, so they couldn't do much in the short term." I rolled my eyes on purpose, trying to lighten the mood. "I have no idea why we even pay taxes."

Knox had told me not to mention Stacey's death for the moment. If the girl realised this was a murder investigation, she might clam up completely.

"Please, will you help us?" I pushed.

"I think... I think..." Her eyes began to glisten. "I think Monique might have vanished too."

Monique? M-O-N. Oh, shit. The *tres bocados* I'd eaten for breakfast turned leaden in my stomach.

"What makes you think that?"

"She said she was going to call Stacey, and we were meant to meet for dinner that night—the Laughing Crab does an all-you-can-eat special on Thursdays—but then she texted to ask if we could get breakfast the next morning instead. This place doesn't open until ten, and the Bluebird Bakery has TFI Fridays. Two pastries and two drinks for the price of one."

"And she didn't show up?"

"I tried to call her, but she didn't answer, and I figured she'd just forgotten. She can be flaky like that, you know? But when she didn't call back by the end of the day, I went to her apartment, and only Cheeto was there."

"Cheeto?"

"Her cat. Usually, Monique asks me to feed him if she goes away, but she has a new neighbour who loves cats, so I figured that she was helping out. But then I spoke with her yesterday, and she said Monique never told her she was going anywhere, and it's been more than three days now. What should I do? Should I tell the police? I guess maybe I should, but Monique didn't trust them."

"Why not?"

"Because a couple of years ago, she went on a date with this guy—one date—and he totally wasn't her type. But he wouldn't take the hint. He used to sit outside her place in his car all night, and it really creeped her out. So she reported him, but the police said they couldn't do anything because he wasn't trespassing on private property. Isn't that crazy?"

"Whether the cops act generally depends on the colour of the stalker's skin and how nice their car is," Knox said. "At least, that's my experience in the United States."

"Oh, he drove a BMW. A nice one. So when the police shrugged their shoulders, Monique got a plank of wood and hammered a bunch of nails into it—she's a carpenter, so she's good with tools—and then she buried it in the dirt outside her place. And you know what? When the asshole got four flat tyres, *she* was the one who got charged."

"Did she get convicted?" Knox asked.

"Thankfully, Judge Morgan was in court, and he just laughed and threw out the case." The girl beamed. "Do you know Judge Morgan? We love him here. Last month, he sent that dumb singer who dressed up a turtle to work at the turtle sanctuary."

"I'm familiar with Judge Morgan. He has a unique approach to the job."

"We definitely need more judges like him. I mean, the creep with the BMW *still* kept coming back. That's when Monique started dating Tomas."

"Tomas?" I asked. "Who's Tomas?"

"He's friendly with Barry."

"And who is Barry?"

"The guy your friend was asking about? With the tattoo? When she came here, I couldn't remember the name, only that it was something fishy, but I asked Monique when I spoke with her."

A spark ran through me. I'd never wanted to be a private detective—I was good at investigating finances, not murder —but this was weirdly exciting. Awful because Stacey was dead, but at least I was helping to find out who killed her.

"The man with the anchor on his hand? His name is Barry? How is that fishy?"

"It's short for Barracuda."

Ah.

"And Monique was dating his friend, not him?"

"I got confused. And Barry might not be his real name," the girl continued, "but it's all Monique ever called him. And she only dated Tomas for a few months. Long enough for him to punch the creep in the face and tell him that if he ever came near Monique again, he'd be eating through a straw, but not long enough for her to introduce him to her family."

Great. So one of our key suspects was a poacher named Barracuda, who was acquainted with a thug who thought nothing of smashing a man's teeth. Oh, that wasn't freaking me out. I realised I was breathing hard and tried to relax, tried to tamp down the rising sense of panic. Two missing women? Stacey was dead, but where was Monique? Had she met the same fate with her body yet to be found? Or was she still alive somewhere?

Tick-tock, tick-tock, tick-tock.

Would we find her in time?

"Does Monique have family close by?" Knox asked.

"Her parents live on Malavilla. That's where she grew up. They're always nagging her to find a nice man and settle down, but she keeps saying she's not ready for that, and Tomas sure wasn't a guy you'd take home to meet Mom and Dad. To be honest, I think she was just using him for the sex, and—" The girl clapped both hands over her mouth. "I shouldn't be talking about her private business like this."

Using him for sex? That sounded familiar, or at least it should have. Last night, Knox had held me until I fell into a fitful sleep, and it had felt like so much more.

"If Monique is in trouble, I think she'll appreciate you doing all you can to help, but we don't need to know the intimate details of her relationship. We only need to find

Tomas, and hopefully he'll be able to tell us more about Barry. Did she tell you why they broke up?"

"Not really? She just said he wasn't the man she thought he was, and that she'd decided to take a break from men altogether. And she did. She deleted her dating apps and bought a Pleasure Master 3000."

Hmm. "Are those good?"

"A-ma-zing. The gold standard of vibrators."

"I've seen them online, but I didn't think they were available in San Gallicano?"

Knox cut me a sideways glare. Yes, his equipment was platinum standard, but he wouldn't be around all the time, and women had needs.

"We picked them up when we took a trip to New York, and then I nearly died in the airport when the TSA guy made me unpack my carry-on bag, but thankfully, the pitcher of margaritas we shared for breakfast limited my capacity for embarrassment. Monique couldn't stop giggling."

"Sounds like a great trip."

"It was awesome, at least, the parts that I can remember. We need to find her. We need to find Monique."

Knox took over again. "Do you know how she met Tomas?"

"Through work, I think?"

"Was he a colleague? A client?"

"I'm almost sure she was doing a job for his boss. He brought her a drink, and they ended up talking. That was either Tomas or hums-when-he-comes guy, but I think hums-when-he-comes asked for her number when he fixed her truck."

Hums when he comes? Yikes. My mind wandered to my own guy. I got a groan and kisses from Knox, or sometimes curses if the moment was particularly intense. And afterward, I'd fall asleep in his arms, wrapped up in the scent of sandalwood and a layer of protection so strong that it kept my nightmares at bay. I was going to miss him like crazy when he wasn't there.

Would the dreams of Aiden return?

The sleepless, sweat-soaked nights?

Knox, of course, stayed focused on the task at hand.

"You said Monique was a carpenter—did she work with somebody, or was she a one-woman band?"

"Oh, it was just her. She used to work with her grandfather, but then he retired, and they sort of...swapped places. She took over his workshop, and he moved to Malavilla to stay with her parents. Poor guy has dementia now—it's so sad."

"Where's the workshop? If we could look through her records, we might be able to track down Tomas."

"You really think Barry is connected to her disappearance?"

"Yeah, I do. Stacey was looking for the guy with the anchor tattoo, Monique knew him, and suddenly they're both gone? At the very least, we need to find him and eliminate him."

I understood that Knox meant "eliminate him from the investigation," but the determination in his voice sent a chill spider-walking up my spine. Knox carried a gun, and he'd worked a job where death was commonplace.

The girl turned things over in her mind and came to a decision. "I have a key to her place. To let the cat out, you know? We can go there on my lunch break, and I'll show you where she keeps past invoices. My name is Angel, by the way."

Angel? It suited her.

"We appreciate your help, and so will Monique."

35

KNOX

"Are you kidding me?"

Knox glanced up at Caro's tone. He didn't know who was on the other end of the line, but she didn't seem happy to be talking to them. And the answer was obviously "no."

"Don't you have better things to do? Like investigating a murder, for example?"

So it was a cop. Vince Fernandez, probably. And if he wasn't asking questions about Stacey, then what the fuck did he want?

"Fine, I'll tell them," Caro snapped. "And you can tell Lyron that I'm never bringing him cake again."

She tossed the phone onto the table and let out a sound that was half screech, half groan. Irritation twisted her face into a grimace.

"What?" Knox asked.

"Lyron's a pain in the ass, that's what. And so is Jason Roy."

"That was Roy on the phone? Not Fernandez?"

"Vince can be a dick sometimes, but he's not a

jobsworth like Jason." Caro closed those topaz eyes for a moment and sucked in a breath. Let it out again. She did that whenever she got stressed, Knox had noticed. "Lyron reported the drone to the police. Apparently, you're still flying it too close to his land, and it's disturbing the peace. Jason said Lyron doesn't have grounds for a complaint, but he also said that you should have a permit, and if you don't get one right away, he'll have to confiscate the drone until whoever is flying it takes the test."

"There's a fucking test?"

"Some multiple-choice thing. They brought it in after idiots kept flying too close to the airport, but it applies to the whole nation. You can take it at any police station, Jason said. Costs fifty bucks."

"So it's more of a revenue generation exercise than a safety thing?"

"Probably."

"Can't we just pay a fine? How likely is Roy to make good on his threat to confiscate it?"

"Pretty likely. He's a by-the-book asshole who dots every *i* and crosses every *t*. Vince says that with his love of paperwork, Jason will probably make chief someday."

"Can't Vince talk sense into him?"

"I'll try calling him, but he's been off with me since I started pushing him on the turtle surveillance. Did you hear anything on Tomas yet?"

"Not yet."

Monique Constantine wasn't a fan of modernisation. According to Angel, she prided herself on doing things the traditional way, which meant sourcing quality materials, using her grandfather's tools, and writing her invoices longhand. Copies were stored in an ancient filing cabinet in a closet-sized office to the side of her workshop, and Knox and Caro had spent an hour yesterday afternoon photographing any from the time period when Monique had been involved with Tomas. But Monique worked hard and seemed to focus on small repair jobs rather than large projects, so there were fifty-seven possible candidates for Tomas's boss, spread mainly across Ilha Grande and Malavilla. Angel said Monique went to see her family regularly and often combined visits with work.

Now the invoices were with Agatha, and she would run a background check on each customer. With hope, they'd be able to narrow down the number of candidates, and someone could pay a visit in person. Probably Knox, possibly Slater. Emily Shadrach was on the way home to her family, and Slater was en route to San Gallicano. Knox had originally planned to leave with Caro right after he arrived, but although she'd spent her nights filling in paperwork for the Blackwood Foundation, she hadn't done much in the way of packing. She seemed more focused on getting justice for Stacey, and Knox knew what it was like to have guilt eating away at your insides like a horde of termites. For years after the accident, he'd lived with the what-ifs. What if he'd had less to drink that night and confiscated Eric's car keys? What if he'd talked his friends out of going to the bar that night, period?

"We should be doing something," Caro said. "I mean, something to find Monique. She's out there missing and—"

"Collectively, we *are* doing something. Blackwood works as a team, and the folks back home are digging through the information as we speak."

"But—"

"The turtles can't feed themselves, and Baptiste is still sick. They need you today." Plus there was this fucking drone issue. "I need to speak with Ryder."

Ryder was in the dining room, which was where he'd spent most of his time since Luna's blow-up with Caro, at least while Caro was at the sanctuary. Luna preferred avoidance over confrontation, it seemed. Sign-ups continued to trickle in for the sponsorship scheme, and the girls were writing up notes for whoever would take over the admin once they'd gone. Fuck, there was still so much left to do. New staff to find, Caro's belongings to pack up, a murder to investigate, plus the ongoing care for the turtles. A juggling act.

"Buddy, there's a problem."

Luna blanched, and Ryder squeezed her hand. "It's okay, moon. What problem?"

"The old troublemaker from next door complained to the cops about the drone. Apparently, we need a permit to keep flying it."

"How do we get a permit? We have less than two weeks left here—wouldn't it be more cost-effective to just pay the fine?"

"We don't get the option of a fine. It's permit or confiscation. One of us has to go to the nearest police station and take a multiple-choice test."

Ryder cursed under his breath. "There must be a way around this."

"Might be faster to take the damn test. We need to pick up supplies anyway, so the trip would kill two birds with one stone."

"If you're going to the store, can I come?" Jubilee asked.

Ryder shook his head. "No, you should stay here with Knox. I can pick up whatever you need."

Jubilee glanced at Luna, and her cheeks coloured. "Uh, so we're running out of sanitary products. A bunch of stuff got left in the bathroom on Kory's yacht, and we need tampons—the ones in the blue box with the pink stripe, regular flow, plus the pads—"

"Okay, you can come," Ryder said hastily. "Just wear a hat so people don't recognise you."

Great. That left Knox to act as referee between two warring women, but at least he didn't have to go to the grocery store.

Luna hummed softly to herself as she scribbled away in her little notepad with a sparkly pencil. She seemed to erase as much as she wrote. What was she doing? Keeping a journal? Or a hit list? Or plotting world domination? Thanks to her "special relationship" with Ryder, Knox hadn't spent much time with her in the past couple of weeks, and she was quieter than she had been at the beginning of the trip. Almost shy.

"Coffee?" she asked, dropping the pencil on the table.

"Is that an offer or an order?"

"An offer. I know you're Team Caro, but you don't always have to think the worst of me."

"But you make it so easy."

She shoved her chair back and smiled sweetly. Too sweetly. "Do you want sugar or salt in your drink?"

"Neither."

He was about to follow her to the kitchen to make sure she didn't add salt or something worse—Borax, for example —when his phone buzzed with a message.

RYDER

The drone test is a joke. On our way back.

KNOX

Hurry. Luna's threatening to make coffee.

RYDER

> Don't forget to say thank you. There's a
> Mexican food stand next to the jetty—do
> you guys want tacos or burritos?

KNOX

> I'll ask. 2 mins…

But before he could call out to Luna, his phone buzzed again, this time with an alert from a motion sensor. They'd been blessedly free of reporters recently, but that didn't mean an enterprising fool with a camera wouldn't try his luck for an exclusive.

"Don't go anywhere. I'll be back in a minute."

"Why? What's happening?" Luna asked.

"Nothing for you to worry about," he told her.

He lied.

The phone buzzed again as Knox passed the first bunkhouse, an alert from a different sensor. The same threat moving around? Or did they have more than one visitor? Knox paused to check his weapon, just in case. He'd carried a SIG P226 semi-automatic during his days on the Teams, and it was still his weapon of choice. The double-stack magazine held fifteen rounds, plus there was one in the chamber.

And he was glad of that. The hairs on the back of his neck prickled as another sensor activated, too fast and too far away from the last to be caused by the same trigger. He heard a motor in the background, high pitched, getting louder, not a vehicle but a boat. Something fast. Powerful. Heading in their direction. Heading for Caro, over in the pool rooms.

Fuck.

Knox tapped his phone, activating Blackwood's emergency alert system. There was nothing good about this.

He was alone with three civilians, one of whom was a clear target. Had that been planned? Had whoever was out there waited until Ryder left the sanctuary to make their move?

The first gunshot rang out at the same time as the first scream.

Luna.

Knox's heart yelled at him to go to Caro, but his head, his training, his professionalism sent him running toward the dining room. Luna was the client. Luna had been threatened. Luna was the woman he'd come here to protect.

Her scream was followed by an animalistic roar, undoubtedly male, and bullets thudded into the surrounding tree trunks as an unseen enemy let loose with a full magazine, taking the "spray and pray" approach. That alone told Knox he wasn't dealing with a professional. He waited for the break as the hostile reloaded, then risked a look. There, a flash of red. Who the fuck wore red to a gunfight? Knox aimed, fired, and the target dropped. Who was he? Or rather, who had he been? The man lay where he'd fallen, legs twitching, a chunk of his brain missing where he'd underestimated his opponent.

Shots came from the dining room, and Knox ran.

"Come out, little girl, and I won't hurt you," a man yelled, then fired again.

Hostile number two was inside, aiming a semi-automatic rifle toward the kitchen, his attention focused on the closed door. On his target. *Luna.* Knox raised his gun, but before he could fire, a volley of shots came through the flimsy wood of the door, and blood blossomed on the man's chest. What the fuck? Shock registered on his face right before Knox dropped him with a double tap to the head.

"Luna?"

The answering call was desperate. "Knox?"

"I'm right here. Put the gun down."

"What about the man? He was shooting at me, and... and..." Her voice hitched, and she choked out a sob.

"He's gone. I'm coming in, so don't shoot at me, okay?"

The door wouldn't open, not until Knox hefted it with his shoulder, and he soon found out why. The body of a man lay behind it, his face red and blistered, his limbs splayed.

"What the...?" There was no time for questions, no time for answers. Luna swung the business end of a pistol in his direction, not on purpose but because she had no idea about gun safety. He caught her arm and pointed it toward the floor. "Careful."

Now she dropped the gun entirely, and it bounced off the man's foot and clattered across the floor. Knox retrieved it, an old Ruger, and checked the magazine. Six rounds left. He tucked the spare weapon into his waistband.

"Stay behind me."

Luna nodded, her face paler than a corpse, and he grabbed her wrist. A shadow moved past the window, another hostile. Tanned skin, short dark hair, black shirt. Yelling came from outside, somewhere near the beach, and Knox's heart stuttered. That was Caro.

His Caro.

A spring fling that meant so much more than he'd dared to admit, even to himself.

He put a finger to his lips and tugged Luna forward. Fear turned her obedient and she followed, trembling from terror or adrenaline or both. Holding fire was the hardest thing in the world right now, but Knox pressed himself against the wall beside the doorjamb, shielding Luna, waiting for this asshole to come look for his buddies. It didn't take long. The muzzle of a gun appeared, then an arm, then a head. One more second, two shots, and then Knox had three guns.

Four hostiles down, but how many more were there? Instinct told Knox at least another three, his brain extrapolating data almost unconsciously—sensors, shouting, shots.

"Luna, I need to go outside."

"No, no, don't leave me."

The dining tables were from another era, made from sturdy timber when furniture was built to last. Knox tipped the nearest one onto its side and heaved it into a corner, forming a triangular sanctuary with thick wooden walls. He lifted Luna inside and checked the latest gun. Nine rounds left.

More yelling, more gunshots, and this time, Knox recognised Baptiste's voice.

"Take this. If anyone but me walks through that door, shoot them."

"I can't—"

"You can. Caro and Baptiste are dead if I don't get out there and help them, and we're sitting ducks if we both stay here."

"Okay," Luna said, so softly that Knox barely heard her above the sound of the boat engine. It was leaving. A retreat? Damn, Knox hoped they were bugging out.

He ran across the room, staying low, and reached the door in time to see Baptiste lurch across the path and collapse, the shoulder of his white T-shirt scarlet, his right arm hanging limply at his side. There was at least one hostile still in the vicinity because dirt kicked up around Baptiste's feet, and the man let out a howl of pain as he was hit again.

Knox saw a muzzle flash in the trees, and he fired back, then ran in a crouch to where the older man lay. There was no time for compassion—Knox grabbed Baptiste by his belt and dragged him toward the dining room. Fifteen yards, ten yards, five yards, another gunshot, and it felt as if a heavyweight boxer had punched him in the leg, then rammed a red-hot screwdriver through the throbbing limb. But he kept going, firing at the trees, knowing a direct hit was unlikely but hoping for a distraction.

Baptiste groaned as Knox shoved him to safety behind the wall.

"Stay there."

"Not...goin' anywhere."

Knox glanced at his thigh. The muscle was on fire, and blood was running down his calf, soaking into his sock and sneaker. How bad was it? Not enough blood for an artery, he didn't think, so he still had time to kill this motherfucker, but where had the asshole gone? There was no movement outside.

But he was still there. Knox could sense him, could feel his malevolent presence among the trees. He was watching. Waiting for someone to emerge from the safety of the dining room so he could put a bullet through their head. That alone told Knox that he was better trained than his colleagues.

But he wasn't special forces.

Knox tore off his shirt and tied it around his thigh, tight enough to stem the flow of blood as he headed to the kitchen and slithered through the gap between the wall and the roof. Luna had her instructions. If anyone but Knox appeared, shoot them.

He slipped through the trees as quietly as a wraith, fuelled by anger and adrenaline. And fear. The silence was unnerving, the stillness a dread that settled in his gut. Where was Caro? He hoped she'd gone to ground, that she was hiding from danger, waiting for him to do his job, but he knew in his heart that she wasn't.

She'd gone.

And that certainty drove him forward.

Knox weaved through the tangled trees, his senses on high alert, thanking the stars above that he and Ryder had scouted every inch of the property soon after they arrived on Valentine Cay. The metallic *thunk* ahead strongly suggested that his target had just tripped over the remains of an old water tank that had been left to rust in the salt-laden air twenty yards from the dining room. And that meant the enemy was at the gates.

Knox had hoped to take the man alive. *Needed* to take the man alive. But pain seared through his leg with every step, blood squelching in his sneaker and spilling out onto the sandy ground. He saw the hostile ahead, dressed in camouflage, dark hair curling over his collar, moving stealthily, differently from the others. They had been cannon fodder. This guy was a soldier, a soldier and a coward who'd waited in the shadows and watched his men die. But now he was making his move, and Luna wouldn't stand a chance if he reached that doorway.

Slowly, carefully, Knox raised his gun and aimed, leaning on a tree for support. Then he gave a whistle that could have been a bird or the wind or a man who'd spent half his life learning to put a bullet into the black.

The hostile whipped around, scanning for danger.

And Knox shot him between the eyes.

36

RYDER

"Ryder?"

Luna spoke in a barely audible whisper, but her distress came through loud and clear.

"Moon? What's going on?"

Thank fuck she'd called. After Knox activated the emergency alert, Ryder had nearly been deafened by gunfire before the line went dead. The ferry didn't leave Malavilla for another thirty minutes, and although he'd begun scouting for alternative transport, the harbour was deathly quiet early on a Tuesday afternoon. The fishing boats wouldn't return until the evening, and the pleasure craft were dark, no owners in sight.

"Men showed up with guns! One of them tried to grab me, so I threw coffee at him and hit him with the kettle. I-I-I think he might be dead."

Ryder had been in many firefights during his varied career, and at the time, they'd been pretty hair-raising. But now he realised there was nothing more terrifying than a woman he cared about facing armed men while he was several miles away.

"Where's Knox?"

"I don't know! There was more shooting, and he...he... he went outside again. Only Franklin is here, and he's hurt."

Jubilee was standing on tiptoes, trying to listen in, but Luna's voice was soft as a breath on the wind.

"Is Luna all right?" she asked.

"Yes, but there's trouble. We need to get back fast."

Jubilee's eyes saucered. "Trouble?"

"Find a boat."

"Okay." She stepped back. "Okay."

Ryder turned his attention back to Luna. There was only silence from the phone now. The gunfire had stopped.

"When did you last hear a shot?"

"A minute ago? Two minutes? What should I do? Knox told me to stay here, but Franklin's b-b-bleeding."

"Are you hurt?"

"Not really."

What the fuck did that mean? "I'm coming, moon. I'm on my way. Where are you?"

"In the dining room. Knox pushed the table over and made me hide behind it."

A male voice spoke. "Emergency services have been alerted, but they don't seem prepared for an incident of this nature, and they won't send medics in without backup."

"Who's that?" Luna asked. "Who's that man?"

"His name is Matt, and he works for Blackwood. They're coordinating a response." Ryder had patched them in to Luna's call—the more information they had, the better. "Where's Franklin?"

"By the door."

"And Caro?"

"I...I didn't see her, not once."

If Caro was sensible, she'd be hiding. Franklin was alive but injured, and Knox... Either he was still hunting, or he was hurt. Hurt bad, because he'd have come back to Luna otherwise, unless he'd gone to look for Caro because it was obvious he was halfway in love with her, even if he wouldn't admit it.

"I need you to listen, moon. Listen to your surroundings. What do you hear?"

"Nothing. I hear nothing!"

"Can you hear the sea? The water lapping at the beach?"

A pause. "Y-y-yes."

"That's your baseline. What else?"

"F-f-Franklin breathing."

"What else?"

"Birds. The ground doves that Caro feeds and...and the gray kingbirds."

In the better days, before that stupid social media post, they'd shared lunch and dinner outside, all six of them. Ryder and Luna, Knox and Caro, Franklin and Jubilee. Franklin had begun teaching the girls about the local wildlife, how to identify different birds by their calls. Ryder had spent time listening to birds too. Hunkered down in the forest with his team in the midst of an operation, waiting to make their next move. Whenever danger approached, the birds fell silent. *If you can't hear me, I don't exist.* If the birds were singing again, that meant the threat had passed, or the enemy was hiding. *Were* they hiding? No, that didn't feel right. They'd come hard and fast, get in, get out. They were either dead or gone.

"Check on Franklin."

"But—"

"It's okay. Check on him."

A long moment passed. "Franklin?" Rustling. "Franklin?"

Ryder heard the faintest groan.

"He's bleeding."

"Where's he bleeding from?"

"His shoulder, mostly, and his leg."

"How much blood? Are we talking a trickle or a gush?"

"It's soaking into his shirt. Like, there's a bit underneath him." So the wounds probably didn't involve arteries. "He has a lump on his head."

"Okay, there's a first-aid kit in the far bunkhouse. You need to—"

Another voice, and not one from Blackwood. Pissed off. Shouty.

"What the devil is going on here? What's all this noise?"

"Who's that?" Luna asked.

"I don't know. Maybe a neighbour." Lyron, the asshole who reported the drone. "Find something you can use as a weapon if you need to. Where's the kettle?"

"I have a gun."

Where the fuck had she gotten a gun from? Ryder took a steadying breath, willing himself to stay calm.

"Do you remember how to use it? Don't put your finger on the trigger unless you intend to fire."

One night on the beach, she'd asked about his gun, and he'd shown her how to handle it safely, oddly pleased that she was interested in his job. He'd never dreamed she'd need that knowledge.

"I already shot at a guy, but I moved my finger now."

Fucking hell.

"Go and see who's out there. Keep the gun at your side."

This was worse than facing a whole army of insurgents. Ryder's pulse thrummed loud in his ears, a soundtrack to the real-life horror movie unfolding on Valentine Cay.

"Who are you?" Luna called, and Ryder was beyond proud that her voice didn't shake. But she was good at hiding her feelings around strangers. "What are you doing here? This is private property."

"So is my land, young lady, and I'm entitled to peaceful enjoyment of my home. Which is what I got until the likes of you showed up. First that drone, and now firecrackers. Where's Franklin?"

"Don't come any closer."

"Is that a gun? I'm calling the police. You can't come to Valentine Cay and threaten people like that."

"Tell that to all the men who just showed up and started shooting at us."

"What men?"

"How the freaking heck should I know? We didn't send invitations."

"Where are they now?"

"Two of them are dead in the dining room, and the others are probably waiting to shoot your stupid ass if you don't get behind a tree or something."

"The dining room? Get out of my way, child. Someone needs to teach you— Franklin? What the...?"

"I think he got shot."

"And you're just standing there? I need gauze, gloves, scissors."

"Do you know first aid?"

"I was a combat medic in Nam. Hurry! And call an ambulance."

A combat medic? That was the first sliver of good news, although the man was still a dick. If Lyron hadn't complained about the drone, Ryder would be there applying compression himself. Hell, he could have taken out the man who injured Franklin before the asshole got off a shot.

"The police are already on their way, medics too," Luna

said. "But this tinpot country doesn't seem to have a SWAT team, so who knows when they'll show up."

"Get the first-aid kit," Ryder told her. "Green bag on the spare bed next to the door. After that, you need to find Knox and Caro. Run." Then, to Matt, "Can we narrow down the location?"

"Working on it. No signal from Knox's phone, but his smartwatch is still transmitting."

Luna's breathing got rougher as she ran to the bunkhouse. She was fit from all the dancing she usually did, but Ryder feared panic was getting the better of her. Jubilee had been talking animatedly with the guy at the burrito stand, and now she was jogging back in Ryder's direction.

"The burrito guy's brother works at the big hotel near here. I offered them five thousand dollars, and he's on his way with the boat they use for wakeboarding. Apparently, it does forty-three knots. I don't really know what that means, but I think it's fast?"

About as fast as they'd find around here. "You did good."

"How's Luna?"

"She's okay. The neighbour showed up, and he used to be a medic before he turned into a whiny prick, so he's helping out."

"Knox is roughly forty yards east of the largest building at the turtle sanctuary. We've overlaid a satellite image, and he looks to be in a forested area. Heart rate one-sixty, blood pressure dropping."

Injured but alive. Heart rate increased with stress and pain, and usually blood pressure did too. If Knox's was dropping, that meant he was losing blood, and if he was still stuck in the trees, he'd lost too much.

"Moon, did you get that?"

"Which way is east?"

"Toward the pool rooms. Head into the trees behind the dining room, and then turn toward the pool rooms. Let Lyron get what he needs from the first-aid kit and take the rest with you."

A boat engine sounded in the distance, getting rapidly louder. Their ride?

"I don't know any first aid."

"I'll talk you through what you need to do. If Knox is bleeding, the key thing is to apply pressure to the wound. Pack it with gauze, and then lean on it."

A boat sped toward them, a young Black man waving from the driver's seat. Colourful wakeboards were stacked in a rack on one side, and electropop blared from bone-shaking speakers.

Ryder covered his ears. "Get him to turn that damn music off," he said to Jubilee as a shriek came through the phone.

"Moon, what is it? What happened?"

"Th-there's a man, and half of his head is gone."

"Do you recognise him?"

"I...I... No."

"Good. Keep going."

The music shut off, and Ryder jumped into the boat, then lifted Jubilee in after him. She collapsed onto a seat and gripped the canopy support so hard her knuckles turned white.

"We need to get to the turtle sanctuary at Valentine Cay."

The driver nodded, relaxed, too relaxed. "Sure, man, that's what the lady said."

Ryder had little choice but to sit as the boat zoomed off, and hearing anything through the phone was a struggle with the rushing wind. But he didn't miss Luna's shout.

"I see him! Oh my gosh."

"Where is he hit?"

"His leg. Like, near the top."

"Is he conscious?"

"Hang on, hang on."

The next voice Ryder heard was Knox's, weak but coherent.

"They...took her. Fuckers took her."

He must mean Caro. Ryder cursed hard. Had they gone by land or by water? He scanned the sea for other vessels, but there was only a fishing boat on the horizon.

"Then let's get you fixed up so we can get her back. How bad are you hit, buddy?"

"Losing...blood. Not...an artery."

Another tiny piece of good news.

"I have the gauze," Luna said. "What do I do with it?"

"Cut Knox's shorts away. Find the wound."

"XSTAT," Knox said. "Find XSTAT."

Knox was in the best position to assess the wound, and he felt a different treatment would work better—tiny sponges impregnated with a clotting agent that were injected into the wound track and would expand and absorb to stop the bleeding.

"Luna, you're looking for a plastic tube, like a fat syringe. It's called XSTAT. Use the plunger to push the contents into the wound."

"I feel sick."

"If...if you need to puke...go over there," Knox told her, and his words were followed by a hissing groan. "Fuck, that stings."

"Now what?" Luna asked. "Should I use the gauze?"

"I'm less than five minutes away. Now we're looking for painkillers and a tourniquet."

A new voice came over the comms. "They're going to fucking pay for this."

Emmy managed to sound both furious and ice-cold at the same time, and Ryder knew one thing with certainty—he wouldn't want to be in the raiders' shoes when the boss arrived in San Gallicano.

"You did amazing, moon. Perfect."

She'd held it together until the cavalry arrived, a coastguard boat with medics on board, plus a dozen armed members of the Special Services Group, the paramilitary force that passed for an army in San Gallicano. When an EMT took the saline bag she'd been holding and told her they had everything under control, she'd sagged into Ryder's arms, and then the tears had come. Apart from quickly hugging Jubilee, she'd been clinging to him ever since. Not that he wanted her to let go. The cops had told them to wait in the girls' bunkhouse, the only place that hadn't been tainted by the armed gang.

"I thought I was going to die. I thought everyone was going to die."

"But they didn't, and a lot of that was thanks to you."

Baptiste was still alive, stable but concussed. Knox was high on ketamine and on his way to the OR. Caro... She'd put up a fight, but she was gone. Perhaps the dog had helped too—there was blood on Tango's muzzle.

The first thing Ryder had seen when they neared the sanctuary was the remains of Baptiste's boat, taking on water and listing badly to port. And when the wakeboat pulled up to the beach, he saw the scuff marks in the sand. The struggle. Caro had fought her captors in the hatchery, that part of the beach where turtle eggs were carefully reburied and monitored. They'd taken her and left six of their teammates behind. Five dead, one unconscious. Knox had taken out three of them with bullets to the head, and the giant in the fifth pool room with the spear sticking out his chest, Ryder had to assume that was Caro's handiwork. A fifth man lay face down in the dining room, but who had killed him was unclear—Luna said she'd fired at him, and he had a hole in his chest, but the neat double tap suggested Knox had also gotten involved. The sixth man in the kitchen, the one Luna had clocked with the kettle—twice, it turned out—had been loaded into an ambulance with skin peeling from his face.

"What will happen now? Am I gonna get arrested again?" Luna asked.

"No. But even if you were, I'd break you out of jail." Ryder kissed her hair. "I swear."

He'd wanted to go to the hospital with Knox, but Emmy told him to stay put. She was in New York with her jet en route to JFK, reading through the files and scheming as she waited to depart. A team was assembling in Virginia. Ryder didn't yet know who would be on it, but Emmy was seething, furious about an unprovoked attack, so she'd want justice to be swift and hard.

"You think the cops are dirty?" she'd asked.

"Some of them, at least."

"Then don't let them cover this up."

Ryder didn't plan on it.

"Where are we going to stay tonight?" Luna asked. "I mean, I'm not supposed to leave, but this is, like, a crime scene."

"I'm not sure yet."

"We can't just abandon the place. What about the turtles? Somebody has to feed the turtles. And why isn't anyone looking for Caro?"

Because nobody knew where the hell to start. She'd

vanished without a trace. And they weren't even certain whether she was the intended abductee. Right before the burned guy tried to grab Luna, she'd heard another man yell, "Get the woman." Had they planned to snatch her and ended up with Caro in a case of mistaken identity? Or was Caro a consolation prize, a desperate attempt not to leave empty-handed? Had they been trying for both girls and only managed to take one?

Knox might know, but he was in surgery. The bullet had gone through his thigh, missing his bone by a fraction of an inch and narrowly avoiding his femoral artery. Ryder didn't have any answers. Sure, they'd found the drives and the possible Cuba connection, but that still didn't explain why more than half a dozen armed men had attacked the sanctuary, conveniently when Ryder wasn't there. And when he thought harder about it, maybe they'd believed Knox wasn't there either? Jubilee had borrowed his ball cap and a bulky jacket to avoid being spotted, and as they drove to the ferry, she'd been slouched down in the passenger seat, fiddling with her phone. Had the enemy been watching? Had they expected to overrun the sanctuary without a fight?

"Wait with Jubilee, and I'll see what I can find out."

"Don't leave me here."

Ryder hugged her tightly. "You've seen enough dead bodies to last a lifetime."

"I'd rather wade through gore than leave your side right now."

He opened his mouth to argue, then decided against it. "Okay, moon. Okay."

Vince Fernandez was standing outside the dining room, talking to the police chief. Hard to trust either of them at this moment. Fernandez looked stressed, raking a hand through messy brown hair and frowning constantly. Concerned that kidnapping and attempted murder had happened on his watch? Or afraid that his links to the criminals would be discovered?

"Is there an update?" Ryder asked.

The chief looked him up and down. "We're not at liberty to discuss this case with civilians."

"We're civilians who had to deal with this for almost an hour by ourselves because the authorities in San Gallicano didn't have an appropriate response team. Our friend is still missing. Don't you think that's earned us the right to know what's going on?"

"We have procedures to follow."

"Procedures?" Luna snapped. "*Procedures?* I was sent here for the heinous crime of putting sunglasses on a turtle, and I told the judge I wasn't safe. But oh, no, he knew best and made me come anyway. Now a psycho tries to kidnap me, and you whine about procedures? You people put my life in danger! I'm going to sue the San Gallicano Police Department for every cent they have, and when I'm done, you won't be able to get a job as a mall cop."

"Ma'am, I—"

"Don't you 'ma'am' me. I'm not my freaking mother. Do your job, if you're even capable. Or are you corrupt too?"

"Ma'am, uh, miss, nobody in the San Gallicano Police Department is corrupt."

"Oh, really? Then explain why all the shooting happened at the *exact* time your officers had called my security away to take some dumb test for a drone permit."

She folded her arms and glared at the man, and Ryder had never loved her more.

Wait.

Did he *love* her?

When it came to Luna, Ryder's feelings were a mess, but he more than liked her. Yet their relationship, if you could call it that, was based on a lie, a lie that he'd been afraid to correct in case he lost her.

The chief glanced at Fernandez, and clearly, this was the first he'd heard about the drone permit. Fernandez tried to explain.

"Jason Roy called me to ask for Caro Menefee's number. Said a neighbour complained about a drone flying over his property, and peacekeeping was needed."

"Peacekeeping?" Luna spat. "Is that what you call this?"

Ryder laid a hand on her arm. "Officer Roy told Caro that if we didn't register for a permit right away, in person, he'd come over and confiscate the drone."

"Understandable," the chief said. "One of those things buzzed my wife by the pool last month, and we're trying to discourage recreational use. I sent out a directive."

"We weren't using it for recreational purposes. As Luna said, a man's been stalking her, and the drone was an important part of our security protocol. You confined us to this location, took away our eyes, and divided our team."

"So you're saying that this young lady's stalker was responsible for"—the chief waved a hand at the devastation —"all this?"

"We don't know. While we were here on the island, we became aware of poaching activity in the local area, and we started looking into it, seeing as the police department didn't have the capability to do so."

"Now, wait a minute..." Fernandez started. "I spent days on stakeouts whenever Caro told me about bait lines, but nobody ever came back to check on them."

"Yeah, funny that."

"Are you accusing me of something?"

"I'm just saying it's a mighty big coincidence that whenever we gave you a lead, that lead became a dead end."

"And that's all it can be—a coincidence. You think I'd

do anything to hurt Caro? She's a friend. A good friend. I'm as worried as you are, and standing here arguing isn't going to help us find her."

The chief held up both hands, stopping the fight. "You're right. Everyone needs to simmer down. Vince, you get on with your work. Mr. Metcalfe, Miss Puckett, wait in the bunkhouse, please. If you have a formal complaint to make about one of my officers, you need to follow proper procedure, and it will be investigated accordingly."

"I'm calling my lawyer," Luna snapped, but the chief just walked away.

This was a damn nightmare. They had carnage, but no clues. Bodies, but no names. Before the authorities showed up, Ryder had taken pictures of the intruders and sent them to Agatha. Blackwood would try to match names to the faces, well, three of them—the guy with the burns wasn't easily recognisable, and two of the gunmen Knox had flanked were missing chunks of their heads.

"Let me check in with my boss first. I bet she already hired a lawyer."

"You think? Because my lawyer isn't very good."

"Emmy Black only hires the best."

"Did you say Emmy Black?" a voice asked from behind. Ryder turned to find a member of the Special Services Group approaching, and he looked serious.

"You know her?"

"I know of her. How is she involved with this?"

"I work for Blackwood, and so does one of the men who got shot. She's pretty pissed."

"Man..." The guy shook his head. "I wouldn't want to be one of those assholes if she shows up."

"She'll be here by morning."

He gave a nervous laugh. "Wonder how soon I can catch a flight out of here?"

Ryder got the impression he was only half joking.

"Did you want something?" Fernandez asked the newcomer. Not quite a snap, but he was definitely riled after their earlier conversation.

"Yeah, so there's been...a development."

"What development?"

The guy glanced at Ryder and Luna, clearly unsure how much he should say in front of *civilians*. What did he know?

"Just spit it out," Fernandez ordered. "We have nothing to hide."

Another glance, but the guy did as instructed. "We think..." He swallowed. "We think we can identify one of the victims."

Ryder's anger came hot and fast. "The victims? Don't you mean the perpetrators?"

"It's the body without a face."

"Which body without the face?" Fernandez asked. "We have two of those."

"The one nearest the dining area."

The pro. Knox had managed to communicate the basic facts before he got carried away on a stretcher.

"You're talking about the dead gunman who was creeping toward Ms. Maara before he turned and attempted to shoot my colleague?"

"I don't know the exact circumstances of his death."

"Who is he?" Fernandez demanded.

"He's...he's one of us. Porter recognised his tattoos. The dead man is Sergeant Ellery Jackson from the Special Services Group."

A serving officer?

Fuck.

This mystery was more twisted than they'd ever imagined.

37

CARO

My head throbbed. My body prickled with pins and needles. I tried to open my eyes, then realised I'd already done that, and I was lying in the dark. Lying in the dark with my legs bound together and my hands tied in front of me.

Metal clinked, and I realised there was a chain involved somewhere.

How?

Why?

The room was spinning.

No, not spinning.

Swaying.

I was on a boat.

In the dark, on a boat.

My sludgy mind struggled to process the details. The horror.

Who did this boat belong to?

Gunfire. There had been gunfire. I remembered that part, or was I imagining it? Men with guns had come to the sanctuary. For Luna? She was the one in danger, she had the bodyguards, so why was I the one tied to...to what?

Body shaking, I worked my way along the chain, hand over hand, and found it secured around a pole by a padlock. I gave the pole a shake. Solid. And a strange texture. Like... like...metal covered in leather. I pulled myself to my feet. Followed the pole upward and found a mattress.

This was a cabin.

A cabin on a boat.

The lack of light, the not-so-muffled thrum of the engine, and the gentle rocking told me I was below decks in the crew quarters on a reasonable-sized yacht. Trying desperately not to throw up, I shuffled around the small room, bumping into things as I went, barely able to move my feet, feeling my way as best I could. Four beds, two up and two down, with a closet jutting out between them at the head end, plus a bathroom the size of a shoebox at the foot. Boxes. Wooden boxes piled on the bunks. I stubbed a toe before I found a light switch and flipped it on.

I saw what I'd expected to see, which was both a relief and a horror. Horror because I was trapped in a cabin. A tiny cabin decorated in shades of brown and beige. Relief because there wasn't a giant three-headed worm stuck in here with me, which wouldn't have been a total shock because this was hell on earth.

My legs had been wrapped in duct tape from knee to ankle, which was why I could only move my feet an inch at a time. Or hop. Or slither. A hysterical snort burst out of me —maybe *I* was the giant worm? Something dry yet slimy had been stuffed into my mouth, and there was more tape around my face. I tried to peel it away, but it was stuck to my hair, and every time I loosened an edge, my scalp screamed.

I took a closer look at my hands. My wrists had been bound with blue cord, and in case I got any ideas about picking the knot undone, the ends had been melted together into one hard plastic lump. The cord was attached to the chain, and I could just about reach the toilet if I stretched my hands out in front of me. At least there was toilet paper. The vaguest nod toward civility.

How long had I been on board? How long since these animals had snatched me from Valentine Cay? Another memory, another horror movie in my head: a behemoth of a man running toward me, arms outstretched, a gun tucked into his waistband. He'd pulled it out, aimed, but Tango had bitten his ankle. My plucky, brave little dog had done her best to defend me. The man had fired at her, and she'd run off into the forest, but the distraction gave me enough time to grab the nearest weapon to hand, which happened to be the speargun I occasionally used for hunting dinner. The behemoth had tried to pull the spear out of his chest, but not for long. He'd quickly lost strength. But before I could reload, one of his friends must have snuck up from behind, because I remembered holding the speargun against my chest and stretching back the elastic, and then everything went fuzzy for a moment. When my mind cleared, I was outside with two assholes dragging me across the sand toward a boat. I'd struggled, desperately trying to keep them from walking all over the hatchery, but my head hurt like hell, and my limbs wouldn't quite do what I wanted. More than human lives had been lost that day, but the others didn't matter to those monsters.

Then the man with the anchor tattoo had run over and jabbed a syringe of something nasty into my thigh.

Then darkness.

Then nothing.

And then I woke up here.

Wherever "here" was.

Knox! Where was Knox? Franklin? Luna? Franklin had

been in his cabin, still sick, and Knox had been wherever Luna was. Probably in the dining room. Knox knew how to use a gun, but the noise... The peaceful sanctuary had turned into a war zone. Had they been injured? Or worse? If I'd been scared before, now I was terrified.

Heartbroken.

I'd told Knox that our relationship was purely physical, but it had evolved into...more. As much as I could offer. If I'd been free of Aiden, I'd have given Knox all of me.

Wait, maybe he was on the yacht too? In a different room? I wanted to believe that, I did, but I still feared the worst. Fingers shaking, I tried again with the tape, beyond caring whether I ripped my hair out. If I could shout, would someone answer?

The pitch of the engine changed, and before I could catch myself, I tumbled forward onto my knees. The yacht was slowing. Why? Where were we? Still in San Gallicano? We could have travelled to a different island, a different country.

How long would it take for anyone to realise I was missing? If Knox and Franklin and Luna were gone, then my hopes rested on Ryder and Jubilee. Hours could have passed before they returned from Malavilla. Jubilee had been excited to go shopping, and it wouldn't have surprised me if she stopped to browse in the stores near the harbour, the ones that sold overpriced souvenirs and trinkets and a hundred other things nobody needed.

For now at least, I was on my own.

38

KNOX

K nox crawled through the trees, dragging his injured leg behind him. Flames burned through his thigh, licking at his insides in white-hot bursts of pain. The dark-haired assassin followed, laughing. They both knew Knox was a dead man. Finally, the assassin had enough of toying with his prey and raised his gun. His finger tightened on the trigger.

Beep. Beep. Beep.

Wait.

Guns didn't go *beep.*

Knox forced his eyes open, then quickly closed them again when the bright lights above made his head pound. The beeping carried on, and the smell of antiseptic told Knox where he was. The hospital.

"Welcome back," Emmy said.

He just groaned.

"Good news. The bullet that hit you was a nine-millimetre full metal jacket, and it went right through. Blood loss aside, you were pretty lucky."

"Where's Caro?"

"We're still working on that."

Knox tried to sit up, but Emmy pushed him down again. "Don't even think about walking out of here. The best thing you can do to help is avoid busting your stitches open and talk to us."

Us?

Knox turned his head to the side and saw Emmy wasn't alone. Black was there, her husband, an ice-capped mountain of a man who scared the shit out of everyone except Emmy. And possibly Rafael, his nephew, who came out of the same mould and was standing next to him, alongside Sky, Emmy's teenage protégé. A real family affair.

"Xav, Dan, and Slater are on Valentine Cay, bugging the police."

"The police...are corrupt."

At least Emmy had brought reinforcements. Dan was one of Blackwood's best investigators, second only to Black, and Slater was a sneaky motherfucker. Xav...was an unknown quantity. He wasn't a Blackwood employee, but he did occasional contract work, and rumour said he used to date Emmy. Rumour also said he was former Israeli special forces and could kill a man without breaking a sweat.

"Corrupt? Yeah, we got that much from Ryder, but one of them—Vince Fernandez—claims to be as concerned as we are. He's promised transparency."

"He's...shady."

Knox's throat felt as if he'd swallowed a bag of nine-inch nails. Every word hurt.

"I understand that. We're treating the information he provides as suspect, but so far, it checks out. Plus he's giving us access to the crime scene, and I'm not about to cut my nose off to spite my face. Knox, we need your input. Ryder and Agatha have told us everything they know, but you were closer to this poaching thing."

"It was...poachers?"

"Are you asking me or telling me?"

"Don't know for sure...who it was. But they knew we were...tracking them."

Emmy held up a glass of water with a straw. "Drink. It'll help your throat. You want me to get you more painkillers?"

"Just the water."

It was cool, and as he sipped slowly, the fire that flared every time he spoke settled to a smoulder. Whoever intubated him hadn't been gentle. Maybe the force had been necessary. Or maybe the nurses had been to the same training school as the San Gallicano PD. Knox wasn't feeling particularly charitable toward the authorities right now.

"We've pieced together a reasonable amount." Emmy nodded to the side, and Knox shifted to see a giant whiteboard on wheels at the end of the bed. He recognised the not-so-neat writing covering it as Black's. "There are three suspects, and as of this moment, we can't eliminate any of them. Luna's stalker, because they tried to take her too, and we know from the messages he sent that he's in the area. Caro's ex-boyfriend, and wasn't that a fuck-up? Walking down the Strip in a bikini?" Emmy shook her head in disbelief. "And then the clear favourite—the poachers. I get them being twitchy, but fuck me, there must be a whole lot of money in dead turtles if that's their reaction."

"They chop them up and sell all the bits," Sky said. "Jewellery made from the shells, leather doohickeys made from the skin, turtle soup made from the insides. Or sometimes they just stuff them and sell them whole. Agatha found a picture of this punch bowl where—"

"Okay, we get the picture."

"It was gross."

Black wasn't an expressive man, but his lip curled in the

faintest expression of disgust. Whether at the fate of the turtles or at Sky's description of it, Knox wasn't sure.

"Until we can eliminate two of the possible suspects," he said, "we're having to split our resources, which is far from ideal. The cyber team is working on the poaching case—the Havana connection, the names from Monique Constantine's client records, and the flash drives—and pressure on the police to clean house will be applied from the top. That leaves us to work the other two angles and either rule them out or track down the culprits. Starting with the ex, I understand that Caro Menefee isn't actually Caro Menefee?"

Knox shook his head. "She isn't."

"So what's her real name?"

"She never told me."

"I thought the two of you were fucking?"

"We were." Was that an eye-roll? "I suppose you've never fucked a woman without knowing her full name and social security number?"

"Never more than once."

Knox glanced at Emmy. Credit to her, her expression didn't falter.

"Well, I didn't push her, okay? She wasn't fond of talking about her past, and I figured she'd tell me in her own time. But I know the Caro part is real, and the ex is Aiden."

"That's a start. Agatha informs me that Caro Menefee also exists, and your Caro adopted her background."

His Caro. "Yes."

"So that leaves us with two possibilities. Either she randomly searched for a woman with an appropriate age, name, and background and came up with a party girl from California, or she was already familiar with Caro Menefee and knew she'd offer a suitable donor identity. If she chose the first option, that makes things more challenging for us, but would also have made things difficult for her. Vance Webber from the LA office is searching for the real Caroline Menefee so we can check out the second option. Is Franklin Baptiste awake yet?"

Emmy shook her head. "Not yet."

"We'll need to speak with him as soon as he is. He spent more time with Caro than anyone."

Knox swallowed through the pain and spoke again. "He did, and they're on good terms, but I got the impression that she always kept him at arm's length. More colleagues than family."

"Which struck you as odd given their living situation?"

"From the beginning, until I got to know her. She doesn't like to let anyone in."

Not even Knox. She'd accepted his offer of help because she had no other choice, not because she trusted him. And perhaps she'd been right not to trust him? If she'd left town when she wanted to, right after Luna's Instagram post, she wouldn't have been abducted. And if he'd—

"Don't do it," Emmy warned.

"Do what?"

"Blame yourself, think about what-might-have-beens, whatever shit's going through that head of yours." Guilty as charged. "Focus on the future, not the past. The stalker— you and Ryder didn't see him, feel him, spot him with the drone?"

"No, and we didn't see any other drones either. Nor did Lyron—he would've kicked off, no question. But there's no way a stalker could have sent such personal messages unless he was close."

Emmy said not to dwell on the past, but how could Knox avoid that? He was losing his touch. First, he'd failed to pinpoint a stalker they knew was nearby, and then he'd been oblivious to the attack on the sanctuary until it was too late.

"What was Luna's reaction to the stalker?" Black asked.

"In the beginning after she found out, she didn't seem too bothered. Acted as if it was a minor inconvenience, treated Ryder and me like servants rather than bodyguards, at least until Ryder charmed her. But the last threat, she was worried about that. I think she'd started to feel safe at the sanctuary, and the intrusion shook her. Ryder says she's not the woman everyone thinks she is. At first, I thought he was bullshitting, but when she stopped playing to an invisible audience, she became human."

"Until she outed Caro on social media?"

"At the time, I was angry with her, damn furious, and her verbal apology wasn't worth shit. But over the next few days, she kept her head down and worked rather than whining, and I think that was as close to an apology as she could manage. She's rich and famous and she can be a bitch, but underneath it all, she's socially awkward as fuck."

"Interesting. And whose idea was the infamous post? I understand Jubilee runs Luna's social media accounts?"

"I assumed Luna thought of it—she was on board with the bikini thing. And even if it was Jubilee's idea, I doubt Luna would have admitted it. Luna's weirdly protective over her, Kory too, that little jackass. The sunglasses-on-the-turtle thing that landed her in court was his idea, and Luna took the heat."

"More interesting. An unexpected conscience. Was the stalker ever mentioned on social media?"

"I'm not sure. I don't think so. Luna's team kept her in the dark about his existence until last month."

"Another question for the research team." Black

checked his watch. "I propose we set the necessary wheels in motion, then get some rest and regroup in the morning."

"What time is it?"

"Nearly two a.m."

"I'm surprised the staff let you stay."

He smiled faintly. "It's funny how attitudes can change when the paediatric unit's fundraiser suddenly reaches its target."

Black, Sky, and Rafael filed out, but Emmy lagged behind. Instead of leaving, she perched on the edge of the bed and straightened the blankets. Friend or not, the fact that she wanted to talk left Knox more uncomfortable than the bullet wound did. He knew he'd pushed boundaries on this job. Getting involved with Caro, going after a band of poachers instead of staying focused on the principal...

"How are you feeling?" Emmy asked.

"Not too bad. Think they gave me the good stuff for the pain."

"I meant, how are you *feeling*? And don't give me some bullshit about this being just another day at work."

"How do I feel? My girl is missing, and I fucked up. I feel like shit." Knox closed his eyes. Took a deep breath, and even that hurt. "I'm sorry."

"Sorry for what?"

"For getting distracted. I was here with a client, and I paid more attention to Caro than to Luna."

"Yeah, well, I think Ryder's paying enough attention to Luna for the both of you. And she said you were with her at the start of the incident, that you only left to go check a sensor. Is that right?"

"Things are fuzzy, but I remember the sensors going off. Three of them, one after the other. I should have gone back to her then. I should have—"

"What did I say about the past? Forget it. Apparently, Ryder told Luna that if a man ever tried to hurt her again, then she should fight back. That's why she beaned one of the fuckers with a kettle. And when he started to wake up a minute later, she did it again, but harder. Broke his damn skull. The docs can't say if he'll ever wake up."

"She did good."

"She did. And she's upset, but she's also not complaining, which is a miracle and also a relief."

"Where is she?"

"At a hotel along the street with Ryder and Jubilee. When I left, the two girls were passed out in the same bed, and Ryder was watching over them. Xav will take a shift later so Ryder can get some shuteye." Emmy raised her gaze to the ceiling. "Assuming Ryder will let him. He's taking it worse than you are."

"But he wasn't even there."

"Exactly. He could hear the gunfire, and he couldn't do a damn thing to stop it. He ended up on the phone with Luna while Jubilee commandeered a boat. Lyron kept Franklin alive while Luna went to find you."

"Fucking Lyron. If he hadn't complained about the drone—"

"They would have found another moment to strike. Whoever it was, you—and I mean the collective 'you,' not you personally—must have really touched a nerve."

"It has to be the poachers."

"I'm inclined to agree with you. But if some asshole with deep pockets and the connections to hire a team of trigger-happy lunatics was sprung for Luna and saw her cavorting with Ryder... Unrequited love can send a person insane." Emmy patted Knox on the leg—thankfully not the one with the gunshot wound—and rose to her feet in one smooth motion. "Get some sleep. We're a team, and we're going to fix this. Shit happens, and instead of beating yourself up and slipping over in it again, you need to focus on getting better. I'll see you in the morning."

She turned off the lights, and the door clicked shut behind her.

39

KNOX

"Carolina Raylene Klein," Dan announced. She'd shown up at the hospital in a burnt-orange skirt that was more of a belt, biker boots, and a tank top that struggled to contain her boobs. So, her normal attire. "Born and raised in California, thirty years old. Nearly thirty-one."

Knox tried to sit up in bed, but the pain medication had worn off, and even shuffling a few inches was an effort.

"That's her? That's Caro?"

"Vance caught the real Caroline Menefee as she fell out of a cab at four a.m. this morning, Pacific time. It took him another two hours to sober her up enough to look at a mugshot. Luna and Jubilee provided a selection."

Black sipped from a mug of coffee. "I hope Vance gave Caroline advice about not getting accosted on the street by strangers."

"Yup, and I understand he was very tactful. He's still there now, making her breakfast and cleaning up vomit in the bathroom, so I expect information will continue to trickle in. But we have the basics. The two Caros went to high school together until Caroline got asked to leave at the end of her junior year."

"What did she do?" Emmy asked. "Just curious."

"Slept with the football coach. Vance says Caroline's talkative when she's under the influence, and she kept whining because the coach kept his job while she had to find a new school."

"I can actually see her point there."

"Same, but the football team was top of the league and Caroline was bottom of the class, so I guess it was a no-brainer. Plus the family didn't want to be the centre of a scandal, so it all got swept under the carpet."

Irrelevant when it came to events in San Gallicano. "Can we get back to Caro?"

"Sure. So, Caroline and Carolina still bumped into each other over the years—they ran in different social circles but had mutual acquaintances, plus they had common ground academically. Not in terms of ability—Caroline attended the University of Coastal California for shits and giggles, while Carolina headed to Stanford on a scholarship." Stanford? Knox's girl was smart, but he already knew that. "Caroline scraped through her degree in marine biology because she liked going to the beach, while Carolina has a bachelor's degree with distinction, major in management science and engineering, minor in biology. They used to chat about the ocean. Caroline graduated and went to parties. Carolina graduated and went right back to Stanford —she also has an MBA and a CPA. The last Caroline heard, she was working for some yacht company and dating a rich guy named Aiden. Caroline described him as hot, charming, and way out of Carolina's league, no offence."

Knox took offence on Caro's behalf. Nobody was out of her league. In fact, she was out of his. An MBA? He'd barely graduated from high school.

"Surname for Aiden?" Black asked.

"We have a possible. When we searched yacht companies in California, Providence suggested AquaLux Yachts, with a former chief operating officer by the name of Aiden Kingsley."

"Can we get a picture to Caroline?"

"We're trying to find one."

"Nothing on the company website?"

"Here's the thing—it nearly went under three years ago. Tax fraud. Three senior staff ended up in prison."

"Kingsley?"

"Not Aiden Kingsley," Dan said. "Don Kingsley, the CEO. Older guy, so possibly Aiden's father. The other two were the finance director and the financial controller, different surnames so probably not part of the family. The guy who owns AquaLux now—one Carlos Davila—says he bought the name and some of the assets and knows nothing about the rest. We're trying to get hold of someone at the IRS who might be able to give us more information."

Three years ago? Knox did the math, but not as fast as Caro would have. "You think Caro got caught up in the fraud?"

Or worse, had she been a part of it? Was she on the run? Was that why she'd come to Valentine Cay and cut off communication with the outside world? Knox dismissed the thought as soon as he'd had it. Caro wasn't a thief. She was a liar—she'd admitted that—but if she was rolling in stolen tax money, she wouldn't be living in a curtained-off corner of a communal bunkhouse and darning holes in her shorts.

"It's possible, but the article in the local paper mentioned a whistleblower." Dan gave him a questioning look. "What do you think?"

Caro had been terrified of Aiden catching up with her. Scared enough to blow up at Luna over a five-second video clip and prepare to flee the country. All this time, Knox had assumed that her ex was just a controlling asshole, but what if there was more to it? What if she'd sent his father to prison?

"I think she's more likely to be a whistleblower than a thief. Where's Aiden Kingsley now?"

"We're working on that. His last known address was in Malibu."

Emmy pushed forward off the wall she'd been leaning against since she arrived. "We'll continue to work on this angle, but realistically, how likely is it that Aiden suddenly showed up here? Does he have any connections to San Gallicano?"

"I asked her that once," Knox said, dredging up the memory from the depths of his still-sludgy brain. "She said the two of them took a trip here, that he liked to travel. I assumed at the time that she meant a vacation, but if he was in the yacht business, maybe they came for work? He could have a few contacts."

"Even so, I'd put him third on the suspect list. Poachers at the top, then the stalker, then Aiden Kingsley."

"Second," Black said in a rare moment of disagreement with his wife.

It seemed to surprise her too. "Second?"

"I have an idea about the stalker."

"Oh?"

"Let's pay a visit to our client."

40

LUNA

"We should be feeding the turtles," I told Ryder. "Who's feeding the turtles?"

Okay, so I hadn't exactly been a fan of the turtles when I first came to San Gallicano, but they'd grown on me. They were kind of cute, the way they waited for their dinner, and they moved through the water with a weird grace. And as long as you didn't stick your hand near their mouth, they were harmless. Plus they helped the environment. They were predator, host, and prey. Who knew sea creatures could be so complicated?

Not me.

Not until this month, anyway.

Each species preferred to eat a particular diet. Hawksbills kept fast-growing sponges from overwhelming the reefs. Green turtles snacked on seagrass and stopped it from getting too long. Leatherbacks kept the jellyfish population under control. Loggerheads ate crustaceans and the digested shells added nutrients to the sea bottom. The turtles were a habitat in themselves—small creatures lived on them, and fish liked to eat those. In turn, birds and fish ate the baby turtles, and bigger creatures such as sharks and killer whales ate the adults. Plus land animals feasted on the eggs, which was why we needed to collect them and bring them to the hatchery at the sanctuary.

The hatchery. Those jerks who shot at us had trampled over the little piles of buried eggs, and when I'd carefully uncovered them with Jubilee, we'd found that Knox and Caro weren't the only victims of the raid.

And maybe it was my fault. Ryder said there were three suspects—the poachers, Caro's ex-boyfriend, and my stalker. At first, I hadn't worried about the man sending nasty messages. I mean, it wasn't exactly hard to spew bile through an online comments form—people did it all the time, and looking back, I couldn't even blame them. I'd done some really dumb things, caught up in an endless quest for likes and attention in a fruitless attempt to make other people happy. But what about me? Had I ever truly been happy? It had taken time on Valentine Cay and all those late-night chats with Ryder to find the answer. To realise that things had to change. *I* had to change them. If I walked right back into my old life as everyone expected, I'd be miserable forevermore.

But now? Now, I was scared. What if I'd brought this chaos to the sanctuary? Franklin was in the hospital, fighting for his life in the ICU, and he was a nice old guy. He didn't say much, but he'd always been kind. Caro was gone. Just gone. She hadn't wanted me there, and maybe she'd been right when she said I was trouble.

The walls closed in as I paced the tiny hotel room. Usually, I stayed in a suite, but this place didn't have suites. The best they could do was a twin deluxe. Which was far from deluxe, but at least Ryder was there to stop any mercenaries from breaking down the door, and Tango was dozing on a blanket by the window, instantly alert at the slightest sound. The dog had grown on me too. I'd never spent time with a dog before, but she seemed to sense when I was super sad and licked my hand.

"Detective Fernandez promised he'd take care of it," Ryder said from his perch on the desk.

"Detective Fernandez? No, that won't work."

Firstly, I didn't trust him. I might not have graduated high school, but I wasn't as dumb as people said. At least, I didn't think I was. Anyhow, the police had called Ryder away, and suddenly people with guns showed up? Right. A total coincidence. And secondly, if Detective Fernandez was feeding the turtles, then who was looking for Caro? He wasn't a great detective, but anyone was better than no one.

"He's volunteered at the sanctuary in the past, and he says he knows what food to use."

"If he's as good at animal care as he is at detecting, he'll end up poisoning the turtles."

Ryder choked out a laugh. "He wouldn't dare to do that with all the eyes on him right now."

"You think?"

"President Harrison called the Prime Minister of San Gallicano and piled on the pressure. The police chief is probably shitting himself."

"Really? The president called? How do you know that?"

"Trade secret."

"I hate this. I hate being stuck here."

Jubilee looked up from her laptop. "Why don't you watch TV? The new series of *The Electi* just came out on Netflix."

I used to watch so much TV, but that was when the most important thing in the world of Luna Maara had been my next TikTok video. I couldn't go back to that life. I *couldn't*. And I had no idea how to explain that to Mom when she got released from jail.

"I don't want to watch Netflix. When can we get out of this place?"

"Kory's on his way back with the *Cleopatra*, and the lawyer has an appointment with Judge Morgan to try and get your sentence shortened. If he agrees, then we'll be able to leave the island right away."

"Leave? I'm not leaving. Not leaving San Gallicano, I mean. I just hate this hotel. It smells weird."

Like old tobacco and Lysol. Hadn't these people heard of fragrance diffusers?

Jubilee's brow creased. She was definitely going to get wrinkles.

"You want to stay? But—"

"Of course I want to stay." Okay, so it would be good if we could skip town before Mom got out of jail, but I needed Ryder to keep me safe, and he wanted to stay with Knox. "Caro's still missing."

"But you don't even like Caro."

I hadn't at first, but after a rocky beginning, she'd been civil. And even if she hadn't been super friendly, she'd been happy to teach me about turtles. Maybe we *would* have become friends if I hadn't given Jubilee the go-ahead to post that stupid video?

"I don't *not* like her."

There was a knock at the door, and when Ryder didn't leap up with a gun in his hand, I had to assume it was one of his colleagues. Probably Black. Which was a weird name, but it suited him because he had dark hair, dark eyes, and a dark aura. Mom said the aura thing was baloney, but I felt what I felt. Anyhow, Ryder said that Black would be coming by to ask more questions, which was pointless because I didn't have any answers, but I'd sit here and listen if it made them happy. Perhaps there would be some news about Caro?

Ryder checked the peephole, then opened the door, and yes, it was the giant. The blonde woman was with him, Emmy, Ryder's boss, the one who made me nervous. He kept his distance from me when they walked in, and I understood why. I'd had enough bodyguards to know that they weren't meant to spend their evenings floating in the sea with their clients, holding hands as they gazed up at the star-freckled sky.

"Any news?" Ryder asked.

Emmy dropped into the chair by the window. "Information is flowing in, but we're no closer to finding Caro."

The giant stayed on his feet. Was he trying to intimidate me? Julius often did that, and it usually worked.

"At the moment, we're having to spread our resources three ways, so we want to get to the bottom of the stalker mystery," he said. "When did you first start receiving messages?"

"I don't know. Nobody told me about them until last month."

Maybe I should have pushed for more details, but honestly, I hadn't wanted to know. Knox and Ryder were there to keep me safe, so what did it matter if there were two messages or two hundred?

"Uh, the first one came in January last year," Jubilee said. "Right after Luna's wardrobe malfunction at the Crystal Beach New Year Party."

Now, that was a night I didn't want to remember. I'd been singing in front of an audience of two thousand, a small crowd by my standards but plenty big enough that there were a hundred videos of the incident. Halfway through the first verse of "Poison," the strap of my halter top gave way, and the flimsy piece of silver cloth succumbed to the lure of gravity. I'd finished the song with a fake grin on my face and one arm clamped over my boobs because what else could I do? Weep in front of the world? I could still picture Jubilee's look of horror as she watched from the wings, holding out a sweaty T-shirt she'd persuaded a poor sound tech to part with. Mom, on the other hand, said I'd handled the situation perfectly. That coverage was through the roof—of the show, obviously, not my boobs—and that little faux pas had probably made me a quarter mil.

Off stage, I'd berated the costume designer, something I wasn't proud of, but it was either yell or cry. And after she examined the garment and basically accused me of unpicking the stitching myself, I'd yelled some more and then run to the bathroom to hide before the tears came. Now I checked the seams on every single costume before I left the dressing room.

"That was the message that said Luna was asking for it, and soon she'd get what she deserved?"

Jubilee glanced in my direction but wouldn't meet my gaze. "Yes."

"And the second message?"

"It came after the Glitz Awards."

Right. Mom had agreed to a collab with an up-and-coming designer, and I ended up wearing a dress made from cotton candy. And do you know what happens when cotton candy gets wet? It freaking melts. Some dumb-ass comedian threw an ice bucket full of water over me as I walked past his table, and I was left standing there in pink lace lingerie. I held it together long enough to collect my award and wave as I exited stage left in ankle-breaking pumps, then I kicked off the shoes and ran. Ran until I slammed into Red Bennett in a corridor and he wrapped me up in his leather jacket and half carried me back to my dressing room.

"And that one said, 'Next time, I'll be the one to wrap

you in a jacket and carry you back home. Then I'll lick you clean and show you what you've been missing.'"

"Yes."

My spine turned to ice. The part with the jacket, that had been private. Nobody knew except a few venue staff, Red Bennett, and my family. And my stalker. I opened my mouth to say something, but all that came out was a sob. I saw Ryder's hands ball into fists.

"That was when Amethyst decided to hire bodyguards," Jubilee said. "But the first ones weren't very good."

Understatement. They were big men, big intimidating men, bigger even than Black. And not in such good shape either. Joe and Harry. Joe never went anywhere without a burger in his hand, and when a pervert walked right up to me and exposed himself, Harry was too busy taking a selfie with a fan to notice. Not until I screamed, anyway. What did I scream? I screamed, "You're fired."

"I've read through the messages," Black said. "And a common theme is that all except the first one contain snippets of information that only someone close to Luna would know. Correct?"

Jubilee gulped and nodded.

"But nobody's ever spotted a common face in the crowd?"

"No."

"Not one of these professional bodyguards has ever raised concerns about a man who's too still, too close, or too interested?"

"Nuh-uh, not that they ever said."

"We've had two highly trained operators specifically looking for threats for the past month. They've used electronic surveillance devices in addition to their own senses, and they haven't spotted anything either. What does that tell you?"

Jubilee squirmed in her seat, and I began to get a tiny bit annoyed. I wasn't paying these people to make my cousin, my best friend, uncomfortable.

"It tells me that the stalker is craftier than you people," I snapped, then wished I hadn't because I'd accidentally insulted Ryder.

"You know what it tells me?"

"No, but I'm sure you're going to let us know."

Emmy's lips twitched, and I wasn't sure whether she was annoyed or amused. I hoped she wasn't annoyed. She scared me more than I'd ever admit.

"It tells me there isn't a stalker at all."

"Then who's sending the messages?"

"Perhaps Jubilee can tell us." He turned back to her. "Go ahead."

"How would she know? She's not a freaking detective. Literally nobody on this whole island is capable of solving a crime."

I looked to Ryder, hoping for support, knowing I wouldn't get any because he was in an impossible position. He wouldn't choose me over his bosses. As I expected, he didn't say a word.

Emmy huffed out a sigh. "Let's quit with the subtle approach. Luna, there are only three people who stay close to you the whole time. You, Jubilee, and your mother. A month ago, my money would have been on your mom because, let's face it, she's a real piece of work, but she doesn't have internet access in jail. We checked. Which means you or Jubilee sent those messages. Do you have something you want to tell us?"

She'd lost her mind. The B-I-T-C-H had lost her freaking mind. "You're crazy! You're all crazy. Caro's missing, and you're in here accusing—"

"It wasn't me," Jubilee whispered, so quietly I almost missed the words. "It was Cordelia."

Emmy just chuckled. "Damn, we were close, but no cigar."

Was Jubilee serious? That filth had come out of *Lady* Cordelia's head? I almost couldn't believe it, and yet...and yet it was exactly the sort of nasty thing she'd do.

"Tell us what happened," Black ordered. "The whole story, start to finish."

Jubilee wouldn't look at me, not even a glance. "Cordelia and I, we talk sometimes. She worries about Luna."

"Worries about me? Worries that I'll damage her precious reputation, more like."

"She thinks you're self-destructive."

"You think I wanted some idiot to throw a bucket of water over me?"

"There were rumours that you paid him to do it."

I spun away, anger balancing on the cusp of hurt. The way she said that...

"And you believed them?"

"He said someone paid him ten thousand dollars."

"Well, it wasn't me. I don't even know how to work a stupid ATM. What was I going to do? Ask my accountant to mail a cheque?"

"Cordelia just wanted you to...cover up a bit. And I didn't totally agree with her on everything because why shouldn't you wear a bathing suit, but..." Jubilee sucked in a shaky breath. "She said it would be for the best if I helped her. That you'd thank us eventually. I know you don't like that the Duke of Southcott is your father, but he did pay so much money in child support when we were little, and without that, what would we have done?"

"I don't know, maybe Mom could have gotten a second job instead of taking me to pageants every weekend?"

"But you loved dressing up."

"No, I loved not getting yelled at. Do you know how much I envied you, being allowed to stay with a neighbour and your books while I had to prance around in swimwear and smile until my face hurt?"

"You...you never said anything."

"I was a child! Whenever I said something negative, I got a lecture, and it was easier to just sing or dance or whatever. And now I'm in so deep I can never get out. Do you know what would happen if I quit? If I walked away from showbiz? People would still follow me. They'd still take pictures and scream my name, except then I'd be 'Luna Maara, failed pop star.' And Mom would probably send me to rehab again."

"I thought you said rehab gave you a new perspective?"

"It was bullshit!" I was screaming now. Screaming and swearing. I clapped a hand over my mouth, relieved when nobody told me off for using foul language. "I just say whatever people want to hear because it's the only way to get out of there. You never got locked up that way. You went to school, and the mall, and the movies. You have friends. You can talk to boys."

Okay, so the "talk to boys" part I didn't envy, especially since her on-again, off-again beau was a little twerp named Benji who somehow managed to be both creepy and super boring at the same time. Thankfully, they were "off" at the moment.

"But you always said you didn't like boys."

"That's not the freaking point!"

Black's cadence didn't change. His voice never rose beyond that soft tone I'd have struggled to hear over the sound of the sea.

"Why don't we give Luna some space?" He hooked a finger at Jubilee. "That means you."

Tears were rolling down her cheeks now, and she opened her mouth as if she wanted to argue, but Black didn't strike me as a man used to being disobeyed. She must have sensed that too, because she picked up her purse and trudged to the door.

A part of me, the part that had leaned on Jubilee for so many years, that had confided in her and shielded her, laughed, cried, and dreamed with her, ached that she looked so broken. But she'd lied to me. Betrayed me. Sided with a half-sister who hated me, and why? Because I showed too much flesh for my stuck-up sperm donor's comfort? I didn't even pick my own clothes.

The door clicked closed, and Ryder reached me in four long strides. I collapsed into his arms.

"How are you feeling?" he asked.

"Like I want to put on a cotton candy bikini and pole dance in front of my father's gates."

"In the rain?"

Ryder got me. He really got me. I hadn't felt this comfortable around anyone in...well, forever.

"Yes, and upload the video to every social media channel that won't ban me for breaching community standards."

He hugged me tighter, and I rested my head against his hard chest, feeling the steady beat of his heart against my cheek.

"Thank you for being here," I murmured. "I mean like this, not just because I'm paying you to be. You're the one person in my life who hasn't lied to me or taken advantage of me, or both."

His heart beat faster, speeding up to match my own.

"I'll always be here for you, moon."

"And then there were two."

Emmy leaned back in her seat and bit into a jelly donut. Knox had just swallowed the last mouthful of his own. Technically, he shouldn't have been eating a donut in the hospital, but Sky discovered that one of the nurses had a son who owned a donut stand and put in an order for three hundred. Now everyone in the damn building was eating donuts—doctors and nurses, admin staff and janitors, visitors and patients.

"Jubilee?" he asked. "You're serious?"

Emmy had finished telling the story of the stalker, and Knox was kicking himself. But who would have thought Jubilee would betray Luna like that? The two of them seemed so close. Was Jubilee jealous of her cousin? Was that why she'd done it? Or did she just have incredibly bad judgment?

"Yup, deadly."

Emmy was always deadly.

"I bet Luna's upset about that."

"I cheated and left Ryder to deal with her. She stopped screeching after we left, so I'm taking that as a good sign."

"Where's Jubilee?"

"We sent her to the sanctuary with Slater. She can clean up turtle shit or whatever."

"Is that safe?"

"Safe enough. The place is still full of cops and crime scene techs, plus there are twenty reporters outside the gates. It would take a special kind of stupid to sail in and start another shoot-out, especially after they lost the last one so spectacularly."

"What access do we have at the sanctuary?" Knox asked.

"Full access, now that the bodies have been removed. Fernandez knows he's out of his depth, so he basically lifted the crime scene tape and told us to have at it."

"I don't trust him."

"Neither do I, not completely," Emmy said. "But we need to know what the police are doing, and he's obliging when it comes to providing information."

"What if it's misinformation?"

"It's a starting point. We're cross-checking with other sources. And either he's the world's best actor, or he's genuinely cut up about Caro."

"If he's involved, he's been lying for years, so he's had plenty of practice."

"True. But there are other possible traitors—he says he told two people about the shark thing and the boat, Officers Roy and Beattie. Roy conveniently removed Ryder from the scene when the sanctuary was raided, and Beattie has a brother named David. Didn't you mention there was a David involved?"

"That was the name I overheard on the beach."

"Fernandez also wrote everything up and sent it to his boss—who is literally called Captain Boss—but he doesn't think Boss bothered to read the report until after the raid. Apparently, he didn't see turtle poaching as a high priority."

"Does he now?"

"I believe so. And if he still needs a push to get off his arse and do his job, Black's working to incentivise that."

"Did he really get James Harrison involved?"

"No, that was me. And I also asked a friend to have a word in the French president's ear, so I guess the prime minister will be getting another call this morning. Did you know that Franklin Baptiste's mum was born in Paris? He has dual citizenship."

Emmy was cunning *and* connected. Thank fuck they were on the same side.

"No, he never mentioned that."

The door crashed open, hit the wall, and bounced back into Dan, who was entering ass-first with a tray of coffee.

"Dammit!" she yelped.

Emmy leaped to help her, probably more out of concern for the caffeine than for her partner in crime.

"Got it."

"They only had decaf."

"Are you kidding me?"

Dan held her "I'm sorry" expression for three and a half seconds before her face creased into laughter.

"Of course I'm kidding. You really think I'd come in here with decaf? I don't want to die." She picked up a paper cup, then cursed again as spilled coffee dripped from the bottom. "We have a call with the IRS in two minutes."

"Cheating on your taxes again?"

"Ha-ha. I managed to get hold of the investigator in charge of the AquaLux case, and he's agreed to speak with us. Tony Goddard. Dana from the San Diego office was acquainted with him, so she did the intros."

The hospital room looked more like a conference room.

A table, half a dozen swivel chairs, and a large screen had appeared while Knox was in the bathroom, and everyone had a laptop. Dan hit a few keys on hers, and Tony Goddard conferenced in from somewhere in California, but he'd changed his background to a Swiss ski resort—Knox recognised the distinctive peak of the Matterhorn. Zermatt was the dream right now. After this trip, Knox never wanted to see the damn beach again.

Introductions were made. Tony Goddard was a slender man in his late fifties, and judging by the deep lines etched into his tanned forehead, he'd spent most of his life frowning. Wispy salt-and-pepper hair curled around his ears, and his bald head gleamed under harsh government lighting.

"I understand you have questions about the AquaLux case?"

Emmy let Dan take the lead. "We do."

"Much of the information was already made public during the trial."

"We're not interested in the nuts and bolts of the case, only in Carolina Klein's relationship with the main players. Specifically Aiden Kingsley. Dana mentioned to you that Caro has been abducted?"

"Abducted? She said Caro had gone missing, but she didn't elaborate on the circumstances. Abducted? Are you sure?"

"Unfortunately, yes. One of our team was shot in the process."

Knox's left thigh twinged at the mention. If the bullet had hit an inch to the right, the doctors said, Emmy would be planning a funeral and not a search-and-rescue operation. Although she'd probably delegate the task to Bradley, and Knox would end up with a glitter-topped casket and fireworks instead of a cremation. Would his mom even show up? He did love her still, his mom, but she'd chosen the bottle over him. Preferred oblivion to her own flesh and blood.

"Your team?" Goddard asked. "Blackwood was providing security for Caro?"

"No, our presence was a coincidence. Our client and Caro were both volunteering at a turtle sanctuary in the Caribbean. We're not certain who the main target was, and we have two suspects for the abduction—a band of local poachers and Aiden Kingsley. Truthfully, the poachers seem more likely, but Caro was scared of Aiden, and there's a possibility her location was recently revealed on social media. So we can't rule him out yet."

"I see. Well, I'm not giving away any secrets when I say he's a real asshole. The consummate businessman on the outside, as crooked as they come underneath."

"But he didn't go to jail?"

"No." Goddard gave a weighty sigh. "No, he didn't, and that's one of my biggest regrets. Aiden Kingsley is a slippery son of a bitch, and he charmed the jury. His lawyer painted Carolina as a bitter ex out for revenge and riled her on the stand."

"*Was* she a bitter ex?"

"Bitter? A little, maybe, but for the most part, she was scared. Scared of Aiden Kingsley, scared of what she'd discovered in AquaLux's finances. At first, she thought she was spotting simple mistakes, and the financial controller provided semi-plausible explanations. But over time, she realised that what she was looking at was systemic, collaborative fraud. Our calls took place over many months, snippets of conversation here and there, often when she went out to grab lunch. Toward the end, she didn't have much freedom. On several occasions, we had a female agent meet her in the locker room at the gym because it was the one place Aiden couldn't watch her."

"He was controlling?"

"Controlling and possessive. A manipulative liar who preyed on a grieving young woman for nearly three years."

"Grieving?"

"Carolina's mother died right after she graduated college. She once told me that if she hadn't been consumed with grief, she might have seen him for the monster he was. Did you know a previous girlfriend of his disappeared without a trace? The sheriff couldn't pin that on him either. Caro firmly believed that she could never be free unless Aiden wasn't."

Every word from Goddard's mouth made Knox's heart ache more despite the heavy-duty painkillers. He hated that Caro had been so terrified of a man that she'd felt she had no choice but to leave her life behind and relocate to the ass end of San Gallicano. No wonder she'd held back with him. The last time she'd opened her mouth, to the IRS, they'd let her down.

"Did you promise her you'd get a conviction?" he asked quietly.

"I never make those kinds of promises."

"Did you tell her it was a sure thing?"

"I told her it was more likely than not. I thought we had enough. So did she, and we *did* have enough. But we didn't count on Aiden Kingsley throwing his own father and former colleagues under the bus while painting himself as an innocent party."

"You brought this on her. You were the one who made her move—"

"Not helping," Emmy said, cutting Knox off. "We get it —Aiden Kingsley is a gigantic shit. But is he a gigantic shit with the connections to hire an armed gang to snatch his ex from a turtle sanctuary in the arse end of nowhere? Because that's what happened. It's a big leap from tax fraud and being a terrible boyfriend to rounding up a band of psychos and riding in, all guns blazing."

Goddard pondered for a long moment, tapping a finger on his bottom lip as he considered. "Aiden's not a man who would get his hands dirty, but your suggestion isn't as farfetched as you might think. AquaLux's clientele... Let's just say that if a businessman of dubious reputation was in the market for a new yacht, Aiden Kingsley was the man he called. That's partly why it was so hard to get a conviction—there was so much cash floating around."

"Is he still involved with AquaLux?"

"Not that I'm aware of, although it's possible he still holds an equity interest. I'm not convinced that Carlos Davila—the new CEO—is entirely aboveboard either, but he's not catering to the same market. He's using influencers and going after celebrity money." Goddard shrugged. "This case is one that stuck with me, so I keep an eye on the company."

"And Aiden Kingsley? Do you keep an eye on him?"

"I believe he moved to New York, but I lost track of him after that. If it would help, I could put out feelers?"

"At this stage, any snippet of information could help. We'd be especially interested in any links he might have to San Gallicano."

"If memory serves correctly, he had a bank account or two there but no office. I'll pull the files and check."

"Where did AquaLux have offices?" Dan asked.

"California, Florida, the Bahamas, and the Caymans."

"Combining their love of the ocean with their love of not paying taxes?"

Goddard cracked a smile for the first time. "I have your number—I'll let you know if I find anything useful."

The screen went dark, and it was Emmy's turn to sigh. "I'd hoped we'd be able to eliminate Aiden. Bloody poachers are still in the wind too."

"How the fuck can they just disappear?" Knox asked.

"Practice. I mean, we thought the Richmond PD under Chief Garland was bad, but those assholes had nothing on the San Gallicano PD. The officers that aren't corrupt are underfunded, undertrained, and unmotivated. A decade ago, things were better by all accounts, but the old chief retired early."

"The job wore him down?"

"Maybe? He quit soon after one of his officers arrested the then-prime minister's son for a drug offence, but I'm sure that was just a coincidence." A shrug. "Bloody politics. The current chief is better at PR than he is at police work, which is why you get show trials like Luna's instead of actual crime-fighting, and when you couple that with the geography... A hundred islands, half of them overgrown and uninhabited, and a populace that doesn't have much respect for authority makes it easy enough to disappear in a small boat. Hell, they could even have transferred her to another vessel."

"Do we have any satellite images?"

Rumour said that Emmy and Black had investments in satellite technology, and they sure as hell had government contacts.

"Not twenty-four-hour surveillance. If Caro had been kidnapped in, say, Russia, we'd have a lot better chance of getting something useful."

"AIS?"

The Automatic Identification System transmitted a ship's position, but it was only mandatory on larger vessels and those carrying passengers.

"On a dinghy? No. We have a list of all the vessels using

AIS in the area, but without anything to cross-reference against..."

Emmy and Dan turned to stare at each other, some silent communication passing between them, and Dan nodded.

"I'll send the list to Goddard."

This felt...wrong. The poachers were the threat. They were the men Knox and Caro had been chasing, Stacey too, and look what had happened to her. Knox wanted to break Aiden Kingsley's nose for treating Caro like dirt, but more than that, he wanted to get her back.

"What about the poachers? We should be spending our time on them."

"We can look at both."

"How likely is it that Kingsley spotted Caro in a five-second video clip on Luna's Instagram account?"

"About as likely as Emmy escaping from an army base with five hundred troops shooting at her." Dan shrugged. "Which is why we're going to follow up on it."

Emmy chuckled and took a sip of lukewarm coffee. "Man, what a week that was. I mean, I nearly died, but I look back on it fondly now."

Gingerly, Knox pressed on his leg, wincing when pain shot through it. No matter, if Emmy and Dan hadn't made progress by tomorrow, he was walking—hopping—out of here and joining the search himself.

"I hope you feel better soon."

Knox stared blankly at the gift-wrapped box of candy Luna was holding out. Was that supposed to help? When he didn't gush thanks, Ryder gently took the box from her hands and placed it on the overbed table that held the dinner Knox hadn't eaten.

The hospital sucked.

"Luna wanted to come by and see how you were," Ryder explained.

"Terrific."

Everyone except Dan had left, to sleep or to scheme or to ask questions. Fernandez had officers going door-to-door on Valentine Cay and the surrounding islands—not Officers Roy or Beattie, he'd been at pains to stress—and Emmy had offered herself, Sky, Rafael, and Xav to assist. Nobody saw much. A couple of folks near the turtle sanctuary thought they might have spotted an SUV around the time of the shooting, but one witness said it was dark green, and the other said it was blue. Dan had spent the last two hours staring at the whiteboard, scrolling on her laptop, muttering to herself, and chewing her hair.

"I'm so sorry," Luna said, sounding oddly sincere. "What can I do? How can I help?"

"There's nothing you can do."

"You can get coffee," Dan said at the same time. "I'll have milk, or whatever passes for milk in this place, no sugar."

Luna disappeared with Ryder as her shadow, and Knox gritted his teeth against pain that throbbed with every heartbeat. He could have asked for more painkillers, *should* have asked for more painkillers, but the guilt was almost as bad as the bullet wound. If Caro was still alive, she couldn't ask for help. Couldn't cheat her way out of her predicament. If she was suffering, then he would suffer too.

This was why he'd vowed never to let anyone else matter. Why he'd sworn to keep his distance. Yes, he cared about his team, about Ryder, about Slater, even Emmy, the cold-hearted bitch. But that was different. With them, he kept a cage around his heart, a bitter edge that sliced away the warmth that had once been his weakness and locked it into a colder, darker place.

Not like Ryder, who let his feelings spill over the sides, a river he sometimes struggled to contain.

When Knox loved, he lost.

Luna returned with Ryder, each of them carrying two paper cups from the vending machine. When were the pair of them going to stop dancing around each other and fuck? Principal or no principal, it was inevitable. Emmy might pretend to be mad, but one night, one freezing night after she'd returned from the type of job she didn't like to talk about, she'd told Knox that love and hate were the two most powerful forces in the world, although she wasn't always sure which was stronger.

But had Ryder even told Luna he was straight yet?

"There were no trays," she said, depositing one of the cups beside Dan. Then her delicate nose crinkled. "Ugh, is that a dating site? You should avoid that guy."

"Why?" Dan asked.

Wait, why was Dan using a dating site? She was practically married, and Caro was missing. There was a time and a place, and this wasn't it.

"Because he's a sleaze," Luna said.

"You can tell that just by looking at him?"

"Okay, so firstly, if a guy's straight and that hot, he's gonna take advantage, trust me on that. And secondly, I'm ninety percent sure I met him at a work thing once, and he was definitely slimy. You can do better."

"Really? What kind of a work thing?"

"Some modelling gig on a boat. I guess he thought his money bought more than the pictures."

"He hit on you?"

"He walked into the cabin I was using as a dressing

room and said there was a limo waiting to take us to dinner. Like, he didn't even ask. Just assumed."

"So you turned him down?"

"Yes, and he didn't much like that. But he was standing between me and the door, so I had to smile and be polite until Mom showed up and kicked him out."

"Can you remember his name?"

"I hardly remember anyone's name, and it was four or five years ago. Mom might know it."

Dan blew out a long breath. "Fuck," she said, and turned the laptop around to face the others.

It wasn't a dating site. It was Providence. And Dan was looking at a photo of Aiden Kingsley.

42

CARO

"Come on!" I growled at the box. Just a little farther...

There were twelve boxes wedged into the cabin, three to a bed, each box roughly two feet square and a foot high. They were made from sturdy, light-coloured wood, and the lids had been nailed on securely. Mostly. I'd found one box with a couple of nails missing, and for the past several hours, I'd been wiggling the lid with my bound hands in an attempt to get it off.

At least, I thought it had been several hours. My watch had broken somewhere between the turtle sanctuary and wherever I was now, and without daylight, I'd lost track of time. Every second felt like an hour, so maybe I hadn't been here for as long as I thought. The tiny cabin had the ambience of a mausoleum. Cramped, grim, deathly. I wasn't certain why I was still alive, but I had no doubt that once I'd outlived my usefulness, I'd be dispatched to join Stacey. The man who brought my food had said as much.

Twice, he'd shown up with water and snacks, the man with the anchor on his arm. Barry. Barry the Barracuda.

He'd open the door and set the bottles and packages on the floor, watching me warily. What did he think I was going to do? It wasn't as if I could run anywhere. I'd managed to unwrap the duct tape from around my legs, taking a layer of skin with it in the process, and I'd peeled the tape away from my face. It was still tangled in my hair, a sticky, messy lump hanging from the back of my head. But my hands, I couldn't free them. The knot was sealed tight, and there was nothing sharp I could use to cut it. Whoever had bound me made sure there was no give in the cord.

"Why am I here?" I'd asked him.

"Because you couldn't keep your nose out of other people's business."

"Are you going to kill me? The way you killed Stacey?"

He didn't bother to deny it, just shrugged. "He wants you alive."

A chill ran through me in the stuffy, hot room. "Who? Who's 'he'?"

"You'll find out soon enough."

The way he said it, I really didn't want to.

The corner of the lid lifted another half inch, and I wiggled my fingertips underneath and heaved. Slowly, one at a time, the nails released their grip, and I tossed the lid to the side. The inside of the box was filled with shredded newspaper, and I scrabbled through it, searching for the true contents. What was so important that it was kept in a box on a fancy yacht? Drugs? No, those got packed in coffee grounds if the movies were to be believed, and didn't the big drugs ring in San Gallicano get busted the year before last?

I dumped paper onto the bed, then dug in again. Froze as my hands hit shell. *Shell.* A carapace.

A sob burst out of me as I dumped the rest of the paper and found a beautiful hawksbill, dead, dried, and stuffed into a box to be sold to some rich asshole who cared more about superstition than ecology. Worse, there were three tiny notches in the back of the shell. This was one of Franklin's turtles. Not a creature I'd helped to raise—judging by its size, around twenty inches, it was roughly six years old—but I still felt the blow personally. There were twelve boxes in this room, and I'd bet everything I owned—which wasn't much, admittedly—that they all contained dead turtles.

These men had no empathy, only greed. No understanding of the bigger picture, only the desire to make a quick buck. They killed with impunity, oblivious to the damage they were doing to the ocean.

And I was about to become their next victim.

A meal for a passing shark, if I was lucky.

A wasted pile of bones if I wasn't.

Would anyone miss me?

Knox and Franklin, if they were still alive, but nobody else. Once, I'd have said Vince, but after everything that had happened, I didn't trust him anymore. Had he ever truly been my friend? Or was he just keeping tabs on me? Making sure I stayed in line?

I had one hope—Ryder. Not that I thought he'd come for me, but if Knox had...if he'd been killed, then Ryder would alert the authorities, and Blackwood, and if Luna was still alive, she'd be screaming from the rooftops. Knox had mentioned his team, his boss too. Crazy, he'd called her. Crazy and deadly. If survival was impossible, I could hope for revenge.

43

RYDER

The "modelling gig on a boat," the sleaziness, the face, it all fit. Ryder agreed with Dan's assessment: fuck. Knox also concurred, or at least his heart rate did. The beeping from the monitor sped up as his pulse went from seventy to ninety in the blink of an eye.

Why? Because if Aiden had hired Luna, had paid her for influencer work, then he would have been following her on social media. Which meant there was a better-than-average chance that he'd seen the post with Caro on Instagram or TikTok.

Had their second-place suspect jumped into first?

"What?" Luna asked him. "Why do you look so horrified?"

"Because that's Aiden Kingsley."

"Huh?"

"Dan isn't looking at a dating site. She's working. And the man on the screen is Caro's ex-boyfriend."

"Really? Gross. She has super bad taste."

Dan snorted as Ryder face-palmed. Usually, he found it cute when Luna blurted out whatever was in that pretty head of hers, but not at this particular moment. She needed to learn that sometimes, it was wise to think before she spoke.

"Get her out of here," Knox growled.

"Moon, we should go back to the hotel."

"Why? We haven't finished our coffee. Not that it's good coffee, but the hotel coffee is horrible too, so we might as well drink this."

Knox looked ready to throttle her. Ryder took her hand and tried to lead her toward the door, but Luna dug her heels in.

"Why is everyone acting so weird?"

Dan shook her head, and her expression said, "How can she be so stupid?" But Luna wasn't stupid. No, she was hella smart, but Ryder had come to understand that she'd never experienced regular human relationships. Never had real friends. She'd gone from the cutthroat world of pageants to showbiz, where folks would be nice to your face and then stab you in the back. Her mom used her as an ATM, and even Jubilee, who was meant to be her best friend, had her own agenda. Who did that leave? Kory? No surprise that Luna had developed prickles.

"Sweetie, you just insulted Caro in front of someone who cares about her," Dan said. "Plus you insulted Knox as well because she chose to date him."

Luna bit her lip as she realised. "I...I'm sorry. I didn't mean bad taste now, only back then."

At least she was getting better at apologising.

"And before today," Dan continued, "we thought there was an outside chance that Aiden Kingsley watched your bikini-on-the-Strip show, but if you have a connection to him, then the likelihood that he saw the clip of Caro just ratcheted right up."

Now the little bit of colour Luna had left drained out of

her face. During the time on Valentine Cay, she'd gotten paler as everyone else had gone darker, thanks to her fake tan wearing off and the sunblock she slathered on religiously every morning.

"I thought she was exaggerating," Luna whispered. "She complained about everything I said and everything I did, so I figured that was just one more screw-up for the list."

"We all did." Dan ignored Knox's glare. "But as information comes in, more and more dots connect to Aiden."

"What about the poachers? Stacey?"

"Personally, I still think they're the culprits, but Aiden's in a close second place. Tell me everything you can remember about him. You said the photoshoot was four or five years ago?"

"Look on my Insta. The pictures will be on there."

Why hadn't Providence picked this up? Ryder didn't use the program himself—that was the domain of the investigators and the research teams—but if Luna had modelled for AquaLux, wouldn't she have tagged the company?

Dan was scrolling. "You have a lot of pictures on yachts."

"That's because people will pay more to see me in a bikini than in a dress."

"Unless the dress is made from cotton candy?"

"I used to love cotton candy. Mom hardly ever used to let me have it because she said it would ruin my teeth and my figure. I was eating bits off that dress all night, but after what happened at the Glitz Awards..." Luna shuddered. "Even the smell of it makes me sick now."

Knox was still watching her, but a little of the animosity faded from his eyes, and Ryder understood that Knox was starting to see the real Luna. The vulnerability she kept hidden from the world.

"Huh," Dan said. "I always figured that was a publicity stunt."

"Maybe it was for the creep who threw the water, but it wasn't for me."

She sounded so fucking sad, and Ryder wished they were still on Valentine Cay. It had been a sanctuary in more ways than one.

"Okay, I've gone back four years. Can you remember anything else about the job?"

"There was a huge hot tub. I hate pools and hot tubs and even regular tubs, but Mom said I was just being a coward and there was a contract. So I had to get in it. Oh!" A pause, and her face scrunched into a grimace. "Tamsin Treska was there, and she kicked me under the water. The bruise went purple and my make-up artist hated me."

"The two of you don't get along?"

"Not since I beat her into first runner-up position at Miss Nevada Teen Radiance. Then her singing career fizzled out, and I hit number one on the Billboard chart, and she hated me even more."

"I think I have it." Dan turned the laptop again, and there was Luna in a hot-pink bikini, laughing as she tossed a volleyball to a pretty brunette with obviously fake breasts. "You were hawking the hot tubs and not the yachts?"

"Maybe? I don't remember. There was another guy there with the sleaze, and Tamsin hooked up with him—like, on the boat—and she was bragging about it afterward. Who does that? Sleeps with a freaking stranger?"

Ryder nodded toward Dan, and this time, Luna turned red.

"Oh."

"Not anymore," Dan said. "I'm very happily not-quite-married now."

"Ethan still hasn't popped the question?" Knox asked, and Ryder was glad for the subject change.

"No, but he's bought the ring, so things are moving in the right direction."

"How do you know he bought the ring?"

"Please. I'm a private investigator." When Knox fixed her with a look, she rolled her eyes. "Okay, fine. I was in Ethan's office, and his assistant was getting lunch, so I figured I'd be helpful and answer the phone. The jeweller said the ring was ready, and I asked if he meant the engagement ring, and he said 'yes.' I'm assuming it's for me. If it's not, nobody will ever find the body."

"At least you don't know what it looks like. That part will still be a surprise."

Dan put her head in her hands. "Platinum band, three-carat marquise-cut diamond in the centre, half-carat tapered baguette-cut ruby on each side."

"Dare I even ask?"

"Well, I couldn't exactly tell Ethan that the jeweller called, could I? So I borrowed his assistant's computer to send an email, and while I was doing that, I might have run a tiny search on his inbox. I just couldn't help it." She gasped and pressed both hands to her cheeks. "Does this work for shocked?"

"You should cry," Luna said. "One time, a guy offered me two hundred bucks to hold up a banner on stage asking his girlfriend to marry him, and she cried loads."

"You charged for a proposal?"

"No, I did it for free, but Mom was mad that I turned down the cash."

"Your mom is a real lowlife."

Luna just looked at the floor. Dan was right, and she'd

said what Ryder had been dancing around for the past three weeks. Amethyst Puckett was a grade-A, first-class bitch.

"Here we go..." Dan went on. "The yacht was called *Bestia*. Same yacht appeared on a cached version of the AquaLux website for sale five years ago. So, Aiden owned the yacht, and some other schmuck installed the hot tub on the upper deck. Five years ago... Aiden was dating Caro then. He's a double sleaze."

Another shudder from Luna, and fuck it, Ryder slid an arm around her waist. She tucked herself against his side as if that was where she belonged. Knox said nothing, and Dan merely raised an eyebrow. Before she could ask any questions, her phone pinged. Ryder knew from her expression that it wasn't good news, and so did Knox.

"What happened?" he asked. "Is there any news?"

"Another body just washed up. Fernandez called Emmy, and she's on her way to meet him."

Knox closed his eyes and muttered something softly, a prayer or a curse, Ryder couldn't tell.

"Is it...?"

"They don't know, not yet. All we can do is wait."

44

CARO

Barry dumped another meal on the floor in front of me. Potato chips, a banana, and a burrito wrapped in aluminum foil. No, not a burrito. A *collito*. Collin, who owned the food stand near the harbour on Ilha Grande, put his own special spin on the dish: shredded meat —don't ask what kind—fries, cheese, caramelised onions, and ketchup wrapped in a tortilla. Which meant we were on Ilha Grande. We were in Half Moon Harbour on Ilha Grande, and down here below the waterline, with the quality soundproofing a fancy yacht demanded, nobody would hear me if I screamed. These arrogant beasts—they were hiding me in plain sight, and all I had to use against them was two bottles of water. Half a litre each—they wouldn't even make a dent if I used one to hit Barry over the head.

"You look like shit," he said as a parting comment.

"Yeah, well, at least I have an excuse. You were just born ugly."

Ugly face, ugly heart, ugly soul. The door closed behind him, and I heard the *click* of the lock. Then the sound of voices. Who was he talking with? I pressed my ear to the wood, straining to hear.

"When can we leave?" Barry asked. "Staying here is dangerous. The police are everywhere, asking questions, and there are people from America with them."

America? A tiny ember of hope sparked. Ryder? Had he brought reinforcements?

"The police are not *here*. They're on Valentine Cay, on Malavilla, on Spice Island."

The newcomer was a local, well-spoken and confident. A leader, not a follower.

"It's only a matter of time. How much longer do we have to stay?"

"Until we find Monique, you know that. If Tomas hadn't been such a fool…"

Monique was still alive? That spark kindled into the tiniest of flames. She'd escaped, and if she went to the cops, if she shared what she knew about Stacey…maybe they'd hand her right back to the poachers. She knew, didn't she? She knew the police couldn't be trusted.

"I didn't know he'd told her so much. If I did, he would have paid the price sooner."

"Always so bloodthirsty."

"Is that a problem?" Barry snarled.

"Not at all, but let's try to avoid any more public shoot-outs, okay?"

"Caro's damn dog started it. If the mutt hadn't bitten Chester, we'd have been in and out, quiet. Everything was under control."

"You lost six men!" the boss snapped. "Six men, including Jackson. Everything was *not* under control."

Six? Knox had taken out five of them? Or had Franklin helped? He kept a gun on the top shelf in his closet, although I couldn't recall him ever using it. Maybe that was why nobody had come to help—they'd been fighting their way forward. I hadn't realised there were so many people on Barry's team. Barry the coward. He'd stayed in the boat until the end, when he'd run over with that syringe.

I hoped Knox had killed them slowly.

Knox. That tiny flame licked a little higher.

"They tricked us," Barry whined. "We thought both of the blonde slut's bodyguards left."

"Carolina *and* Monique—your team is making too many mistakes."

"We'll find Monique before she goes to the police. They're not even looking for her."

"I thought that idiot Fernandez sent Jason and Maceo to ask questions on Treasure Atoll?"

Jason and Maceo? Was that Jason Roy and Maceo Beattie? It had to be them. And he'd called Vince an idiot, so did that mean Vince wasn't involved? Wasn't dirty? And maybe not such an idiot either if he'd sent the two officers to Treasure Atoll. That was nowhere near Valentine Cay. Was he trying to keep them away from the investigation?

Perhaps...perhaps there was a chance for me?

"They're only asking about Carolina, and they have no idea where to start. Fernandez told Maceo that they're focusing on the smaller islands."

So, Officer Beattie was definitely involved. That no-good — Wait... Ice prickled over my skin. Carolina. The man outside had called me Carolina. Not Caro or Caroline. *Carolina.*

"Better that Maceo is out of the way. He's getting nervous, and we have other eyes and ears."

"Any word on what we should do with the woman?"

"The boss just arrived—he can deal with her while you search for Monique."

This man, this *monster* who owned cops and ordered

Barry the Barracuda around, who didn't have a problem with bloodshed, he wasn't the boss?

A new voice entered the conversation.

"You can go now. I'll take it from here."

And that flame, that precious flame, it stuttered and died.

45

KNOX

Fuck, that hurt. Knox glared at the crutches the nurse had brought and continued to hobble around the bed. The doctors didn't want him to leave, not yet, but they'd also admitted they couldn't stop him.

"What are you gonna do, tough guy?" Dan asked. "Hop into another gunfight?"

"I can't just sit here doing nothing."

He could join the canvassing team on nearby islands. Head out to the sanctuary and search for missed clues. Something, anything that might help to find Caro. This morning, when Fernandez had called to say the body found last night was an as-yet unidentified male, he'd also told them that whoever took Stacey didn't kill her right away. She'd been alive for at least a day after she was last seen, but the things they'd done to her... Knox shoved his injured leg into a pair of shorts, making a conscious effort not to wince.

"We're not doing nothing in here. We're sifting through clues. Not all investigation involves legwork."

That was true—Agatha had finally wormed her way into SG Telecom's records, and now they knew that Stacey's cell phone had last pinged a tower on Malavilla. Sky, Rafael, Emmy, and Xav had taken the first ferry over there while Dan focused on the search for Aiden. Knox didn't want to voice the fear at the back of his mind. That if they didn't find Caro soon, it would be too late.

"It *feels* as if I'm doing nothing. Somebody has to have seen something. A diver, a swimmer, a fisherman. Have we been to the fish market?"

"Yes," Dan said, her tone condescending. "And every harbour, tavern, and chandlery." Her phone rang. "Give me a second."

Knox stiffened, hoping for news, but it was just Slater calling from Valentine Cay for an update. Dan put him on speaker.

"Try to talk some sense into Knox, and then find Jubilee," she told him. "I want to know how Luna was paid for the hot-tub thing. There's a tangle of companies, related party transactions galore, very incestuous. No wonder the IRS struggled."

"How does that help to find Caro?" Knox asked.

"If Aiden's involved, he must be getting money from somewhere."

"Jubilee's right here," Slater said. "Come and talk to Dan."

Out of the corner of his eye, Knox saw Jubilee walk into view on Dan's screen, then focused on finding a shirt. The EMTs had cut his clothes away, but Slater had brought some of Knox's belongings from the sanctuary after Emmy refused to help and told Knox to stay put. Kory had shown up with the *Cleopatra*, and Ryder had made sure there were rooms ready for both of them, although getting down the stairs promised to be a challenge. Still, Knox would cross that bridge when he came to it. After he made it across the passerelle, obviously.

"How did Luna get paid for that modelling shoot?" Dan asked. "A cheque? A bank transfer?"

"I don't know. Our accountant would have handled that, but I can ask him. Although I think he might be sick this week. Usually, he replies real fast, but I emailed him about a payment a few days ago, and he hasn't gotten back to me yet."

"Try calling him. Wait... Can you hold that mug closer to the screen?"

A mug? What did that have to do with anything?

"It's just coffee."

"Havana Hills Cigars? Where did that come from?"

"The kitchen."

Dan tapped at the keyboard, and Knox paused his shoe hunt to watch her. Why was she so interested in...? Right. Havana. The note on the pad in Stacey's hotel room had mentioned Havana. Blackwood had been tracking ships bound for Cuba and Miami, but nothing had shaken loose there.

"Hmm, the Havana Hills plantation is in Ecuador. Does Franklin Baptise smoke cigars?"

Knox shook his head. "Not that I ever saw."

"Okay." Dan blew out a breath. "Okay. Jubilee, find me that banking information."

After the call ended, Dan stood, and she had a faraway look in her eyes. Unfocused. As if her thoughts were elsewhere.

"What?" Knox asked.

"I'm going to speak with Franklin."

The older man had come off worse than Knox in the Battle of Valentine Cay. He'd taken a round to the chest and another to the calf, and if Lyron hadn't jumped in to help, Baptiste wouldn't have made it to the hospital. Knox had visited him briefly yesterday, assured him that the turtles were being cared for and folks were searching for Caro, but Baptiste hadn't been up to talking much.

"I'll come with you."

Dan didn't seem thrilled, but she also didn't try to stop him. "Let me do the talking."

Baptiste wasn't looking much better today, still deathly pale, but the nurses had propped him up on a pile of pillows, and he was awake. Dan took the seat beside the bed, leaving Knox to lean against the wall by the door. He could have limped over to the chair by the window, but sitting somehow felt like admitting defeat.

"How are you feeling?" Dan asked.

Baptiste ignored the question. "Caro?"

"There's no news yet, but we have a whole team of people looking. I'm hoping you can help me with some information."

Baptiste nodded. "Anything."

His voice was hoarse, every word an effort. If Knox ever got his hands on the remaining men who'd invaded the sanctuary, he'd make sure to kill them slowly.

"Does the Havana Hills cigar company ring any bells?"

"The place on Malavilla? Been closed for years."

Knox's spine went rigid. Malavilla? Havana, Malavilla? Once, he'd asked Dan why she loved her job so much because, let's face it, there was a fuck of a lot of boring shit involved, and she'd said that in every successful investigation, there was one moment. A moment when everything changed, and that moment was better than sex. Knox figured she was talking crap, but now he understood exactly what she meant.

But Dan's expression didn't change. She didn't show a

glimmer of the frantic hope Knox felt. "Can you tell me about it?"

"Not much to tell. They used to grow tobacco there. Make cigars. But then Leopold passed on, and his son decided it was too expensive to run the business here. He kept the name and moved production to Ecuador."

"What happened to the place on Malavilla?"

"The house is still there, last I heard. The fields are gradually returnin' to the way nature intended. Guess that's no bad thing."

"I didn't see the house on the map. Havana Hills?"

"The official name is Turtle Bay, on the north side of the island, but there ain't no turtles there, not anymore. The locals still call it Havana Hills."

The locals. Monique Constantine had grown up on Malavilla. Her parents still lived there. If she'd spoken to Stacey about the place, there was a reasonable chance she might have called it Havana Hills.

"You said the old owner's name was Leopold? Do you have a surname?"

"Voss. Leopold Voss."

"And his son?"

"Theron Voss."

Dan's smile was quick and, if Knox wasn't mistaken, satisfied. She squeezed Baptiste's hand gently.

"I hope you make a good recovery."

"You'll find Caro?"

"We're doing everything we can to bring her back."

Out in the hallway, Dan was hustling. Back to Knox's room, back to her laptop. She plopped into her seat and started typing before Knox made it through the door.

"That's it, isn't it? Havana Hills?"

"Voss was one of the names on the list from Tony

Goddard. Aiden Kingsley sold three yachts to people in San Gallicano, and... Yes! Theron Voss. He's there."

"Wait, wait, wait... I thought Havana was part of the smuggling case?"

"Yeah, well, maybe it's part of both." Dan already had her phone in her hand. "Emmy? Head to an estate called Turtle Bay. North side of the island."

46

RYDER

Luna squashed against Ryder's side as Emmy appeared on the screen. Technically, Luna shouldn't have been at the briefing, but Black was also in the grand saloon on board the *Cleopatra*, and he didn't tell her to leave. Neither did Knox. He just kept giving her dirty looks, and although Ryder didn't like that, he understood. He understood why Knox held a grudge. Dan's working theory was that Aiden Kingsley was connected to Theron Voss, who owned an estate linked to the smugglers. Theron Voss was also on Monique Constantine's client list.

Jubilee was wisely keeping out of the way, up on the sundeck with Kory. Slater had been released from babysitting duties and headed over to Malavilla to help with surveillance duty.

"The place is wild," Emmy said. "As in overgrown, neglected, and full of hazards. Oh, and there are trail cams. Don't forget the trail cams. The house is in good shape, plus a small area of garden around it, but other than that, we're talking thirty acres of undergrowth. Sky, Rafael, and Xav are still holed up there, watching. We've counted eight outbuildings, including two giant barns that were probably used for processing or storage or something."

"People?" Black asked.

"Seven males so far. And they definitely have sentries. Pairs seem to be walking the same pattern around the buildings, but the intervals aren't regular."

"When are you going in?" Knox blurted.

"If nothing changes, tomorrow evening."

"Why not tonight?"

"Because I don't like suicide missions."

"Another day could cost Caro her life."

"So could an attempted rescue if we go off half-cocked. Right now, we're digging up intel and satellite photos, plus Gage is on his way from Virginia. We could also do with Ryder. Luna, how do you feel about that?"

"Huh? Why are you asking me?"

Black answered for Emmy. "Because you're Blackwood's client, and we don't break our contracts."

"I'll be safe here on the boat, right? And I don't even have a stalker."

"Knox will stay with you."

Ryder saw Knox's jaw clench. He wanted to be a part of this operation, *he* wanted to be the one to sneak into Havana Hills and get revenge for Caro's abduction. It sickened him that he couldn't go. Ryder knew that because he'd feel exactly the same way in Knox's shoes.

"Will Ryder be safe?" Luna asked. "I mean, is this dangerous?"

Neve hadn't loved the idea of Ryder joining the Navy, but she'd accepted his chosen path. Understood that it was their best chance of a new life together. Having another woman worry about him felt...weird. But a good weird.

"I've spent my life training for this, moon."

"I..." She faced him, and he saw the apprehension when she bit her lip. But she nodded. "Okay. If you want to go, then that's what you should do. Just get Caro back."

"Good." Emmy flashed a smile. "Then the team tomorrow will be me, Xav, Sky, Rafael, Slater, Ryder, and Gage, with Dan on comms."

Black wasn't going? Knox glanced at him, and he answered the unasked question.

"We're on foreign soil, and if we're mounting a rescue operation, we need political leverage. Tomorrow afternoon, I'll be informing the prime minister that for as long as San Gallicano's environmental credentials are in question, the consortium he's been wooing to invest in a significant green energy project here will not be handing over the cash he wants." Black's flicker of a smile was more cunning than his wife's. "Money talks. By the time we've finished rounding up poachers, he'll be thanking us."

"We'll hold a full briefing in the morning," Emmy said. "Get some sleep."

Sleep didn't come easy that night, not to Ryder and not to Luna. At the sanctuary, they'd grown used to each other's company, so when Luna walked tentatively into the room Kory had assigned to him—a cramped cabin near the stern with two narrow beds—and said she didn't want to be alone, he hadn't argued.

She lay facing him, moonlight slanting across her make-up-free face, hands clasped under her chin.

"Are you scared?" she asked.

"About tomorrow, you mean?" He was due to travel to Malavilla in the morning. His kit was packed and ready.

"What if people shoot at you?"

"I'll shoot back, and I have good aim."

A long pause. "I wish I'd told Emmy that I wanted you here. Would you have been mad if I did?"

"Not mad. Disappointed that I couldn't go and do my job."

Another pause. "I'm freaking terrified."

"Why?"

"Because...because I don't have many friends, and I hate the thought of saying goodbye tomorrow and never seeing you again." She rolled onto her back. "I sound like such a loser."

"No, you don't, and that won't happen."

"How do you know? Knox left Caro in the pool room, and now she's gone."

"That was different."

"But the ending could be the same."

Ryder rolled out of his own bed and sat on the edge of hers. He wanted to be close to her. Wanted to wrap her up in his arms and hold her. Wanted to— Fuck, he shouldn't be thinking about that. He was already jacking off four times a day to keep his cock under control, and picturing Luna naked underneath him sure didn't help matters.

"I promise you that this time on Saturday, I'll be right here."

Even as he said it, his stomach rolled. There were no guarantees, not in this world, although if he'd known what Saturday would bring, he wouldn't have used a word as strong as "promise."

"Don't leave me," she whispered.

He wasn't sure whether she meant tonight or in general, but he stretched out on her bed, perilously close to falling off the edge, and brushed a few stray strands of hair away from her face.

"I'm right here. You're not alone."

"Soon I will be. You won't stay, and Jubilee... I thought she was on my side, but she was helping Cordelia. To *scare* me."

"By her twisted logic, she thought she was helping."

"Do you really believe that?"

"Do you want the truth? Or do you want me to make you feel better?"

He used to ask Neve that, ever since the day she got a shitty haircut and asked, "Is it really that bad?" She'd always told him to be honest when she asked for his opinion on dresses, but that day, she'd burst into tears. Turned out that she'd just wanted him to hug her and tell her she was beautiful. Which she was, even with lopsided hair that had gone a weird shade of orange.

"The truth. Always the truth, even if it's not pretty. People constantly blow smoke up my ass, and I hate it. *Hate* it. There's nothing worse than a liar."

Shit. Well, he'd walked right into that one.

"I think... I think that Jubilee is easily led, and our research team said that Cordelia has a strong and forceful personality. It wouldn't have taken much for her to manipulate Jubilee into doing her bidding."

Luna didn't say anything, not one word. The silence stretched, taking Ryder's nerves along with it, a tangible thing that tightened around his gut, squeezing.

"You okay?" he finally asked.

"It hurts," she whispered. "I don't know if I can forgive her."

"Take some time. Time heals."

"Hmm," was all she said, and then she snuggled against his side.

He stayed there. Heaven help him, he stayed there the

entire night, under false pretences, knowing that this could be the only time they shared a bed. If he told her the truth, she'd hate him, and if he didn't, he'd hate himself.

47

CARO

I *will not cry.*
   The door closed behind me, and I heard the lock click.

I will not cry.

Aiden had left me in a crumpled mess on the floor, blood trickling from my lip, more bruises than unmarred skin, every muscle aching. This was the second time he'd raped me on the boat, face-down on the floor, wedged between the two bunks so I couldn't fight back. The second time of many, he promised. He'd done it before, back in California, but he'd always apologised afterward, sworn he wouldn't do it again, or occasionally blamed me for leading him on. Here, the mask was off. Funny, I'd feared death for so long, but now I realised I'd welcome it.

And I wouldn't give him the satisfaction of seeing my tears.

Of knowing how angry I was with myself.

I will not cry.

He hadn't tried to stick his dick in my mouth—he knew I'd bite it off—but nor had he gagged me. No, he'd taken pleasure in my pain and laughed when I cursed him. And because he knew that he was going to kill me eventually, when he'd had his fun, when he'd destroyed every last fragment of my soul, he'd taken great delight in telling me that I hadn't broken him the way he planned to break me. No, he'd just pivoted, gotten dirtier, and used the money he'd squirrelled away offshore to invest in a new business venture. His good buddy Theron had already been supplying turtles on the black market, but they'd expanded. Grown from a few local sales to an international network. Aiden had the contacts; Theron had the foot soldiers. When I agreed to talk with Stacey, I'd thought we were taking on a handful of two-bit opportunists, when in reality, we'd been wading into my worst nightmare. Theron's men had been watching. Spying on Knox and me when we went to Monique Constantine's workshop to find her customer list. They'd been looking for Monique, Aiden said. Imagine his joy when they'd sent a picture of me instead.

All this time, I'd blamed Luna. I'd blown up at her for that stupid Instagram post, but it hadn't been her fault that Aiden found me; it had been mine. My fault the sanctuary had been invaded. Had Luna even survived? I hoped she had.

Muscles screaming in agony, I rolled onto my side, my watery eyes meeting the dead turtle's blank stare. Aiden had chuckled when he saw I'd opened the box. Left it there, the beautiful creature another reminder of my failure. I'd considered clocking him with it, swinging that hard carapace into his head and hoping he died, but what was the point? Where could I go? My hands were still bound, my wrists raw where I'd struggled to free them, and the sharpest thing left in the cabin was the disposable wooden spoon Barry had brought me alongside a bowl of gross-looking stew. The stew had come from Pescado, a tourist joint renowned for its shitty hygiene, and I'd puked without taking a mouthful.

"Sorry I screwed up," I told the turtle, and a sob escaped. "I tried."

Of course, it said nothing, and that was when I realised I was losing my mind. Three days of hell, and I was talking to a freaking turtle. At least, I thought it had been three days. They'd brought me six meals in total, and Barry referred to them as dinner and breakfast. No lunch.

"I don't suppose you have a knife?" The sob turned into a laugh, slightly hysterical, and the turtle just stared back at me, its expression snooty. Sometimes, when hawksbills opened their mouths, they almost looked as if they were smiling, but I figured the taxidermist or whoever Aiden had hired to create this abomination thought it would be too difficult to—

The hawksbill.

Hawk's bill.

They'd gotten their name because of their beak. That sharp, curving beak, reminiscent of their namesake, so perfect for digging food out of hard-to-reach crevices. A hawksbill had bitten me once, soon after I arrived at the sanctuary and before I learned how to handle turtles properly. That bite had hurt like hell. The edge of its mouth had sliced into my finger, sharp as a blade.

I scrambled to my knees, my hands numb from being trapped underneath my body while Aiden punished me. The rope was nylon, made of a thousand twisted strands, as tough as steel when it was twined into fishing nets and used to pillage the ocean. I rubbed one edge of the cord against the turtle's beak, and the tiny strands began to fray.

Something exploded in my chest, and I realised it was hope. If I could get my hands free, then maybe...maybe... All I had to do was get to the main deck. We were in the harbour in Ilha Grande; I was sure of it. Pescado was right there. If I screamed, one of the tourists who roamed the promenade gawking at the yachts would hear me. People would notice. I mean, Aiden had shredded my clothes, so my boobs should raise a few eyebrows, at least.

Once, I'd hoped Aiden would forget me.

Now I was going to make sure he didn't.

48

KNOX

This wasn't what Knox had signed up for. He'd joined Blackwood to help people, to save people, rules and bureaucracy be damned. But now, for the most important job of his life, he'd been sidelined. Forced to watch from the in-your-face extravagance of Kory Balachandran's father's yacht. Six times, uniformed staff had asked whether he wanted a snack, a drink, anything at all, and he'd struggled to rein in his temper as he banned them from the palatial saloon. Jubilee was still keeping out of the way on the sundeck, and Kory had made himself scarce. Five minutes after Knox snapped at the last unfortunate steward, Luna had tiptoed in, carefully placed a bottle of chilled mineral water at Knox's elbow, and asked softly if there was any news. When he said there wasn't, she'd left as quietly as she arrived.

Emmy and the rest of the team—minus Black—were on Malavilla, putting the finishing touches to tonight's mission. Ingress, egress, ten different backup plans. The men at Havana Hills were still an unknown quantity. Because of the circumstances—a barely sanctioned op in a foreign country

—they needed to avoid bloodshed, broken bones, and dead bodies, which was somewhat of a disappointment. Lynching was too good for Aiden Kingsley.

Knox only hoped that the man did something stupid, like pulling a gun on Emmy. She'd mentioned that she wouldn't hesitate to shoot in self-defence, and she'd said it with a glint in her eye.

Caro deserved justice. So did Stacey and Monique, the latter of whom there was still no sign. With Blackwood handling the visit to Havana Hills, Fernandez had focused on the search for the missing woman, but her friends and family claimed they hadn't seen her. For the most part, he believed them, although there was one guy, an ex, who Fernandez thought might be lying. Not "involved in her abduction" lying, but "covering for a woman he still cared about" lying. Knox hoped he was. Hoped that Monique was safe and far away from San Gallicano. At least Wednesday's body hadn't been her. The ME had identified the man as Tomas Laker using a print from his one remaining finger. Dental records had confirmed the match. He'd been a petty criminal, in and out of jail since he was eighteen and a guest at San Gallicano's one and only juvenile facility before that. Coincidentally, he'd gone to school with Officer Jason Roy. Roy, of course, denied having anything to do with him, but all the tiny pieces of circumstantial evidence were piling up.

Knox switched to a live view from Sky's bodycam. She was hunkered down in the undergrowth, watching the largest outbuilding at Havana Hills. Barely fifteen yards away, a mean-looking motherfucker carrying a sidearm was smoking—a cigarette, not a cigar—but Sky didn't flinch, didn't waver. Knox saw a lot of Emmy in her, and he knew Emmy did too. She learned quickly, mentored by both Emmy and Rafael, although her relationship with the latter was still a mystery. The two of them finished each other's sentences, and Rafael would kill to protect her, yet Sky was dating Asher, an up-and-coming racecar driver who spent more time indulging in his love of cars than his love of Sky.

Knox snorted quietly to himself. Who was he to criticise someone else's relationship when his own pitiful hookups rarely lasted more than a week? Until Caro... He thought he might love her. Knew that if she came back, he'd move heaven and earth to make her happy.

"Do you want any lunch?" Luna asked from the doorway.

"I'm not hungry."

"Is there anything I can do to—?"

"No."

"Uh, okay."

She backed away, and Knox tamped down the guilt that niggled. Sure, Luna was trying to help now, and maybe there was truth in Ryder's claim that she was a different person under the brattish exterior, but she bore some responsibility for what was happening today. If Aiden was involved, if he'd seen that fucking social media post...

Knox turned back to the screen and watched the guard puff out smoke.

49

LUNA

"That's gross."

Kory gagged and backed away from the kitchen until he trod on my foot. I yelped and shoved him, but my bigger concern was the smell.

"Shit, sorry," he said.

"What happened?"

Kory was twenty-six, the same age as me, but when he crinkled his nose like that, he looked twelve.

"Jacques decided to sample the local cuisine yesterday. Some kind of fish soup. And I guess it was bad because he just puked all over the stove."

Kory was absolutely right—that was gross. "So we're not getting lunch?"

"We'll have to go out."

"I can't go out—Knox is busy, plus he has crutches. Is Jacques okay?"

"Malinda's going to take Jacques to the doctor, and the rest of the staff are going to deep clean the kitchen." Kory paused. Grimaced. "Maybe I'll call Dad, see if we can get the whole lot ripped out. How long does it take to fit a new one?"

"How should I know? Don't you think replacing the whole kitchen would be kinda wasteful?"

A month ago, I'd probably have been on board with the plan, but now...now I'd seen the kitchen at the sanctuary, which had to be fifty years old, and not only was it still going strong, but I hadn't gotten food poisoning from it either.

"Do you want to eat vomit?"

"They said they'd clean it, dumbass."

My stomach grumbled, and I knew I should have ignored it, but I'd grown used to eating proper meals. *Tres bocados* instead of black coffee for breakfast, stew and flatbread instead of a salad and ice water for lunch, grilled fish and a baked sweet potato or rice for dinner instead of tofu and steamed vegetables. Mom was going to yell at me because I'd put on weight, but I also felt stronger. Both mentally and physically. Deep down, I'd always been scared of change, scared that even though I hated my life, the alternatives would be worse, but now I realised that change might not be the monster I'd always feared. A lot had happened in the past month, bad stuff like nearly being kidnapped, but there had been good moments too. And I was still alive, still breathing, looking at life through fresh eyes.

"How long do bacteria take to die?" Kory asked.

"That wasn't a question that came up at pageants."

"I'll google it. What do you want for lunch? There's a weird burrito place along the promenade. Not real burritos —they put French fries in them—but the guy who runs the place is hot."

"Do you ever not think with your dick?"

"Just because you're a eunuch doesn't mean everyone else has to be."

"I'm, like, eighty percent sure that women can't be eunuchs."

"Nah, someone wrote a book about it. *The Female Eunuch.* Go put on sunglasses and a hat or whatever."

"I already told you, I can't go out. Not without Knox."

"Why? We're barely leaving the boat, and I thought your stalker was just Cordelia being a bitch?"

Kory did have a point. The only reason Mom had hired bodyguards was because I'd received threats, but those had all been down to my horrible half-sister. I'd sent Cordelia an email telling her precisely what I thought of her, but she hadn't bothered to reply. Not that I was expecting her to. She'd have her butler craft a suitably snotty response on personalised stationery and mail it sometime next month. Although now that I'd seen the messages she'd crafted on behalf of my stalker, I realised that she wasn't quite the prude I'd always assumed. She was just a sick witch who liked to pretend she was better than everyone else.

"Okay, fine. As long as we go straight to the burrito place and nowhere else."

"The place next door does the best strawberry daiquiris."

"Do they do takeout?"

"You're so boring these days."

Once, I'd have taken offence at that and come up with some outrageous stunt just to prove him wrong. But today, I simply nodded.

"I learned a bunch of stuff in the past three weeks. Not only about turtles, but about myself."

Maybe I should write Judge Morgan a thank-you note?

Kory just rolled his eyes. "Sounds like a freaky rehab program."

"Don't mention freaky rehab. I've had enough of that to last a lifetime."

I considered telling Knox where I was going, but he had enough on his plate. The look in his eyes earlier, it had been...haunted. I wished there was something I could do, some comfort I could offer, but he didn't want me around. That much was clear. Emmy said I was the client, but...but I also wanted to be a friend. Ryder, Knox, even Caro, they were the first people to look beyond my money and my stupid reputation and treat me like a regular human being. Okay, so Caro hadn't exactly been nice, but she'd been honest. And I valued honesty above everything.

San Gallicano was hardly South Beach, but there were enough people around that I dug out a floppy hat and oversized sunglasses and pulled on a loose cover-up over my pink bikini. Kory had taken a few photos of me earlier to use for my socials, but my heart wasn't in it. Now that I'd had a taste of privacy, I was reluctant to let it go.

He was waiting for me on the swim platform, and we hurried across the gangway, keeping our heads down, Kory because he wanted to believe people might recognise him, and me because people *would* recognise me. It felt like a lifetime since I'd last walked along the promenade. The place was busier this time around—more boats, more tourists, more locals hawking beaded necklaces and sunglasses and bags of dubious spices. Kory would be devastated that the *Cleopatra* was only the third-biggest yacht in the harbour.

The biggest was named *Kraken*, and as we walked past it, a man dressed in white linen pants and a pale blue polo shirt crossed the gangway and clipped me with his elbow. I was about to demand an apology when I realised two things. One, I was supposed to be staying incognito. And two, he looked familiar.

It took me a moment to place him.

And then I remembered. My stomach, it was like a lake and someone had just tossed a boulder into the middle. Ripples of nausea spread out to the edges.

"That's him!" I grabbed Kory's arm and whispered frantically. "That's the guy!"

"What guy?" Of course he turned to look. "His ass isn't bad."

"The guy Knox and everyone else is looking for," I hissed. "Aiden the sleaze."

"You think?"

"I'm seventy percent sure."

I'd only gotten a quick glimpse, but as he breezed past, I'd caught a whiff of his cologne. Something spicy and overpowering. The same scent I'd gagged on five years ago when he hit on me on his stupid boat.

"So go tell Knox."

I took a step toward the *Cleopatra*, but what would Knox do? He couldn't go after Aiden himself, not with his injured leg, and everyone else was on Malavilla. On Malavilla looking for Aiden and Caro. But Aiden was here. What if Caro was here too? Aiden was gone right now, but he'd probably be back by the time anyone made it over from Malavilla, and then searching for her would be a heck of a lot harder. The yacht looked quiet. If Aiden was up to something sketchy, like kidnapping his ex-girlfriend, for example, surely he wouldn't have a dozen staff around to witness the crime?

"Wait here," I told Kory.

"What the hell are you doing?"

"I'm going to check if Caro's on that boat."

Now Kory grabbed my arm. "Have you lost your mind?"

"If Aiden comes back, distract him."

"What if someone sees you?"

"I'll just act dumb and say I'm looking for a friend. Call Knox, okay? Tell him where I am."

The "looking for a friend" story wouldn't be that farfetched, would it? People already saw me as a dumb blonde, so they'd totally believe I was on the wrong boat. I ran onto the *Kraken* before Kory could stop me and headed into the main cabin. The stairs would probably be in the middle, and the sleeping deck would be the best place to keep a prisoner. My pulse raced as I paused beside a polished wood bar, listening for signs of anyone else on board, and I realised I was actually freaking terrified. Was it possible to break a rib from the inside? My heart was pounding so hard that I was about to find out.

Above the soft classical music that played in the background, a *thunk* sounded from someplace deep in the boat, and I almost ran right back to Kory. But I'd come this far. I grabbed a bottle of champagne—not a regular bottle, but a magnum of Dom Pérignon—and hefted it in my hands. Then I tiptoed forward.

50

CARO

"Thanks, buddy."

I carefully placed the turtle on the floor. If it had been a living, breathing creature, I wouldn't have been able to pick it up, but dried, desiccated, whatever they'd done to preserve it, the beautiful animal was lighter than it would have been in life. Not so carefully, I stepped over Barry's lifeless body, pausing to kick him in the balls as I went.

"That's for the fish stew," I muttered.

There was a glimmer of light to my left, and adrenaline fuelled me as I ran toward it, desperate to get out of this hellhole. For a moment, I wondered if I should search the other rooms for Knox, but head overruled heart. I'd be better off finding help. If I stuck around longer than I had to, I'd only get caught again.

Plus I knew Aiden. If he'd caught Knox, the chances of him being alive were slim. I fought back tears as I crept forward.

The door led from the crew quarters to the guest accommodation, a portal between utilitarian practicality and opulence. My bare feet sank into the expensive carpet as I paused to listen. Music played softly, but the loudest sound was my own rough breathing.

Quiet, Caro. Do you want to die?

No, I wanted to get up to the main deck and scream for help. Surely there had to be one cop on this godforsaken island who wasn't corrupt? I took a step forward, then froze as a voice came from my right.

"What was that—"

I had no time to run, no time to hide. The stranger did a double take as he saw me sneaking forward, naked and bloody, and we both moved at the same time. I barrelled forward, hoping to barge past him and reach the stairs, but he lunged for me, his fingers digging into my bruised flesh as he grabbed my arms. I began yelling, hoping someone might hear me, even though I knew there was a better chance of alerting a friend of my new captor than a rescuer. Whoever this brute was, he was stronger than he looked. Or perhaps more determined. He dressed like a frat boy, but he fought like the Hydra.

And I was losing. He forced me back a step, back toward my prison, back toward death.

Then...maybe I was dead already. Or hallucinating. Because Luna was there. Standing behind the Hydra, her eyes wide, her face pale. She raised her arms and whacked the monster with a magnum of champagne, glass against bone, and when the bottle didn't break, she hit him again. The *crack* would later haunt my nightmares. He crumpled to my feet, eyes vacant.

"Run!" I told her. "How do we get out of here?"

"Uh..."

I grabbed her hand and pulled her forward, but my legs hurt so badly that I cried out in pain. She overtook me, and then I saw stairs. Saw hope. The music grew louder, and I recognised "Winter" from Vivaldi's "Four Seasons." One of Aiden's favourite pieces. He'd taken me to hear it in New York.

"Who else is here?" I asked as we burst into a good-sized saloon. This was a bigger yacht than I'd thought. "Where are the others?"

"It's just me. And Kory, and I asked him to call Knox, but now that I think about it, I'm not sure he even has Knox's number. Anyhow, we should get out of—"

More music, but this time it came from Luna's pocket. She cursed—far too mildly for our current situation—and fished out her phone.

"Kory, I can't talk right—"

She never got to finish the sentence. I tried to scream as Aiden grabbed her, but no sound came out. Luna, on the other hand, began shrieking like a banshee. I looked at the open deck beyond the saloon, and I almost ran to it. But I couldn't leave Luna behind. I owed her. I'd been a bitch, and she'd still come into the monster's den to rescue me.

Finding my voice, I roared and charged Aiden, but what I thought was a wall turned out to be a door, and when he stumbled back, it popped open. Then he was on the gunwale, still with Luna in his arms, and momentum carried them both over the railing. There was an almighty splash as they tumbled into the water of the vacant berth beside us.

Shit!

Could Luna even swim? When she came to the sanctuary, she hadn't been able to, but Knox said Ryder had been teaching her. How far had they gotten with the lessons? Fuck it. I dove in after her. Aiden could swim well; I knew that for certain. He'd been captain of the swim team in college. He was still fighting with Luna when I popped up beside them, and I grabbed his wrist, trying to unpeel his fingers from around her arm. Maybe I'd break one or two in the process? I hoped I did.

"Hey!" a guy yelled from the promenade. "Hey! Luna Maara's in the water!"

Suddenly, there were men everywhere, diving off the promenade fully clothed, yelling about various lifesaving qualifications. Luna's bikini top had disappeared somewhere, and she was still screaming blue murder. Aiden knew he was beaten, at least for now. He released his grip and treaded water while he got his bearings, surveyed the chaos before he began swimming smoothly in the opposite direction.

That bastard! For a moment, I considered going after him. Considered trying to drown him, to hold him under until he breathed his last. But he was bigger, stronger... And he was getting away. If I didn't act now, he'd come for me again, he'd—

A hand grabbed my shoulder, and I nearly punched its owner. "Get off me!"

"Ma'am, I'm here to help. I worked a summer as a lifeguard."

"I'm fine. Leave me alone."

"Your face is bruised."

And my strength was ebbing. The panic that had driven me was gone, and I couldn't catch Aiden. Only a miracle would help.

This wasn't over.

51

KNOX

"Uh, excuse me."

Knox looked up to find Jubilee gripping the doorjamb, her knuckles white.

"I don't want another drink."

"I think Luna fell in the water."

What the actual fuck?

"You *think* Luna fell in the water?"

He repeated it slowly because the idea was ridiculous. Luna wouldn't even go near the edge of the boat. When she boarded, she scooted over the passerelle so fast you'd think it was on fire.

"Or maybe someone pushed her?"

Fuck, fuck, fuck. Knox grabbed a crutch, then dropped it and just gritted his teeth as he half ran, half hobbled out of the room behind Jubilee. She pointed over the railing, beyond the smaller boats berthed next to them to a commotion in the water. Splashing, shrieking, there had to be twenty bodies in there. All male apart from Luna, and where the hell were her clothes?

"Who are those men?"

"I don't know—I think they jumped in to save her."

Great, someone had already done the hard part. "Maybe you should take her a towel?"

And Knox would prepare a lesson about the dangers of getting too close to the edge, right after he delivered a lecture on never, ever going ashore without the bodyguard she was paying to accompany her at all times. Shit, he'd have to explain this to Emmy.

Then his heart stuttered.

Luna *wasn't* the only woman in the water.

He saw the face he'd been dreaming of for the past three weeks, the lips he'd feared he'd never kiss again. Only Caro's head was visible, and one of the wannabe heroes was with her, but she wasn't looking at him. No, she was staring at something else. *Someone* else. A dark-haired man stroking through the water, heading away from the scene. Aiden Kingsley. That motherfucker. Even from the deck of the *Cleopatra*, Knox could see the dark bruises marring Caro's beautiful features.

He also saw red.

Walking might have been a problem, but he could still swim, and he dove off the yacht, calculating speed and trajectories in his head. He could catch that asshole. Catch him and make sure he never got his hands on Knox's girl again.

Because Caro *was* his girl.

She might not realise it yet, but he'd convince her to come around to his way of thinking, and he'd do it with love, not by force and manipulation.

Aiden Kingsley was so focused on his destination, so convinced by his own immortality that he didn't look back. Didn't see Knox heading toward him, low in the water. When Knox got close, he ducked beneath the surface, propelled himself forward, and dragged Kingsley under like a shark snatching a turtle. After a moment of shock, the fucker began to struggle, fast realising that he was fighting for his life. Did he know who Knox was? Recognise him as the man who spent time with Caro? Knox hoped he did, wanted Kingsley to understand with his last breath who had killed him and why.

The two men grappled, experience and skill versus raw desperation. When Kingsley tried to kick for the surface, Knox pulled him under again. Kingsley was more proficient underwater than Knox had expected, but that didn't matter. This would still be his grave. Gazes met, and Knox saw the spark of recognition. But his satisfaction was quickly damped when instead of swimming upward, Kingsley dove down, arms reaching out, and grabbed Knox's thigh. Fuck. The man homed in on Knox's exit wound and pressed, forcing his thumb inside, and it was all Knox could do not to roar in agony.

He fought the inferno that shot up his leg, that weakened his hold, that flooded his brain with signals to *get away, get away, get away*. Knox stretched for Kingsley's head, feeling his way, ready to force nails into his eyeball. He needed a miracle, an unearthly intervention to help him fight against this blackout pain. An arm snaked around Kingsley's neck, but...but it wasn't Knox's arm. No, he was still gripping the motherfucker's head, and this arm belonged to a giant.

No, it belonged to Black.

Emmy's husband tightened his chokehold and motioned Knox away with his other hand. *Get out of here.* His calm, almost bored expression said he had everything under control. Knox wasn't about to disobey a direct order just to prove a point. He released his prey and shot upward, gulping in mouthfuls of air when he surfaced, keeping his face hidden among the wind-blown ripples.

The crowd's attention was still fixed on Luna and Caro, but Knox still didn't want to risk being spotted. Once the pain had turned from white hot to red, he submerged and headed back to the *Cleopatra*, one useless leg trailing behind him.

He had to find his girl.

Jubilee gasped when he hauled himself onto the promenade, hand over hand up the trailing end of the mooring rope, and dripped blood and water across the passerelle. He scanned the shore for Caro as he grabbed a towel from a sun lounger and used it to stem the flow from his wound.

"What...what happened?" Jubilee asked, ashen.

"Tore a few stitches, that's all."

"Should I call an ambulance?"

There she was. Caro stumbled toward him like a baby fawn. Someone had given her a towel, but every bit of skin he could see was covered in bruises, some purple, some already yellowing around the edges. Her bottom lip was split and swollen, and she winced with every step she took. But she kept going.

"Yeah, call an ambulance," Knox said and limped back across the passerelle.

He wanted to gather her up in his arms and kiss her senseless, but he couldn't, not without hurting her more, plus he was still holding the damn towel against his bleeding thigh. Instead, he had to settle for running one finger down an undamaged part of her cheek.

"Did you...?" she whispered.

Knox knew exactly what she was asking. "You're safe."

She took a shaky breath and then began crying. Fuck. That wasn't the reaction he'd hoped for.

"I thought you wanted that?"

Through the tears came a barely audible "Thank you."

Better. "I'll ask 'what the fuck?' later, but for now, I'm just going to say that I love you."

A sharp intake of breath.

"I don't expect you to say it back, not yet, but maybe someday."

"I love you," she blurted. "I can't... I can't believe I'm here."

Luna, also with a towel wrapped around her, was posing for pictures and signing autographs for her rescuers. Nobody noticed when Knox and Caro slipped back onto the *Cleopatra* and into the saloon. Would his blood come out of the carpet? If not, they could deduct from his paycheck because he needed to get Caro away from the cameras.

"Medics are on the way. How badly hurt are you?"

"Nothing...nothing life-threatening. A lot of bruises."

"Tell me he didn't..."

Caro cried harder, and fury boiled through Knox's veins. Now he did hug her, but ever so gently, and peppered her wet hair with soft kisses.

"I wish I could go back and kill him again, but slower."

"He's really dead?"

Knox nodded. He absolutely trusted that Black would have finished the job, but if there was any comeback, it was on him. He'd take the heat.

"Then that's all that matters. I'm here, and he's not. We won. He lost."

"We're going to get through this. Together."

She hugged him tighter. "Are the police coming? There are still men on the boat, at least two of them."

"Fuck, I should—" Knox took a step toward the stern, but Caro clung to him.

"They're not going anywhere. I hit one with a turtle, and Luna got the other with a champagne bottle. I think she might have broken his skull. The second *crack* sounded odd."

"A turtle?"

"I felt bad about it, but it was already dead, and I didn't want to join it. Where's Franklin? The shooting... Did he...?"

"Still in the hospital, but he's expected to recover. Volunteers have been feeding the turtles at the sanctuary."

Luna strolled in and flopped onto the nearest couch with a heavy sigh. "In ten minutes, everyone on the internet will have seen my boobs."

And Ryder would probably go feral.

"Not everyone," Knox said, trying to make her feel better. "Maybe just a few million." That didn't help much, did it? "Where's Kory?"

"Talking to the hot guy from the burrito stand. Can you save the lecture about boarding strangers' yachts for later? Because I know I'm gonna get one."

Even Caro smiled at that.

"Sure, I'll let Ryder do the honours."

Luna rolled her eyes, but then she turned to face Caro. "I'm so, so sorry I made that post. If I'd known it would lead to...to this..." She gestured at the chaos outside. "I think I might just quit social media altogether."

"It wasn't your fault."

"Really?"

"A member of the smuggling gang saw Knox and me when we were looking for Monique. They took a picture, and it found its way to Aiden. It's all connected—him, the poaching, some guy called Theron. The cops. Not Vince, but Jason Roy and Maceo Beattie, plus a bunch of others."

"Aiden told you that?" Knox asked.

"He's so fucking arrogant. He wanted me to know how successful he'd been after...after I reported him to the IRS."

Another sob escaped. "I thought he'd go to prison. He cheated so much, and I spent a year gathering the evidence."

"We know," Knox said gently. "We know everything. Stanford, huh?"

She covered her face with her hands. "I should have told you. I just found it so hard to trust anyone."

"A wise woman once told me not to dwell on the past, and she was right."

"What woman?"

Was that a hint of jealousy? If it was, Knox kind of liked it.

"Relax, she's my boss."

Sirens were coming from all directions now, and as they grew louder, Caro sank onto the couch beside Luna. Fuckin' Luna. Ryder was going to lose his shit when he found out what she'd done. That she'd risked her own safety to help Caro. Maybe they could wait until tomorrow to tell him? Until after the— Shit, the operation on Malavilla.

"I need to call Emmy," Knox said, mostly to himself, but it was Black who answered. The big man strode in shirtless, drying his hair with a towel. Relaxed, casual, no hint that he'd just strangled a man and left his lifeless body for the fishes.

"I've already spoken with her."

"She's calling off the operation?"

"No, we're going ahead. Theron Voss was on the *Kraken*, so it's fair to say he's involved, as we suspected."

"You went on board?"

"I got curious. Thought I'd take a look around before the police arrived and tainted the scene." He glanced at his watch. In a nod to practicality, today he'd worn a Panerai Submersible, which retailed at more than Knox's monthly salary. And Knox earned good money. "I need to change. There will be questions to answer this afternoon."

Luna had one. "Did...did those men on the *Kraken*... Are they still alive?"

Black smiled, and his smiles were rarer than the hawksbills Caro had worked so hard to save.

"If you're ever looking to change career, I'll give you a job."

52

CARO

"**G**ood morning."

The voice was British. And female. A doctor? I heaved my eyelids open—even my lashes seemed to hurt—and took in my visitor. Definitely not a doctor. She was close to my age, maybe a year or two older, with good skin and an athletic figure. But her eyes had a deepness to them, a haunted quality that said they'd seen a lot, none of it pleasant. And they were the strangest colour. Almost violet. She wore casual clothes—denim shorts and a tank top—and her blonde hair was piled on top of her head in a messy bun.

I was almost certain that I didn't know her. My head was fuzzy, but wouldn't I remember the accent? Wait, what if she was part of the mob of paparazzi that followed Luna around? This was exactly the sort of juicy story they'd love.

"No comment," I snarled, but she just laughed.

"I'm not a reporter."

"Then who are you?"

"I work with Knox."

My heart skipped, and not in a good way. "Where is he? Is he okay?"

"Relax, he just went to hunt breakfast. The food here is shit, and he knows that firsthand."

"He said he got shot. It was bad?"

As he limped to the ambulance yesterday afternoon, he'd insisted it was no big deal, but I saw the pain he tried to hide. The doctors had stitched up his leg again, and now I was stuck here for "observation," which I suspected wasn't really necessary, but they liked to cover their asses. Somehow, I'd ended up in the fancy, private part of the hospital with my own room and a TV, so it wasn't as bad as it could have been. Where had all those flowers come from?

"Knox lost a bit of blood on Valentine Cay. Would've been worse if Luna hadn't got to him quickly."

"Luna?"

"She called Ryder, and he told her where to find the first-aid kit."

"I was worried they'd killed her. There was so much gunfire."

"Oh, they tried. Nice work with the speargun, by the way."

"Is he dead? The man I shot?"

I was almost certain he was, but it paid to make sure.

"As a doornail, whatever one of those is. You did a good job."

"Not good enough. They still took me."

"Eh, shit happens to the best of us." There were a few strands of hair stuck to my cheek, and she brushed them away, her touch featherlight. "How are you feeling?"

She wasn't asking out of obligation. Her tone, her expression, they suggested she genuinely cared. Her hand twitched toward mine, but she didn't touch me again.

"I... Not so good. Did they...did they tell you what he did to me?"

"It's a good thing Aiden's communing with the fishes. If he wasn't, I'd rip his fucking head off." She grinned, and the effect was chilling. "I'm speaking metaphorically, of course."

"I still keep expecting him to walk in."

"Rest easy." Her voice, her expression, her demeanour softened. "Words are inadequate at a time like this, but all I can say is that it will get better."

Was she saying what I thought she was saying? She seemed so strong, so confident.

"You were...?"

"Karma took longer to catch up with the men who raped me, but he got there in the end. Just know that people have your back."

Knox. By "people," she meant Knox, didn't she? When it came to my problems, he and karma were one and the same thing. I closed my eyes for a moment, processing. My brain was still running at half-speed today, tired after little sleep, emotionally drained after surviving the impossible. Was this a dream? The aches that spread through me every time I moved said otherwise.

"I...I don't understand what I did to deserve Knox. At first, I tried to keep him out, but..."

I'd told myself it was just a fling. A fling had been easy. But a relationship? The thought of getting serious scared me, but not as much as the prospect of losing him.

"The heart needs what the heart needs." The blonde rolled her eyes. "Sometimes that's a shiv, but Knox isn't one of those guys; don't worry."

"How can I not worry? He offered to help me, but we barely know each other. I love him, but is it enough? My judgment when it comes to men is terrible."

"Mine isn't, and he wouldn't be on my team if he was an arsehole."

So this was his boss? Emmy? He'd mentioned her once or twice, and he said she was crazy.

"I met Knox less than a month ago."

"Sometimes you have to take a leap of faith."

"Would you?"

"Eighteen years ago, I crossed paths with a guy in London, and a week later, I moved to Virginia to live with him."

"Love at first sight?"

"Hell no. I broke his nose." *What?* "But two years later, I married him, and I haven't killed him yet, so I guess things can work out."

"You *broke his nose*?"

"Yeah, but it healed pretty straight. Now it's a fun story to tell at parties." She studied me carefully, and her gaze crawled under my skin. Yes, this was definitely Emmy. "But you're right to be nervous. It's a big change, and I'd be more worried if you jumped in with no reservations, especially since you have a fuck ton of trauma to work through."

"I have so much baggage that I'd get thrown out of the airport."

"And you think he doesn't have any?" She chuckled softly. "The irony—you're wary of commitment in case you can't get rid of the guy later, and Knox holds back because he's scared of losing someone else he cares about."

"You mean the car wreck?"

"He told you about that?" Emmy seemed surprised.

"A couple of weeks ago."

"Then he's definitely decided you're the one because he never discusses that with anyone. Are you coming back to Virginia with him? Or do I need to brace for a flexible working request?" She sucked in a breath. "Or a resignation?"

"I…I'm not sure. I didn't feel safe here after Luna posted a picture of me online, but I was still deciding where to go. We spoke about Canada. Knox was going to visit."

"There's nothing stopping you from coming back to the US now, if that's what you want."

"I guess. But I don't want to be *that* woman. A burden. I mean, I have nothing. *Nothing.* What if he offers me a place to stay out of obligation, and it doesn't work out, and…and… I met Aiden when I was at my lowest point. My mom had just died, and he said he'd help me, but he broke me."

"Firstly, Knox isn't Aiden. Secondly, you met him before the latest round of shit happened. Thirdly, if he tried to fuck you over, he'd have me to deal with as well as you. Close your eyes."

"Huh?"

"Close your eyes. Do it." I obeyed because Emmy didn't seem the type of woman you argued with. "We're three months into the future. What does your life look like? Where do you want to be?"

"I can't… I don't know…"

"Focus on your breathing, and then let your mind wander," she told me.

So I did. *In and out, in and out, in and out…* And I saw…Knox. Sleeping beside me in a huge bed, one that didn't have a bunk above it. He looked so peaceful, sunlight slanting across his golden skin. I'd wake him with a soft kiss, and we'd eat breakfast together before we both headed to work. Or maybe I'd eat him instead? Work… I'd be back in an office again, but perhaps I'd choose a non-profit this time, so I could still help animals but without cleaning out turtle pools from dawn till dusk. I'd miss the turtles, but…

three years of that life was enough, and...and I wouldn't be able to go back to the sanctuary without thinking of what happened that day. The way I'd been dragged across the sand toward a waiting boat, helpless to escape. If the grant from the Blackwood Foundation came through, I could leave without guilt.

Once, I'd focused on material things. Mom had worked in a high-end hotel, bowing and scraping to the rich and famous. With a start, I realised that maybe my past was the reason I'd pre-judged Luna. Not only due to her antics with the turtle, but because I'd spent my childhood listening to Mom's tales of celebrity excess. I'd been brought up to believe that they were better than us, that their life was something to aspire to, but now I understood that money couldn't buy happiness. I still craved security, but I wanted a simple home, one that could be filled with memories rather than shiny trinkets. And I wanted to make those memories with Knox Livingston.

I didn't need the kind of life I'd once wished for.

I just needed him.

I needed to know that whenever the past got too much for me to bear, he'd wrap me up in those strong arms and take the pain away.

And I'd do anything to get that, even moving to Virginia.

I'd been murmuring my thoughts to Emmy as I went, words pulled out of me by an invisible string mingling with the beep of machines and the squeak of shoes on tile in the hallway outside the room. The scrape of a pencil on paper. When I opened my eyes, Emmy handed me a note.

"What's this?" I asked.

"Security. You're worried things are moving too fast."

"I don't understand."

"It's an IOU for an apartment in Richmond. One year,

rent-free. Either use it right away or save it for a rainy day. There's also a number for Corazon da Silva. She runs the Blackwood Foundation, and the last I heard, she was starting the search for a new accountant. The current guy is due to retire at the end of the year."

"You mean—"

The door cracked open, and Knox appeared. My heart lurched. This man...he'd set me free. Did Emmy know he'd killed Aiden? She'd said he wouldn't be back, so I had to assume that she did. Knox had a crutch in one hand, coffee and a grease-spotted paper bag in the other, and I felt the smile spread across my face. His expression mirrored mine.

I had to try. I *had* to.

Emmy backed toward the door. "I'll leave the pair of you to it."

53

KNOX

A hundred and seventy-one hawksbills, sixty-three green turtles, eleven loggerheads, thirty-seven leatherbacks, and five olive ridleys, the last of which weren't even native to San Gallicano. That was how many turtles Emmy and the team found when they incapacitated the guards at Havana Hills and took a look through the barns. Plus a stash of shark fins and a narwhal tusk. Nobody knew where the fuck that had come from, and Theron Voss wouldn't be telling anyone—he was on ice in the mortuary, along with Barry the Barracuda and Aiden Kingsley. Kingsley's body had washed up this morning, minus an arm. Detective Fernandez had called to tell Knox.

Forty-eight hours had passed since Luna ignored all sensible courses of action and boarded the *Kraken*. Her boobs had indeed gone viral, but thankfully, that would be the worst consequence of her actions from that day. With help from Black, she'd explained to Detective Fernandez that she thought she'd heard a scream as she walked past the *Kraken*, and being a good citizen, had hurried on board to offer assistance. It was close enough to the truth, and the only men who would contradict her story were dead. Kory had backed her up.

In the eyes of the San Gallicano authorities, she was a hero, and most importantly, Judge Morgan agreed with that assessment. Luna had been released from her sentence, although she wanted to return to the turtle sanctuary to help out for a few days before she left the country. She and Kory planned to skip town on Thursday, right before Luna's mother got released from jail. Yes, Thursday. Amethyst's sentence had been extended from thirty days to thirty-three after she spat at a guard.

What did Ryder plan to do? That was anyone's guess.

He'd been predictably horrified when he found out Luna had gone head-to-head with a member of Aiden Kingsley's gang for the second time, and groaned long and loud when he saw her boobs doing the rounds on the internet. Headlines included *Lovely Luna frolics with friends in San Gallicano, Luna Maara flees shark while vacationing in the Caribbean*, and *Spotted: Fuller-figured Luna Maara— is she pregnant?*

Only if it were the immaculate conception. She was still sharing a room with Ryder, but he swore they weren't exchanging bodily fluids. Knox believed him, mainly because he'd overheard Luna and Kory having the "gay, straight, or bi?" conversation earlier. Luna swore that Ryder was too sweet to be straight, but Kory wasn't convinced he was gay, despite Ryder's claim about a boyfriend. When the possibility of bisexuality was mooted by Kory, Luna had shuddered and said no way, Ryder definitely wasn't into women.

Could she really be that oblivious? Yachting activities aside, Luna wasn't stupid, but the woman was so socially inept it made Knox want to face-palm.

The shower stopped, and a minute later, steam billowed

into the bedroom Knox was sharing with Caro on the *Cleopatra*.

"Could you pass me a hair tie?" she asked.

He rummaged on the dressing table until he found what she wanted. This whole domesticated thing was weird, but he kind of liked it. Sharing his space, his life, with a woman. They'd talked last night, talked for hours, just lying next to each other, barely touching, and while the sex on Valentine Cay had been great, this new connection, it was...more. Caro told him about her childhood, her mom, and the struggle through college. Not so much about Aiden—that was still raw—but she let him see the real her. And he spilled his own secrets. The difficulties of growing up with an alcoholic mother, his escape in music. Opening up left him feeling lighter inside, as if he'd finally let go of a weight that had been dragging him down. Huh. Maybe Ryder was right and there was something to that therapy shit after all?

The hardest part had come later, after they'd fallen asleep. Caro thumped him in the early hours, flailing in the throes of a nightmare. He'd tried to catch her hand when it came for him again, but then he pulled back, letting the blow land. What if his touch scared her? Made things worse? In the end, he'd splashed cold water on her, then held her while she cried herself back to sleep.

But things would get better.

They could only get better.

"Are you sure you want to go back to the sanctuary today?" he asked as she emerged in a bathrobe.

"If I don't do it now, I never will. And my stuff is still there. I need to pack and also check that Tadie's doing okay."

Tadie lived on Valentine Cay, and she'd been volunteering with Franklin since she was fourteen years old, although not so much lately because her job got too demanding. Some remote customer service role. People complaining the whole time, she said, and when she heard there were openings at the sanctuary with a decent salary on offer, she'd gladly handed in her notice. Two students on a gap-year trip were arriving tomorrow, which gave Baptiste time to find a second full-time employee and focus on his recovery. Plus the locals had rallied around, helping to collect eggs from beaches all over San Gallicano and cleaning up the mess left behind after the raid.

Today, Luna and Ryder would be at the sanctuary, plus Jubilee, Kory, and Slater. The others had flown back to the US, but Emmy had told Knox to take a couple of weeks to get himself and Caro sorted out. Luna was happy with that, as long as Ryder could stay with her until the end of the contract, although how much bodyguarding he'd be doing was debatable. He seemed to be acting as more of an emotional-support commando.

"Speaking of packing, we still need to work out where you're going to live."

Knox hadn't pushed the subject, but time was ticking, and even a hotel room needed to be booked in advance.

Caro gave a tentative smile. "How about Richmond?"

Knox stilled, hoping he hadn't misheard, fearing she meant Richmond, UK, and he'd be spending a lot of time over the Atlantic. Caro mistook his surprise for reluctance.

"I don't mean we have to live together, not yet. We can take things as slow as you want. But I spoke with Emmy, and she offered me somewhere to stay and basically arranged a job interview, so..." She took his hand. "I really want to make a go of this."

Emmy had done what? That crazy, meddling...genius.

"Where's the job?"

"At the Blackwood Foundation."

"That..." That would be perfect. Cora and Mercy had

been through similar experiences, and it wouldn't be a high-pressure environment. They spent their days planning fundraisers to disguise the fact that they were giving away over a billion dollars that Blackwood had liberated from organised crime. "That position would suit you very well. Did Emmy offer you an apartment? Or room and board at her place?"

"An apartment. But if I get the job, I'll pay her back for the rent. I don't want to be a charity case."

"She wouldn't take the money. All she'd ask is that you pay it forward someday."

"I like her, but she scares me a bit."

"You and me both, baby. Where you live is up to you, but I already spoke with Ryder and Slater. If you want to stay with us for a while, they're good with that."

"Is there enough space?"

"Ryder and I moved to Richmond around the same time, and Slater's lease was up. We all travel regularly, plus we were hanging out together after work anyway, so we figured that instead of renting three apartments that would stay empty half of the time, we'd get a nice house and split the rent three ways." Knox grinned. "We have a great pool, and if you need space, there are two spare bedrooms."

"I want to sleep with you." Caro's face flushed. "I mean share a bed. And have sex, obviously, but...but..."

Don't cry, baby.

"We have all the time in the world now. When it happens, it happens." He held her close and kissed her wet hair. "Never thought I'd do the boyfriend thing, but here we are."

"Here we are," she echoed.

Knox never wanted to be anywhere else.

54

KNOX

"I think I'm gonna fire Mom," Luna announced over lunch, and Jubilee began choking. Slater thumped her on the back, and an olive flew across the table. Kory just gaped, and even Ryder looked mildly surprised.

But good for Luna. Amethyst Puckett was toxic.

"Can you even do that?" Jubilee asked. "I mean, she's your mother."

"Which means she should have my best interests at heart, right? So why have I spent the whole morning dreading tomorrow? Feeling sick that there are only four days left until she gets out of jail and I have to see her? Four days until I have to join her stupid circus again. I don't want to hawk hot tubs on Instagram. I don't want to wear clothes made out of food. I don't want to get recognised everywhere I go. All I ever wanted to do was sing, and I'm not even allowed to perform my own songs."

Knox glanced sideways at Caro, and their gazes met as she did the same thing. Who knew a casual picnic could bring so much drama? They'd schlepped the food with them from Ilha Grande, cleared space in the shade under a mango tree, and dragged the bigger of the two dining tables outside. Someone had tried to patch up the bullet hole in the other, but there was no way to hide it completely. As for the outdoor dining set Jubilee had bought, that was covered in bloodstains—Knox wasn't sure whose—and was now residing in the forest out of sight. Tango was lying beside Caro, her head resting on Caro's foot, and Knox figured he should research pet import regulations. Cora wouldn't mind a dog in the office. She liked animals.

"It's been a stressful month," Jubilee said. "Maybe if you take a few days when we get back... Should I book—"

"No, no, no! You sound just like her, do you realise that? There, there, stop acting out, I'll book you into rehab *again.*"

"Sorry, I—"

"And don't think I've forgotten the way you schemed with Cordelia, or that Mom employs you, not me."

Jubilee gasped. "Well, what about Julius? You hate speaking with him, and Mom always handles those calls."

"Until I can get rid of him too, I'll hire a go-between. And then when I've made my last two albums with Sonic Flare and survived the world tour I never wanted to do in the first place, I can reevaluate my life."

"But what about the money?"

"I've been working since I was four years old, and Mom keeps bragging that I'm a millionaire ten times over."

Support came from a surprising corner.

"There's nothing harder than living a lie," Caro said. "It's not just having to constantly remember who you told what; it's the darkness that builds up inside. The misery. You should go with your heart."

And then an unsurprising corner. Ryder.

"Caro's right. Your mom won't make things easy, but you're strong. You'll get through it."

"Does anyone know a good lawyer? Mom hired mine, and I think—"

Knox's and Ryder's phones pinged at the same time, and Knox knew that sound. The sensors. He was on his feet in a heartbeat, gun in hand, Ryder and Slater following suit.

"Dining room," Knox said. "Now."

His damn leg throbbed as he herded the girls and Kory to safety, Ryder heading along the driveway and Slater slipping through the trees to the beach. Paranoia, perhaps, but they weren't expecting visitors, and nor were they taking any chances. Caro looked as if she was fighting back tears, but Luna grabbed the kettle and hefted it in her hands. Fucking hell.

"Maybe you could put that down?" Knox suggested. "I have a gun."

"Or maybe I could just keep hold of it. Caro, you want a frying pan? There's a frying pan in there, and it's heavy."

By the time Ryder called to say it was a false alarm, Caro was armed with a frying pan, and Jubilee and Kory had saucepans, but they quickly returned them to the kitchen when Ryder appeared with a pretty but nervous-looking brunette in tow. Knox raised an eyebrow.

"This is Monique," Ryder introduced. "She heard it was safe to come out now."

"I..." She smoothed the fabric of her flowery sundress with her hands. "I don't know where to start. I guess by saying thank you? And sorry. I'm so sorry if anything I did made this worse."

Well, damn. This was the last thing Knox had expected today. "Where have you been?"

"Staying with a friend." Her smile was shaky. "In his attic. I wanted to go to the police, I did, but Stacey said they couldn't be trusted, and I was just so scared. Terrified. I heard they found her body."

Stacey's remains had been formally identified through dental records now. Blackwood was assisting her parents with getting her body repatriated, and Caro wanted to pay her respects at the funeral.

"Were you with her that night? At Havana Hills?"

Monique nodded. "I guess we tripped an alarm because they came out of nowhere. We both ran, and I thought she was right behind me, but when I reached the sea, I realised she'd gone. And then a guy started shooting, so I jumped off the cliff. I didn't see her get caught. Honestly, I thought she'd escaped too, but when I finally managed to call my friend, I found out she hadn't made it."

"It took you three days to call someone?"

"The currents took me away from Malavilla, and I ended up on Monkey Island. It's uninhabited. Stacey said the shark sightings were probably fake, but..." She shuddered. "Anyhow, after two days, a boat full of Japanese tourists showed up, and I told them I'd fallen off my paddleboard."

"They gave you a ride back?"

"To Ilha Grande. I didn't want to go anywhere near Malavilla."

"How did you find out about the turtles at Havana Hills?"

"Through gross stupidity. I lost my mind and dated the bad boy. I thought it would be an adventure, you know? And he did treat me okay, better than the last... Never mind. Sometimes, I used to go to Havana Hills with Tomas and use the pool while he did...well, he said he worked with the maintenance team, which I guess on a deep level I always thought was odd because the place was kind of overgrown, but I figured he was trying to clean up his act. Anyhow, we were there one day in the winter, and it was cold, so I didn't swim for long. And I figured I'd go find him. Just to see if he wanted a drink or something to eat. And that's when I saw the turtles, and I realised he hadn't changed at all."

"You didn't report it?"

"I was scared." She looked at her feet. "Scared that Tomas—or worse, Barry—would know it was me and retaliate. I should have told someone."

"You told Stacey?"

"A few months ago, I watched one of those nature documentaries. I honestly didn't realise how rare turtles were getting, and... Yes, when Angel called and said a journalist wanted to speak with me, I told her. And I offered to show her where the barn was. I'm so, so sorry."

At least they'd cleared up the last piece of the puzzle. Fernandez and the coastguard could stand down—everyone had feared they were looking for a body, despite the detective's suspicions that Monique's ex was acting cagey.

Caro got up and gave her a hug. "The only people to blame are the men who did this."

"Maybe a woman too. Tomas's boss was married, and his wife was always around. Lucinda. Lucinda Voss. I saw her walking to the barn once."

Okay, it seemed there were a couple of puzzle pieces left.

"Will you talk to the police now?" Knox asked. "There's at least one detective who isn't dirty."

Monique nodded. "I'll tell them everything."

Fernandez sent the coastguard to Valentine Cay to pick up Monique. The cutter had been out looking for her body, and all the officers were mighty relieved to see her alive. And there was more news—the men Emmy's team had captured at Havana Hills were starting to turn on each other, tripping over themselves in their efforts to win the top prize of an immunity deal from Judge Morgan. Seven dirty cops had been suspended so far. Blackwood's cyber team had cracked the passwords on the flash drives, and Stacey's own notes would help to put her killers behind bars, those that were still alive anyway.

It was almost over. A few days of packing and goodbyes, and they'd be heading back to the US.

Luna's phone rang. The screen had lit up three times while Monique was talking, but Luna had ignored it and then finally turned the phone over. But now she grimaced and growled, "Get lost."

"Who is it?" Jubilee asked.

"Julius."

"Why is he calling you? He knows you never answer."

"How should I know? Probably because he can't get hold of Mom, and there's some mega urgent deal for a plushie toy that he wants me to promote in Japan."

"So you're just going to keep hanging up on him?"

"You can answer if you want to."

"Uh, no."

The phone kept ringing.

"How about I answer?" Ryder offered. "I'll even tell him to go to hell if you want me to."

Luna leaned against him, her head on his shoulder. "You'd really do that?" she asked dreamily.

"Sure."

"Can you find out what he wants first?"

Ryder put the phone to his ear. "This is Bentley Throckmorton, Ms. Maara's communications assistant. On a scale of one to five, with one being a sales pitch for cryptocurrency and five being a world-ending catastrophe, how important is this call? She told me to only take a message for the fives."

A pause.

"A five? Really? Well, go ahead."

He cocked his head to one side, listening, and the amused smile slipped off his face. Luna became more anxious as she watched, gripping his hand hard enough that her nails dug into his flesh.

"Yes, I'll relay the message. Yes, she has your number. Now you can go to hell, one-way ticket. Yes, she told me to say that too." He hung up and gave a weighty sigh. "Well, fuck."

"What? What is it?"

"There's...news."

"Good news or bad news?"

"I'm not entirely sure. So, the first thing is that the record label saw the memes of your boobs and decided you were bringing the company into disrepute. They're abrogating your contract, effective immediately."

"Abro-what? I don't even know what that means."

"Revoking it. Apparently, they can do that. Clause thirty-two point eight or something." Ryder twined his fingers through hers as she digested his words. "You okay?"

"Uh, maybe? I...I'm not sure. What's the other news?"

"The Nile Palace wants to offer you a four-month residency. Six shows a week, and you'd have creative control."

"The Nile? What, in Egypt?"

"Sin City, baby. The Nile Palace Hotel and Casino."

"I... Wow. What about the tour? Did Julius mention the tour?"

"Cancelled along with the two albums and all the promo."

She sagged in her seat. "Thank goodness."

"Amethyst is gonna be furious," Jubilee warned.

"You know what? I don't even care."

55

LUNA

"**Y**ou're very quiet tonight," Ryder murmured as Kory told everyone the story of his disastrous trip to the Blayz Festival. I'd already heard it twice, so I'd mostly tuned him out.

"...and I guess the organisers thought that if there was a big enough crowd, it wouldn't matter that they didn't get the proper permissions for the event. But it did, and a thousand cops showed up halfway through the first day. When the bands ignored them and carried on, they cut the power. Can you believe that? Then they started arresting people for drugs. I didn't get to play my set, but man, I'm glad they didn't find my weed. Chad Bassington had, like, one joint in his pocket, and he spent three days in jail."

Slater was leaving tomorrow, so we'd booked a table at Coletta's Bar and Eatery for one last dinner together. Tadie had recommended the place—Coletta was her aunt, but she swore that didn't sway her opinion on the food, which was excellent. Plates piled high with fritters, deep bowls of rice and peas, dishes of spicy chicken and pork. My clothes were getting quite tight now.

"I'm okay. Just thinking."

"About your agent's phone call?"

I nodded. "This time yesterday, I had all these commitments. Studio time, live shows, interviews, personal appearances... And it's just...gone. I'm free, and I should be happy because wasn't that what I'd been dreaming of? But I also feel like a bit of a failure. Professionally, I mean. We've already established that my personal life is a disaster."

"You're not a failure, moon. You've been working for twenty-two years, and you've made more money than most people do in a lifetime."

"But I've never had an empty schedule before. It's weird."

"What about the Nile Palace thing?"

"Jubilee emailed Julius and told him to send the details. They say full creative control, but I bet they don't really mean it."

"You could always take a break. Reevaluate."

"Maybe? I'd settle for partial creative control if the show wasn't in Vegas."

"Isn't it easier having a show so close to home?"

Despite the heat and the endless humidity, I shuddered. Yes, I owned a house in Las Vegas, but it hadn't felt like home in a long time.

"Mom will be there, and believe me when I say she's not going to take my change in direction well." I clung to Ryder's hand, and a shiver ran through me when he brushed his thumb over my knuckles. "If she forces me back into rehab, promise you won't believe the stories you read in the papers? I'm not exhausted or suffering a breakdown, and I don't have an eating disorder or a substance abuse problem. Unless you count acetaminophen because she gives me a constant headache."

"I understand where you're coming from."

"Ryder, who do you work for?" I asked. He'd been at my side for over a month, but I had a sickening feeling that his contract was with my management company rather than with me. And who owned the management company? My mom.

"Blackwood Security." He gave me a puzzled look. "You know that."

"Yes, but Mom hired you, and she signed the contract. You're here to protect me, but I think you're working for her."

"Moon, I don't give a fuck about the contract. I'm working for you."

Ryder said it with such vehemence that I sagged in my seat. He was on my side. Not Mom's, not Cordelia's, not his own, mine. I'd never had an actual ally before, and the revelation made me want to weep with relief.

"If I left here tomorrow and flew to Vegas, would you help me to grab as much of my stuff as I can from my house? I think I'm gonna check into a hotel for a while."

"I'll be by your side the whole way."

"Do you think I'd be doing the right thing?"

"Yeah, I do. Moon, you're a different person than you were a month ago. Back then, you were only focused on making other people happy—your family, your record label, the world. Now you've learned to think about yourself too." He hooked an arm around my shoulder and squeezed. "I'm so fucking proud of you."

The words were foreign. Despite all that I'd achieved, the trophies I'd won, the charts I'd topped, the shows I'd sold out, I'd never once heard those words from the person who I thought mattered. My mom. She always wanted more, more, more. Nothing was ever enough. But now, I realised who truly mattered, and that was the man sitting next to me. Go figure. My new bestie was a guy. I'd seen those magazine articles that said every girl needed a gay best friend, but I hadn't believed them. Were we supposed to go shopping together now? What did Ryder know about colour? He mostly wore grey and black.

He kissed my hair in that sweet way of his. "If you ever need a bolthole, there's a spare bedroom at our place in Virginia. Knox and Slater won't mind if you stay there for a few weeks."

Really? A month ago, I would have said no way, but Knox had never acted sleazy toward me, and Slater seemed to come out of the same mould. And I trusted that Ryder wouldn't put me in danger. Mom wouldn't be able to track my credit card and find me, and I wouldn't have to deal with strangers poking around my room every day. Plus Caro was slowly becoming a friend. We'd gotten off to a shaky start, but that had been my fault as much as hers, and now we'd bonded over turtles and skinny-dipping. She'd left her chair to sit on Knox's lap, and I envied her that closeness. She'd been through the same thing I had, even worse seeing as she'd been kidnapped too, but she didn't have that mental block that stopped her from having a relationship.

"Can I sleep on it?" I asked Ryder.

"You can do whatever you—"

The slap came out of nowhere, right across his face. He jumped to his feet in an instant. Slater too, then Knox a second after that, once he'd deposited Caro back into her own seat. But none of them seemed to know what to do about the small but furious brunette standing before us with her hands on her hips.

But I knew. "Don't you touch him!"

I was ready to claw her freaking eyes out when Knox's arm snaked around my waist and hauled me back against him.

"Easy, Luna."

"Let go of me!"

"There are enough pictures of you on the internet already this week."

Okay, so he had a point, but the woman had just hit Ryder. Who even was she? Later, when I looked back on that evening, I wished I'd never found out.

"I've been waiting for over two years to do that," she hissed, her eyes narrowed to tiny slits.

"Do we know each other?" Ryder asked.

"I was one of your bridesmaids, you asshole!"

Was this an April Fools' joke? Today was April first, but weren't the pranks supposed to finish at noon? Slowly, Ryder's expression turned from confusion to recognition to shock, and I realised that whatever was going on, it was real. He glanced at me, then looked back at the brunette.

"Mia?"

"That was for Shylah."

"Who's Shylah?" I asked.

"His ex-wife. The one he abandoned in Iowa. He was supposed to stay home with her after he quit the Navy—her daddy even bought them a house—but oh, no, he just had to carry on gallivanting. Jerk."

Ryder had been married? Like, to a woman? The news sent a chill through me, a cold, crackling wave that threatened to snap my spine. He was straight? Had he lied to me? Or...or... I clutched at straws. Maybe he'd felt pressure to conform, from family, from the military, from society, and he'd worried about coming out. So he'd married a woman, a woman he loved in a different way, until he found the courage to be true to himself. Hadn't he said he was proud of me for doing that? What if he'd been speaking from experience?

"I never should have married her," he murmured.

"No, you shouldn't. She cried for months after you left.

Months. Lost thirty pounds, stopped getting out of bed, all because you're a jackass." She turned to me. "Take my advice and escape while you can, girl. He'll only break your heart in the end."

"We're not dating, and I'm actually proud of him for finally coming out."

"Coming out? Wait, you think he's gay?" Mia snorted. "Ryder isn't gay. He's just a filthy liar who's obsessed with his dead girlfriend, the one he'll never get over. *Never.* You're competing for his attention with a ghost."

I opened my mouth to snap back at her, but then I looked to Ryder, and I saw from the horror on his face that it was true. It was all true. He'd lied to me. Lied to me about the most important of things and left out a whole lot more besides. The green tinge suggested he was going to puke.

Mia just picked up his glass of water and threw it over him.

"Have a nice life," she snapped and stormed off.

"Moon..." Ryder started, but I cut him off.

"Don't you call me that. You don't get to pretend to care anymore. Was this a game to you? Let's mess with Luna's head? You know how I feel about men. I told you things I've never told anyone before, and all because you gained my trust under false pretences." He took a step forward; I took a step back. "Get the heck away from me."

I ran for the bathroom, the only place where I could hope for some privacy. People already had their phones out, recording us. Recording me. I locked myself into a stall, and then the tears came. The moment I finally found a tiny glimmer of happiness, a sliver of hope for the future, it fell apart. My body shook as I sobbed, and now I had no one. Not one single person I trusted.

Minutes passed. Somebody came to use the toilet, and I kept a hand over my mouth until they flushed, then let myself cry again. How was I even going to get out of here? Wait until the restaurant closed and then sneak through the window?

A soft knock sounded, and I jumped.

"Get lost."

"Are you okay?" Caro asked.

"Of course I'm not o-freaking-kay. Just keep him away from me."

"Knox made him leave."

"He'll probably circle back, the sneaky, conniving jerk."

"That's what Knox figured, so he went with him to make sure that didn't happen. Can I do anything to help?"

"N-n-no. Did you know? That Ryder likes women? Am I the only idiot?"

"Not for sure, but I saw the way he looked at you."

"How did he look at me?"

"As if...as if he was the night sky and you were the stars."

"What does that even mean?"

"It's a metaphor. Like he was the darkness, and you were his light."

"I'm not his anything." Not even his friend, not anymore. How could I be when he'd broken my trust? "I need to get away from this place."

"Slater's waiting to take you back to the *Cleopatra*."

This time, it was Caro by my side as I hurried past people who wouldn't stop staring at me. Kory tucked my pashmina around my shoulders and gave my arm a sympathetic squeeze.

"Guess you'll be on Insta again tomorrow."

I was so, so sick of social media. Of belonging to everyone but myself.

Jubilee was paying the bill, and I kept my head down, using Caro as a shield. My life was out of control. This was what I'd always feared—that if I pulled back from writing my own story, then the narrative would take on a life of its own. That my vulnerabilities would be laid bare for all to see.

"I'm sorry, ma'am," the waitress said. "Your card's been declined."

"Huh? It definitely shouldn't have been. Could you try it—"

"Use mine." I fumbled for the little purse that held my phone and a few other essentials. "Just hurry up."

The waitress took my card, only for the embarrassment to continue as my card got rejected too. If this wasn't the worst night of my life, it was undoubtedly in the top five.

"Did your accountant forget to pay the bill?" Kory joked as he handed over his own Amex.

Jubilee bit her lip. "I don't know. He hasn't been replying to my emails."

"Maybe he died? Has someone checked his office for a corpse?"

"Can we not talk about death?" I shuddered. "Don't you think we've all had enough of that?"

Finally, we managed to escape from the restaurant, and Slater walked two steps behind as Caro shepherded me back to the *Cleopatra*. The whole way, I was on edge, nails digging into my palms as I waited for Ryder to leap out of a souvenir store or pop up from behind an ornamental flower box. Even after we boarded, I still felt strung out, a rubber band waiting to snap. I sat on a bar stool, shaking as I drank neat vodka from the bottle while people I barely knew and didn't trust talked about me behind my back. Part of me wanted to run to my cabin, to cry alone, but it hadn't only been my cabin. It had been *our* cabin. Ryder had slept on my bed. I'd woken with his arm across my stomach, trapping me, only I hadn't felt trapped, I'd felt protected. Now I just felt betrayed.

Finally, Caro came over.

"Jubilee's asking if she should book flights for tomorrow," Caro said.

"Yes, she should." As long as she could get her stupid credit card to work, anyway.

"Where do you want to go?"

That was a good question.

56

CARO

"Do you think we should...I don't know...pull him out of the water or something?"

Knox snorted. "Good luck with that."

I felt sorry for Ryder. Yes, he'd been an idiot, yes, he'd lied to Luna, but he hadn't meant to hurt her. He should have owned up to his lie, but the way the truth had come out... Neither of them had deserved that.

Mia Yates, she who'd ruined dinner and so much more, was a friend of Ryder's ex-wife from their college days, and while Shylah had stayed in San Diego with him, Mia had followed her dream for a greener future and taken a job at a company that built wind turbines. And who was about to become the company's biggest customer? The government of San Gallicano. When Black threatened to hold up the funding, the CEO had gathered his best and brightest, hopped on an airplane, and rushed to Ilha Grande in an attempt to salvage the deal. Mia and her colleagues had been checking out the menu board at Coletta's when Mia happened to glance inside and...yeah. Disaster.

We knew that because Shylah had actually called to

apologise. Mia had always had a fiery temper and a protective streak, apparently, and she'd been one of the women who'd rallied around in the aftermath of the split. Shylah said she was in a better place these days. She'd even met a new man, one who wanted the same things that she did.

As for Ryder, he spent his free time floating in the pool, staring blankly at the sky, miserable as fuck. Knox said he still did okay at work. It was as if he switched himself on and off.

And now he was off.

Just bobbing around in the pool.

"Ryder, dinner's ready," I called.

Nothing.

I'd been in Virginia for a month, and although I loved the turtles, it was good to be home. And by home, I meant both in the US and with Knox, because wherever he was, that was home now. Our relationship was comfortable and easy, with none of that crushing pressure I'd experienced during my years with Aiden. I came and went as I pleased, I wore whatever I wanted to, and Knox encouraged me to make friends rather than cutting me off from them. Cora and Mercy had invited me out a couple of times, and I'd been able to enjoy myself without constantly looking over my shoulder.

We'd stayed in San Gallicano long enough for the grant money to come through, for Franklin to leave the hospital and begin his recuperation. Tadie loved her new job as much as I was enjoying mine, and I'd definitely go back to Valentine Cay to help out in the future, but just for a week or two, not for three more years. The Blackwood Foundation had even worked out a deal with Emmy where they'd sponsor the flights for any Blackwood employee who wanted to spend two weeks or more volunteering with the turtles. Six people had signed up so far.

Originally, I'd planned to bring Tango to Virginia with me, and she'd had her rabies shot to prepare, but when Tadie sent me videos of her running around at the sanctuary, she'd looked so happy that I didn't want to unsettle her. She loved the beach. She loved swimming in the ocean. Last night, Knox had suggested adopting a dog in Virginia if I wanted company while he was away, and we planned to visit the shelter at the weekend. Cora said it would be fun to have a dog in the office. We worked out of a townhouse near the Blackwood branch in Richmond, and there was a park opposite, plus a small courtyard out back.

"Just leave it—he'll eat if he wants to," Knox said. "I think he's in a funk because he saw the news about Luna."

It had been all over the internet today, the big announcement. That she'd be performing in Vegas for four months in a show billed as a pop extravaganza with old favourites and new surprises. I'd known it was coming. Known she'd signed up to sing at the Nile Palace, and keeping the secret had nearly killed me. But she'd been let down too many times, and I wasn't going to become the latest in a long line of people to break her trust.

We spoke every few days, not for long, but enough that she knew she wasn't alone. When we first met, I'd thought she was the ultimate spoiled brat, a princess used to getting her own way. But now those walls had been broken, and I saw her for what she was. Scared, used, and alone. She'd stuck to her guns and parted ways with her mom, a decision I knew had cost her most of the strength she had left. Amethyst wasn't making things easy, and the lawsuits had already started, but what were they fighting over? Nothing. Because Luna's accountant hadn't died, although she'd said more than once that she wished he had. No, he'd waited until the Puckett family was out of the way, and then he'd emptied all the bank accounts and left the country, heading first to New York, then to New Jersey, to London, to Zurich. Blackwood was tracking him, but he seemed to be taking a tour of the world. At least the theft hadn't made the headlines. That would have been the last straw on Luna's back. The one that broke her.

She never mentioned Ryder, and if I brought him up, she changed the subject. He'd hurt her badly, but I could see things from both sides. What she viewed as an egregious breach of trust, he'd seen as a way of protecting her. Initially, he'd figured that his sexuality didn't matter, that she was just a client who he'd wanted to feel safe, so why tell her the truth? It wasn't as if he'd ever have touched her in a way that made her uncomfortable. But then his heart got involved, and the hole got deeper and deeper until there was no way out. Luna never mentioned why she was so twitchy around straight men, but I could guess. A little of what I saw in her, I felt in myself, but while I pushed through my fears, she shied away from hers.

"She's not doing the show because she wants to. She's doing it because some asshole stole her money, and she needs to pay her rent. Is there any news on that?"

"Not yet. Ryder would be in Zurich, tearing the place apart, if Emmy didn't keep him on a short leash."

"Better than being in Las Vegas."

"Slater had to talk him out of buying tickets to her show."

"He seriously thought of going? That would have been such a bad idea. I'm still trying to explain his side to Luna, but..."

"She doesn't want to know?"

"Not at the moment. Let her focus on the show for a while, and maybe the hurt will fade."

"They would have been good together."

"Yes, they would."

They'd been so close on Valentine Cay. Soulmates. That was probably why his lie had stung her so badly, why she'd reacted the way she did. Perhaps the stars would someday align and they'd find their way back together? It was getting dark as Knox rose to his feet and offered me a hand. I left the outside light on, left Ryder floating in the water, staring up at a glittering sky.

And went to mend one more crack in my own damaged heart.

WHAT'S NEXT?

The Blackwood Security series continues with Luna and Ryder's story in *Blue Moon*...

You know what they say about showbiz? They love to build you up, and then they tear you down.

Luna Maara never wanted to be a star, but by the time she realised she hated the limelight, she was in too deep. Sold out concerts, fans screaming her name on the street, memes going viral whenever parts of her fell out of a costume. Oh, and stalkers. Don't forget the stalkers. The latest one calls himself Mark Antony, and he sends her linguine carbonara and...dog treats?

Most people think she has it all—the fame, the money, the luxurious lifestyle. But under the facade, there's nothing but an empty shell. Everyone close to her lies, or takes advantage of her, or both. Her family, her friends—she can't trust anyone. Not even Ryder. Somehow, her former bodyguard's betrayal hurt most of all.

Former SEAL Ryder Metcalfe never meant to fall in love again, but during a nightmare trip to the Caribbean, a prickly pop princess wormed her way under his skin. And then she ditched him. Which was his own fault, and also his biggest regret. He can't turn back the clock. He can't change fate.

But somebody else can.

When Luna's scared, there's only one person to call. Only one man she trusts, with her body if not with her heart. Mark Antony might gift Ryder a second chance, but he's determined the star-crossed couple won't get a third.

For more details:
www.elise-noble.com/blue-moon

If you enjoyed *The Devil and the Deep Blue Sea*, please consider leaving a review.

For an author, every review is incredibly important. Not only do they make us feel warm and fuzzy inside, readers consider them when making their decision whether or not to buy a book. Even a line saying you enjoyed the book or what your favourite part was helps a lot.

WANT TO STALK ME?

For updates on my new releases, giveaways, and other random stuff, you can sign up for my newsletter on my website:
www.elise-noble.com

If you're on Facebook, you might also like to join Team Blackwood for exclusive giveaways, sneak previews, and book-related chat. Be the first to find out about new stories, and you might even see your name or one of your suggestions make it into print!

And if you'd like to read my books for FREE, you can also find details of how to join my advance review team.

Would you like to join Team Blackwood?

www.elise-noble.com/team-blackwood

facebook.com/EliseNobleAuthor

x.com/EliseANoble

instagram.com/elise_noble

goodreads.com/elisenoble

bookbub.com/authors/elise-noble

tiktok.com/@EliseNobleWrites

ALSO BY ELISE NOBLE

Blackwood Security

For the Love of Animals (Nate & Carmen - Prequel)

Black is My Heart (Diamond & Snow - Prequel)

Pitch Black

Into the Black

Forever Black

Gold Rush

Gray is My Heart

Neon (novella)

Out of the Blue

Ultraviolet

Glitter (novella)

Red Alert

White Hot

Sphere (novella)

The Scarlet Affair

Spirit (novella)

Quicksilver

The Girl with the Emerald Ring

Red After Dark

When the Shadows Fall

Phantom (novella)

Pretties in Pink

Chimera

The Devil and the Deep Blue Sea

Blue Moon (2024)

Blackwood Elements

Oxygen

Lithium

Carbon

Rhodium

Platinum

Lead

Copper

Bronze

Nickel

Hydrogen

Out of Their Elements (novella)

Blackwood UK

Joker in the Pack

Cherry on Top

Roses are Dead

Shallow Graves

Indigo Rain

Pass the Parcel (TBA)

Blackwood Casefiles

Stolen Hearts

Burning Love (TBA)

Baldwin's Shore

Dirty Little Secrets

Secrets, Lies, and Family Ties

Buried Secrets

A Secret to Die For

Blackwood Security vs. Baldwin's Shore

Secret Weapon

Secrets from the Past

Blackstone House

Hard Lines

Blurred Lines (novella)

Hard Tide

Hard Limits

Hard Luck (TBA)

Hard Code (TBA)

The Electi

Cursed

Spooked

Possessed

Demented

Judged

The Planes

A Vampire in Vegas

A Devil in the Dark (TBA)

The Trouble Series

Trouble in Paradise

Nothing but Trouble

24 Hours of Trouble

The Happy Ever After Series

A Very Happy Christmas

A Very Happy Valentine

A Very Happy Halloween (2024)

Standalone

Life

Coco du Ciel

Twisted (short stories)

Books with clean versions available (no swearing and no on-the-page sex)

Pitch Black

Into the Black

Forever Black

Gold Rush

Gray is My Heart

Audiobooks

Black is My Heart (Diamond & Snow - Prequel)

Pitch Black

Into the Black

Forever Black

Gold Rush

Gray is My Heart

Neon (novella)

A Very Happy Christmas

A Very Happy Valentine

Dirty Little Secrets

Secrets, Lies, and Family Ties (2024)

Printed in Great Britain
by Amazon

41595634R00254